A DECEPTIVE DEVOTION

THE LANE WINSLOW MYSTERY SERIES

———

IONA WHISHAW

A
DECEPTIVE
DEVOTION

A LANE WINSLOW MYSTERY

TOUCHWOOD

TouchWood Editions
touchwoodeditions.com

This book is a work of fiction. Names, characters, places, and incidents are either
products of the author's imagination or are used fictitiously. Any resemblance to
actual events or locales or persons, living or dead, is entirely coincidental.

LIBRARY AND ARCHIVES CANADA CATALOGUING IN PUBLICATION

Title: A deceptive devotion / Iona Whishaw.
Names: Whishaw, Iona, 1948- author.
Description: Series statement: A Lane Winslow mystery
Identifiers: Canadiana (print) 20190051671 | Canadiana (ebook) 2019005168X |
ISBN 9781771513005 (softcover) | ISBN 9781771513012 (PDF)
Classification: LCC PS8595.H414 D49 2019 | DDC C813/.54—dc23

Cover illustration by Margaret Hanson
Design by Colin Parks
Edited by Claire Philipson

TouchWood Editions acknowledges that the land on which we live and work is
within the traditional territories of the Lkwungen (Esquimalt and Songhees),
Malahat, Pacheedaht, Scia'new, T'Sou-ke and WSÁNEĆ (Pauquachin, Tsartlip,
Tsawout, Tseycum) peoples.

We acknowledge the financial support of the Government of Canada through
the Canada Book Fund, the Canada Council for the Arts, and the Province
of British Columbia through the British Columbia Arts Council and the Book
Publishing Tax Credit.

PRINTED IN CANADA

23 22   3 4 5

To my great-grandmother, Lucy Addison (1861–1946)—
brave, amusing, loving, an articulate diarist in dire
times, and a guiding inspiration in my life.

PROLOGUE

September 1947

THE HUNTER STOPPED AND STARED at the thing in front of him, so familiar, but so out of place. Puzzled, he looked toward the whispering forest and at the meadow, just visible under a golden blanket of sun on the other side of a shadowed gully. He could hear the creek below him. He strained his ears, alert now. His best buddy had operated one of these in Sicily. Why was it here? He scanned the forest in front of him again as if it might yield an answer and then reached for his rifle and dismounted, letting the reins drop. He propped the rifle against the rock and knelt down to see better. He only looked up when his horse whinnied and skittered sideways.

"Don't turn around."

The voice, sudden, surprising, utterly unlikely, made him want to laugh.

He felt only shock, not pain, as his head was yanked backwards by his hair. He could hear the slide of the gun along the rock as it toppled. In an eternity of time, he wondered at how his hat had come off, at why it didn't hurt to have his hair pulled this way. His eyes wide, head held back at an impossible angle, he saw the sudden glimpse of heaven and then pitched forward, surprised by the warm, draining finality of death.

CHAPTER ONE

July 1945

THE DACHA GARDEN, SLIGHTLY UNKEMPT, was a lush emerald green of grass bordered by the wildflowers that the deputy director liked to grow: yellow buttercups, blue cornflower, nodding chamomile. The air was the very scent of summer, Stanimir Aptekar thought. He was so strongly assailed by a memory of his childhood in his garden at home near Saint Petersburg that he was momentarily in its complete possession. He was running joyfully through the trees to the river, his brother Stepan in full pursuit. He pulled himself back to the present with some effort, drinking the vodka remaining in his glass to anchor himself.

The four men sat in white wicker chairs around a small table under the shade of an ancient and spreading apple tree. Its living branches were filled with tiny green apples; its dead branches untrimmed, provided a suggestion of decay. The men leaned back, all of them smoking. The vodka bottle was depleted to below the halfway mark, the plate of sausage and loaf of bread nearly spent. Despite the languid comforts suggested by this scene, there was a sense of urgency about the meeting.

"It has been going well," Ivanov said. "We have people in place in Britain and, as you know, some important defections. It is excellent that we had the foresight to begin this process before the end of the war. We are in a consolidating phase, yes? Koba is pleased that we are finally getting some traction. But the next moves are critical. Our ability to build a nuclear capacity depends on what happens now. If we are exposed, it will mean critical delays. And he will not stomach delays."

There was a dark obviousness to the implications of Stalin's impatience. Ivanov, the assistant deputy director of the MGB, the Ministry of State Security, leaned back in his chair, looking at his comrades as if challenging them for their potential failures.

"We could have been saved some of this extra work if we'd been fast enough when the Americans and British were scooping up physicists from Germany."

Ivanov reached forward to put his cigarette in the ashtray on the table, and then thought better of it and flicked it into the bushes instead. It was his dacha after all.

"Stanimir?"

He had a high-pitched, snivelling voice that irritated Stanimir Aptekar.

Aptekar leaned back. The other three seemed to move imperceptibly forward. He was aware of the deep blue of the sky against the green of the tree that shaded them. So much beauty, he thought.

"In Canada, we are operating out of the embassy in Ottawa. We have people in the very centre. I have their names in my dossier. I have also put in place a failsafe plan. Should something go wrong, it will take little time to assemble a back-up group. This I keep in my head." Aptekar tapped the side of his head with his long index finger.

"Is that wise? If something should, God forbid, happen to you?"

"With any luck, God is forbidding. Comrades, these are new and delicate times. Here, among ourselves, in this trusted circle, I recommend caution to everyone."

He thought with a deep well of sadness of Stepan, a hero of the war, picked up one afternoon from his apartment where he celebrated the birthday of his wife with his daughter and her two small children. No one had seen him again, not until the state presented a red box with a hero's award from the People to his grieving widow. She had shown it to him, wordlessly, her expression devoid forevermore of the humour and intelligence that had once animated it. What had his brother done? Whom had he offended? There would never be an answer. Aptekar had gazed at the silver medal, a momentary fantasy that his brother and all his life had been physically compressed into this metal disk, the image of Stalin stamped forever on his remains.

He looked at the smiling faces of his comrades. Masha Ivanova came out of the house with *sushki* and tea. No circle could be trusted. Certainly not this one.

"So, Comrade Aptekar." Ivanov, now deputy director, interrupted his walk back and forth across the room, his brown boots gleaming in the sunlight that poured in the east window of the Kremlin office Aptekar had been called to. "Tea?"

"Thank you." Such sinister courtesy, Stanimir Aptekar thought. "Congratulations, Deputy Director Comrade Ivanov, on your promotion."

That meeting in Ivanov's sunny garden two years before seemed a lifetime ago.

A samovar stood on a long table pushed against the wall. The commander acknowledged this compliment with a nod and then lifted his hand; a soldier at attention by the door clicked his heels quietly and began to pour tea into two glasses waiting on a tray.

Dismissed, the soldier saluted and withdrew, closing the door quietly. He will be right outside, Aptekar thought wearily.

"You have done great service over a long career, comrade."

"You are kind to say so," Aptekar said.

"Your dossier reads like an adventure book for schoolboys. Such exploits! They don't make spies like you anymore."

The deputy director lifted a manila folder, which Aptekar did not doubt was a prop, like everything else in the room. He knew this strategy well. He had employed it many times over the past fifty years—goodness, was it fifty years he had worked for intelligence, first for Mother Russia, and now for the Soviet Empire? He inclined his head, his hand partially on his glass of tea. He would drink when Ivanov did.

"Berlin recently, I think?" Ivanov sat down, smiling benignly at his guest. "Such a messy arrangement! We are delaying the inevitable, I think. The West is delaying the inevitable."

"It is indeed. East Germany will be the envy of the West, Deputy Director Comrade Ivanov."

"We should never have conceded any part of Berlin. You agree, I think?"

"Yes, comrade. Certainly."

Ivanov dropped a lump of sugar into his glass. "I'm glad you agree. Westerners are pouring in and out of there with ever-increasing zeal, as if they suspected that Berlin might become a problem. As if their increased presence in the city was a precaution of some sort. And we are letting them traipse across our sectors unhindered!" Ivanov momentarily lost his composed demeanour.

A cool head was required in this moment. Aptekar focused all his attention on appearing interested, while his mind sorted through two piles: what might be coming next, and what he might be able to do about it. His escape to the West was planned, everything in place. No one knew except the British director, who had arranged to have him met at the border. This ceremony, or whatever it was, here with Ivanov, represented his last feigned look of earnest commitment to the aspirations of the Union of Soviet Socialist Republics.

"What we are wondering, Comrade Aptekar, is why so suddenly? We are hoping, because you had your ear to the ground in Berlin as recently as June 20, you might be able to provide insight."

June 20. The day he met with Lane Winslow. He had been assigned to bring her across, but he had seen immediately that she had no appetite for double agency, or indeed, any sort of espionage. The outcome of the fateful evening had been very different from what he had intended, and yet . . . he had made that sudden decision. Now it seemed that history, so out of his or anyone's control, shone a light on that moment at dinner when he had said, surprising even himself, that he might like to retire in the West. Why had he done it? Was it a sentimental attachment to the past, to the years he had worked with her father when Russia and Britain were on the same side of things?

He reasoned that they had not discovered what he had said specifically, but the increased activity in Berlin made them question why he had failed to bring the British agent over and what he might have said to her about their plans for Berlin. There was something in Ivanov's voice that made his heart sink. He knew that his autonomy was at an end. Even this handsome talk of his heroism would not protect him now, any more than it had his brother, Stepan.

"I do not believe the West is any more zealous than it was before. When I was there, the traffic on the corridor into Berlin, both by road and rail, was extremely heavy. I can assure you, the West has been suspicious and anxious to keep its presence sturdy from the beginning. They bargained for half of Berlin, and they intend to keep it, no matter what happens."

Ivanov shrugged in agreement. "I expect you are right. There are those, however, who take a more sinister view. I do not say I do, but others. They have concluded that there has been a leak, that our intentions with regard to Berlin, and even our plans to build networks in the West, were passed on to a British agent. Of course, the world is full of paranoia. Everyone makes much too much of the smallest things. I expect a careless word, a stolen dossier, something for which our agent would not have been culpable." Ivanov smiled at Aptekar. "But, comrade, I am forgetting myself! This is not why you were invited here! The People, in recognition of your long and storied service to the country, are at last going to allow you to retire! What are you now, nearly seventy? You are legendary, inspirational! You have a home in the countryside near Leningrad, do you not?"

Aptekar smiled as well. "I do, Deputy Director. A nice little place with a small garden." Why had he talked about plans to build a new network in the West? Aptekar searched his mind to remember who should know about these plans. Ivanov had not been included in the final proposal made after that summer meeting, but here he was talking about it as if he were talking about the expansion of the Kremlin parking lot. Perhaps, since his promotion, he'd been brought into the need-to-know circle. Whom had Ivanov knocked out for that promotion? Almost with resignation, Aptekar listened to that high-pitched voice he disliked so much, and knew he would be next.

"Ah! Then you shall garden! How enviable. How little time one has to be close to the earth, and yet such a life is quintessentially Russian, do you not agree?"

"Very much so," said Aptekar. "I expect it is the reason that we call her our 'motherland,' unlike our recent enemies with their 'fatherland.' I shall look forward to returning to her bosom."

"And so, Comrade Aptekar, today has a special significance." Ivanov stood and went to the sideboard where a red, satin-covered box waited. The door to the room opened, and a man in a dark serge suit and holding a camera came in, as did the soldier who had been waiting outside the room. "Comrade, please." Ivanov signalled with a little flick of his hand that Aptekar was to stand and approach him.

"Comrade Stanimir Aptekar, it gives me great pleasure to present you with the Red Banner medal for service to the Motherland and the defence of the Union of Soviet Socialist Republics." Ivanov opened the box, turning it slightly toward the soldier and cameraman, as if they were a large audience, and then removed the medal and pinned it on the lapel of Aptekar's jacket. He reached for Aptekar's hand and shook it vigorously, turning them both toward the camera and smiling broadly. The flash emitted only a soft *pfft*, as though downplaying the occasion taking place.

WHEN APTEKAR HAD been escorted out into the hall, Ivanov waited to hear the footsteps recede and then went to the telephone on his desk, tapping his fingers impatiently on the desk's surface. The man on the other end had been told to pick up on the first ring, but it rang three times before Ivanov heard "Da?"

"Now. Have him followed. He has the name of every potential agent in our outpost in Ottawa in his head. Do not kill him, and do not let him disappear. We will pick him up soon. Do you understand?"

APTEKAR STOOD ON the embankment of the Moscow River, watching a barge move slowly south. He had removed his medal and slipped it into his pocket. On the whole, he thought, I am alive. My brother had to be executed before he got his hero's medal. There would be no cottage in Sussex, that was certain. It had been something he'd begun to envision for himself, almost as if it had been a real possibility. Someone had found out and was going to make sure it never happened. Lane Winslow would have told her people that she was bringing him over, but how would someone here in Moscow have found it out? He doubted there would even be his own little house outside Leningrad. He heard the car pull up and stop on the street behind him, but he did not turn. It would not be taking him to the western border in Yugoslavia, where he was supposed to be by the end of the week.

CHAPTER TWO

September 1947

LANE PICKED UP THE EARPIECE of her old-fashioned wall phone and spoke into the trumpet.

"KC 431, Lane Winslow speaking."

"Ah, Miss Winslow. It's Al Stevens. How are you?"

"Good morning, Vicar. Very well, thank you. How nice to hear from you. How are you?"

A September sun shone through her living room window and shot a band of light down the hall where she stood.

"Fine. Yes, thank you. But I'm wondering if you can help me. You see, through a rather peculiar series of circumstances I have an elderly Russian lady . . . in my charge, I suppose you might say, and if I'm honest, I'm not quite sure I know what to do. She doesn't speak a word of English." The vicar sounded harried and seemed to be talking quietly in case his guest might turn out to speak English after all.

"Goodness! How did you come to be in possession of an elderly Russian lady?"

"She was dropped off here by a taxi. Our parish has a little charity for Russian refugees that has practically ceased operation since its heyday in the thirties, and the taxi driver thought the best thing would be to bring her to me. I gather she must have come in on a train and managed to find the taxi outside the station. And there you are, you see. She's sitting primly in my sitting room dressed from head to foot in black and looking expectant. It was the taxi driver who remembered you might be able to help."

Lane looked at her watch, and then longingly out the door at the end of the hall, which was open and letting in warm September air. It was just ten, and she had planned to spend the morning in the garden, starting with running the mower over the unkempt grass.

"I can be there in about an hour, Vicar. Can you keep her entertained until then?"

"She seems determined to entertain me. She's been talking very slowly and patiently in Russian and showing me a photo of a man and saying something like 'mert.' Can that be the fellow's name?"

"Mert?" said Lane. "Unlikely his name."

"It's more like 'mertf.' Well. Never mind. You'll solve the mystery when you get here. I'll ply her with cake until then. She seems very partial to cake."

Lane was just taking her car keys off the hook by the door—and wondering why a Nelson cab driver would know about her and her ability to speak Russian—when it came to her. Whoever was in that woman's photo was not called mertf. He was *mrtvý*. Dead.

INSPECTOR DARLING OF the Nelson Police was relieved that, for the last week at least, crime in Nelson and environs appeared to be taking a well-earned rest. His usual partner, Constable Ames, was away in Vancouver on a sergeants' course and would not be back for a fortnight, and if he examined his own conscience honestly, he would admit he missed him. They worked well together, and Ames was willing to put up with a good deal from Darling, something Darling knew would not last forever. Ames would grow into his own, but they might, he reflected, find a new balance as equals. Well, equal-ish.

The paperwork Darling had intended to tackle lay untouched on his desk, and he himself was standing in front of his open window with his hands in his pockets, looking down on Baker Street, where people were moving briskly about their business, still in their summer clothes. The air was soft and warm. It will be another one of those glorious Septembers, he thought, when we all live suspended for one last delicious moment above the coming fall and winter. He smiled benignly upon the street below. And anyway, he was getting married in just a few short weeks. The thought made his heart flutter in a way completely unfamiliar to him up until the time, over a year before, when he had met Lane Winslow.

His happy rumination was interrupted by the jangling of the phone on his desk.

"Darling."

"Darling indeed. It's me. I'm sorry to interrupt your progress on your paperwork."

"You interrupted it long before you called. I was thinking happy thoughts of being married to you."

Darling could see her, standing in her hallway speaking into that ridiculous ancient trumpet telephone, her chin tilted up to reach the horn, her auburn hair falling back behind her ear, the light from her front door catching her beautiful cheekbones, and her green eyes full of light and humour. She was the most beautiful woman he'd ever encountered, and he was going to marry her.

"Ah. You'll get over that when we are married, and the sober reality of it hits home," Lane said. "As it happens, I'm not calling idly. At least I think I'm not. I've just had a call from Mr. Stevens, our padre."

"He's found a reason why we two may not be joined in holy matrimony?"

"You do have a one-track mind. No. He's found an old Russian lady and doesn't know what to do with her. She doesn't speak a word of English, and she keeps showing him a picture of a man and saying he's dead. I mean, I think that's what she's saying. When the vicar told me the word she keeps using, I realized it must be that."

"Miss Winslow, if it is your intention to clutter up our wedding with dead bodies, I would like to register my protest now."

"Very funny, Inspector. No. I am coming up to town to visit the vicarage to help the vicar and the old lady understand one another. I'm merely telephoning you to let you know I'm coming up, and to warn you in the off-chance that there's something fishy about the man in the photograph being dead. If that's what he is."

"Well, let me remind you that many people are, perfectly legitimately, dead. And now I intend to get back to my paperwork and not spend another moment thinking of you. Anyway, why are you wasting time talking to me? The poor vicar must be beside himself trying to communicate with her."

"Oh, that's all right. He's plying her with cake. I'll come by and see you in any case?"

"Yes, you will."

"AH, AT LAST!" the vicar said when Lane appeared at the door. "Please do come in." There was an imploring quality to the "please" that suggested the last hour had been a strain.

Lane followed him into the sitting room where a small, neat, and aristocratic-looking woman, easily, Lane thought, in her late sixties, sat very upright on the edge of the two-seater sofa, as if she could not let her guard down. She had her hands in her lap, and she looked up with an almost supercilious air when Lane appeared, as if Lane had better explain herself. There was a depth and alertness to the Russian woman's eyes that belied her age. Lane smiled at her, in part out of courtesy, but in part because she was genuinely delighted to meet a type of person she never thought she'd meet again: a Russian aristocrat.

"Madam, my name is Lane Winslow. I am most pleased to meet you," she said in Russian.

At this the woman looked at Lane with surprise and relief.

"Countess Orlova," the woman said, offering a gloved hand. "I am pleased you have come. I cannot make this gentleman understand me."

"I will do what I can. My friend, the Vicar Stevens, called me, but I live an hour away. I'm sorry it has taken so long. How may I help?"

There was an almost happy familiarity to speaking Russian again, a language she had spoken equally with English as a child.

"I have come in search of my brother."

She reached into a small black handbag and pulled out a photo. Lane took it. The man in the picture was standing next to a car that would have been an absolute luxury in the twenties. Long, sleek, a pale colour with a black convertible roof. She did not recognize it but thought it might be German. The man, dressed in hunting clothes, appeared to be in his mid-forties and was looking directly at the camera. He was handsome, with perhaps sandy hair parted in the middle, and he had, Lane thought, a wary expression. The car appeared to be on a gravel driveway with a bank of trees behind it.

"Where was this taken?" Lane asked.

"In Shanghai, in 1922. We fled there and found some refuge in an émigré community."

"But you have come here?"

"The curse of Communism is coming to China as well. One has to go somewhere." Here Countess Orlova looked toward the window as if this was one more inadequate refuge she was forced to endure. "My brother disappeared about ten months ago, and I managed to trace him to Vancouver."

"But you think now he has come here?"

"This is what I learned from the Russians there. Many are White Russians, still supporting czarist pretenders who are waiting for the return of the empire. They collect money for this purpose. They are fools." The countess said this bitterly. "They are throwing twigs at a fortress wall. I am afraid that my brother has become involved with them and that, as a result, he is dead." She glanced at Lane and then looked down again.

Why? Lane wondered. It is as if she doesn't think I'll believe her. She has been a refugee. It must have been very hard for her. Refugees are so much flotsam and jetsam scattered on the perilous shores of political changes. Hard up and considered a nuisance wherever they go.

"What makes you think he might be dead, Countess?" Lane asked.

Orlova turned away at this question and was silent. Finally, she said, "Just call me 'madam,' please. 'Countess' is so formal. In Vancouver they lost track of him. He disappeared. Someone suggested he might have come here. That he was running. They said he was being pursued by Soviet agents."

Lane had a momentary thought that this was ridiculous, but a Soviet agent had engineered the killing of a Russian dissident right in the local hot springs the previous year. Canada, which had seemed to her such a refuge, so far away from the torments of European upheavals, now felt much too close to the world.

Seeing the vicar shift impatiently on the chair by his desk where he had been watching this exchange, Lane said, in English, "Madam Orlova is in search of her brother. She seems not to be sure if he is dead or has managed to come here. I'm not really sure how we can help her. I can take her to the inspector so that he can look at her picture and perhaps broadcast it around the area. Oh, gosh. And I wonder if she has someplace to stay?"

"I could, of course, canvass around the area, but it might take some time . . ."

Making a few mental adjustments, Lane decided there was nothing for it.

"She can stay with me until something turns up." She turned back to the countess and spoke again in Russian.

"I have a friend who is in charge of the police here. He can help find your brother if he is anywhere nearby. I propose that we stop by and see him, and then you must come and be my guest. I'm afraid I live very far out of town, but it is beautiful and quiet."

"Why must I see the police? I don't wish to." Madam Orlova seemed to recoil and delivered this in an aggrieved tone.

"He is a very good man. The police here are not like those in the old country. You need not fear them," Lane said, knowing that that was not always necessarily true, but confident, in any case, of her policeman.

Suspicious, Countess Orlova indicated reluctant consent to the plan by turning her mouth down at the corners and standing up and waiting by the door while the vicar took up her two small, battered valises. Lane opened the car door for her and then turned to look at the vicar.

"Thank you so much. I suppose the inspector can help to find her brother if he's even around here, and then we'll have to see what she's intending to do. If you do hear of any place, please let me know. And I guess we'll see you next week."

Lane and Darling were scheduled to meet the vicar to discuss their wedding plans, and no doubt take some religious instruction, on the following Wednesday afternoon.

"Yes. Well, good luck. Very nice to meet you, Countess Orlova." The vicar leaned down to address Lane's passenger with a slightly forced smile that suggested Lane would need all the luck he had wished her.

Orlova turned her head slightly and inclined it toward the vicar.

"Be good enough to thank him for the cake," she said, unsmiling. "He is most kind."

"The countess liked the cake and thanks you for your kindness," said Lane, getting into the car.

"YOU'VE DONE WHAT?" Darling asked through pinched lips, looking past Lane with a fixed smile at the countess. "Are you mad?"

"A little, yes, I'm afraid," Lane allowed. "But it shouldn't be for long. The vicar is hard at work looking for a suitable place for a gentlewoman down on her luck. In the meantime, she has to be somewhere. Now, for the business at hand. She has a photograph of her brother, whom she is seeking. She has followed his tracks all the way from Shanghai and believes he might be here."

Lane moved to Madam Orlova. "I have explained to Inspector Darling about your brother, as far as I know it. May I have his photograph to show him?"

The countess clamped her hands tightly on the top of her handbag, as if she meant to deny the request, and then slowly opened it and pulled out the picture.

"It is an old picture, tell him. It is almost twenty-five years old, but he does not look so terribly different. He is called Vassily Mikhailov."

"Can you spell that?" Darling asked. He wrote the name down and then took the picture and studied it. Expensive car, expensive suit. The air of a confident man. Where his jacket was open, a heavy watch chain hung from inside his vest to his waistcoat pocket. "May I keep this picture for a couple of days? I need to make copies to share with my colleagues at the Mounted Police."

The older woman frowned at this request. "Why is this necessary? He has seen it. What more does he need? It is the only artefact I have of my brother. Can he not just show it to these other policemen here?"

"I understand, Countess. But he will bring it back to us, or I will come myself and get it. This is a very big country, as you know. Like Russia. The police that operate outside this town will need to have his picture."

"How do I know he is not just collecting evidence to arrest me?"

This distrust of the police was genuinely earned, Lane thought. They had been relentless in their pursuit of the aristocracy and eliminating White Russians or any other resistance to the revolution.

"He would have no cause to arrest you, madam. Even if you managed to come here illegally, I am sure that you could be granted status as a refugee. His prison cells are very tiny. He has plenty of local criminals to fill them with."

This remark elicited a slight smile, and Orlova inclined her head in a little nod.

The business concluded, Lane said, "We'd better be off. I'll have to stop and get some proper food if I'm to have a guest, and I'm sure the journey has been tiring."

"It will be good practice for you," Darling said. "We shall want proper food, I expect, when we are married."

"Ha! And don't forget next Wednesday. Mr. Stevens is expecting us. No. I won't kiss you. My guest will think we are in cahoots."

"I can't wait to get into proper cahoots with you," Darling said.

"Goodbye, Inspector."

CHAPTER THREE

DARLING WATCHED LANE HELP COUNTESS Orlova into the car down on the street below his window and shook his head. She was always impetuously close to offering people refuge in her beautiful house with the view of the lake in King's Cove, but this time she'd actually done it. He shouldn't be annoyed, he knew. It wasn't his house after all, but the prospect of having Countess Orlova looming like the Queen of Spades over his visits and, more importantly, the preparations for his wedding, was discomfiting. The wedding was October 18. Less than a month away. The vicar would surely have found a place for her by then.

He was on the verge of shouting "Ames!" when he recalled the other fly in his ointment. Ames was away. Instead he put his head out the office door and shouted, "Oxley!"

"Sir?"

The young man who was temporarily occupying Ames's desk appeared in the hall. Oxley had transferred to Nelson from somewhere in Ontario—Darling was at a loss to remember where—just after Ames had left to go to Vancouver for his sergeants' course. He was shorter than Ames, and compact, with black hair brilliantined into submission, and a respectful tone that Ames had never managed to achieve. Darling wasn't sure it was an improvement.

"I need this photograph replicated, and I'd like it sent to the RCMP divisions in the area, along with the message that we are looking for this man who has gone missing. Oh, and can you get me an extra for Ames? And try not to ruin the photograph. It belongs to an old lady who's attached to it."

"Sir," Oxley said, infusing into the word a sense of reproach that he'd ever damage anything.

This accomplished, Darling took up his hat and went down to the front door. "Going off to send a wire," he said to O'Brien, the desk sergeant.

"One of the boys can do it for you, sir."

"Thanks. I need the walk."

"Missing Ames, aren't you, sir," O'Brien said, very nearly winking.

"Certainly not. And I don't have to put up with any backchat from Oxley," Darling said.

"Yet," muttered O'Brien under his breath as he watched Darling go out the door.

Once outside, Darling indulged in trying to weigh how September created its own magic. That heat that could be, no, is, summer, and yet the cool suggestion of melancholy, or perhaps a coming out of the doldrums into a fresh, clean time of change and possibility. He had studied literature at university before the death of a friend during a bank robbery pushed him to become a police officer. He remembered a line of poetry: "Sorrow and scarlet leaf, sad thoughts and sunny weather. Ah me, this glory and this grief agree not well together!" An American, he recalled, a translator of Dante. Parsons? But it was not grief he felt but elation. Not just because of his wedding but because he realized that this turn into the fall always filled him with elation.

He entered the train station and approached the telegraph window. A small girl in a green dress and a little white hat, swinging her legs on the bench, sat with her mother. He guessed, from the lack of luggage, that they were waiting for someone to arrive. Darling winked at her, and she smiled shyly and pulled closer to her mother.

"I need to send a wire, please," he said, leaning down to the level of the man sitting behind the grill. He gave the address. "Ring me. Stop." He looked at his watch. "Three PM. Stop. Darling. Stop."

That dispatched, he walked the short distance to his favourite dining establishment, Lorenzo's Restaurant. It was early afternoon, and the dining room was empty. Lorenzo was setting out cutlery for the evening seating.

"Inspector! So good to see you." Lorenzo greeted Darling, as he always did, with enthusiasm, and then looked toward the door. "Alone today?"

"I'm afraid your Miss Winslow couldn't stay in town today. She has a guest to attend to. Unfortunately, I can't stop either. I just wanted to check something with you. Last year you mentioned that among the people who come here there are Russians. Is that still the case?"

"A few, yes. They are, how would I say? Very European, maybe. For example, old clothes, but very good. They are not practical like the local farmers, the Doukhobors. I know that man who works sometimes at the court, he comes."

"Ah. Mr. Stearn."

Darling had visited Mr. Stearn, the official court translator, the winter before. He'd been keen to keep Lane Winslow away from any official standing in the case of the death of a Russian, and he had sought out Mr. Stearn to do the translating for his interviews with local Russian speakers. He was a somewhat querulous older man who had refused the long drive along snowy roads to New Denver and seemed to have a strong prejudice against Doukhobors. Darling didn't look forward to another interview with him, but he was a place to start.

"Thank you, Lorenzo. I shall pay him a visit," Darling said, putting on his hat and turning toward the door. Then he stopped. "Did I say, by the way, that Miss Winslow and I are to marry?"

Lorenzo put down the knives he was holding and clutched his hands together, his face wreathed with delight.

"Oh, Inspector! This is the best wonderful news! Wait, please," he said, waving his hand, and rushing toward the kitchen. "Olivia, please come, important news!" he called into the open door.

Olivia, Lorenzo's wife, came out into the dining room pushing a dark strand of hair away from her face. She wore a white apron tied around her slender and wiry body and a smile that lit up her striking features.

"The inspector has just told me the most beautiful news,

my dear. He and Miss Winslow are going to be married! Eh? What did I always say?"

"Tanti auguri, Inspector! Lorenzo always say you must be in love. Now I see is true." Olivia shook Darling's hand. "She is so beautiful and such a kind face. Bravo!"

Still warmed by the effusive happiness of Lorenzo and his wife, Darling made his way back up the hill toward the station. Should he have said anything? He would like to have invited them to the wedding, but he and Lane had not really discussed the guest list, and he worried that it was a lot to ask to have them close the restaurant and drive all the way to King's Cove. He reasserted his dour inspector mien as he approached the station. He'd told no one there yet. He wasn't sure entirely why. He looked at his watch. He had time before Ames called to pay a visit to Mr. Stearn.

"Keys, O'Brien," he said. His desk sergeant, amazingly, seemed to be going through some files, doing police work for a change.

"Going up the lake, sir?" O'Brien asked him, winking.

"If you wink at me one more time, Sergeant, I'll have your stripes. I will be back in half an hour. You better have that lot done when I get back."

He knew why he hadn't told them.

COUNTESS ORLOVA SAT primly in the passenger seat as Lane drove them, and the bags of groceries she'd bought, to King's Cove. She had not spoken since they had exchanged the communication necessary for determining what sort of food to buy at the nearly brand-new supermarket. Lane tried to imagine what question she could ask about the countess's life that would not be intrusive, when her guest finally spoke.

"It is beautiful. It is a little like Russia, with all these trees." Orlova spoke in Russian.

"Yes," Lane said, smiling. "Perhaps that is why I love it. I knew the minute I came here that this was where I wanted to be."

"You were smart not to choose to live in that miserable little town. I grew up on an estate along the Neva River. We too had to drive up to town for things. But it was Saint Petersburg. We went in the late fall for the season, the opera, ballet. They call it Leningrad now. A travesty. But the city was ruined by the war. Saint Petersburg is no more. They can call it anything they like."

"How very distressing," Lane said. She wanted to dispute the "miserable little town" designation the older woman had given Nelson, but she sensed that Orlova, having started on her own past, might need to share her bitterness.

"One can never escape," Orlova continued. "It was not enough that our parents were made to disappear, our house taken over by officers pretending to be egalitarian. It is not enough that my brother and I were forced to flee all the way to Shanghai. No. Now they must pursue us still."

"Why now, do you think?" Lane asked. They were climbing the hill upon which the little Balfour store and gas station sat. She slowed down because Mr. Bales's black Lab often lay in the middle of the road.

"My brother foolishly cast his lot with the anti-Communist groups in Shanghai. He wrote articles, drew attention to himself. Now with China on the verge of embracing the red star, well. There you are. He fled without even telling me. He must have been in danger of his life. He would never leave without taking me unless that were true."

The black Lab was lying at the side of the road for a change and lifted his head lazily as Lane drove by.

"I'm so sorry," Lane said. "I can't imagine the worry you must have endured."

She really couldn't. In spite of her dangerous war work, she hadn't had to suffer exile and flight, only to find herself still hunted by people who wanted her dead. She was not surprised at Orlova's bitterness. And to have to endure the uncertainty and anxiety of having a brother disappear like that, with no warning.

The birch and alder leaves rustled in the breeze as they drove up the hill toward the junction that would take them to Lane's house. Some leaves were just beginning to turn yellow, warning of the coming fall.

"But this is beautiful!" Countess Orlova said, clasping her hands under her chin. "I have brought my little water-colour kit and some paper. I will paint here and give some paintings to you. That will be my way to thank you!"

Carrying her guest's two small suitcases to the house, Lane said, "You paint. How wonderful! Come. Let me show you your room and where you can freshen up, and then I will show you around."

The second bedroom off the hall had not seen use since Lane had moved to King's Cove, but she kept it more or less at the ready in case of a visit, in particular from her friend Yvonne, who promised often that she would descend on Lane from France one of these days, but instead had buried herself more and more in horses and, recently, a new love interest. Lane unlatched and pushed the window sash up and put the suitcases on the bed. She must have books in one of them, she thought. It weighs a ton. How far had the old lady had to drag them on her own?

"Will this do? I'm afraid it looks out on nothing but trees."

Countess Orlova stood at the door and scanned the room, looking at the pale green walls and the ceiling, the simple green and orange curtains in broad vertical stripes, the side table with a lamp, and then she smiled. It was the first real smile Lane had seen from her.

"This is like the room in a summer dacha. Simple, peaceful, calming. Thank you. I don't think I realized until this moment how completely weary I am, and the prospect of being in this restful place for even a short time fills my heart."

Leaving Orlova to settle in, Lane went back out to the car to pick up the groceries. She was feeling uncertain. She was so used to being alone, to suiting herself and coming and going without reference to anyone else's comforts or needs. Still, she reminded herself, this was only until Stevens found something for her guest. More worrisome was that these same anxieties might hold when she was married. How would she adapt to giving up this complete sense of independence, even given that she loved Darling? Up until now she had, she realized, assumed that the love alone would ameliorate any losses she felt. That her new identity as part of a couple would open for her a new way of being happy. Putting these anxieties firmly out of her mind, she began to sort the food into cupboards and the fridge. She told herself it would be jolly good for her to get into some sort of normal routine of breakfast, lunch, and dinner.

DARLING HEARD THE latch being pulled from inside after his second bout of knocking on Mr. Stearn's door. The door opened a fraction and a man peered suspiciously at Darling.

"Yes? Oh. It is the inspector, is it not?"

"Yes, Mr. Stearn. Inspector Darling. I wonder if I might come in? You may be able to help me with some information."

Stearn, who had looked on the verge of opening the door wider, frowned and seemed to recede slightly. "What sort of information?"

"Really, Mr. Stearn, this might be easier if I could come inside. It is your expertise on the local Russian community I need. We have a woman who has come from Shanghai in search of her missing brother. I thought you might be able to help me understand how to proceed, as you understand the complications best."

This appeal to his expertise seemed to do the trick. Stearn opened the door and stepped aside to allow Darling to enter. The room had a murky feel, which Darling took a moment to identify as coming from nearly closed curtains, cigarette smoke, and unopened windows, as if Stearn recoiled from both light and air.

"Please sit down, Inspector. I can offer you tea," he said, glancing with evident reluctance at the kitchen visible at the end of a short dark hall.

"That's quite all right, Mr. Stearn. I won't keep you long."

This assurance caused Stearn to sit on the edge of a faded easy chair with his hands folded on his lap. "Yes. How can I be of assistance?"

"A woman in her sixties has come here looking for her missing brother. They are, she told me, White Russians from somewhere near Leningrad. They were forced to flee in the twenties to Shanghai. Her brother left suddenly, and she traced him to Vancouver, and there she was told he had come here. Who are some of the people I should ask about this? Indeed, do you know of anyone who might have come into the community recently?"

Stearn shook his head. "I know nothing of this. Most of such people stayed out on the coast. Why would anyone come here?"

"You did," Darling pointed out.

"Inspector, you know nothing of our situation. The people who came away from Russia were aristocrats, professors, writers, scientists. People who had real standing in the old Russia. We had to flee, leaving everything behind, or risk imprisonment or death. We arrive in China, or here, with nothing, and we are nobody. I taught philosophy at the university in Moscow until I was unceremoniously turned out. Why did I come here? Because I must eat, Inspector. I decided that my best chance would be to hire myself out as a mere translator in a place far enough away from the coast that I would not meet any competition from my fellow refugees. As for others like me here, there are very few. Understand, I will not give you their names; however, I am willing to contact them and encourage them to call or visit you at the police station if they know of anything that will help you. I'm afraid it is all I can offer."

Darling, not for the first time in his work, was struck by his own ignorance of the greater circumstances and backgrounds of the many people whom trouble had thrown into involvement with the police. Stearn had been to him a somewhat tiresome and resentful person to whom he'd had to apply from time to time to translate in courtroom or interview situations. He imagined him now at the height of his powers as a prestigious member of a doomed society, brought to these threadbare circumstances.

"That will be wonderful, Mr. Stearn, if you could organize people to contact us. Thank you so much for your time." He stood up and offered Stearn his hand.

"I do not promise anything will come of it, Inspector."

PRECISELY AT THREE, Darling's phone rang, and he was put through to Constable Ames, who was calling, he said unnecessarily, from Vancouver.

"I know where you are, Ames. What are you doing?"

"Working hard, as instructed, sir. Do you miss me?"

"Certainly not. Your replacement is a respectful young man who doesn't put his feet up on desks. I need you to do something for me. I want you to nose around the recent émigré community from Russia. I want you to find out if there is, or has been, anyone there by the name of Vassily Mikhailov. An old lady called Countess Orlova has turned up here from China, saying she is looking for her brother and that she heard in Vancouver he had come here."

"Well, if he's supposed to be there, why am I looking here?"

Ames heard Darling sigh on the other end of the line.

"I'm trying to help her find her brother, using the resources of our exemplary police system. You wouldn't mind just doing what you're told and getting what you can?"

"Sir. Sorry, sir. What's his name again, silly-what?"

"Don't try me, Ames. This is costing money. Vassily Mikhailov." Darling followed up by spelling the name out. "Wire me when you have something."

"Righty-o. How is Miss Winslow?"

"Thriving, somehow, in the absence of your constant worship. Ames, I, uh, never mind. Just get to it."

"Yes, though you do know I'm trying to study for my exam coming up," Ames pointed out.

"Yes. So you say. Now run along."

He had been about to tell Ames about his upcoming wedding and ask him to stand as his best man. That effusion of whatever Ames was going to say on the subject could wait.

CHAPTER FOUR

A MES CLOSED HIS BOOK AND looked at his watch. He was scheduled to have a drink with another aspirant called Tompkins and then go for a bite. Tompkins was a local and might know where he could start with the Russian émigré community, something that, until that moment, he had not known existed.

The bar was noisy and smoky, and Tompkins was holding up his end, talking loudly between puffs on the subject of the study material they were being subjected to. "I mean, you read that stuff, and you think, it's all common sense, isn't it? They can ask me anything about a situation, and I could give them the right answer."

"Yes, I suppose you're right," said Ames. "There's all the regulations to remember exactly as well, though."

Tompkins offered him a cigarette, which Ames declined.

"Listen, my boss needs me to look into something." Ames leaned forward. "I need to look for some Russian who might be here as some sort of immigrant."

"Ruski, eh? Mostly here as displaced persons. They have a church near Hastings somewhere. I don't know why people don't just stay home. Do we need all these DPs who can't talk English? They never adapt or mix in. Just stick to themselves and never learn the lingo. Funny you should ask about them, actually. A buddy of mine told me one of them ended up dead a few days ago."

"Do you know the name?"

"Even if I'd heard it, I wouldn't be able to say it!"

Siberia, August 1947

"WHY ARE WE stopping?" someone asked. The question seemed to slowly penetrate the consciousnesses of the people dozing and ill in the train car, and they began to stir, coughing and struggling up off the floor.

Aptekar, who had been crammed into the corner, opened his eyes, and followed the upward movement of the others. He had been asleep, finally, after what had seemed days of rocking back and forth in the wooden confines of the cattle car, and he longed to return to sleep's forgetfulness. The energy, suddenly, of people getting up, pressing to peer through the cracks in the boards, asking each other questions, finally reached Aptekar, and he pushed himself to a standing position, slapping his legs to return circulation. The train certainly was slowing.

With a shriek of scraping metal, the train came to a complete halt, followed by the sound of steam releasing. The prisoners fell quiet, trying to hear the subject of the shouts now going on outside.

"We are nowhere," a young man, who still sported a bruise from a beating that covered most of the side of his face, called out. "You can see. It is some tiny station. They are running around outside like chickens. Something has happened." This statement caused another push to look through the slats. Aptekar didn't bother. Something was amiss. He could hear it in the voices of the soldiers outside the train. He primed himself to full alertness.

"We have to put these swine somewhere," he heard someone say just outside his corner of the car.

"We can't reach anybody," another complained. "Even the telephone is not working at this piss-pot of a station."

"Why can't they stay where they are? What's going to happen in the next hours? How far are we anyway? We've been travelling for more than a week."

There was a shout and then the talking soldiers receded. The prisoners could hear the sound of boots on the wooden platform. "There's an old fool of a telegraph operator," someone called.

"They've gone inside, no doubt to decide how best to eliminate us," the young man said, spitting out the words.

A woman sobbed and began to pray in a high-pitched voice, rocking back and forth.

"You call on God? Really? Have we not had proof enough of His non-existence over the last years? Shut up!" someone shouted. The woman reduced her praying to tearful whispers.

Aptekar kept his ear to the wall of the car and looked around at the people who had been unceremoniously pushed into the train by armed soldiers in Moscow with bundles of bread and sausage, some buckets for latrines, and a barrel of water with a metal cup. Re-education begins with the complete removal of all human dignity, he thought. The food was long gone, and the water sloshed in the bottom of the barrel, where the taste of rust and gasoline was intensifying. Aptekar thought that wherever they were being taken, they must be near. He had made the trip across the country more than once, and a week would get them nearly to Vladivostok, where he knew there were at least five labour camps, and on the way, many more.

He felt weak and leaned against the corner and closed his eyes, trying to recapture the oblivion of being asleep as he stood. Sitting down again felt like giving up and he wanted to be ready for whatever was about to happen.

It was dusk when the door of the car was slid open. People stood momentarily frozen, looking at the row of armed soldiers watching them, feeling the sudden gust of cool pine-scented air. Then they began to press forward. A young man, pushed from behind, tumbled out onto the rocky bed of the rails and cried out.

A soldier prodded him with the butt of his rifle to get him up, then shouted, "Everyone is to come out in an orderly fashion. You are to proceed over there to the station room. You will rest overnight, and we will continue in the morning on foot. There is a camp near Svobodny. And, *comrades*, do not attempt to leave. You will be shot." The sarcasm of that word, "comrades," was not lost on them.

Some of the young soldiers turned their faces away, closing their eyes and covering their noses, as the stench of unwashed people and overflowing latrines billowed out of the car. Aptekar was one of the last out. A young woman climbed down and then turned to help him.

"Leave him! Move on!" someone shouted at her.

"But he is old," she protested.

"Go, young woman. Do as they say. I thank you," Aptekar whispered to her. "I can manage."

Reluctantly she turned away, and Aptekar slid off the car on his stomach so he could slow his descent. He fell to his knees, and rose slowly to look surreptitiously at where they were. A small wooden train station, a water tower, dense, rapidly darkening forest. There must be a road, but he could not see it. Thank God it was not winter. He had seen people clinging to the outsides of trains freeze like blocks of ice.

"There are sick people," he said to one of the soldiers. "They need warmth, food, medicine. One of the women is pregnant."

"Do I look like a doctor to you? No one asked them to get sick. Now get inside."

Aptekar nodded his head once. It could have been acknowledgement, it could have been an expression of his feeling that this response was about what he'd expect from one of these soldiers of the revolution.

"He won't last ten minutes," a young soldier said, lifting his chin toward Aptekar. "He's old. Why do they bother? No bullets in Moscow?"

They want to see regret in our eyes before we expire, Aptekar thought. It is revenge for a thousand years of feudal repression. Somehow it is never enough for them, though.

At dawn, the soldiers, exhausted from having to be on guard all night, began to shout and kick the sleeping prisoners to get them up. Aptekar had found a corner again, having decided on the train that having no people on two sides was preferable to being hemmed in on all sides. He rose and slowly put on his jacket, which he'd used as an inadequate blanket during the cold and uncomfortable night. He did not at the moment know how, but he would not spend one night in the camp they were bound for. The soldier was right. He would not last ten minutes in one of the Soviet Empire's labour camps.

AMES WAS IN the morgue looking at the face of a man of indeterminate age who looked like his last few years had been difficult. He was gaunt and had an unkempt stubble on his chin as if he had been able to shave only intermittently. His hair was thinning and lank. "What's his name?"

The attendant looked at the label on the dead man's toe. "Goo something . . . Gusarov, Bogdan."

"How did he die?"

"Nothing obvious. He's pretty undernourished. Most likely natural causes. Post-mortem still to be done."

Ames nodded. "Where was he found?"

"No idea. I just look after them. Check upstairs."

Ames considered. It wasn't the man Darling was looking for. He'd have to go and find out if the party his boss was looking for was alive somewhere. "That's okay. Thanks for the time."

"You're welcome. Thanks for the visit. It's usually pretty quiet down here."

AMES GOT OFF the Hastings streetcar at Campbell and walked south. The church he had been directed to was a few blocks down and across from Georgia Street, and while he wasn't a connoisseur of churches in general, this one was quite beautiful on a sunny afternoon. White paint with a striking sky-blue bulb on the top with a cross on it. He hoped someone was there. The front door looked locked, and rather than try it, he went around to the back, hoping there might be some sort of office. He was in luck. The door was ajar, and when he climbed the steps and knocked, a heavily bearded middle-aged man in a black robe appeared.

"Yes?" He was smiling with what struck Ames as cautious politeness.

"I'm Constable Ames." He fished into his breast pocket for his identification. "I'm just trying to locate a Russian gentleman, and I wonder if you can help."

The priest nodded. "I am Father Petrov. What is the name of this man?" He had replaced polite with guarded. He had a strong accent, and pronounced each word carefully, as if he were still practicing English.

Ames pulled out the scrap of paper he'd written the man's name on and read it. "Vassily Mik . . . Mikhailov. Sorry. I can't say it very well."

The priest reached for the paper and read it. "Why would you be interested in this man?"

"My boss in Nelson is, actually. Apparently, his sister is looking for him."

"And why should he be here if she is all the way in Nelson?"

"Yes, sorry. Apparently, she came here from China and someone told her he had left here and gone farther inland to Nelson. I just need to find out if he was here, or what you can tell me."

"And her name?"

"Oh, gosh. Sorry. Countess something. I didn't write it down. I think my boss just wants to find anything he can to help her."

"Well, I'm sorry to tell you we will not be much help. I have never heard of this man. He might not even have been a true believer. If that is the case, he would never have come here to the church."

Ames, who'd wanted to have something to give Darling, was disappointed. "Oh. Well, thank you very much for your time." He put on his hat and offered his hand to the priest. He was at the bottom of the steps when the priest called out.

"Listen. I will ask around. Better me than you. People in my community are very suspicious and fearful of the police and people they don't know. No one will tell you anything. Where can I reach you?"

Buoyant again, Ames bounded back up the stairs and waited for the priest to find pen and paper, and gave him the number of his rooming house and the Nelson Police along with Inspector Darling's name.

Father Petrov walked Ames back to the sidewalk, watched him go back up the street toward Hastings, and tightened his lips.

LANE WAS SITTING on the porch with a cup of coffee and a book when she heard the countess coming through the French door.

"Good morning, Miss Winslow."

"Please," Lane said, getting up. "Sit here. May I get you tea? Coffee?"

"Tea, thank you. I slept very well. It must be the air." Orlova settled cautiously into the canvas deck chair. "I will paint today. I will start with this view." Lane's guest was wearing a wool skirt and a cream-coloured blouse and heavy beige stockings. She pulled a black hand-knit cardigan around her body and sat looking out at the lake.

While Lane was making the tea, she struggled with the details of being a host. How long had her guest been travelling? Should she offer to do her laundry? Would she want to visit the local people with her? Would she want to nap in the afternoon? On Wednesday, Lane was scheduled to meet the vicar with Darling. Would Orlova wish to come into town? On Saturday Darling was scheduled to come out to spend the day with her. How would they include her? She poured water over the tea leaves and then idly wondered if she ought to haul her samovar out of storage in the attic, and in the same instant rejected the idea. If she examined her motives, she guessed that she was being churlish—not wanting to establish any comforts that would make her guest stay longer. Right, she thought. Let's start at the beginning. Breakfast. She had lovely eggs from Gladys Hughes's chickens, and a boiled egg and piece of toast was the place to start.

She topped up her coffee and then put the tea and some sugar next to Orlova on the metal table she had brought from France when she first moved here.

"Why did you come all the way here?" Orlova asked Lane.

"I just wanted to do something new, I suppose. I can't go back to my childhood home in Latvia. I don't really want to be in England. So here I am."

The countess turned and looked at her. She was holding her mug of tea in both hands, warming them in the cool air of the morning. Lane looked up and was held by the penetrating dark eyes that examined her. She's intelligent, Lane thought. What could she have been if she had not spent her life in privilege? Then she looked away. It was not like she had been doing much with whatever intelligence she had, since settling into her comfortable country life in King's Cove.

Countess Orlova sat back and looked out at the lake. The sun skittered across the water, and light was beginning to climb up the mountains on the opposite shore, changing the charcoal shadows of the morning into the blue-green of the day.

"I never wanted to leave my home," she said. "When the revolution came, I lived with my family in our home by the Neva. My father was a count, but he worked for the diplomatic corps. My own husband, a count also and a major in the czar's army. I had a child, did I tell you? A little girl. She died of diphtheria in 1917. I moved back to my family and was so bereft that I did not think of what was going on outside until the day they came.

"The only reason I am alive today and not rotting in some prison is because my brother and I were out riding. I did not want to go or do anything because I was inconsolable, but he had begged me so much that I agreed to go with him. It was like something out of a story. There is a little hill behind our house, and we had ridden up from the river to the top of that hill and we saw it. Our house surrounded by soldiers, our servants, our farm workers pulling our possessions out the doors and throwing them into the yard, going through them, shouting, taking whatever they wanted.

"You can't even think when you see something like that. You can't comprehend the sudden end to all you've known. I wanted to rush down, find Mother, make them stop. But my brother held me back. He took me to a cabin in a wooded area of our land where he used to go drinking with his friends sometimes, and he told me to wait. When he returned, he had peasant clothes for me to wear and some food, and he said we had to leave. With the confusion of the revolution and the war, we were able to get out. And that was that. So here I am, drinking your tea."

Ignoring her own curiosity about how Orlova had filled the intervening thirty years, Lane said, "I am so sorry, Countess. I just think of Russia today as being the Soviet Union, impregnable, socialist. My own grandparents had their house taken over but were allowed to live there until they couldn't stand it anymore, so they returned to Scotland with what little they had. But to think about how it began, the countless agonizing stories like yours . . ."

Orlova sighed and shook her head. "It is in the past. We must carry on, have a purpose. My purpose is to find my brother, and bury him or look after him, whichever will be required of me. And now, you must help me out of this chair, or I will remain here all day."

CHAPTER FIVE

London, August 1947

"**H**E'S DISAPPEARED, SIR."

The director looked up. "What do you mean, disappeared?"

"I mean, we sent someone to the contact point at the Yugoslav border near Trieste, and he wasn't there. Our man asked around discreetly, and there was no sign he'd ever been there."

"Thank you. That will be all," the director said.

When his secretary was gone, the director rose abruptly and stood looking out the window at the clouds gathering above the buildings across from his offices on Curzon Street and put his mind to trying to frame the next steps. Thanks to Lane Winslow, a possibly very useful ageing Soviet agent had asked for sanctuary in England, and now it would appear they'd bungled it somehow. It was a sacrifice, and it had better be worth it. Regardless of the sequence of events, he had to try to assess how they might be exposed by this. What did this Aptekar know about the workings of British intelligence? And what was he, the director, losing in the way of Soviet clandestine knowledge? All he had in hand was what Winslow had told him: that she had told Aptekar nothing but that she had no intention of becoming a double agent, and in turn, the Russian agent had offered to come across and retire in England—but had given her nothing.

Had his contact been pulling the wool over his eyes? Perhaps that agent never had any intention of crossing. Perhaps it was a ruse to test the porousness of British intelligence. It was infuriating that he had no way of knowing if he could trust his contact. The agency was already under the gun because they didn't seem to be able to keep up with the machinations of their counterparts on the other side. The Soviet state security apparatus, the MGB, was evolving fast, changing tactics. It didn't seem to be interested in labour unions or other ways to spread socialism on foreign soil. Since the thirties, they had been setting their sights on turning high-profile members of British society for the express purpose of strengthening the Soviet hand over the West, and there was no indication that they were going to stop. It was these latest names he had bargained for. Otherwise it would all have been for naught.

He would have to get hold of Lane Winslow and ask her to go over everything that had transpired in Berlin between herself and Stanimir Aptekar again. He wouldn't go himself this time. He had a man in Vancouver he could send, though he regretted this; he still had fond memories of his long wartime affair with her, despite her palpable dislike of him now. In fact, he was happy that he could inconvenience her, when all she wanted to do was get away completely and forever from her old life. No doubt she saw herself immersed in domestic bliss with that prat Frederick Darling. The director's ability to disrupt the lives of people far away pleased him, and he turned, optimistic again, and pushed the call button on his desk.

"Better bring in the Yugoslav file," he snapped into the microphone. Might as well make it look good, and in any case, he might have missed something. He was surprised not to have heard from his contact.

"AND THAT'S IT, sir," Ames finished. "I mean, someone might get hold of me, but the priest didn't make it seem very likely."

"Well, it was a long shot. I'll send you out a picture of him anyway. I've got others out with the RCMP."

"What about the dead guy, sir?"

"What about the dead guy, Ames? He's dead, and he's not our man. What are they teaching you out there, anyway?"

Ames cleared his throat nervously. "You're the one who always told me that coincidences should be paid attention to. I just wondered if it was important that just when we're looking for a Russian, one turns up dead."

"I also always told you that sometimes coincidences are just coincidences," Darling pointed out. But he was thoughtful; Ames had stumbled into the right idea from time to time in the past. "Why? What are you thinking?"

Asked directly like that, Ames was suddenly not really sure what he was thinking. "I think I was thinking that it might matter how the guy here was killed. I mean if he died of starvation, and he could have by the look of him, then okay, it probably means nothing. But what if he was murdered? Then you have something more like one man missing and one murdered."

Darling made a noise that sounded like acknowledgement. "When are they doing the post-mortem?"

"I can find out, sir."

"Do that and get back to me. How are your digs?"

"I have a very sweet-looking landlady who is as ferocious a woman as I've ever met. No visitors, no food if you're late, no smoking, no drinking, and a sharp rap on the knuckles if you don't make your bed on the way out."

"It's good for you. Your mother is much too indulgent. Nose to the grindstone, Ames. We're paying for you to get this promotion. And keep away from girls with flower names!"

"Yes, sir," said Ames cheerfully. When he hung up, he left the telephone booth and put his hands in his pockets and turned toward Cordova Street, where the Vancouver Police were housed, and began to whistle.

THE COUPLE LAY, familiar and lazy, in the afternoon heat, which was only slightly mitigated by the shade of the tree they stretched under. The air carried the sweet scent of cottonwood. The blanket they lay on was disordered.

"I wish this would never end," the woman said, her arm across her lover's chest.

He turned and propped his head on his hand. He could feel the pebbles in the sand under his elbow. "It wouldn't have to if you just left him. You don't even have children.

There's nothing to keep you there." His voice, starting soft, began to take on frustration as it did whenever the subject came up.

The woman pulled away from him, lying back with her arm across her forehead. "You know I can't. He, well, you know what he's like. Let's just leave it and not ruin what we have. Please. He'll be hunting again soon, and we can be together then, like usual."

The man did know what he was like. They had been friends and had hunted together. That was before he'd fallen for the soft and gentle promise of his friend's wife.

"I hate him," the man said simply.

He stood up and began to put his clothes to rights.

"YOU HAVE A Russian lady staying with you?" asked Eleanor, surprised. "You must bring her around. How long is she staying?" She looked up as the door to the post office swung open, and Mabel Hughes came through. "Hello, Mabel. Lane has a Russian lady staying with her. She was just about to tell me about it."

Lane smiled. Her neighbours in King's Cove included Eleanor and Kenny Armstrong, who nurtured her and fed her tea and sandwiches like loving grandparents, and the Hughes ladies, Gladys in her seventies and her two daughters, Gwen and Mabel, in their late fifties, who were vigorous no-nonsense women in rubber galoshes who created the most divine gardens. She had grown extremely fond of them and used to the intense gossip they all indulged in.

"Well, it's just an odd series of circumstances, really," Lane said. "She apparently lost track of her brother and is trying to find him. She turned up at the vicar's in Nelson, and he hadn't had time to find her anything, so she's staying with me. She's busy painting a picture of the lake as we speak. She doesn't speak much English, so she was a bit reluctant to come out and meet people. She does very nice watercolours. She showed me some she brought with her from China."

"China! And a missing brother. How interesting!"

Trust Eleanor to leap to the mystery, Lane thought, smiling.

"You'll need more eggs," pronounced Mabel practically. "And we none of us fool ourselves that you cook very much at your house. You'd better have a few vegetables and some bread as well. We've bottled the beans, and always have more than we can eat."

"You're not far wrong there," Lane admitted. "But I'm going to pull up my socks on that front. I bought proper food in town, and I intend to produce proper meals. You're very kind, Mabel. I will buy the vegetables from you as I do the eggs. I may need to get a few recipes as well."

"When are you going to need a few recipes for that nice inspector of yours is what I ask myself," Mabel said, nodding her thanks to Eleanor for the bundle of mail, and then turning to Lane.

Eleanor leaned over the counter with interest. She'd been wondering the same thing but was much too respectful of Lane's privacy to ask it in the public venue of the post office.

Lane was acutely conscious that she had told no one in King's Cove about her upcoming marriage, especially when it was less than a month away and to be conducted in King Cove's own St. Joseph's, the little Anglican church by the creek near the turnoff to the Nelson road. The vicar came there most weeks to conduct a service. Had he hinted anything? She doubted it. He was a man of utter rectitude and restraint. She supposed the rumour mill was fed by the fact that Darling had been visiting her so often over the weekends. She longed to say something now, especially as she hoped to invite everyone anyway, but she felt she couldn't until she'd told Angela Bertolli, her great friend who lived on the upper road, and Eleanor herself, who seemed as fond of Lane as her own grandmother in Scotland was.

"I'd better get back to my guest," Lane said, and gave everyone a cheerful wave.

Eleanor had given her a lovely nosegay of orange mums and blue mist that would go into Lane's deep blue glass vase, which she had brought with her wherever she moved. Perhaps Countess Orlova would like to paint them, Lane thought as she made her way back over the simple wooden bridge that crossed the narrow gorge between her house and the post office.

THE COUNTESS WAS sitting on the porch with a board on her lap, looking out at the lake scene before her. She had taken two kitchen chairs out with her, one to sit on and one to hold her metal box of paints, a glass of water, a cloth roll of brushes, and pencils and a rag. She had washed the paper with a translucent sky blue and was now sketching in the lake, the mountains, the frame of the nearer forest. She could hear Lane coming back into the house but did not turn away from her work. She suspected her hostess would have the kind of manners that would leave her in peace until she was finished. She stopped drawing and sat back. She felt, as she always did, subsumed into the landscape she painted. It freed her from thought and anxiety like nothing else. It made her real, legitimate. At the moment, it allowed her to forget her fears that she had been misdirected and that he would not come here—and what would she do if she did find him?

Orlova shook her head and refocused on the lake. One thing at a time, she told herself. If there was anything she had learned in her life, it was that you could plan your life all you wanted, but fate was a wave that swept all before it. To survive you must swim with the current.

Russia, 1895

"WHY DOES VASYA get to go to school and I have to stay here?" Tatiana asked peevishly. She had slung herself sideways into an armchair, her feet dangling toward the open French doors. It was early September, and her brother was preparing to return to the General Staff Academy in Saint Petersburg, where he was in officer training and studied surveying.

"The same refrain from you every year, my dear girl. Why do I spend a small fortune on tutors for you if you are going to complain? If anything, you are better educated than he is."

"No, but seriously, Papa, why can't girls be officers? Think of the things someone like me could do if the men were at war, organizing people back at home to support the war effort."

Her father shook his head and laughed. "I did not think, when your mother first presented me with a girl, that she would produce such hours of entertainment and amusement . . . and such a rebellious spirit. If your mother comes in here, by the way, she will not be amused to find you with your feet all over the furniture."

Tatiana swung her legs off the chair and put her feet sedately on the floor. With an exaggerated motion she composed her skirt over the laces of her shoes. "You see, Papa, it makes me think you do not take me seriously. Am I not as smart as he is? Admit it, smarter, even though I'm younger? I want to be something important."

The count folded his newspaper carefully and put it down on the table beside his chair. He looked with affection and concern at his daughter. She was right.

"You are much, much smarter than your brother. And you mustn't think you are not important. You are vastly important to us. And wait," he put up his hand. "Before you say it, not just because of how you will marry, but because when you go into society you can have enormous influence. The whole empire is run by women from the drawing rooms. There. Is that not enough ambition for you?"

"That is a fairy story, Papa. I've seen those women in our drawing room. They talk of nothing but clothing and the servants, and they gossip viciously about each other, 'My Nickolas said this, my Sasha said that.' They have no minds of their own, they just parrot whatever their husbands say." She leaned forward and whispered angrily, "Does my own sainted mother have one original thought?"

She threw herself back into the chair and gazed out at the garden. She could see the fields, a sea of gold, beyond the hedges. Soon it would be harvest, and the hapless peasants would be slaving over the scything on all the neighbouring estates. There was a beautiful painting of a harvest done by a friend of her father's hanging over the fireplace. Two women were bent over the golden wheat with hand scythes, their clothing white, their faces plump and rosy. She had always loved the painting. It had made her want to paint. But of late she had seen the lie. Those women were no better than slaves, to their fathers, their brothers, their husbands, their landlords. They were exhausted, and they and their children were perpetually hungry because they had no time to farm their own puny plots.

"I am sorry, Papa. I should not have said that. I was thinking about the harvest, and I am happy to have a papa who brings machinery so that people do not have to break their backs. I see your kindness to them, and I want to be like you. I am terrified of becoming someone's wife, and my only contribution to this world being to gossip about my neighbour."

Her father looked sad. She was not wrong. Her idealism came from him. It surprised him to see it in this wiry, dark-eyed, beautiful fifteen-year-old girl. But she was doomed to disillusion, as he had been. The world would not part for this giant of a girl. It would slowly and irrevocably reduce her to its demands. He only hoped that when the time came she would find a husband equal to her and that children would engage her passions. He shifted uneasily in his chair. If his wife had anything to do with it, it would be sooner than later. "She is ridiculous with her airs," his wife had said to him. "Marriage will take care of that. It is not too early to find someone. I've told you before. What are you waiting for?" The count stood up and offered his hand to his daughter.

"Come, show me your latest. The sketch of the cook's daughter was excellent. M. Benet must be very proud of you!"

CHAPTER SIX

—————

THE PATHOLOGIST SAT AT HIS desk leafing through the papers on a clipboard.

"I did this one this morning as a matter of fact. Nothing unusual. Heart attack. Why do you need this, again?"

He looked up at Ames, who sat expectantly opposite him. He was young, not much older than Ames, which surprised the constable. He always assumed pathologists were staid middle-aged types like Ashford Gillingham, affectionately known as Gilly, in Nelson.

"My boss in Nelson, sir. He likes to dot his i's and cross his t's. There's a search on for someone from this Russian community here who might have gone inland. He has a sister looking for him."

"If this isn't the same man, I don't see how it helps. In any case, nothing unusual, no wounds, gunshots, evidence of beating, and so on. He had a faint rash on his neck from the heat, probably. His heart stopped suddenly. He was undernourished and had a weak heart. Chapter and verse. Case closed."

Ames sat silently for a few moments, making pleats in his trouser leg, and then, anxious not to be a nuisance, but suddenly quite clear on this point, he said, "Would you mind if I had a look? I mean, I'm not a medico or anything, but I'm imagining my boss giving me what for if I don't."

"It's not very inspiring, but if you insist. No skin off my nose."

They made their way down the stairs to the basement morgue.

"What made you go into this racket?" Ames asked.

"I had a professor who was very interesting on forensic science. He made it seem like discovering what people die of was the most fascinating job in the world. I like mysteries, and being able to be at the centre of them seemed like a nice way to make a living."

Ames wrinkled his nose. "That's a lot of time with dead bodies."

"True, but you have to deal with their grieving families, and find their dangerous killers. My end of it is very peaceful and quiet."

The pathologist pulled the drawer and exposed the corpse. Ames looked at it. This time he saw the rash on the neck and leaned in, trying not to breathe. The area looked raised, and its pink colour was in contrast to the pale skin around it. "Is it surprising that this rash is just on this one part of his neck?"

"Ever had a rash? It's usually in patches."

"I suppose you're right. I got a rash from nettles on my arm when I was a kid. It should have died down in a couple of hours, but I had some sort of reaction and got these sort of raised welts." Ames walked around the rest of the corpse. "Does he have it anywhere else?"

"No, but it wasn't the rash that killed him, may I remind you. It was his heart."

Ames nodded. "Right. I don't know why I got fixated on it. My boss has a real thing about looking at anything unusual. But as I said, I'm not a doctor. Okay, thanks. That should soothe the savage boss back home."

"That bad, is he?" the pathologist said as he wheeled away the last remains of Bogdan Gusarov.

"No, not really. I shouldn't say that. He does razz me a fair bit, but he's a damn good detective."

"I SHOULD LIKE to walk," Orlova said.

The painting she had done while Lane was at the post office was on the window seat in the sitting room, where she had put it to dry thoroughly.

"Yes, a walk before lunch is just the thing. Let me—"

"No, no," Orlova said. "It is not my intention to derange you by dragging you around the countryside. I need only some instructions, and I will go on my own. I will take my painting case and may need to sit to capture a scene."

"Oh," Lane said, nonplussed. "Are you sure? I'm quite happy to come with you. I generally walk a good deal myself. There are a number of paths here that—"

"Am I likely to become lost?"

"No. I mean, whichever path you take it ends up back at either someone's house or the main road. Here. Let me draw you a map."

If her guest wanted to walk on her own, Lane thought, she must certainly do it. Lane understood well the desire to be alone with one's thoughts, and poor Orlova must have many disturbing thoughts to be alone with. She took a piece of paper from the pile by her typewriter and quickly sketched out the main road system of King's Cove and all the paths that she herself had trodden, including her two favourites: the one that looped up to the old schoolhouse, and the one that went through the meadow on the way to Angela Bertolli's house.

"You can also go down to the lake, but we usually drive there as it's an awful climb back up. Perhaps we'll do that tomorrow if the weather holds. And perhaps, this afternoon, we could stop by to see my friends, the Armstrongs. We've been invited for tea."

"I see," said her guest in a non-committal tone.

Lane watched her tie her laces and affix the crumpled black hat that she had been wearing when Lane had first met her in Nelson—which was only yesterday but already seemed like days ago—and then stood by the door as Orlova marched firmly up along the driveway and out the gate, the map and a cane in one hand and one of her small, brown suitcases, converted to a paint box, in the other.

"I will be fine!" Orlova called back when she got to where the car was parked.

Earnestly hoping this would be so, Lane went back to the sitting room and sank into her easy chair, watching the sky through the open window. It would be a right nuisance to have to drag her guest along a path if she collapsed. And that was only assuming she'd be able to find her. After some moments of reflecting on how strained she already felt after only one day, Lane pulled her socks up and went to the window seat to look at the painting. It was absolutely marvellous. The lake lay in perfect crystalline stillness in the morning sun. Orlova had managed to capture the soft scattering of cumulus cloud in the intensely blue sky high above the distant mountains. Wishing she could accomplish such artistic magic, Lane held the painting up and turned to each of her walls wondering where she would hang it if it were hers. Then she remembered the countess had said she would paint some pictures as a thank you—and settled on the south wall.

With a residue of anxiety about how the countess would cope on the narrow winding paths of the Cove, Lane turned her mind to the business of meals, a much more anxiety-inducing proposition. She had bought a small chicken, and she presumed she would roast it in her oven without too much difficulty, but for how long? She had made a few things in the oven since she had arrived. A roast beef once for Darling, and she had attempted brownies with Angela's encouragement the year before. Perhaps she should spend her morning making brownies so they had them for after dinner. She would have to go upstairs to the attic and pull out the box her books had come in from England. She had left her two cookbooks in the box, but with a marriage in the offing, it was time to pull them out. It would be extremely instructive for Darling as well, since he had less idea than she did, if that were possible, about how to put a meal together.

"YOU AGAIN. YOU'RE supposed to be studying."

Darling had been contemplating whether it made sense to drive up the lake and perhaps do the loop around New Denver to Slocan and back with the photograph of the missing man. There were a number of Russians living along that route though they were not the émigré Russians Vassily Mikhailov was likely to seek out. For that more elusive group, he would have to hope that Stearn would be successful in getting someone to contact him at the police station.

"I would be studying, sir," said Ames, "if I weren't off on goose chases for you."

"Nothing doing then, on the Vancouver corpse?"

"There never was, sir. It's the wrong man, but I did go back and had the pathologist read me the report, and then I actually asked to see the damn thing. I expect a raise when I get back."

"I've never known you to be squeamish, Constable."

"No, sir, but you can hardly expect me to love looking at dead people."

"Then you should have trained as a teacher. Have you got some brilliant insight, or not?"

"No, I'm afraid not. The guy evidently died of heart failure. Of course, trust me to get off on a side road. The guy had a rash on the back of his neck, and I thought it was odd, so I kept asking questions about that instead of focusing on the fact that the guy died of a heart attack and that's that. I think I wanted to, I don't know, have this corpse be related to your missing brother."

As soon as Ames had said this, he wished it unsaid. It would make him look foolish in his boss's eyes.

To his surprise, Darling grunted at the other end of the line. "No harm in that. Always looking for a connection. It's what you're supposed to do. And not hang on to an idea when it's the wrong one. It seems to me you have again stumbled on the right course of action. Look at something that might be relevant, think it through logically, and then discard as necessary."

"Thanks, sir. I think I felt a bit of an idiot. Like the country bumpkin policeman in the city."

"Listen, Ames," Darling was suddenly serious. "We never, with all that we do, can know the full story of someone's murder, the full deep reason why someone would kill someone else, what those last minutes were like. But we are humans, and there is a certain amount that we know about the world around us from what we feel, and while these feelings do not constitute forensic evidence, they can sometimes be an indicator that we need to look more deeply. You had a feeling about that rash, but it was just a rash, and you know that because the pathologist told you how he died. But if he were our case, those feelings might cause me to leave the door ajar and wait to see if something comes through."

Ames was silent for a moment. "Thank you, sir. Obviously not a murder, and as you say, not our case." Ames paused. "I don't think that part about feelings is in the sergeants' manual, by the way."

LANE WAITED ANXIOUSLY for the return of her guest and breathed a sigh of relief when she heard her come in the door a little after four.

"Countess, you are back! I worried that you might have got lost," she exclaimed. Not to mention banging about in the woods lugging her suitcase-cum-painting box around, Lane thought.

"I am sorry to worry you. I found a lovely place to paint, and I lost track of time," Orlova said. "Dear me, look at my clothes covered in plant life. Let me change quickly, and I shall be ready for your friends."

Lane thought again, as she sat near the weeping willow by the front door, about what it was like to live with someone else and have to take on this whole new layer of accommodation: being quiet in the early morning, waiting in the afternoon to go to tea. It suddenly seemed to her a massive risk to take Darling permanently into her life. What if she hadn't the patience for it?

AS SOON AS Lane and Orlova arrived at Eleanor's home, Eleanor graciously opened the screen door wearing her broadest, dentured smile. Her brilliant white hair had been carefully treated with a blue rinse and then coiffed; she'd put on the frock she wore to church on summer days.

"Welcome, Countess!" she said. "Come in, come in!"

Orlova nodded at Eleanor with a slight smile and stepped up into the kitchen. "But it is a charming cottage," she said to Lane, her smile more genuine, as she saw the polished iron and white enamel of the stove, and the long sink under the window that looked out on the north garden and the lake far below.

"She says it is a lovely cottage," Lane translated. "Where's Alexandra? Usually she is part of the reception committee."

Eleanor smiled and nodded and then extended her arm through to the sitting room. "We thought she might be a bit much, so we've put her into the bedroom with a snack. Kenny is through there. We couldn't decide whether to have tea in the garden because the weather is so fine, or use the sitting room, but we've opened the windows and really, one forgets how lovely it can be. You know how often we use it!"

The little-used parlour had been aired and a formal tea table set near the window seat along with two beautiful chairs from the previous century, the dust covers removed, exposing the fine green damask upholstery on the seats.

Kenny looked up from setting out the cups and smiled broadly, the skin around his eyes wrinkling, and he bowed slightly. "Welcome," he said, holding out a chair.

Orlova composed herself on the chair and looked around the room. Lane tried to imagine how Orlova would see the room. There was a glass-fronted cabinet full of photos and treasures brought from the old country, a round wood stove that was used only in the winter, and only to bring down the damp. A dark inset in the wall was given over to shelves of books, which Lane realized she had never looked over. What sort of reading did the Armstrongs do? She only ever saw them reading the *Nelson Daily News*. Judging by the spines, many of the books must have belonged to Kenny's deceased mother, Lady Armstrong, in whose house Lane now lived. There was a row of photographs of the early years of King's Cove on the wall against which the sofa lived and a round table with only the silver-framed photograph of Kenny's brother, John, who had died in the Great War.

A sharp yapping suddenly rose up from the bedroom. "Is there a dog?" Orlova asked, surprised.

"Yes. A lovely little thing. Our hosts thought she might be too much excitement," said Lane.

"May I not see her? I have a great fondness for dogs."

"Countess Orlova would like to meet Alexandra," Lane translated.

Looking relieved not to keep their West Highland terrier incarcerated in the bedroom when she had been used to having the run of the house, Kenny went off to release her.

For the first time since Lane had met her, Orlova looked genuinely pleased and relaxed as the dog wiggled around her feet and sniffed at her shoes. "What is she called?"

"Alexandra," Lane said. "I want one myself."

"The name of an empress!" Orlova said, ruffling the dog's fur.

The tea, which had threatened to be a strain with all the exaggerated formality and difficulty of translating back and forth, proved to be very pleasant after all, thanks in large part to Alexandra, admiration for whom required no translation. Orlova, so reserved and restrained, made an effort to make herself agreeable and, sparing no compliments for the excellent sandwiches and walnut cake, got up and began to smile and point at objects around the room. She admired the regimental sword that had belonged to Kenny's father and pointed with interest at a picture of Eleanor as a nursing sister with her colleagues that was taken in France in 1915. Then she stopped at the picture of John.

"That is Kenny's younger brother. He died in France in the Great War," Lane said.

Orlova picked up the picture carefully and gazed at it and then looked at Kenny with an expression of deep sympathy. "It is terrible to lose a brother," she said softly.

Lane translated this and explained that her guest was seeking her own brother and didn't know if he was alive or dead.

Kenny nodded, then sighed. "Well, then. Shall we have a look at the garden?"

ON THE WAY back to Lane's house Orlova said, "You are lucky. They are good people. Kind people. What a life you live here, you cannot imagine!"

"They are very kind and are good friends."

Orlova shook her head as they emerged from the little copse of trees that separated Lane's house from the post office.

"Friends." She stopped to gaze at the weeping willow and pond by the side of the house. "You know, we had friends. These friends were the ones who reported us to the commissariat. People who had eaten at our table, drunk my father's brandy, smiled, and simpered. I know I should not be bitter. We would have been tossed out sooner or later. And they were no doubt looking to protect themselves. I don't even feel satisfaction that it did them no good. One of them survived. I met her in Shanghai. I don't doubt she was informing there as well. You see. You are lucky."

Lane nodded, struck forcefully by the vast difference in their circumstances. The great socialist paradise bred distrust and fear at every level. She tried to imagine how people might be changed by living in such a society every day of their lives. How could one grow up to be honest and straightforward, if one had to combat potential treachery on every side?

"What would you like to do now?" she asked.

"I think a nap, if that is all right. And if I may use your basin to rinse one or two things."

"I can throw them in with my laundry. I'll probably do a wash in a couple of days."

"No, no. I am used to this from travelling. I take very little with me, and just wash and dry as I go."

"Well then," Lane said, relieved by her guest's independence. "The clothespins are in a bag by the line. And I will pop up the road to return some things to my friend Angela and leave you in perfect peace."

THE DARK WAS absolute in the forest. He had his knife in his belt, but instead of his rifle, he had his revolver in the pocket of his jacket. He was hunting, after all. Verne Taylor had been on this trip with Brodie many times. He'd begged off the last couple of years, though. Work, he'd said. But it wasn't that. It was her.

He knew it was wrong, but he loved her, and he could not bear to watch Brodie hit her and treat her like a slave. Hesitating, he thought of the last time they were together, alone in the wooded glade in a remote cove, making love. Afterward, she had said it was no use, that they lived in a fantasy. That it was too risky to go on. His heart ached remembering the hopelessness in her sweet eyes. He took a jagged, anxious breath and picked his way forward with his flashlight. Near the creek, he would turn it off. He could find his way blindfolded.

He felt the tension that was akin to alertness, excitement even. He was used to this, though it had been thirty years since his war. He was eighteen again suddenly, still lying on a hill in the dark, still picking off the Boche when they struck a match or looked over the trench wall, the wavering light of the kerosene lanterns below, outlining the dark and unmissable target.

He could hear the creek in the distance, behind the line of trees. He turned off his flashlight and stood, waiting for his eyes to get accustomed to the dark. Listening.

CHAPTER SEVEN

August 1947

THE FIVE SOLDIERS WHO HAD been assigned to guard the transport of prisoners to Svobodny prison camp were tired. Aptekar could see that. Tired and unhappy. They were young and had been given a job they no doubt thought would be easy. Transport the prisoners by rail, deliver them, get back to their barracks outside of Moscow. By rights they should be on the train going home by now, laughing through the smoke of cigarettes hanging carelessly off their lips, drinking vodka, playing cards, taking advantage of the week it would take to get home. Instead they had been obliged to try to stay awake in shifts to guard the prisoners and were now forced to walk with their charges along the dirt road, probably experiencing the same dogged weariness as their prisoners, through the unchanging scenery of the dark and looming forest.

Aptekar had heard them talking. They had been told by some commander by telegraph—and then reported brusquely to their prisoners—that they should arrive by nightfall if they kept moving. One of the soldiers suggested that any stragglers would be shot. So here they were, two at the front, two at the back, and the threatening one looking, Aptekar thought, like he'd enjoy the opportunity to shoot someone, if only to relieve his own feelings of anger.

They were shambling in an ever-lengthening column as older people, the sick, the pregnant woman lagged further behind. Someone asked if they could stop. The answer came in the form of shouted instructions to keep moving. Aptekar tried to keep himself in the back third of the line and along the edge. If any opportunity arose, he would take it. There had been quiet yet aggrieved conversation among the prisoners as they had started out in the morning, but now only the shuffle of feet was audible, even the guards having given up on conversation.

"Hey!" one of the guards at the rear exclaimed.

Just ahead of Aptekar a man had stumbled and fallen and was making no attempt to get up, forcing the shuffling mass to split and move around him. Both the rear guards moved forward, holding their rifles at the ready. The commotion had not yet reached the front of the line.

"Get up!" one of them shouted while the other prodded the fallen man with his boot.

"You can shoot me if you want . . ."

What else the man was saying was lost on Aptekar. This was what he had waited for. Both guards were now in front of him, and the prisoners were distracted. The young soldiers looked angry and confused, maybe not so sure about shooting. Aptekar slipped out of the line and made for the forest, his heart beating wildly with the sudden need for speed and the fear that someone would give the alarm, perhaps another prisoner hoping to gain favour or one of the guards from the front of the line who had been forced to turn back and look at what the trouble was.

He stumbled through the underbrush at the edge of the road, feeling it grabbing at his legs, and then he was in the forest, where there was only silence. Winded by his sudden acceleration, Aptekar stopped and fell to his knees on the deep blanket of pine needles, his chest heaving as he tried to catch his breath. He was too old for this sort of thing. He looked back in the direction from which he'd come and was amazed that there was no one in pursuit. He could still hear shouting, but he did not bother to listen anymore. Pushing himself back to his feet, he began to move deeper into the forest, travelling parallel to the road, and back toward the train station. It would be night before he got there. He would consider his options then.

The spaces between the trees were densely packed with dried underbrush impeding his progress and causing him to stumble, but he knew if he was to have any chance, he could not stop. The shot, when it came, sounded farther away than he expected. It was a crack, like someone hitting a tree with a metal pole. Aptekar stopped, noticed the pounding of his heart, and waited. The forest seemed to press closer and wrap around him, muffling any further sound. He forced himself to move again, farther from the road, but still in the direction of the station. If they had shot the prisoner, then someone would notice he was gone. They would know he would have bolted into the forest nearest him. If they had the will to look for him, that is where they would go.

He travelled for another quarter of an hour and then stopped. The silence was total. Even birds do not like to be in here, he thought. He felt sure that he would hear people if they came after him, but in the next moment he was not sure. He suddenly felt that the dense forest stifled even the sound of his own breath. He made an abrupt decision to go in a direct line back toward the road. He was sure that he had passed the point where the road took a slight bend toward the east. When he reached the ditch that marked the edge of the gravel road, he stopped and listened again.

Nothing.

Cautiously he walked forward and peered in the direction the column of prisoners had gone, but they had disappeared. With alacrity he hurtled across the road and charged into the forest. He would continue his journey on the other side. He thought for a moment of the man they must have killed, pushed perhaps into the ditch. Well, Aptekar thought, once again moving toward the train station, he took his way out. Now I take mine.

"WHAT HAVE YOU done with your guest?" Darling asked. Darling and Lane were walking companionably to their appointment with the vicar.

"She seems quite happy being alone. She spends her days painting. She's really very good. If she gets bored, I have a few Russian novels in the bookshelves, though I'm sure she's read them all. She's quite a vigorous old thing. Goes for a long walk every day."

"Well, isn't that nice."

"I don't know why you're taking on. She's not staying with you!"

"No, indeed," Darling conceded. "I'm not a big enough human being, I'm afraid, to throw my doors open to a complete stranger. You know nothing about her."

"I do too. She's a sad and harmless old lady who lost everything in a revolution. She has terrible stories to tell." Even as she said this, Lane thought about the focused, piercing quality in Orlova's eyes.

"There is nothing more terrifying, in my view, than an old lady. They depend for their camouflage on the innocence of their looks, but I've seen old ladies wield umbrellas and canes with lethal effect. We had a case before the war of a gang of well-armed hold-up artists who were run out of a mountain hideout by an old woman of eighty."

"Really, Inspector. Are you quite finished?"

"Yes, darling. But I speak only partially in jest. If the vicar doesn't find her someplace, she could become a fixture. We'll have to move the furniture around her," he said. "Though she could be useful holding a lamp, I suppose."

Lane stopped and put her hand on his arm. She could see the vicarage half a block along. "Darling, are you sure about the house? I feel such a brute saying I won't move."

She and Darling had discussed where they would live when they were married, and Darling had said instantly that he would be happy to move out to King's Cove. He could keep his little house on the hill in town for when his work required him to be nearby, but otherwise he was quite prepared to commute. After all, David Bertolli, Angela's husband, drove into town every day to teach music, and he seemed happy enough.

Darling took her hand and kissed it. "I don't really know what is meant by the phrase 'to make someone happy.' They always say that, don't they, when they talk about people being in love, and I'm not sure that it is possible for, or really the job of, any one person to make another happy. But I am certain that you are happy there, and that that house means everything to you. I want more than anything for you to be happy," he said, "as happy as I am because you have consented to love me. So yes, I am sure. Anyway, the views are great, and I will get much-needed exercise cutting wood for the stove."

Lane beamed. "We are in such good agreement that I can't see the vicar will have anything left to do."

The vicar's office was panelled with dark wood and book shelves so crammed with books that all those that didn't fit were piled on top of the shelved books. More books were stacked precariously on the side table under a reading lamp.

"What a massive collection of books!" Lane said. "Are they all ecclesiastical?"

"In one way or another, I suppose they are. World religions and whatnot. I like to know what the opposition is up to." Stevens smiled. "Now then. Sit down over there. Tea will be along shortly."

Lane and Darling sat side by side on the leather two-seater, and the vicar settled in a deep chair opposite. Darling found himself relieved that Stevens was not sitting in his desk chair, which would have caused him to loom over them.

"Now, I do see you, Miss Winslow, at St. Joseph's of a Sunday, but are you are a regular churchgoer, Inspector?"

"I am not," replied Darling.

"So direct! How wonderful. Such a lot of time is wasted with protestations of one kind or another. While I know it is my duty to encourage people to attend, I must confess that I don't believe God really minds about that sort of thing. He is much more concerned with what is in people's hearts. Still, marriage is a sacrament ordained by God, and I must explore with you your understanding of what it means to be joined together before God, your understanding of the proper roles of husband and wife." The vicar hesitated. "Have you discussed this? For example, Miss Winslow, your role as a wife. To be a happy presence when your husband comes home, with a hot meal ready? I do have some pamphlets that may be of interest and provide some guidance."

Lane could feel the fixed smile on her face. She dared not look at Darling, who must be on the verge of hysterics at the thought of the so-called hot meal he was likely to get from her.

"I live in a beautiful place, so I am certain I can manage the happiness. I'm afraid the proper cooking might be a bit beyond me just at first. But Frederick and I will be learning to cook together, so if we don't poison each other we should make out very well." She very nearly added, "Will God be happy with that?"

"Ah. How very modern of you, Inspector! Now, I know you live in town. Have you fully decided on where you will live once you are married? I only ask, you see, because we want to be alert to any feelings of resentment you may have at giving up a good deal in this marriage."

"We have settled on living in King's Cove," replied Darling. "I can't imagine feeling any resentment, Vicar. I love Miss Winslow and freely enter into the marriage on these terms."

"Splendid. Yes, absolutely splendid. If I am going to marry you, I should like to think that you are truly compatible and will have a long and joyful married life. Divorce is rare, of course, and we frown upon it, but I wonder if it should be," he said. "So many couples find too late that they have made a mistake and feel forced to spend the one life God has given them in misery without seeking spiritual help."

"Oh, quite," said Lane uncertainly.

It occurred to her that, when one is in love, one never thinks one will be miserable. She looked at Darling. Try as she might, she could not imagine being miserable with him. But she could not have imagined it with Angus either, the man with whom she had had a wartime affair and who had been so deceptive. Well, she never would have had the chance for matrimonial misery with Angus, she thought. Unbeknownst to her, he had been married the whole time.

As if reading her mind, the vicar asked, "Of course, I must ask if you are both free to marry legally?"

They nodded.

"Good! Now then, I could ask you if you have thought about children, but in the case of two people who are a little older and more mature than some of my parishioners, I can see that you are quite capable of sorting that kind of thing out. I must remind you that the early flush of love may not always be equal to the stresses of married life. You must be prepared, to endure, well, difficulties. Disagreements, differences in values perhaps. The church is always there to . . ." But he stopped, his expression taking on a worried cast as though he'd suddenly forgotten where he was in the instructions he was to give.

Darling felt his face flush. "Yes, of course. I, we—"

"I mean, we are here as a support if things get rocky. But I can see that I've no need to worry. You've both perhaps been . . ." The vicar felt a little off his game and decided to change his tack. "Should we perhaps go through the ceremony itself so that you know what to expect? There is the little matter of 'obey,' which does give difficulty from time to time."

At the door later, as Lane and Darling were leaving, Vicar Stevens shook them both warmly by the hand. "God is very well satisfied with what is in each of your hearts, I am surc of it."

AT THE WINDOW table in Lorenzo's, where they had bccn welcomed with cries of delight and a glass of congratulatory white wine, Lane sat with both her hands in Darling's.

"What can he have meant by our being 'capable of sorting it out'?" she said. "Can he have meant what I think?"

"I can't imagine what dark avenues your peculiar mind travelled. I'm sure it was perfectly innocent," Darling said. "I should not be drinking in the middle of the day," he added.

"For a moment I thought he was going to say we'd both 'been around the block.'"

"We have," Darling said, putting his glass down and looking into her eyes. "I can't wait to begin sorting things out. It's all I can do not to start now. You are especially beautiful when you are about to get a plate of whatever Mrs. Lorenzo has in store for us."

Darling was forced to relinquish Lane's hands when Lorenzo arrived. "We made pasta this morning. A very simple dish, fresh pasta, butter, sage, ricotta."

"As usual, it looks and smells divine," Lane said.

Lorenzo hovered, as if undecided, and then folded his hands together and looked earnestly at Lane.

"Mrs. Lorenzo and I are—I hear this expression—over the moon. The inspector is a very, very good man, and now I see he is also very smart. We wish you a long and happy life together, Signorina Winslow."

When he had gone, and Lane had recovered from the tears Lorenzo's words had induced, she said, "That's all anyone needs to say, isn't it? I feel if the vicar had said just that, our marriage would have been full of sunny blessings, instead of all that stumbling about with oblique hints about values and God apparently insisting I be a good cook and that business about 'sorting things.'"

"Don't forget that God expects you to be a happy presence," Darling reminded her. "I suppose he is duty-bound to hint at the impediments life strews along the path of happiness. Fallings out. You, perhaps, growing tired of my recalcitrant nature."

"He is a very good man, the vicar. He is kind and worries about all his parishioners up and down the lake. I imagine it was difficult to be confronted with us. I'm sure all the rest of his soon-to-be-newlyweds are barely out of their teens." She reached across and took his hand again. "I will only grow tired of you if I discover that your decency and humour turn out to have been an act. By the same token, you might find that, in the end, my fits of insecurity and indecisiveness are too tedious for words."

"Only if you have been feigning intelligence and kindness."

Lane smiled with such sweetness that his heart turned over. Then she took her napkin and spread it across her lap primly and nodded toward the door of the kitchen.

"Should we eat, do you think? Poor Mrs. Lorenzo will be wild if she thinks we've let her lovingly prepared meal go cold."

CHAPTER EIGHT

CONSTABLE AMES OPENED THE MANILA envelope handed to him by his landlady, who wore an expression of someone expecting the worst sort of material would be sent to a young man.

"It came in the mail," she said.

"Thanks. From my boss."

He pointed at the return address, smiled in as trustworthy a manner as he could muster, and went upstairs, ripping open the seal. Sitting on his bed, he pulled out a photograph of a dapper, not to say rakish, man, well-dressed and leaning against an expensive-looking car. As old as the car looked, Ames thought he wouldn't mind driving that thing around.

There was a note attached to the photo.

This is the brother of the Russian woman, Countess Orlova. She's already tried to track him down in Vancouver, and discovered he came this way, so the

*whole exercise is probably moot. However, this is just
in case she missed something.*

Ames chuckled. So like Darling. No salutation, no
"study hard" messages. Just business. He looked at the
pile of books on the little desk by the window. He hadn't
the energy to go back into them. He'd go over the notes
from the lecture he'd had about arrest, search, and seizure
later. He looked at his watch. It was only five o'clock.
There might be time to take the tram down Hastings and
visit the Russian church again. It wasn't until he was
getting off at his stop that he wondered if anyone would
be at the church. As it happened, he was there just ahead
of an evening service, and he found the priest readying
himself in the vestry. Another man in a suit was with him,
holding a robe. Both looked up when Ames knocked on
the open door.

"Ah. Constable. You are back so soon. I have nothing for
you, I'm afraid." He said this with a slightly interrogative
uptick, as if buried in his statement was the question of
why Ames should be there at all.

"No, no. I wasn't expecting anything. My boss sent
along this photograph of the man whose sister is looking
for him." Ames pulled the photo out of the envelope and
handed it to the priest. Both men leaned closer to look at
the picture. "I guess you've seen this already, as the lady
was probably showing it around," Ames added.

Finally, the man in the suit shook his head.

"I never see this," he said. His voice was unexpectedly
deep coming from a small slender man.

The priest handed back the picture. "You know, I never saw this either, and I do not know the man. Mind you, I did not meet the lady, for that matter."

At this, Ames frowned. He remembered that the priest had not mentioned meeting anyone like this Countess Orlova on their last meeting.

"That's strange, now that I think of it. Would she not have come here first if she had traced her brother to Vancouver?"

The priest shrugged. "I suppose, yes. But there is another parish. Holy Resurrection on West Seventh Avenue. You should go there as well."

With instructions for getting to the other church, Ames sat on the rocking tram, looking out at the street scene going by. He had never been to a big city and, except for the centre where the main hotel and the rail terminal were, Vancouver felt more like a small town with its rows of wooden houses. He hopped off near his rooming house and decided it might be too late to go to the other church. He would go directly after his session the next day. It was only a week until his exam, and he thought he'd better have some supper at the diner he'd come to like on Main Street and then go home to study. But he was musing as he ate his bowl of beef stew at the counter. Why had the priest of one of the two Russian churches in Vancouver not seen the picture of the man his sister was so keen to find?

Saint Petersburg, 1897

TATIANA STOOD AT the back of the room, transfixed. The hall was packed with men—though some young women dotted the crowd, some not even wearing hats—shouting and raising their fists. It made her heart swell with a thrill she had not experienced before. The man on the stage was named Ulyanov. He was not handsome, exactly, but passionate. His dark eyes had a quality, she thought, of boring right into your soul. He was talking about the corruption of the tsar and of the cruel oppression of the peasants, no better than slaves at the hands of the wealthy landowners. Capitalism, he said, is the source of the suffering of the people of Russia. Tatiana wasn't quite sure what capitalism was, but she understood his cries of anguish on behalf of the peasants. Didn't she feel it herself? Didn't her father? But now the suggestion that her father was in the wrong after all. It was not enough to be kind to the farmers, to make their burden lighter. They should not have farmers at all. Farmers should be in charge of the means of production, should be working for themselves.

She could feel her heart filling. At that very moment Ulyanov seemed to be looking right at her, into her eyes. He was speaking directly to her, she was sure. It took a moment for her to realize that there was a commotion at the door, shouting, banging, the doors being pushed with the butts of rifles. In a moment her passion was replaced by panic. She had to get out. Thanking God that she was by the door, she pressed her body against the back wall and waited for the soldiers to get in and begin pushing through the crowd—then slipped out and ran back toward the street.

She looked around, frantic. She had got away from her chaperone, Madam Rykova, as a lark because she had seen a flyer stuck on a wall: VLADIMIR ULYANOV, THE NEW

WORLD. Now, in the bustle of the street, Tatiana wondered where she would find her again. There was nothing for it but to go back to their apartment. Madam would have to go back there eventually.

"My God, where have you been?"

Tatiana felt her arm wrenched, and she was pulled away from the line up for the tram. She set her face in defiance to whatever her governess was about to say to her.

"You nearly made my heart stop!" her governess gasped, with a tone between fear and fury.

"I just went to look in some shop windows. I don't know why you're making such a fuss. It's the middle of the day. No one is going to hurt me!"

"If your mama hears of this, I will be put out onto the street!" Rykova said, looking furtively around, as if someone from the household might have followed them.

"Who is going to tell her? I'm not. And no one's going to put you on the street. You're a relation, after all."

"Yes, a poor relation. The most disposable kind. I will explain our lateness by saying we both went to look at the shops. You'd better tell me what you saw."

"That's the spirit! Now what shall we tell her we saw? She is most interested in evening gowns. Let's talk about those."

Madam Rykova stopped. "You didn't go look at shops, did you? Where have you been? Oh my God, not a young man? How could you have conducted a correspondence with a young man without my knowing? Oh my God, your papa—"

"Madam, please stop!" Tatiana could not shake the sound of Ulyanov's voice, the searing gaze of his eyes. *There* was a man! "When have you known me to be interested in young men? Have you ever met a young man in our house, or in any other, that wasn't insipid and boring? Who could be interested in such hothouse specimens? Men without passion or heart. Really, madam, sometimes I think you don't know me at all!"

They resumed their journey, but Madam Rykova was not at all easy in her mind. That was the problem, really. She did know Tatiana, very well. All this talk of passion and heart convinced her that she should talk with her charge's mother as soon as possible on the subject of getting Tatiana safely married. They had delayed too long already.

GLENN PONTING, A geologist turned prospector who lived in a small but comfortable cabin a short distance from King's Cove along the road to Adderley, was taking samples a mile up the steep mountain behind his house. It was getting late, and the shadows would soon start to fall across the clearing he was working in. He would finish labelling the last couple of samples and start back down. His mare was tethered nearby and had been grazing peacefully when something alarmed her. Her head came up, and she lifted off her front legs in a little dance and whinnied. Ponting, who had a small canvas bag in his hand and was writing in a notebook, looked up at the sound.

"What's up, little lady?" he said, looking across the meadow toward the woods that encroached on them from above. He put down his things and walked over to her and stroked her nose. "You hear something?"

Fearing it might be bears or a cougar, he took his rifle from its holster on the saddle and continued to talk quietly to the horse. The sound of crashing in the underbrush just south caused them both to turn and see another horse, clearly in some distress, burst out of the forest and then stop in confusion at the sight of them. Ponting put his rifle down and approached slowly. It was a black gelding, complete with saddle and saddlebags, and a bedroll that had come loose and was swinging near the horse's back legs, adding to the animal's panic.

"Whoa, there, calm down," Ponting said quietly, as he sidled forward and reached for the reins that dangled off the bridle of the anxious beast.

The horse moved his head up and down and fidgeted anxiously, but seemed soothed by Ponting's voice and finally allowed himself to be taken. The prospector led him to where his mare watched the proceedings and tied him nearby. He fixed the bedroll so that it was secure on the back of the saddle and then looked the whole thing over.

"You lost your rider, eh?" he said.

He looked out in the direction the horse had come. Why had he bolted? Either the rider was, even now, crossly tramping out of the bush cursing his mount, or he'd been hurt, and had possibly even sent the creature for help. Most animals head home. Was this the way home for him? But there was nothing much north of King's Cove until Adderley. More likely he would come from along the lake, or one of the farms near Balfour. Or even King's Cove itself—though he was pretty familiar with the equine residents of King's Cove, and this fellow didn't look familiar.

Deciding at last that he'd better ride back in the direction the horse had come from, Ponting repacked his sample bags, hung his geological pick, thermos, and rifle back onto the saddle and mounted. He set out toward the woods in the south leading the riderless horse. They had not gone a hundred yards into the bush when the black horse stopped and pulled back so suddenly that Ponting nearly dropped the lead.

"Come on," he coaxed, making a chucking noise, but to no avail. He could see a clearing up ahead. The horse would not budge. "Spooked by something, eh? What's happened?" He dismounted and tied the lead around the trunk of a slender tree. "You're going to stay here and behave, and I'll go look and see what's happened to your master, agreed?"

Ponting rode into the woods and across into the meadow.

Once in the forest, he tried to follow the path the gelding must have taken and was forced to dismount so that he could see the ground more closely. On a forest floor already covered in needles, dead branches, and fallen trunks it wasn't easy. They continued until Ponting's eyes began to blur, and he had no idea if he was following a trail, or simply imagining he was following one. How far away had the horse been when he lost his rider? Or was the rider fine and even now looking for a horse that had been spooked and pulled away and bolted?

He estimated they'd travelled to the north edge of King's Cove, maybe a quarter mile above the abandoned cabin up the hill from his own snug cabin, when his mare suddenly pulled back and became skittish, snorting anxiously. He tried to still her to listen.

"What now?" he asked softly, stroking her neck. "Do you sense something?"

He could see a small clearing ahead, and at first glance, nothing seemed amiss. A substantial downed tree lay across the middle of the clearing, but nothing else. The horse was unwilling to move another step, so Ponting wound the reins around a slender tree and walked toward the log. It was then that he heard the distant gurgle of a stream. It must be the upper reaches of the small creek he drew his water from.

He looked across the meadow and walked toward the sound of the creek. Why was the horse spooked? He got to the edge of the clearing where trees marked its southern boundary and spilled down a sharp, shaded incline to the creek below. He walked along the top of the rise, trying to see through the thick growth of trees to the water below.

The creek and its underbrush looked undisturbed. But something felt wrong. If the person who owned the horse was a hunter, he could have wounded an animal near here somewhere and then perhaps set off on foot to finish it off. He moved forward to see if he could spot a trail of blood anywhere and then stopped. With a wave of horror, he thought, what if the tables had turned, and somehow an enraged bear or cougar had attacked and dragged the hunter into the bush? If that were the case, the hunter would have dropped his rifle, the underbrush and grass would be disturbed. But in deep contrast to what he was feeling, the meadow and the creek below gave no indication of any disturbance.

"Hello! Hello . . . is anyone there?"

The forest, deeply shadowed in the dwindling afternoon, was silent but for the faint whispering of the tops of the trees as the breeze moved through them.

"SIR." IT WAS Thursday morning, and Oxley had put his head in Darling's door.

Darling was still unsure about Oxley. He wasn't Ames. He was too—well, what was it, Darling thought—too earnest perhaps? Was he too lacking in humour? Yes, he decided, maybe that was it. Still, he'd have to do.

"Yes?" Darling said without looking up.

"We've had a call about a hunter who hasn't returned."

"Chalk one up for the beasts," Darling muttered under his breath. "Where?"

"Somewhere in the mountains above Balfour. It's not unusual for this person to be away overnight on a hunt, but it's been a couple of nights, and his wife is worried."

"We'd better go along and see her. Did you get her address?"

"Yes, sir," Oxley said with a slightly offended tone. "Shall I get the car?"

"Yes, fine. Oh. I have the keys." Darling reached into his jacket pocket and tossed the keys across the desk. I'll meet you outside."

He looked at the nearly empty Mikhailov file on his desk. He'd had the pictures of Madam Orlova's missing brother sent out to nearby RCMP detachments two days before and he'd heard nothing yet, nor yet from any contact of Stearn's. Well, the lost Russian would have to make way for the lost hunter. Wondering if Oxley was going to adopt the air of a resentful puppy for the whole trip, Darling took his hat from the stand.

"ONTARIO BOY?" ASKED Darling while they waited for the ferry across on the west side of the lake to empty of cars.

"No, sir. I'm from Cranbrook originally, but I went to Carleton. It was brand new, and then I just stayed on. You're going to be able to fly to Cranbrook soon on a passenger plane."

"Oh goody. Why does every town in this province have a name beginning in a K or a C?"

"Nelson, sir? Vancouver? Fernie? Victoria?"

"The question was rhetorical, Oxley. Were you in the Ontario police?"

"Ottawa, sir. After my university, I joined up there. But I naturally jumped at the chance to be nearer home."

Bit eager, Darling thought. He'd be jumping at chances everywhere. Ames had better mind his p's and q's.

"What do we know about this hunter?"

"Right, sir," Oxley said. He'd made notes in his little notebook and had them fully committed to memory. "His name is Raymond Brodie, forty-eight, works in a local mill. He's an experienced hunter and has never had a mishap before. He left his home on horseback," Oxley looked at his watch, "exactly fifty-three hours ago. He's five foot eleven, weighs about a hundred and seventy pounds, and has dark brown—"

"All right, Oxley, thank you. You're a very proficient note taker. Well done."

Darling felt mildly bad about being so short with his new driver. He didn't have far to travel down the circuitous mental streams of his own consciousness to understand his ill humour. He was worried about telling people he was getting married, he was worried about Lane's house being cluttered for what was beginning to feel like an unlimited time with a Russian émigré, and he was missing Ames. It wasn't fair, and he knew it. None of these irritations was a life-threatening condition, after all. Perhaps he needed a cup of coffee.

Darling tried again as pleasantly as he could. "What made you decide to go into policing?"

They were now on the road and travelling at a sedate pace toward the outskirts of Balfour, where Brodie lived. Too sedate. Darling quelled another tide of irritation.

"My life was saved by a policeman, sir."

"For a minute I thought you were going to tell me you were a Boy Scout."

"It would have been better if I had been. I wouldn't have been so dumb. When I was eight, I was playing with my friends along the Bull River, and we'd built a sort of raft out of driftwood, and we pushed it out onto the river and it broke up pretty quickly, and the two of us who were trying it out fell into the drink. I think I hit my head because I could feel myself face down in the water, and then everything went dark. The policeman was fishing nearby and got us both out. My parents weren't too sympathetic, I can tell you! But the policeman came to visit me a couple of times to make sure I was okay. I thought that was pretty nice."

"So you wanted to be a nice policeman."

"Well, I mean, yes, if you put it like that. I wanted to help people."

"Very commendable. You can help Mr. Brodie now by picking up the pace, if you don't mind."

"OH, THANK YOU so much for coming. I wasn't sure if it had reached this stage yet, but I'm terribly worried about him. It's very unlike him."

"I understand he set out two days ago on horseback?" said Darling.

"He saddles up Monty. He usually takes a sleeping bag, his rifle, food, water, ammunition. He likes to think of himself as a pioneer. He does it a couple of times a year." She couldn't keep the disapproval out of her voice.

"Does he go alone?"

"Yes, that's part of his pioneer fantasy. Alone against the elements sort of thing."

"And he's hunting what at this time of year?"

"Brown bear, mostly. I dread what he brings back, if I'm honest, because I have to dress it and prepare it. I prefer if it's deer, frankly, but I've learned to get used to it." She didn't sound like she'd learned to get used to it.

Oxley was scribbling industriously. "Mrs. Brodie, horses usually try to get home if something's happened to the rider. No sign of the horse?"

Mrs. Brodie was a thin woman who wore her hair in curls so tight they looked like a cap. She wrung her hands. "That's just it. He hasn't come back, the horse, I mean. I'm afraid that he will come back without Ray, but I'm terrified something's happened to the both of them."

"I can get some men to comb the area," Darling said. "Do you have some neighbours who might be able to help?"

"Oh, yes, I'm sure Clarence would, and Leonard and his boy. They're all good in the bush."

"Excellent. Could you get them organized? And if you

give me the use of your telephone, I'll organize some of my men to come out."

"THERE, CONSTABLE OXLEY. You have a chance to be really helpful. I hope you have a good stout pair of boots," Darling said when he had put in his call to the station and was standing with Oxley by the car, waiting.

"My uncle used to hunt like that, but that was in the old days, before the war."

"As long ago as that?" Darling said. "Did he survive?"

"He did, but he ended up having to put his horse down on one of the trips because it broke a leg in a fall. He had a long walk out of the bush and lost the heart for it afterward."

Darling looked up at the mountain looming behind them. "I suppose that could have happened here. Depending how far in he got, it would be a slower trip out on foot."

"Inspector?"

Darling turned and saw two men carrying rifles and outfitted for the bush.

"Yes. You must be Mrs. Brodie's neighbours. Thank you for coming along."

"It's only our duty, sir. I'm Leonard, and this is my son Ben. I've been out with Brodie, so I may have an idea what his usual route would be. Typically, he goes up through here," Leonard pointed toward the mountain, and then moved his arm to the north, "and then he goes north and does a kind of loop above the cove. He's good in the bush, but it is unusual for him to be gone this long."

"My constable was wondering if something might have happened with his mount, and he's having to walk out,"

Darling said, nodding toward Oxley, who reddened at the sudden praise, however oblique. "My men should be here momentarily. I wonder if I could put you in charge of directing their efforts, as you have such a close knowledge of Brodie's usual movements? I've instructed them to bring an ordnance map of the area."

"Yes, sir. Pleased to sir," said Leonard. "The map will be a big help. Ben, go saddle up the horses."

CHAPTER NINE

———————

"**THE BALLET IN RUSSIA IS** very famous, is it not?" Gladys asked. The warm September was holding, and they were seated around a table outside, innocent of the drama beginning to unfold nearby. Gladys had marked the occasion by pulling out a lace tablecloth. One of the two cocker spaniels had taken up a position next to Countess Orlova, sensing perhaps, that this new guest might be charmed into dropping bits of cake his way. The patient wait had yielded nothing, and the dog now collapsed with a *humph* and put his head on his paws.

Orlova looked toward Gladys and smiled slightly. "Ah! Is this lady interested in the ballet?" she inquired of Lane. "This is excellent cake," she added.

Lane translated.

"I studied ballet as a girl before I came out here," Gladys said. "I wanted to teach dance. Of course, English ballet is unequalled, but the Russian ballet was considered quite good. I get papers from the old country, so I am able to follow what is being done and who is who in modern ballet." She said this with a slight sniff, causing Mabel to direct a warning look at her mother.

Lane smiled and exclaimed, "I didn't know that! How wonderful. You certainly have the grace and carriage of a dancer." She turned and explained to her guest, reducing the impact of Gladys's evident view of the inferiority of the Russian ballet.

"There you are, Mother. Grace and carriage. Well done," said Gwen, dropping a morsel of chocolate cake onto the grass.

Orlova again nodded and smiled almost sadly. "We attended the ballet at the Mariinsky Theatre in Saint Petersburg. It was beautiful. A vanished life."

Lane handled this part of the conversation carefully, so as not to ignite any disagreement about the merits of the English system over the Russian. "Your garden looks magnificent," Lane finished, adding in Russian, "these ladies are quite the best gardeners in the community. Would you like a little tour?"

"Yes. Perhaps there will be something to paint."

"Countess Orlova would love to see more of the gardens. She is in search of a lovely vista to paint, and one can hardly turn around here without tripping over a vista."

With Gwen, Mabel, and the dogs walking Orlova around the garden, Lane took the opportunity to enjoy a break from the delicate and exhausting job of translating and instead helped Gladys take the tea things into the house.

"Extraordinary woman," Gladys said briskly. "How did you come to be saddled with her again?"

Lane explained about the vicar and then about Orlova's missing brother.

"Another mystery for you to solve," said Gladys, stoppering the sink and turning on the tap. "Although, no one is dead, so perhaps it won't interest you."

"You do have a morbid view of me! I'm afraid I'm not much use in the missing persons department."

"Nonsense. You speak Russian. That inspector fellow will beat a path to your door. Not that he doesn't already." Gladys looked over her glasses at Lane as she handed her a dish towel. "She's a funny old thing, isn't she? I mean it's not the sort of thing you expect to trip over in King's Cove, a Russian countess."

"No, I suppose not. I hope someone finds her brother. I feel quite sorry for her," Lane said.

"Absolutely fatal, feeling sorry for people," Gladys declared. "If you aren't careful you never get rid of them."

Lane hoped it wouldn't be as bad as all that.

"Thank you so much for having us, Gladys. I imagine she may want to come back and paint at some point, but if you don't mind too much, it shouldn't really involve any language complications. I'm sure she likes to sit quite undisturbed."

"Anytime. The dogs won't eat her," Gladys said. "Though I must say, she certainly kept every morsel to herself."

"Yes. Poor puppies. You have them on starvation rations here! I'll just send her up on her own then, next time, and I'll pack her some sandwiches so she won't require any feeding."

Lane, waiting for her guest's tour to be over, stood next

to the fence that looked out over the much broader view of the lake enjoyed by the Hugheses because they were higher up the hill. The beauty of it filled her, and it was at that moment that she thought about Gladys's remark about how odd it was to have a Russian countess at King's Cove.

It was odd.

From this vantage point, looking down on the little post office, and her own house, and across the lake, she saw suddenly how odd it was. And there was something Orlova said. Had she not asked her about Gladys's interest in the ballet? Lane remembered clearly that she had not translated Gladys's question about the Russian ballet. Did the countess speak some English after all?

COUNTESS ORLOVA WAS napping, and Lane had been moving quietly around the kitchen, thinking about what she ought to prepare for their supper. She would have liked to go upstairs to the attic and spend part of the afternoon browsing through Lady Armstrong's boxes, but she worried that the creaking of the stairs would disturb her guest.

The afternoons seemed to come on faster now, and she could feel the temperature beginning to drop. She would shut the windows though she was reluctant to close the French doors just yet because the afternoon sun was full on the porch, still providing a soothing warmth. She stepped out and crossed her arms, looking out at the quiet lake. She mustn't, she thought, be churlish about her guest. The countess was quite pleasant after all and fretted about being any trouble and was really very entertaining with her stories of her old life as a girl in Tsarist Russia. But at the same time, Lane felt at every moment that her house was not quite her own. Look at her now, creeping about, worried about waking the old lady. Would it be like this sharing a house with Darling?

"God, I hope not!" she muttered aloud.

She was just turning to go back in to tackle the still completely unresolved issue of supper—and wondering if she should call the vicar to see how he was getting on with finding a place for her guest—when she heard horses coming down the road at a good clip. She was certain from the sound there were two of them, and they were making their way past her place and going toward the Armstrongs'. Delighted at having something to distract her, Lane tiptoed down the hall and sprang out the door. She ran across her little bridge and arrived at the road in time to see the unusual sight of Ponting leading a second horse along behind him. He was throwing himself off his mare, clearly in a hurry.

"Good afternoon, Glenn! Where did you get that nice-looking fellow?" She came out onto the road and walked along beside him.

"I need to use the telephone. I found him wandering in the bush and couldn't find the rider. I'm afraid something's happened to him."

"Here," Lane said. "You go on. Give me that, and I'll find a place to tie him."

By this time, the commotion had brought Kenny Armstrong out of the cottage along with Alexandra, who set up a chorus of high-pitched barking. Alexandra seemed undaunted by the horses. Kenny picked her up, trying to shush her. The dog glared at the interlopers from the safety of Kenny's arms.

"Oh, hello, Mr. Armstrong. I'll need to use your telephone if you don't mind. This fellow," he nodded at the black horse, "was loose in the bush without his rider. I'm afraid something's happened."

"Good God! Yes. Come right in. Go through to the parlour over there. Just ring once to get the exchange."

Eleanor came through from the rear of the cottage, holding a bunch of carrots.

"Glenn's found a riderless horse. He's calling the police. He's brought the horse here with him," Lane said.

Kenny had gone through to make sure Ponting was having no difficulty with the telephone.

"Great heavens!" exclaimed Eleanor. "So much for the quiet country life. Riderless horses and Russian countesses everywhere."

"Yes, I'll hold!" Glenn seemed to be enunciating loudly and clearly, as if he were not used to being on the telephone. He came from a very well-off middle-class family in Toronto, but perhaps all these years without a phone had made him forget how to use it.

Lane moved toward the parlour, followed by Eleanor, who had put aside the carrots as if they would have no place now, in this time of disaster. Ponting put his hand over the receiver and looked at his audience.

"Apparently the police are out conducting a manhunt. They aren't sure how to reach them."

"Oh. I shall go at once! Did they say where?" Lane asked. Ponting put up his hand.

"Yes. I see. Just past King's Cove. I'm at the village post office. I can take someone there." Glenn hung up and turned to the others. "Apparently the inspector has a team out near Balfour looking for a missing hunter. They're going to try to reach him, and I guess he'll be on his way here. Nothing to do but wait."

DARLING LOOKED ANXIOUSLY at Mrs. Brodie as he spoke to O'Brien. He'd have liked to ask him more questions but did not want to frighten her unnecessarily.

"Right. I'm on my way. Thanks." He hung up the phone.

"I'm just going over to King's Cove. One of the local prospectors has found a horse in the bush." He tried to say this in a matter of fact way, but he could see the look of alarm in Mrs. Brodie's face.

"It's Monty, I know it!" she said breathily. "I'm coming with you!"

"We don't know that. I'd like you to stay here by the phone. If any of the party comes back, I'll want you to tell them where I've gone. King's Cove post office. Tell me again what your husband's mount looks like."

"Black gelding, small white patch on his forehead. Um . . . the saddle blanket is dark brown and orange." She said this in a rush, as if the panic was making her forget things.

Darling could see the shadows beginning to move up the mountains on the other side of the lake as he sped toward King's Cove. He hadn't wanted to say anything to Mrs. Brodie, but the riderless horse did not bode at all well, and it was getting late. By the time he could get his party reorganized and back into the area where the horse had been found, it would be dark.

LANE LOOKED AT her watch. She had better get back. Madam Orlova would be awake, and she'd left no note to say where she was.

"Let me know if there's anything I can do. I'd better get back to my guest," she said, trying to hide the reluctance in her voice.

"Right you are. Perhaps if it ends up being a lot of people, we could gather them at your house. I can help you keep them fed and watered," Eleanor said. "I'd better bring my medical kit as well, just in case." She'd been a nursing sister in the Great War, and her kit had been useful more than once in the intervening thirty years.

Lane smiled as she crossed back toward her house. There wasn't a crisis in the world that Eleanor couldn't handle, she thought. The house was completely quiet, and the hall was dark in the late afternoon. Lane went through to the kitchen and looked at the clock. Orlova didn't usually sleep this late. Had she better wake her up? With some trepidation she went down the hall and stood in front of the closed door. Finally, she knocked quietly.

"Madam? Are you awake?"

There was no answer.

She knocked again and then very cautiously opened the door. The afternoon sunlight drew a line of bright green across the lawn visible through the spare room window. The room was empty, the bed as tidy and untouched as she had seen it in the morning. What if the countess was off on one of her walks? Lane normally wouldn't worry, but with a hunter missing, she wondered if she should be concerned about cougars or even bears. Perhaps Alice Mather, with her history of mood swings and her conviction that any day someone was going to be hurt by a cougar unless she kept their numbers down, was on to something when she went on her crazy cougar hunts.

AMES WAS HAVING trouble concentrating. He bet that the lamp on the desk provided by his landlady contained the lowest watt bulb she could find. In a pique he stood up and looked over the lampshade at the top of the bulb. Twenty watts. He sat down again, not enjoying having been right. He really had to study, but he was puzzled. He'd been along to the church on Seventh Avenue and spoken with the priest there, who had seemed surprisingly young. The priest thought he had a vague memory of seeing an older lady in the back row who didn't look familiar.

" . . . but you know these old women. All the same."

The priest had tried to get to her at the end of the mass, but she had disappeared. He said refugees had started coming again, this time from China, where some Russians had spent the war. He assumed she was one of these. He certainly did not remember ever seeing the picture of the man with the car.

It was too late to telephone through to Darling, and in any case, he'd like to have more to tell him. Perhaps he should try talking to some ordinary parishioners. If the priest noticed someone new in the church, maybe someone sitting near her would remember her. He should talk to the man leading the investigation into the death of that Russian as well. This struck him immediately as ridiculous. It was obvious the two matters were not connected except by their Russianness. Still. It ought to have been easier, and this was rankling. The Russian community in Vancouver wasn't that big, and Darling had said the old lady had asked people here and had gotten a lead that her brother had gone to the Nelson area. Why did no one here remember talking to her? Or what if she had talked to people, and they wanted to cover it up, or pretend they'd never talked to her? Why? What would they be afraid of?

The younger priest—damn, but he had trouble with these Russian names—had seemed less standoffish. What was the name? Ames found his notebook where he'd laid it at the end of the desk and flipped back through his notes. Dmitry. He'd go see Father Dmitry after class the next day and see if the priest could explain why people were so suspicious of the questions he was asking.

CHAPTER TEN

August 1947

THE RUMBLE WOKE APTEKAR FROM a dream—he was standing on the edge of a cliff above a fjord, roiling water impossibly far away below him. In the swirling darkness, he could hear the distant call of someone whose voice he recognized but couldn't place. He opened his eyes and looked, momentarily uncomprehending, at the grey light filtering through the trees. Then he came to, and the cold and damp of the overnight dew brought back memory of his escape, along with the instinctive fear of the noise that woke him. He was stiff and pushed himself slowly off the forest floor. His coat, under which he had slept, smelled of wet wool and damp soil. In a moment, he was collected.

A train headed east.

He had been surprised to find the train they'd arrived on gone when he got to the station, and he wasn't sure when another would be along. He had positioned himself two hundred yards west of the station house so that he would be near the hind-most cars, those farthest from the engine, when the train stopped. He watched the train approach, smoke belching, sullying the morning, the metallic screeching of its wheels ripping at the silence of the forest. It was slowing. That meant it would take on water. Whoever was on it would get off, unless it was carrying prisoners. They would not get off, unless it was to endure the march he himself had been forced to set out on the day before, but their guards would, no doubt, to shout and harry them.

But this train did not seem to carry prisoners. The cars were packed with crates. Men dressed in the baggy blue suits of rail workers dropped onto the tracks, stretching. They complained that the station would provide no coffee or bread, and then spit and drank from bottles of vodka and brandy being passed around. Someone in charge called out to them to get a move on, and the men began to move down the tracks looking into the cars, pulling open the doors, giving a cursory look and closing them again. Aptekar waited patiently while the train took on water, praying for the usual inefficiency of the rail workers, who were, he knew, badly paid and spent weeks away from home at a time. He moved slowly farther west, closer to the cars with the wooden slats, cars which had been pressed into service to move the machinery that would power the growth of the latest five-year plan for the great Soviet economy across the vast expanse of the empire.

And then, the luck he hoped for. The cursory inspection at an end, a car only three from the back had no door and appeared nearly empty. The rail workers had begun to drift back, and then the shriek of the whistle caused them to pick up their pace and climb back on to the cars in the front. He had to time his next move carefully. If the train began to move before he was next to it, he would never be able to run, as the younger men did, to leap on. When the workers seemed to be in, he darted out of the forest and made for the car. With his heart pounding—expecting to hear the alarm raised at every second—he scrambled up the two rusted metal footholds and threw himself onto his stomach on the wooden floor of the car, panic giving him strength to pull himself in. Panting and gasping, he could feel the train begin to move, and he closed his eyes.

The train rocketed east. His fear of being discovered dissipated and was replaced by hunger and discomfort. He lay stretched out with his coat under his head, trying to find a position that did not make him ache. At some stops, station employees again walked along the rails giving the cars a cursory check, and Aptekar positioned himself behind a crate that purported to contain a printing press. He wondered if they were looking for stowaways, but the heyday of people jumping trains across the country was nearly over. People were beginning to settle into the economy of factories and collective farms. They were tired of war, and they were tired of disruption. He could hear the workers talking, planning for what they would do in Vladivostok with their days off.

Vladivostok. He too must make plans.

He had the night on the swaying train to contemplate how far he had fallen, even in his own estimation. Once at the pinnacle of the organization, he'd miraculously survived the change of regime and had been contemplating a retirement far from the socialist paradise he'd come to despise. In the moment that he'd been arrested and marked for deportation to a gulag, he had, he thought, become a slouching, exhausted, and anonymous prisoner, like all the others who marched through Russia's history to their confinement and death in some faraway prison. Russia, with its tens of thousands of miles of space, had an infinite capacity to hide all its inconvenient people out of sight. He knew, in his darkest moments, that he was only trying, like the fool in the stories, to outrun Death—a battle no man could ever win. And yet, he thought, shrugging in the dark, it is the duty of a man imprisoned to try to escape. He may yet hold his head high when he turned a corner one day soon and met Death, with his scythe and his patient hollow eyes, and deliver himself a whole man.

"IT IS A setback, I agree, comrade. But he will never survive on his own in the wilderness. He is old."

"He *has* survived, though, comrade." The commander seemed to heap derision into the word. "He was seen in Vladivostok, and now there is no trace of him there."

The commissar, who was of third rank, clamped his lips shut, frowning. He did not care for, nor was he used to, being spoken to in this way. Still. He had to be careful. Clearly he was being held responsible for Aptekar's disappearance from a prison train when it was only miles from the prison, and clearly the commander had better sources of information. He was surprised to learn that their prisoner had been seen in Vladivostok because he scarcely believed the old man could have made it there.

"I will institute a search," the commissar said finally.

"I've already instituted a search, comrade. That's how I know he's disappeared. I don't think you understand who this man is. He may be old, but he is the wiliest, most resourceful operative this country ever had. He's a survivor, Pankov, and his head is full of our secrets. Believe me, disappearing from a column of prisoners, and making his way to Vladivostok, no doubt hiding on the next train that came along, would be child's play for him. Try Shanghai. He could doubtless hide out there."

"Have you thought of America, comrade? Ships in Vladivostok go quite often to Western Canada. There is some sort of arrangement where our ships dock in Vancouver and are repaired."

"What are you waiting for?"

"I have a good officer I can send who—"

"He'd better be good."

Pankov stood up to take his leave. No point in bothering the commander with details. The British might know something. Not usually, in his experience, but best to cover all the angles.

WORRIED NOW, LANE went outside. Perhaps her guest had woken up and gone into the garden to enjoy the remains of the afternoon, but a quick tour around the house showed no signs of her. How far might she have gone on one of her walks? Lane reminded herself of how groggy she herself felt when she overslept. It was likely that Orlova had set out just to clear her head and might not have attempted more than that. That partially comforting thought freed Lane to go back inside and think about what she ought to prepare if a search party descended on her.

As if she'd summoned it, the search party began to arrive. Darling had Oxley park his car at the top of Lane's driveway, and at the same time, she heard the clatter of horses. Ponting was mounted and leading both Raymond Brodie's mount and Kenny's horse—the latter appeared bemused at finding herself suddenly saddled and being led away from the fenced field that had served as her retirement from the mail-wagon Kenny had replaced with his new truck.

"The best way to make any kind of time in the bush is to get up there on horseback. We can cut around up by the top road and across the meadow. We'd be approaching where I found this fellow from the south side instead of the north," Ponting said. "It will start to get dark soon, so we'd best get on with it."

Darling stood, concern on his face, looking at the horses, and then turned to greet Lane. "Ah. Miss Winslow. This is Constable Oxley. I can't recall if you met when you came into the station. We are going to ride into the bush. I have a couple of flashlights in the car. Do you have another we could use?"

"How do you do, Constable? Certainly, Inspector. What else can I get you?"

"Flashlight will do. And before you ask, I have ridden before. We patrolled on horseback in Vancouver," he added under his breath.

"Right. Flashlight it is," Lane said, smiling briefly, and went into the house to fetch it.

111

When the men had disappeared up the road, Lane disciplined her wayward mind away from the stirring sight of Darling on horseback, something she'd never expected to see, and back to the troubling matter of her missing guest. Then she slapped her forehead and remembered that Countess Orlova had a standing invitation to go and paint at the Hugheses'. Feeling some relief and chiding herself for letting the concern about the missing hunter infect her thinking, Lane went back into the house to begin her supper preparations—though she did have a passing thought that her guest could have left her a note. As she passed the guest room, she was about to close the door. It wouldn't do to have Countess Orlova think she'd been nosing about in her bedroom. Thinking to just double check, Lane went into the room and saw one of her guest's two suitcases was pushed under the bed. She had a quick look for the second one, but it was not in evidence. Good. It was confirmation that she was painting somewhere. She would have taken her painting equipment in it. Closing the door behind her—and wondering if the countess would prefer to borrow her light French shopping basket or a cloth bag to cart her painting supplies in—Lane turned her mind to food. She had intended to roast a chicken, but it was getting late. Perhaps she could cut it into bits and roast it with some carrots and potatoes. It would take less time and would also feed the men if they came back late and hungry.

CHAPTER ELEVEN

LANE HEARD THE DOOR AND her guest's footsteps along the hall, and she breathed a sigh of relief. At least nothing had happened to the old lady. Her anxiety had been ridiculous, but it had mounted as she'd been preparing the chicken and still, an hour after the men had left, Orlova had not returned. She had thought of phoning the Hugheses and then decided against it. Her guest would not want to feel herself hounded, but with time ticking away, Lane had finally resolved to phone when she heard the door.

"Ah, Countess! You are just in time to supervise my supper preparations," she called out.

"No 'countess,' please. It smells very good. I am sorry I am returning so late. When I awoke, I felt heavy, you know, like I needed to clear my head. I very much like that route past the old school. There is a lovely view of the lake from up there. I lingered too long."

"You have nothing to apologize for." By the old school? Lane felt a frisson of anxiety. The old school was far from the settled houses. She would have been more likely to meet cougars on a walk like that. If a cougar had been wounded by the missing hunter, it would be in a very dangerous frame of mind.

"Why is there another car in the driveway?" Orlova sat at the kitchen table, with a nearly imperceptible *oomph*. "My old bones. I forget I am no longer a girl."

"Ah," said Lane, thinking of the possibly greater tragedy that might be unfolding in the bush above King's Cove. "Apparently a local hunter has gone missing in the woods above here somewhere. His horse was found by a neighbour who was working in the bush. The car is Inspector Darling's. They've gone up on horseback to look for him. Oh, I'm sorry. I didn't think to ask him whether he had any news of your brother."

"Oh dear, I should so like to hear. But they have much more urgent things to think about. If my brother is dead, he is dead, and there is nothing that can change that. If he is alive, I will find him. They will come back here, yes, when they have found the hunter?"

"Or not found him. They have flashlights, but I wonder if they will search all night or mount a bigger search with more men in the morning? Madam, I wonder if you should be more cautious? Granted, the hunter may have been thrown, but cougars are known to attack at times. I never thought the possibility very real until this poor man went missing."

Orlova shook her head. "I certainly haven't seen any wild beasts, but I am anxious not to be attacked, so I will be more careful. I will stick to painting your neighbours' gardens instead of the wilder parts of the forest. There!

Now, this unfortunate hunter. What can have happened?"

"His poor wife. She must be beside herself," Lane said.

"Yes. There is always the tragedy, is there not? The women left behind."

Lane set the table. There was none of the relaxed atmosphere of the first days her guest had been there because hanging over them was the uncertainty of when the men would return, or with what result.

IT WAS NEARING eleven o'clock when the search party came back, exhausted and discouraged. The two policemen dismounted gingerly, unused to the new exercise. Lane and Countess Orlova, who had been reading in the sitting room, quickly set the table and laid out some plates.

"Oxley found a path trampled through the high grass heading north, so he must have gone in that direction at some point, but then it just vanishes, as if he'd been lifted up and placed somewhere else," Darling said. "Thank you. Brandy is a godsend. Not you, Oxley, you're driving."

"What will you do now?" asked Lane.

"I'll have to go talk to the unfortunate Mrs. Brodie. I'll bring the police dog out first thing."

They ate in silence. Ponting was the first to push his chair back.

"I'd better get the horses over to the Armstrongs'. Brodie's horse can bunk in with Kenny's."

Darling followed, and this caused Oxley to jump up with alacrity.

"Thank you, Miss Winslow. We'll be along first thing, but we won't bother you."

"Nonsense. I must be of some use. Would it help if I brought Mrs. Brodie here? She might feel better being nearby."

"Yes. That's a good idea. I will ask her now when I go deliver the bad news that we were not able to find him. I only hope he is as resourceful as the pioneers he so admires and has found a safe place to overnight, or better yet, has walked out and is even now on his way home."

"Well, you let me know. Have a hot bath when you get home. Your muscles will thank you. Goodnight, Constable Oxley," she called out to where Darling's driver waited by the car at the top of the drive.

"It's a dreadful situation," Orlova said when she and Lane had returned to the sitting room. Neither of them felt quite ready to go to bed. "That poor man." She shook her head and clucked quietly. "Why does he go on his own? Even my brother, who thinks himself such a man, did not hunt alone. He took his friends with him. Once one of them was thrown and hit his head on a rock, but at least his friends could carry him out." Orlova stopped and moved toward the window and pulled the curtain, looking out into the darkness. "I no longer believe my brother to be alive, if I am truthful. If your inspector has found no sign of him, then I must suppose he did not come this way. I'm no longer certain what I am doing, sitting here with you in this beautiful place, as if I were suspended out of time somehow. The truth is, I have nowhere to go. Where could an old woman like me find a home anymore?" Orlova moved a hand to her cheek as if to wipe away a tear. "But for now we must think of this poor hunter. After a good sleep, perhaps what I should do will become clearer. There, now. No more gloomy thoughts, eh?"

"I suppose we had better go to bed," Lane said. "As you say, tomorrow things might be clearer. At least you do not have to be caught up in our drama but can resume your painting. You could go up to the Hughes place at the top of the hill. In fact, that's where I thought you'd gone today."

"Yes. That is an excellent idea. No one needs an old lady underfoot!"

Lane turned out her bedside lamp. She had tried to read but could not shake the sadness she felt. The countess whose home was taken from her, the hunter's wife. How could a man ride off on a sunny morning and just never come back? She turned in the dark so that she could feel the cool air coming in the window. As she began to drift off, it came to her that she had thought Orlova had disappeared for a moment as well, but instead she'd been up the hill painting, enjoying the scenery with her little suitcase of paints. Or had she? Lane opened her eyes and stared into the darkness and frowned. Why did she think that? With the discomfiting thought coming unbidden into her mind that Orlova's presence suddenly seemed to her more than a little strange, she turned on her side and tried to sleep.

"IS ALICE OUT with her trusty rifle again?" Angela asked. "There was a shot the day before yesterday in the afternoon that nearly took a year off my life. I had to run around and count the boys." Angela Bertolli, who had come with her husband and three small boys from New York to live in King's Cove, had once had Alice Mather practically in her yard during one of her shooting sprees. Angela had had to order the boys to stay indoors and away from the windows until Alice's son had come to fetch her home.

Eleanor frowned. "I don't think so. Alice was in yesterday and seemed quite calm. More likely to have been that missing hunter."

"Missing hunter?" Angela asked. She leaned on the counter and shook her head. "What's that about? And why do you have two horses this morning? The boys would be crazy about the two horses. Too bad they're in school."

"Dear me. It's a dreadful business." Eleanor explained about the missing hunter, and then asked, "What time was that shot you heard again?"

"Gosh. I don't know. Late afternoon? I'd picked the children up from school at Balfour, but David wasn't home yet from Nelson. Four? Four thirty? It came from way up, past that dreadful abandoned house at the top of the road. Do you really think it might have something to do with the hunter?"

"It could. He could have gotten one shot off at an animal. Glenn found the horse spooked and wandering northward up on a meadow where he was working. That's roughly up that way. You probably want to keep an eye on the boys, if there's a wounded animal around."

"That funny old lady Lane has on board had better be careful as well. She's always walking around on her own. And I wonder if she knows about Alice? Alice could bump her off without hesitation just because she's foreign."

The conversation about Lane's guest made Angela resolve to stop by. She realized she'd been rather avoiding

118

Lane because she felt awkward about her guest's inability to speak English—she wouldn't be able to chat freely, as she was used to, without taking the guest into consideration. But now, with the new activity around the missing man, she thought she'd better get caught up. Maybe the inspector would be interested in the gunfire she'd heard.

"Oh, you needn't worry about the countess," Lane said when Angela poked her head in her friend's front door and looked nervously down the hall. "She's gone off to paint. She wanted to catch the morning light on Gladys's lupines."

Angela emitted a relieved breath. "So, what's going on? I heard about that poor hunter."

"Yes. It's horrible. The police will take their German shepherd out today. He's apparently a sniffer dog. I'm going to bring poor Mrs. Brodie, the hunter's wife, here. I expect the search party was in the bush before dawn. I have coffee ready for them. Can you stay and have a cup?"

Though Angela had laundry waiting, she decided she would not move from Lane's house for the world just then. She saw the painting Countess Orlova had done of the lake from the front porch and picked it up.

"My goodness! Is this one of hers? She's very good, isn't she? I should invite her over to see some of my work. Would you come if I did that? Otherwise we'll be gasping like fish, trying to communicate."

"That's a very kind and generous idea. I haven't even seen all your work. As soon as this crisis is over, let's plan it." Lane was carrying the coffee to the porch. "Phew," she said, settling into her deck chair. "It's nice to have a moment of quiet. Such a beautiful morning, and all the while some poor man is lost or injured in the woods."

Angela sat down and took her coffee. "I was telling Eleanor I heard a shot at four or four thirty the day before yesterday. I thought it must be Alice, but Eleanor tells me Alice is in good shape right now. If it isn't her, do you think it might have anything to do with the hunter? I was just telling Eleanor that your Madam whatshername should be careful on her walks."

"Yes, she should, especially if people are shooting. I'm terrified he's wounded a bear or a cougar and the countess will meet an enraged animal on one of her walks."

"I don't know. If the hunter was attacked, so might any of us be by a wounded animal. Why will people hunt so near where people live? The children don't go far into the woods, but your old lady was striding along in her sensible shoes way up my road yesterday. The first time I saw her, she was carrying a little suitcase. She looked so comical," Angela said, "an old lady in the middle of nowhere with her suitcase, but I realize now those must have been her painting supplies. I should take a leaf out of her book. I don't know . . . with the kids getting older, my whole life seems to be about the care and upkeep of the family, and I never seem to get to the easel."

AMES WALKED OVER the Burrard Bridge, and then down toward Hastings and onto Main Street from the diner on Fourth Avenue. He was perplexed and too full of coffee. He thought the long walk would do him good. Did what he'd learned today merit a call to Darling? It struck him that the more he investigated, the less he knew or understood. It meant going back to his rooming house to use the phone, and he quailed at calling anyone from his landlady's sitting room because she'd hover suspiciously, thinking that he was up to no good. Honestly, he thought, if she believed young men so wicked, why did she put them up? Maybe they'd let him use one of the phones at the police station. It was police business after all.

Once he arrived at the station, no impediment was offered to his using the police telephone, and he was shown into a small office.

"Reverse the charges, though!" the officer said.

"Well, I'm sorry, Ames, but he's not here, and no amount of you needing to speak to him is going to make him appear. There's a missing hunter up the lake, and everyone, including the dog, is out on this one." O'Brien had the air of a man who was relieved not to be scrabbling about in the underbrush. "Is it important?"

"No, I'm calling to ask about the weather. When will he be back?"

"I'll get out my crystal ball. Why don't you tell me, and I'll pass it on?"

"No, that's all right. It's a bit complicated. I'll phone first thing."

"Suit yourself. I suppose you expect we'll be paying for this call, now."

"Yup."

Later, in his favourite diner, he contemplated what he'd learned. He realized that this meant there was more to the story than Darling had told him, and he was preparing to be slightly peevish about being kept in the dark, when a more generous spirit, perhaps fed by the unequalled chicken and dumplings provided by the Chinese chef in the kitchen, made him think that perhaps Darling himself had no more information than he had given Ames.

There was one more class the next day, and then Monday morning was the exam. His fellow students had all decided to go out for the night to their local, but his anxiety about the exam swept all before it, and he paid for his meal and walked back to the rooming house to study.

The class the following morning on forensic ballistics proved more engaging a topic than he had anticipated, and Ames was talking animatedly in the hallway with a couple of other officers about how a really scientific approach to ballistics could help the rate of arrests, when the pathologist he'd spoken with about the dead Russian approached him.

"Constable Ames, soon to be sergeant without a shadow of a doubt, you're sharper than you look. If you've got a moment, there's something you might like to see."

CHAPTER TWELVE

————

THE DOG RAN FORWARD, HIS nose to the ground, and then ran up a long outcrop of open granite with a low *woof*, and then back toward where the men were following on horseback.

"What is it, Bailey?" his handler said. "I think he's got something, sir."

Bailey rushed forward again and stood on the top of the outcrop overlooking a gully. The men could hear the gurgle of a creek. Darling dismounted and hurried after the dog, who was barking at something below, hidden from the men.

"Here!" Darling called back to the search party and scrambled onto the outcrop and looked down to the base of the rock.

He could see that it was already too late. The man was stretched out, face down, his head turned away from the rock at an angle that looked much too loose. Dropping down near the man's feet, Darling could see that it was painfully evident that this was not an accident. The great rend across the man's throat was black and encrusted with flies. Dried blood gave evidence that blood had drained and pooled under his head, soaking into the grass where he had fallen. Darling closed his eyes and turned his head away for a moment to take a breath.

"Police only, please!" he called out. And then on consideration added, "Mr. Leonard, we have found the remains of a deceased individual. I will want you to verify if this is Brodie. Can you just wait there in the meantime?"

Ponting, Oxley, and the neighbours of the dead man, who had come because they knew his usual routes, were beginning to scramble onto the outcrop.

"Oxley, camera," Darling commanded.

Constable Oxley pulled his equipment off the horse, pocketing some flash bulbs in case they were needed, and took the camera out of its leather case. As he made for the scene, he stopped, frowning, and looked around, as if trying to penetrate the surrounding forest, then he hurried on to where Darling was crouched by the body. Ponting and the neighbours occupied themselves with the horses and spoke in low voices trying to piece together how a man who had gone hunting on his own had managed to shoot himself. Constable Ward, Bailey's handler, had called the dog and was calming and stroking him.

Darling looked up as Oxley clambered down with his equipment.

"He's had his throat cut." He said it quietly, so the others would not hear.

"Oh." Oxley stopped, frowning, and seemed to want to look away.

"No time to be squeamish I'm afraid. The whole thing, Constable. The lay of the body, the wound, the ground around here. Damned grass will probably mean no nice imprints of the killer's shoe. We need to look for the weapon."

Darling looked around at the encroaching forest and the dense underbrush. How had the man come to die here? Was he with someone he knew? Or had someone discovered him here and, for some reason, killed him? Or could someone have come into this dense and remote bit of bush to kill this man deliberately? And why? Oxley got to work with the camera, and Darling called back up to the waiting men.

"Mr. Leonard, would you mind? It's not a pleasant sight, I'm afraid."

Leonard made his way around the outcrop and positioned himself near the head of the body and then turned away, swallowing. "It's him. That's Brodie. What happened to him?"

"Thank you. Can you go back and wait with the others now?" Darling said gently. "When we're done here, we'll have to bring him up and pack him out. Mr. Ponting, where did you find the man's horse? Was it close to here?"

Ponting surveyed the area. "It was on the other side of this creek, I'd say half a mile north of here."

Darling looked at the other side of the creek. "He fell forward, facing the creek. Was he on his way to water his horse? The horse must have bolted down this slope, across the creek, and up to where he was found."

Darling climbed back to where the other men were

standing. "His throat has been cut. It may have implications about how we get him out. Have we got a blanket or anything?"

The news seemed to strike Ponting like a blow.

"Throat cut! I've been riding and working these mountains for years and never heard of such a thing. Never felt in any danger."

Ponting dismounted and approached the neighbours who, after the initial effort to see, had moved away and were standing quietly holding their mounts. Leonard had his hand over his mouth as if trying not to be sick. His son Ben, with the imperturbability of youth, was looking eagerly toward the rock.

"You heard, I guess. Did either of you bring blankets?" Ponting asked.

Seeing that Ponting looked in control of himself and seemed disposed to organize something to contain the corpse, Darling went back to check on Oxley.

"He could have been resting here, sir, when he was surprised from behind." Oxley was leaning forward, trying not to breathe, to get a close-up shot of the dead man's neck.

"It would have to have been a tallish man to pull this off. The way he's lying suggests he was standing and then pitched forward," Darling commented. "Let's get that dog on to seeing if he approached the area from this side."

Darling realized that they would need a spare horse and saw that Brodie's neighbour still looked green.

"Mr. Leonard, can you and your son and Mr. Ponting ride down to Miss Winslow's? We'll need a horse to get him down. Not Mr. Brodie's. I doubt he can be made to come any closer to where his master fell. Perhaps, Mr. Ponting, you could bring one of the mounts back." He thought for a moment about the next bit. "Miss Winslow will have Mrs. Brodie with her there. She'll have to know, I suppose, but please leave the details to me."

"Yes, of course, Inspector."

Both men looked relieved about the instructions to keep the information to the minimum.

"Is there anything else, Inspector?" Ponting asked, as he handed Darling his blanket, the only one they had among them.

"Yes. Can you ask Miss Winslow to telephone the police department and have them send out a van? Then can you ask her for one of her largest sheets?"

"How long shall I say it will be for you to get him down?" Ponting asked.

Darling looked back toward the body where Oxley was still squatting with his camera. Who knew how long here? Some time to get the body up and secured, the ride back. "It'll be a couple of hours at the very least. That should be time to get the crew out from town and have it all ready when we arrive. It will be beastly for that poor woman."

Ponting mounted and joined Leonard and his son, who had already moved farther from the scene. He was not at all looking forward to being the bearer of bad news. At least if something ever happened to him in the bush, he'd leave no broken-hearted widow.

"Ward," Darling said to the handler, who had been watching Oxley with professional interest. "Can you take that dog and see if he picks up the scent? I'd like to know how the man got here. Let's work from Mr. Ponting's theory that he was approaching the creek from this side. Oxley, how are you getting on?"

"I've got a full set of photos of the scene, sir. I'm not seeing his rifle. It wasn't with his horse, so he must have had it with him."

Darling rejoined the constable, and together they warily lifted the stiff torso away from the ground to see if the rifle was under him. Even this small movement made the head shift grotesquely. The gun was certainly not under him.

"Let's think through this. The man wants to water his horse, so he dismounts and begins to lead him down the gully toward the creek. Perhaps he is carrying the rifle and props it up somewhere while they head down. But why is he here behind the outcrop where he is obviously surprised by the killer?"

Oxley, who had begun packing the camera equipment, looked down toward the creek. "Maybe he's taken the horse down and left him to drink and has come up here to stand against the rock in the shade? That could put the killing in the afternoon."

"Because?" asked Darling.

"If he's looking for shade, the sun is behind him toward the west. That would make this side of the outcrop shady."

"Hmmm," Darling said.

"I'll put this stuff up top and go have a look around for the rifle." Oxley bent over to take up the camera bag, looking once more at the body and giving an involuntary shudder.

Darling watched Oxley for a moment as he was beginning to move back and forth near the outcrop, looking for the rifle. He could see where their two horses were munching unconcernedly on the high grass. He looked back at the body. Gillingham, the local pathologist, wouldn't have much difficulty with cause of death. The cut looked clean, from what he could see through the caking of blood and flies, but Gilly could probably determine more clearly what sort of weapon was responsible. Darling sighed. It looked expertly delivered. The end of the war had disgorged experts in every form of death back into the country—though admittedly this close-quarters sort of killing was more rarefied. Some sort of special operations person would know how to deliver this kind of death, he reasoned, an experienced hunter would as well, and he had no doubt there were plenty of those up and down the Kootenay valley.

Whatever the case, it didn't look as if the body had been moved, and though it was difficult to really read the ground with its accumulation of dense grasses, twigs, and so on, all the blood was pooled under the victim's head, which meant that he was surprised from behind, most likely. Random? Deliberate? Someone would have had to follow him or know where he was going in the latter case. Random was more worrisome; it suggested a madman on the loose. Something the residents of King's Cove would not like to hear.

Curving well around the scene, Darling descended to the creek and found a place to ford the water. He crossed and, keeping the same distance relative to the body, moved up the other bank and approached the ground directly opposite where the body lay on the other side of the creek.

From this vantage point, he could see Ward and the dog on the open area on the opposite side of the creek. Bailey was following a scent away from the outcrop and the creek that suggested the hunter had never been on this side of the gully. He looked back across the creek and could see the outcrop with the body still lying in the shade, now under Ponting's blanket, and waiting to be transported out. He narrowed his eyes and tried to imagine the scene. Perhaps it was about this time of day. The hunter has led his horse to the creek and scrambled back up to sit with his back against the rock, enjoying the shade. In his mind's eye, Darling could see that the hunter would have had his gun with him. He would not have left it in the holster on the horse, nor would he have propped it up somewhere away from him. There are cougars and bears to consider. So he is sitting with his gun by his side or across his knees. He's closed his eyes. The killer has climbed the outcrop and reached down to cut the hunter's throat. No. It's an uncomfortable reach, and why would the hunter not have heard him coming? The killer must have approached from around the low side of the outcrop, so the hunter must have had his back to him. What was he doing? Perhaps Gilly would be able to tell something from the angle of the cut. Why did he not hear someone approaching? Could he have gotten up from his rest and crouched down to pick up his rifle? And of course, the rifle was missing. Had the killer kept it, or merely gotten rid of it for some reason? Or could someone else have picked it up?

With a sigh, he looked behind him toward the meadow. The horse had bolted across the creek and up the bank into that meadow and wandered until Ponting had found him, spooked and lathered. Had the killer tried to go after the horse? If he was intent, for example, on robbery, he might have. The saddle bags were still on the horse when he was found and seemed to have nothing of value, but that was not to say they hadn't had something worth stealing.

More carefully now, Darling walked along the bank looking down, and found where the ground had been disturbed by the fleeing horse. The twigs and dead leaves had been trampled, exposing the soil on the bank. No sign of human prints. He stood looking down at the creek, his brow furrowed, and then he shook his head, smiling grimly. If I've cut someone's throat, he thought, I need to wash up. He scrambled down the bank to the other side of the creek and walked along it until he saw exactly what he wanted.

"Oxley, when you're finished over there, I think I have something."

From somewhere above he heard Oxley, his voice muffled as if he'd been looking away.

"Coming, sir."

"It looks to me like someone, let's say the killer, washed up just here. You can see where they've wiped their bloody hands, or the knife, on this grass here. It's faint because they've washed up first, but it's there."

CHAPTER THIRTEEN

1918

"**I DON'T KNOW WHY WE HAVE** to be 're-educated' by people who can't even put an X for their own names."

Tatiana looked up from swilling the mop along the surface of the stinking concrete around the toilets. She didn't know who the girl was and didn't care. She whined every day in that weepy voice, and every day Tatiana ignored her.

"You shouldn't let your blond hair show through your head scarf. You've heard what they're doing," Tatiana said.

The girl didn't seem to have one iota of practical good sense. She threw the bucket of water, already black from the floor, over the toilet and jumped back to avoid getting splashed. It stank no matter what they did.

"And by the way," Tatiana said, "who do you think cleaned your toilets? Maybe it's our turn."

"It's disgusting! I never left my toilet like this." The blond girl's voice broke. "I'm going to die!"

"Probably," said Tatiana.

She took up the bucket, stepped on the strings of the mop to get the last of the water out, and walked out and up the stairs to the cleaning closet. The blonde was slow to follow. She ought to feel sorry for her, Tatiana knew. The girl was obviously sick, and she didn't know where her family was or whether they were alive or dead. Tatiana was better off because it was no mystery for her. Her parents were dead. Her husband was dead. Her daughter was dead. Only Vasya was still alive somewhere.

The woman who looked back at her in the broken mirror was barely recognizable. She was old at thirty-eight, her face thin, with deep lines and a bitter look. She took off her head scarf and pushed her hair back, re-inserting the pins, and then replaced the scarf. Her pinafore stank of sewage as she slung it into her bag. She would report to the supervisor and get back to the rooms to wash her clothes in the tin basin with a cracked and uneven bar of lye soap and cold water. She hoped that the bread she had left would still be under her bed in her box. There would be nothing else.

In the hallway, she passed two men she had seen before. They were in charge of something, she didn't know what. She moved close to the wall and looked down. Suddenly one of them grabbed her by the arm.

"Where are you off to, then?"

"To the supervisor, comrade."

"Listen to that voice, eh, Sasha? The music of the decadent aristo!"

"Please excuse me, comrade. I am expected." Tatiana pitched her voice low, respectful.

Her persecutor pushed her up against the wall, his face looming in front of hers.

"Yes, by me."

His hand went up under her skirt grabbing at her thigh and something snapped in Tatiana. She brought her knee up as hard as she could, hoping she hit something that mattered. The man cried out and let go, and Tatiana tried to make a run for it.

She could hear the other man saying, "Comrade, leave it. Not this one. We're late ourselves."

Tatiana felt her arm yanked again, and she was pulled around so violently that she dropped her bags. The man brought his arm up and hit her across the face with the back of his hand, spitting out an insult. Her head flew back, and she felt her skull crack against the wall, and then she crumbled.

LANE HAD A feeling of everything being up in the air, indeterminate.

"I don't know where I am, just now," she said, putting her cup on the table. "That poor hunter is missing, Countess Orlova's brother is missing, the vicar hasn't called about a place for her to live, and I even have to wait till ten to go pick up Mrs. Brodie. Just up in the air, that's all. And now you're telling me that my guest is wandering much farther away than I thought, with a hunter missing and possibly a wounded animal loose."

"I know what you mean. It's hard to even think of doing the dishes with all that going on," Angela said.

Lane smiled in spite of the seriousness of the situation.

Angela famously hated doing dishes and sometimes left them piled in the sink and on the counter for days. "I'm waiting for the boys to get old enough to wash them," she had once told Lane.

"Angela. I . . . I do have some news, of a sort," Lane said. "It's not the most auspicious time for it, really."

"Oh, God, you're not going away again, are you? I couldn't stand it. I'm much too used to you being here now."

"No. Not exactly. Darling and I are going to marry." She rushed the last part of the sentence. Rip the bandage off.

Angela shrieked. "Oh, Lane, sweetie! That's the best news ever! I told you, didn't I?"

"All right. Keep your hair on. No one knows but the vicar. I haven't told anyone yet."

"You told me first?"

"I wondered if you'd, you know, stand up with me, be my matron of honour."

"Would I! Oh my God! What will I wear? When is it? Oh, gosh, I'm so happy." She had reached across the table and was kneading one of Lane's hands.

Lane was embarrassed by Angela's delight but, much to her consternation, felt herself about to become tearful. She used her free hand to keep her tears at bay.

"Okay. This is ridiculous. Let's not make a fuss. Eighteenth of October, right here in St. Joe's. You have plenty of time to find something to wear. I haven't even thought of what I'll wear. It's to be very quiet. No one wants a big palaver."

"Oh, there will be a palaver, mark my words!" Angela got up and began to pace across the porch. "Flowers, a

135

dress, reception. Where shall we have the reception? A dinner, do you think, or cocktails? Are you inviting this lot?" Here Angela waved her hand to encompass the residents of King's Cove.

"Angela, please. Slow down! I'm sure Darling doesn't want a big fuss either."

"Well, it's not his wedding, it's yours! Anyway, I think you have him all wrong. I think he's the kind of man who'd like the biggest possible brouhaha made out of his wedding. I certainly would if I was marrying you! Who's he having as his best man? Does he have a brother, or something?"

Lane was a little reluctant to say, but Angela was a ship in full sail at the moment, and she would be bound to get it out of her. "I think he might be going to ask Ames."

"How absolutely adorable! David picked his favourite cousin who was as useless as a lump of potato. He got so drunk before the ceremony that he was actually fishing around in all his pockets looking for the ring. It was touch and go, I can tell you! Daddy had to make the speech. Constable Ames, on the other hand, would be much too respectful to behave like that! I am so excited!"

Excited enough for the two of them, Lane thought. "Back to reality. Are you coming with me to get Mrs. Brodie? I think she'll need a lot of support."

FELIX HUNT STEPPED onto the platform, watching the busy Nelson train station materialize as the steam cleared. Charming, he thought. He'd been delighted to get the assignment from the director because his work in Vancouver had devolved into almost one job, passing himself off as a member of a repair crew and inspecting Soviet ships docking at the harbour. He knew émigrés were still dribbling in, and sailors had to be accounted for so that as many as arrived also left. And he knew he had a counterpart on each ship. An arrogant man in a suit who was always full of confidence because he would have suborned ordinary crewmen to spy on their mates. Sometimes he thought it would just be easier if they shook off their disguises and dealt directly with each other. They had the exact same interests after all. The Soviet minder wanted every sailor who arrived to leave again when the repairs were done, and so did he. But Hunt was also looking for likely informants.

He had spent the trip to Nelson admiring the mountains and wilderness. He would have loved to retire to Canada, but his wife was hankering to be home. They'd sent their only son to school in England, and she pined for him. She was being plucky, but he knew he should ask for a transfer back, sooner rather than later. He asked directions to the Dade Hotel, took up his suitcase, and went into the sunshine. He had received meticulous instructions from the director about how to find Lane Winslow. He would settle in, have a good meal, and then hire a car and drive out first thing in the morning.

The director was quite specific: find out everything she knew about the Russian operative Aptekar. She had been the last one to see him, and he had not turned up at the meeting place in Yugoslavia. The director had emphasized that she could be found to have nothing to do with it, but they needed to be sure that Aptekar had not decided to fade back into the woodwork with British secrets. Hunt was disappointed to learn from the director of this woman's possible duplicity. He had learned enough in Vancouver about the dangers of the Soviet menace to British outposts like the Dominion. He wondered if her supposed "retirement" was genuine. She spoke Russian, she might need money. And there was that business of the Russian staying in her house. An old lady, to be sure, but Russian. The director had said Lane Winslow had been an outstanding operative during the war and was intelligent. More's the danger, he thought, pausing outside the doors of the hotel and looking up. He'd get a room on the top floor. He'd like a view of that beautiful lake.

Early September 1947

"WHAT ARE YOU doing here? You look like hell. Is this some undercover operation?" Igor Dudin stepped aside to let Aptekar in.

His old colleague's apartment felt crowded and overheated to Aptekar. "Something like that. I need a bath and some help."

Dudin looked quickly into the hallway and then closed the door. "Were you followed?"

"I certainly hope not. If I was, I am a dead man."

Putting his hand on Aptekar's arm, Dudin said, "I know. Everybody knows."

"Then I am a dead man now." Aptekar sighed and leaned against the wall, suddenly aware of his exhaustion. He'd given it a good try, he thought. He didn't blame Dudin for what was about to happen. It was how things worked. His friend also had to look out for himself.

"What will you do?" he asked, resigned.

"Vodka, bath, good feeding. In that order. Then we'll have to find clothes and get you out of here."

"Are you sure? It is not safe for you." Aptekar felt a mix of hope and suspicion.

"When is it ever safe for us? I can tell you, the knives are out for you. Betraying the motherland. Come. I will run the bath, and we will drink while it fills. You are lucky. Today happens to be one of the two days a week when there is hot water. You are also lucky because I have been assigned a flat with my own bathroom. The reward from a grateful nation."

Aptekar lay in the bath, his jangled nerves soothed by the vodka and hot water. He could hear his old companion in the kitchen, frying something that smelled like sausage, and it made him think that none of it mattered, that anything would be worth one final good meal. They would not send him to a prison camp this time, he knew. Execution. He hoped Dudin would get the credit for his capture and not be dragged down with him. He would help him, turn himself in, make it look good. He sank under the water to soak his head and rubbed soap into his hair. In the end, it is creature comforts. They matter more than ideals, loyalty, some improbable long and peaceful retirement. He did not, he reflected under the influence of the truth-inducing vodka, merit a peaceful retirement after what he had spent his life doing.

CHAPTER FOURTEEN

GLASSES IN HAND, LANE AND Orlova sat exhausted in the sitting room. The temperature had fallen enough by nightfall that Lane had lit the stove. She was conscious of a pall of sadness at this first hint of the coming winter cold. It seemed to underscore the chilling and exhausting activities of the day.

Mrs. Brodie's shock and sorrow at the sight of her husband's body wrapped in a sheet, so suggestive of a shroud, being removed from the horse and placed in the van had been heart wrenching. Angela had gone home by the time the men returned from the bush, so it was up to Lane and Countess Orlova to try to comfort the widow. Her choking cries had no adequate response. They could not understand why anyone would have killed her husband any more than she could.

Lane had given her brandy and made tea and tried to keep her warm, but nothing stemmed the flow of tears or questions, or prevented her near collapse at the sight of the van being driven away. Lane had finally been able to get hold of a cousin of Mrs. Brodie's, who agreed to meet them at the Brodie farm. Darling had forsworn to ask Mrs. Brodie the necessary questions to begin piecing together the events surrounding her husband's death, but he told Lane to tell the cousin that he would be out in the morning to talk with her. It was a murder investigation.

"That poor woman," Orlova said, shuddering. She pulled her black sweater more tightly around herself.

"I feel drained," Lane admitted. "But, madam, you must be careful; we all must be, at least until they find out why that man died."

"You don't need to warn me! I will go nowhere but here, or up to that Mrs. Hughes to paint her flowers."

Lane stood up. "I think that is wise. I'm for bed, I think. Would you like anything else?"

"No, thank you. You must rest and not think of me. I am just fine."

Lying in the dark, Lane felt Mrs. Brodie's sorrow like a dark mantel. It reminded her of the cost of love. She had loved and lost herself once, a circumstance that had been sullied by deceit and manipulation. Now she loved, she knew, for real. And the man she loved was a policeman. Please, she whispered into the darkness, never let this be me.

THE SOUND OF the phone pierced her consciousness, and she pulled herself, bemused, from a deep sleep. She pushed herself slowly out of bed and listened. Two longs and a short. It was for her. She glanced at her bedside clock. It was well after nine in the morning, but her dismay, her memories of the day before, and her worry about her guest were all pushed out by the insistent ringing. In the hall, she picked up the earpiece and spoke into the receiver. "KC 431. Lane Winslow speaking."

"Ah. Miss Winslow. Good morning. My name is Felix Hunt."

An English voice. Lane frowned and then turned to look at the kitchen. She could hear Orlova turn the tap on.

"Miss Winslow?"

Lane turned back to the phone. "Yes. I'm sorry. Who did you say you are again?"

"Felix Hunt. I work at the British Consulate in Vancouver."

"I see."

But she didn't. She could think of no reason she should be contacted by anyone at the consulate.

"I'd like to come out to see you. It shouldn't take above an hour."

"You are coming from Vancouver?" She shook her head, trying to feel less groggy.

"No. I should have explained. I'm here in Nelson. I was asked to come by and just, well," he hesitated, "clarify a few things. Is there a place we can go where we will be . . . uninterrupted?"

Dunn! she thought, feeling herself come fully awake.

"I see," was all she offered.

She was fully conscious of her guest in the kitchen. Dunn, her deceptive and manipulative ex-lover, now in charge of, she guessed, counter-intelligence at MI5. She had thought, hoped, that she had seen the last of him during the summer when he had tried to manipulate her into returning to work for him as a double agent with a promise to save Darling, who had been wrongfully arrested for a wartime murder. Instead, she had brought the British a defecting agent, Stanimir Aptekar. Why could she never seem to get clear of Angus Dunn?

"Would you be able to see me today?"

Stilling with great effort a desire to ask if they had no working telephones in Vancouver, she said, "What time were you thinking? I have a guest at the moment, and we are expected somewhere for lunch."

They weren't, but Eleanor could always be counted on to provide a lunch.

"Ah," he said. "When then?"

Conscious suddenly of her anxiety about Orlova, she could feel herself revert to the secrecy she'd been used to when dealing with British officials. Her guest, she reminded herself, might understand more English than she was letting on.

"Oh, I see. You want to see the wharf. You won't need anyone to show you where that is. It's about an hour out of town. Just before you get to the King's Cove turnoff. You'll be able to see the sign just ahead of you. There's a little lane that goes down toward the water on your right. Just follow that." She stopped and listened, and then added, "About three, I'd guess, all told."

"Are you saying you will see me at three?"

"That's right," Lane said, trying to sound bright. "Good luck. No, no trouble at all. Oh, and say hello to Marion for me. Bye now."

She knew her deception was unnecessary, but it came to her naturally, a circumstance that made her cross.

"I have put the tea on, Miss Winslow," Madam Orlova said, coming to the door.

"Good idea!" Lane said. She retrieved her robe from the bedroom and padded down the hall to the kitchen. "Someone wanting direction to the wharf where the steam boat docks. I completely overslept. How did you sleep?"

"Like the dead," said Orlova. "It was cool this morning, but the sun is already warming everything up. I am very determined. Today I will not move from the bottom of your garden. The light is wonderful, and I have seen the angle of your house I would like to paint."

"Yes. Of course. Wonderful. And perhaps today we will hear if anyone has any news about your brother."

"Or if that priest of yours has found me a place to stay? I am sure you would like your house to yourself again." Here Orlova's seemingly cheerful mood seemed to dissipate, as if it had been merely put on. She wrung her hands and sighed. "I am so worried about poor Vasya, if I tell the truth. When this is over, I don't even know where I will go. I feel as if there is no home in this world."

Lane was stricken again by her guest's troubles. "You are most welcome here, for as long as it takes. You remind me that you too are facing your own kind of sorrow and anxiety."

Orlova shrugged in a way Lane remembered so well from Russians she knew as a child. A tilting of the head with downturned lips, as if to say, "We are powerless against the fates."

LANE WATCHED MADAM Orlova from the window. The old lady sat with her board on her lap, and at that moment, she had a pencil in her hand and was drawing with confident sweeps, looking continuously up to the house. It must be wonderful to have such focus, Lane thought, to be able to lose yourself in a task and have something beautiful at the end of it. To be able to forget your sorrows if only for an hour. She had been made to sketch as a child by one of her governesses who believed it was what young ladies should do, but neither she nor her sister had exhibited any talent for it, though Lane had enjoyed sitting outside trying. But she had preferred to read, and her sister had preferred to be out in the stables. She picked a pillow up from the window seat, gave it a couple of pats and put it down. Somewhere, at the very same time as she was enjoying the peace of a sunny day, she thought, poor Mrs. Brodie was suffering the horror of losing her husband to an act of unspeakable violence.

She would make her bed and try not to think of the fate of the sheet she had provided for the transport of the hunter's body. Then she would go investigate her much-neglected stand of apple trees. Robin Harris, who lived down the hill from her, had been quite scornful of her apple crop. He had shown her that the trees were already being taken over by pests and various sorts of who knew what. But she could at least still get some apples off them. There were some early apples already ripe. She would attempt a pie. She started toward the bedroom and nearly got entangled in her guest's black sweater, which had slipped off the back of a chair onto the floor. Scooping it up, she stopped at the guest room and worried for a moment about whether it would be rude to intrude on her guest's privacy by barging into her room, and then she thought there would be no harm in laying the sweater neatly on the bed.

She certainly had no cause to complain about her guest. She washed her own clothes in the sink, though Lane had offered the washing machine, and hung them neatly on the clothesline. Stockings, blouse, underwear. The bed was made with military corners, her hairbrush and personal items were lined up neatly on the little dresser. She had Lane's copy of *The Government Inspector* by her bed. Suitable reading for a woman disillusioned by politics. Lane put the sweater on the bed and was about to leave when she saw that one of the two suitcases Orlova had come with was standing behind the dresser. It must be the one where she kept her paints. Unsure why, really, she leaned over to look under the bedspread and then stood up again, and surveyed the room. It was a sparsely furnished room. A bed, a bedside table, a dresser she had cleared two drawers of, and a chair from the kitchen. Lane had provided a small pot of daisies to brighten up the otherwise austere look of the room. She opened the closet door a smidgeon, feeling fully guilty now, and glanced at the two dresses and jacket hanging neatly. She closed the door quickly and beat a retreat from the guest room, closing the door behind her. She stood, momentarily nonplussed. Madam Orlova was outside in her front yard painting. But of course, she would have taken her paints out in her suitcase. She turned her mind instead to the disturbing circumstance of the phone call from Mr. Hunt, apparently from the British consulate.

It was only as she was getting dressed that she recalled something that the man had said: "A place we could go where we would be," Lane remembered his hesitation, "uninterrupted." Why would he think they would be interrupted in her own house?

FELIX HUNT HAD put down the phone and sat on for a moment in the phone cabinet off the hotel foyer. Lane Winslow had been pretending to talk to a friend. Was this a sign that she was covering something up; had she learned something about her guest? Or was this just the natural caution of an ex-British agent?

"AMES." DARLING LOOKED at his watch. "Shouldn't you be writing your exam?"

"Yes. It's in half an hour. I've been trying to reach you."

"I've been thrashing about in the high bush finding dead hunters, not that you should concern yourself about it in any way."

"Oh. That's interesting," Ames said, wishing his exam was over and he was back at his post helping Darling.

"Yes, it is, Ames, and unless you have something equally interesting, I have to go meet with the grieving widow to find out more about who might have wanted to cut her husband's throat."

"Ugh. Sorry, sir. But this is about the Russian thing, and I thought it was surprising. First, when I took the picture around to the priests in the two parishes that seem to serve most of the Russians here, no one had heard of that Madam Orlova, and no one had ever seen her brother. I thought that was surprising for a start because you told me she'd been looking for him here. Then I got a call from one of the priests. One of the men who'd seen the picture when I was showing it around came to see him saying he had seen the man before and was really afraid and didn't know if he should say anything. The priest persuaded him to talk to me. According to him, the man in the picture you sent me is a member of the Soviet secret police, and he had been interrogated by him when he was arrested back in Russia. He was really scared because he was worried something would happen to him, even here in Canada."

Darling frowned. This was not how he thought the thing would go at all. His mind leapt to Madam Orlova. Was she who she said she was?

"This is unexpected, Ames."

"Yes, sir. There's more."

"You have been busy. Go on."

"That dead Russian, the one who supposedly died of a heart attack? The pathologist caught me in the hall yesterday and told me that I had been right about there being something funny about the rash on his neck. He'd decided to have a closer look, took some sort of scraping and analyzed it. It apparently contained a deadly poison that may have caused the heart attack. They're moving the death into the 'suspicious circumstances' category."

"This shows you stumble into being clever from time to time, but it does not necessarily suggest any connection with the secret policeman."

"No, sir."

"Unless—"

"That's exactly what I was thinking, sir. What if the secret policeman is actually here in Canada and the dead guy recognized him? That would mean the man who spoke to me was correct to be anxious."

"You'll need to get the Vancouver Police Department involved. Your job is to get your exam done and get the hell back here. Give them the photo, tell them what you know, and good luck. I'll need to think about the whole thing from this end. It's a nuisance, with this murder to deal with."

Darling hung up the phone, paused for a moment, his lips set in a grim line, then stood up and got his hat off the hat stand. He had not shared with Ames his now-growing anxiety. He sat back down and stared at the phone. If Lane's guest was not quite who she said she was, she had to be rooted out of there. Reaching for the receiver, he was about to dial, and then he put it down again. He would have to be careful. Resolved, he put his call through.

"KC 431, Lane Winslow speaking."

"Lane, don't talk. Just listen, make the right kind of noises."

"Oh, hello," Lane said. The second time in one day she had to pretend on the telephone.

"Ames has dug something up in Vancouver. That picture your guest is showing around may be her brother, but according to at least one frightened man, he is an MGB interrogator."

"Yes, of course," Lane said, glancing down the hall.

"I'm due out at Mrs. Brodie's, but we'd better call the vicar to see how he's getting on with finding a place for her. She may not be all she seems."

"Oh, yes. A good deal more in my cupboard. I'll take care of it."

Darling hung up. Whatever that was supposed to mean. He'd warned her.

"Oxley!"

Silence.

Darling went into the hall and looked into Oxley's temporary office, then he went downstairs. "Where's Oxley?"

"Washing the car, sir. He's around in the alley. He's quite thorough. He's been out there for ages."

Boy Scout, thought Darling again. "Too bad. We're going up that long dusty road to interview the widow."

"You sound pleased, sir," O'Brien said, not a little pleased himself, at the thought of all that work going to waste.

"I am a bit, yes. And I see it might rain. We can blame him for that, and all."

MRS. BRODIE LOOKED as though she had slept only fitfully. She sat at her kitchen table in front of a cup of coffee, and though she reached for it from time to time, she did not drink. Her cousin, who was introduced as Arlene Taylor, leaned against the sink, arrayed in a clean starched apron, looking the complete antithesis of the dishevelled and listless widow.

"I'm sorry to intrude, Mrs. Brodie," Darling began. He had asked Oxley to find a seat behind him somewhere for his note taking, so that she did not feel overwhelmed by the two of them.

Mrs. Brodie only shook her head, either to say it was

all right, or she wasn't ready to cope. Her cousin came to stand by her and put her hand on her shoulder.

"Can this wait, Inspector? You can see the state of her." But Mrs. Brodie patted her cousin's hand.

"It's all right," she said quietly.

"Mrs. Brodie, can you think of anyone who would want to harm your husband?" Darling asked.

Tears sprang into her eyes and she shook her head again. "I knew you would ask me that question. I lay awake all night, knowing there was no one. Everybody," she hesitated, "loved Ray, they did. I wanted to think of someone. I wanted this to make sense."

Darling nodded. "Can you—"

"Nobody even knew exactly where he went," she said. "He must have met someone up there. They must have fought or something. What about that man who found his horse? Maybe he was up to something and Ray ran into him."

"We will be looking into every circumstance, Mrs. Brodie. Most people are murdered by someone they know, so we always like to start in the middle of the circle. Is there no one he has ever had a dispute with?"

At this the cousin turned away and looked out the window. The sky had greyed over so that it felt as though an untimely dusk was encroaching. Both women sat silent.

"Mrs. Taylor?" Darling asked the cousin. There was something in her movement that seemed to Darling like an attempt to stifle something.

She turned back, her arms crossed tightly. "Things haven't always been that great between Ray and my ex-husband."

Mrs. Brodie put her hand on her mouth. "No, Arlene. That . . . you can't."

"Can't I? It was okay with us all pretending before. But this is different. Ray is dead. God, he's not even my husband, and I feel like I've got more sense than you!" She walked over to the table and pulled out a chair. "The truth is, Inspector, that my husband and Cassie here had an affair about five years ago. It wasn't a good time in any of our lives. Cassie and Ray managed to get through it, but we didn't. In fact, I couldn't wait to get rid of my husband. I couldn't wait to get rid of Cassie, either, if you want to know the truth." Then she shrugged. "But blood is thicker than water."

Darling glanced at Mrs. Brodie, who was staring at her hands in her lap, and then addressed Mrs. Taylor again.

"Does your ex-husband—what is his name?—live in the area?"

"Verne Taylor. No. He moved into town. He has that boat repair shop just off Lakeside."

"Have they spoken recently, do you know?" He looked at the widow.

"I don't think so. Why should they?" Mrs. Brodie said, looking up. Her words contained a challenge. "But you're barking up the wrong tree if you think it's Verne. He wouldn't hurt a flea."

"Just his wife," said Mrs. Taylor, folding her hands on the table and looking away from her cousin.

"Just to be clear, Mrs. Brodie, your husband did take his rifle with him?"

She frowned. "Yes. He was hunting. Why?"

"We haven't found the gun," he said. "Do you know what kind it is?"

"I think it was an Enfield S something. What do you mean you haven't found it?"

Oxley's pencil could be heard scraping over the page in his notebook.

"It was not at the scene, nor was it with his horse, or anywhere near where the horse was found."

"Then whoever did it, took it," said Mrs. Taylor.

"That may well be, though he did not die of a gunshot wound," said Darling. "The weapon used was a knife. Did he have a hunting knife?"

"Oh," said Mrs. Brodie, looking white. "Yes, I think so. I don't really know what he takes, but no hunter would go without a knife, would he?"

Strictly speaking he hadn't heard from Gilly as to what sort of knife had made the wound, nor the possible position of the victim when it happened. He got up, and Oxley, taking the signal, stood as well, closing his notebook. Rain was beginning to patter on the windows. Even in the house, the drop in the outside temperature was palpable.

"We will keep you posted as we go along, Mrs. Brodie. Please feel free to call the police station at this number if you think of anything at all that may be relevant to the investigation."

As they were leaving, Oxley turned and touched the brim of his hat. "My condolences, ma'am."

Inside the car, brushing off the heavy drops of rain, Darling nodded toward the house, where the door had been shut almost before they were fully off the front steps.

"That's got to be awkward."

"It opens up a couple of possibilities, doesn't it, sir? The ex-husband and that prospector. I never trust the guy who is first to the scene."

"This is from your vast experience as a murder investigator, is it? Back to town. We'd better visit the faithless Verne Taylor."

CHAPTER FIFTEEN

"**N***U?*" **SNAPPED THE COMMISSAR. "WELL?**"

"He was seen to board a ship bound for Hong Kong. I suspect he has connections there among the ex-patriots."

"Who do we have there?"

"I'm not sure, sir. I will find out. When I do, what would you like me to direct him to do?"

The commissar made a face and looked at the big picture of Lenin on the wall opposite his desk. "I don't really see the point of him anymore. He's old. He should have been allowed to retire. And he's cost us too much."

"Sir," began his deputy. He was anxious not to anger his superior. The commissar had a reputation for showing no feeling, so that you never knew where you were before it was too late, and you were on a train bound to some godawful place.

"Yes, what is it?"

"He may still have active connections with that British agent. I agree that eliminating Aptekar would end the problem of his taking secrets anywhere; on the other hand, he also could lead us to the agent. What was his name? Winslow?"

"*Her* name," the commissar corrected. "The agent in question now is the daughter. Stanton Winslow, the man he dealt with before and during the war, is dead. I don't see why you think he will lead us to her, if he is busy going to Hong Kong. He should be going the other way. Unless. Ah, I see your thinking. Hong Kong is a British protectorate. He could get safe passage to England from there. He could then reconnect with her there and be brought safely into their fold by her.

"I want him eliminated. Put someone on it. In the event that he slips through our fingers, we need to figure out where he will take asylum. Find out where she is exactly. We can put someone to work in London doing something useful instead of costing us money gallivanting around the city going to the theatre."

"WELL, MR. HUNT. What can I do for you?" Lane and Felix were sitting under the overhang of the apple shed on the wharf. It was cool after the rain, and the lake was still agitated from the earlier storm.

"I have been asked by the director to have you just go over again the substance of your conversation with the Russian operative Stanimir Aptekar. You met him in June of this year in Berlin."

"You astonish me. He's sent you all the way out here for that? I gave a full report. And anyway, why can't you ask the Russian operative? He must be settled in London or the southeast by now. I understood he was going to try to get out almost immediately."

Hunt shifted uneasily on the bench, imagining what the pile up of dust and splinters was doing to his trousers. "That's the problem. He hasn't. There was a plan to meet at the Yugoslav border and he never showed up. We don't know if he was duping us by pretending to agree to this arrangement or if he has been apprehended by the Soviets, who might have got wind of his plans to escape. If the latter is the case, he may be even now, depending on your conversations, spilling valuable British intelligence."

"Ha!" Lane barked. It was unbelievable! "You think I gave him valuable British intelligence? Like what? Where to find a public loo in London? The director has obviously not furnished you with all the facts. No, of course not. This whole system works without anyone anywhere having all the facts. The director himself knows very well I had no intelligence to give. I was asked to become a double agent, and for reasons I cannot explain, I agreed and was sent off to seduce the Russians armed with a story about my dissatisfaction with the West and missing my Russian nanny. It was only a stroke of luck that, instead of being seduced by my story, the agent I talked to wanted to defect. I placed the necessary information in the hands of Mr. Dunn, and that was the end of my involvement. And will, by the way, be the end of any involvement I will ever again have with British Intelligence. I am sorry you have been put to the trouble of a long journey for nothing."

Hunt sighed. He was a good judge of character, and he did not doubt Lane Winslow's story in any particular.

In fact, she was not the first person to express frustration about their director.

"I think the problem is that we don't know what's happened to him. If he's been captured, he will either be executed or sent to a gulag."

"Since when has the intelligence branch cared about that?"

"You have a point. As I'm thinking through this, I'm wondering if it is possible that he was alerted to some danger, some betrayal of his intention to cross over, and has had to go into hiding. You met him. Could he pull this sort of thing off? I understand he's getting on."

Lane thought about the Aptekar she had met. Confident, wiry, supremely aware, and intelligent.

"It is possible," she said. "I don't know how much physical strength he could bring to bear on something like escaping from capture. But he is very urbane. If he could get into a community of displaced White Russians somewhere, he could pass himself off as an aristocrat with no difficulty. In fact, I expect he is an aristocrat. Even if he had no money, it wouldn't matter. All of them must be as poor as church mice, wherever they are." Her own countess, for example.

"Is there any possibility that he might try to contact you?"

Lane was about to protest the absolute impossibility of this, but then she remembered that in the previous winter Aptekar had been as close as Vancouver and had known how to reach her then. He had sent her a letter, saying he'd been a colleague of her father's and even suggested then that she might like to come over to the Russians, when she had become involved with the death of a Russian at the local hot springs. If she agreed that it was still possible, it would almost certainly mean that she would not be out of the clutches of British Intelligence. She rubbed her eyes. She was still bleary from lack of sleep. An impossible idea worked its way up. She turned and looked at the agent, searching the profile he was presenting her.

"Is this why you've come? You think he's here? All this probing and these hypothetical questions! Why don't you just ask? And I'll save you the trouble now. He's not here. He hasn't contacted me, and I certainly don't expect him to. I'll grant you that it is theoretically possible. He knows more or less where I live. He was out in Vancouver during the winter. He was running an incompetent local asset who was working with the Russians. However, his contacting me assumes that he could get all the way to Western Canada while on the run."

"There is the possibility that he is not on the run at all, but still in the pay of his original masters," Hunt speculated, ignoring her outburst.

"In that case, he would have no need to find me. He'd be busy working operatives in Germany and even England. If there was an arrangement to pick him up somewhere in Europe and he didn't turn up, then you might want to worry about who betrayed him, if he was captured before he could escape. I was under the impression you people don't like loose ends. The betrayer, if such a one exists, is a loose end." She stood up and brushed off the back of her skirt. Rain was beginning to spit down again. "One thing is certain, Mr. Hunt. I am not your loose end. Everything I know, you now know."

Hunt stood up, followed Lane's lead, and brushed off his behind, and then looked at his now-dusty hand in distaste.

"Is there the slightest possibility that he will try to contact your guest?"

Lane stopped still and then turned slowly and looked at him.

"My guest?" Of course, she thought, she'd mentioned her guest when she'd spoken to him on the phone. "I shouldn't think so. Why should he? What an odd idea."

"I was under the impression she is Russian herself."

"Were you? How, I wonder?"

Hunt smiled and shook his head. "I have no idea how I got that impression. All this talk of Russians, I suppose. Thank you, Miss Winslow. I will let you know if we require anything else."

Well, Hunt thought, opening his car door. Had he wasted his time?

"Please don't," Lane said, with her brightest smile. "Can you find your way back? Oh, and don't pass on my best regards to your boss when you speak with him."

Hunt nodded and got into his car. "Right. Duly noted. Well then, goodbye, Miss Winslow. Oh, and congratulations on your upcoming wedding!"

Chilled by more than just the rain that was beginning to fall in earnest, she watched Hunt's hired car labour up the steep road from the lake. His congratulations—so cheerfully delivered—had stopped her breath. The tiniest handful of people knew she was getting married. How had *he* come to know? She turned the engine over in her car. She had better go to Bales's store for some biscuits to give legitimacy to her having driven away suddenly in the afternoon. But she sat, her engine running, rain beginning to fall more persistently, blurring her windshield.

She tried to assess how she felt. Newly frightened about the reach of her former employers, certainly, but there was also melancholy at the thought that perhaps Aptekar had not managed to get out. She pushed away her concerns about what British Intelligence seemed to know and focused on Aptekar. Perhaps his story to her about wanting to end his career on a nice farm in Sussex was all a fairy story. Spies rarely told the absolute truth. On the other hand, if he had been planning to defect, the thought that someone might have betrayed him disturbed her. Who? It was possible he had been under surveillance the whole time in Berlin, after Berlin, or even before. Who knew what he got up to? Certainly, during the winter when he was in Canada, he had seemed to be a trusted and hard-nosed Soviet agent.

It was the sudden thought that she herself somehow might be responsible for his fall from grace that caused her to put her forehead on the steering wheel and close her eyes. It was at that moment that she began to wonder why Hunt had really come all this way. And she didn't buy for a second that he made a mistake about her guest. How had he known? And how had he known about her marriage?

With a groan she realized that she was now forced to keep more secrets from Darling. She would not be able to tell him about this meeting, or anything that was said in it. She had thought the whole business of the Official Secrets Act—to which she was bound for the next fifty years—was finally behind them. She recalled how it had created the great cavern of doubt between her and Darling right from the beginning and had nearly got her charged with murder. Bloody British Intelligence!

AMES CLOSED HIS exam paper and looked around the room. He appeared to be the first one finished, and he immediately became uneasy. He glanced at the enormous clock at the front of the hall. There were more than twenty minutes remaining. He should do what he learned to do in school: go back and check his work. It wouldn't hurt. He opened the booklet to the first page again and carefully reviewed his answers on a series of questions about the Criminal Code as it governed arrests. His mind wandered to his conversation with the local police about the dead Russian man. The constable he had talked to had listened patiently and taken notes, looking with interest at the picture and commenting on the car.

"So you think this is a suspicious death and that this fellow might be behind it? Do I have that right?" he'd said to Ames.

This was such an oversimplification of what Ames had swirling around in his mind that he had to think about what to say next. "It's not that I think it's a suspicious death—your coroner does. You could have a word with him. There is at least one very frightened citizen who recognized this man in the photograph from back home as being a member of the secret police."

"If this 'secret policeman' of yours is back home, why do we need to worry about him, again?"

Ames had felt a little foolish.

"Look, I think, my boss thinks there might be something going on here among the Russians, so he wanted to make sure you had all the information I collected."

"If we have a suspicious death, we'll look into it, rest assured, and if it leads to any of the rest of this, we'll look into that as well. Will that do? Oh. And good luck with your exam."

Ames had stood up and thanked the constable, who was already being distracted by the tea cart. "Can you let my inspector know if you find anything?" He'd pulled a used envelope out of the wastebasket, jotted down the information for getting hold of Darling, and pushed it toward the constable, who had picked it up impatiently and put it on top of his notes.

Thinking about this now, Ames did not feel reassured and, indeed, had begun to wonder how important it really was. Looking at the infinite details of the Criminal Code, he thought about how easy it was to go down a rabbit hole when you were investigating something. You could talk yourself into believing some detail meant something and work to make it fit into a pattern that might be entirely of your own invention. You needed, he thought glumly, to both look into rabbit holes and keep the big picture in mind in case you were looking down the wrong hole.

"Gentlemen. Time's up," the invigilator said.

The sound of paper rustling and pencils being put down and chairs beginning to scrape on the wooden floor interrupted his thoughts. No matter how well he did on this exam, it was a long way from guaranteeing he'd be any good at the job, he thought, nodding at the man who came by to pick up his test.

APTEKAR WALKED OFF the gangplank onto the solid wooden pier of the Vancouver port. Despite the maelstrom of truck engines and men shouting and all the business of crates being loaded and unloaded, chains rattling, and horns honking, gulls circling and squawking, the scene seemed quiet to him compared to the insistent metallic thrumming and banging of the engines in the ship that never let up during the whole of the trip. His quarters had been in the bowels of the ship, crowded in with ten other sailors near the echoing steel engine room.

He stood, trying to orient himself. He'd been here less than a year ago, he thought, under such different circumstances that his past appeared to him like a fictional story. He was the prince in the tale, living in luxury at the great Hotel Vancouver, being waited on, wearing an expensive Italian suit and English shoes.

He looked down at his borrowed and collapsing boots and laboured to see himself as anyone else might see him, an ageing Russian sailor coming off the ship for a night on the town. He'd wanted to bring his rucksack with his only change of clothes, but the sailors were not permitted to carry anything off the ship. One of the young men he'd befriended on the crossing came up behind him and pounded him on the back.

"You should come where we're going, comrade. Girls and drink, or are you too old, eh?"

Aptekar smiled. "Maybe, maybe not."

"That's the idea! Tomo over there knows the places. He's been here before."

"Ah. Good. So we don't have to waste time being lost. Is the minder coming as well?" Aptekar could see the commissar standing at the top of the gangplank looking over the scene, his hands behind his back, a look of supreme confidence on his face.

"He doesn't have to, does he? He's already got one of us on the job."

Maybe even you, Aptekar thought. Well, I know the places, too. "All right, then, let's go," he said.

The waterfront hotel bar was raucous with good spirits. His companions had put together four tables and sat in front of now-empty plates but full glasses, all talking at once, shouting over each other. In another hour, Aptekar thought, it will tip, and tempers will begin to rise, arguments about money, disputes over the girls who had begun to gather. Glasses would be broken and sailors tossed out. He staggered drunkenly toward the dark hallway where the sign of the pointing finger indicated the location of the toilets down some stairs.

Once in the dimly lit hallway, he paused, completely sober, and looked behind him. No one had followed, but it wouldn't be long. He hurried down the stairs to the first landing. Now he could hear talking above him at the hallway entrance. On the bottom landing, he could smell the acrid bathrooms, combined with the kind of permanent mouldering damp of dockside hotels the world over. A door at the end of the little passageway had a small filthy window. Thank God, an outside door. Heavy steps were beginning down the stairs. Two men, talking pornographically about their plans for the rest of the evening in loud Russian.

Aptekar darted to the door and slipped out into the dark, closing the door quietly. A cold clinging fog had moved in off the water. It was not yet ten. He could still get a tram east.

CHAPTER SIXTEEN

A **PARK BENCH. WHAT A BLOODY** cliché! The green at Russell Square was nearly uninhabited except for one stout matron under an umbrella impatiently waiting for her toy poodle to perform. It wasn't fully raining, but the spitting of drops made the director turn with irritation to see if the man he was meeting was coming. He put up his own umbrella and took a folded newspaper out of the inside pocket of his raincoat. It was open to an article about Harold Wilson possibly getting an appointment to the board of trade.

The director looked up. Where was his counterpart? Who the hell was Harold Wilson? Maybe he should get a quiet desk job like the board of trade. He stared unseeing at the paper again. The whole bloody thing could fall through. The first name they'd given him had been a bust. A pretender from Exeter, who was too cowardly to do anything but talk big about the virtues of socialism. He'd never have made a real agent for the Russians. Well, the director thought,

I've done my bit by giving them Aptekar's name. It wasn't his fault the Ruskies had bungled it.

A man in a black trench coat sat down next to him, and the director felt a burst of anger because he'd not seen him till he was on the bench next to him. The man pulled the sides of his coat over his lap and folded his hands. After a few moments he spoke, in a deep voice with a thick Slavic accent.

"I hope you are not planning to keep me out here all day. It will be raining hard soon."

"It will take no time at all. Your first man was a waste of time."

The other man shrugged. "I can only give you what I know. If he is not everything you hoped for, then I am sorry you are disappointed. We are disappointed, too. You did not hold up your end of the bargain."

"Not my fault. You lost him. I did hold up my end. You promised a second name." The director wanted to look at the man beside him on the bench but continued looking at the picture of Harold Wilson. The portly woman had scooped up her dog and was walking past them to the near gate onto Guilford Street.

"We are working on it." The director could sense his counterpart shaking his head.

"That's rubbish. What work is required?"

"A good deal if it is to be the right one. All you've really offered is an ageing spy. One we were prepared to cashier and allow to live a quiet old age. Now we are forced to arrest him and house him somewhere in Siberia. If we find him. We in turn must find the right inside man for you. One who is of diminishing use to us but will be enough to make it look like you are on the job."

The director stood up. "This is nonsense."

"Sit down," the Russian ordered. "How do we know you have not gone back on your word? We don't. In fact, we now have reason to suspect he is here in your country somewhere, no doubt sequestered by you."

The director sat down and stared across the park. The low shrubs were beginning to glisten with the rain. What his counterpart said surprised him. Would it be useful to have him continue to believe this?

"How so?"

"He was followed to Vladivostok. He likely shipped to Hong Kong and made his way here."

The director clamped his mouth shut and took a deep breath. Then he turned to look at the Russian.

"There is another possibility," he said, "but I'll need that second name."

LANE PACED IN her kitchen. Orlova was still in the garden, but she was rinsing her brushes. She poured the water, now a murky green-brown, onto the grass, made a point on the hairs of each brush in succession with her lips, and put them handle-side down in the glass. Lane wanted to talk to Darling, but he was occupied with the case of the hunter. She needed, she decided, to get away to think, to try to understand. She felt badly over her sudden doubts about her guest. Normally she would write through it, make a map, try to fit things on it, but her house was not her own, and the things that were happening were so disparate they had yet to coalesce into a firm narrative.

The glass with the brushes was sitting on the lawn. Lane had thought the cleaning was a prelude to coming back into the house, but the artist sat on, looking at the painting, turning her head this way and that and glancing up at the house. Decided, Lane went out the kitchen door and down the stairs. She walked around the sheets she had hung out to dry in the morning, taking a handful of cloth in her hand. They were drying nicely. In another month she would have to revert to hanging her washing in the kitchen on the laundry frame above the stove.

"May one see?" she asked as she walked across the lawn toward her guest.

"Yes. I cannot decide about one of the lines over here." She pointed at one side of the paper. "But I think it is all right. You will tell me." Lane walked behind her and looked at the painting. It was her house, gleaming white in the sunlight, her weeping willow, even a few errant daisies in the foreground. There was still a slight gleam of wet paint above the roof.

"It is perfect!" Lane exclaimed. Her anxieties as she had paced in the kitchen moments before seemed, in this moment, to be madness. Here was what mattered, surely. An old woman who was an artist in search of her missing brother. Why did it suddenly have to be more complicated?

"You shall have it," Countess Orlova said. She stood up and stretched her back. "This is the trouble with being old. You think you are tired and will be more comfortable sitting, only to find your back seizes up and you must stand, which also makes you tired." Then she smiled. "Is there still some coffee left? I would like some cold, with ice in it."

"That sounds perfect. I've never thought of that. Let's do that, and then, do you mind awfully? I have to go back into town to meet with Darling and the vicar again about some details. I'll ask him again about any progress on a place for you. With any luck some information might have come in about your brother." Though Lane knew that even with the ongoing murder investigation, if there had been any news, Darling would surely have let them know.

The old lady waved her hands. "No, no! You go. I will take one of my little walks to loosen up and then have my usual nap. And I can start supper. May I use that beef I saw? I can make a nice soup for us. The nights are becoming colder."

"I'll bring some bread back with me."

Having finished her coffee with ice—a fine innovation—Lane took up her handbag and cardigan. "You know, we have a very interesting Russian community here called Doukhobors. They promised to teach me to make that wonderful brown bread of theirs. Perhaps we can go and visit and get hold of some borscht. It will be half a day, but if you are up for it, it is a nice drive."

"Those who wrestle with their souls. I remember learning about them. From a time when peasants could only look to heaven for freedom from the burden of their lives." She smiled. "Brown bread and borscht. It will take me back to my childhood. Now, that I would like."

"Good. We can plan on it, then, before you leave."

Lane backed the car through the gate and turned it so that she was headed up the road to the turnoff. She glanced in her mirror and could see Madam Orlova standing on the porch under the blue spruce, watching her, her arms at her sides, her black cardigan pulled over her shoulders.

"MY GOD! HOW did you get here? I almost don't recognize you! Come in, come in."

Aptekar offered his friend his hand and then collapsed onto a chair by the fire in the sitting room of a modest house on Frances Street. "I know, Sergei Alexandrovich. I am nothing like the man I was the last time we met."

"Darya, look! It is our old friend. Can you make tea?" Sergei's wife was standing in the doorway to the kitchen, wiping her hands on her apron. She came forward, her face clearing as she recognized their visitor, and held out her hands.

"You poor man! You are so thin! I have soup, and while you eat, I will make up the spare bed."

Closing his eyes as Darya bustled off to the kitchen, Aptekar felt his first moments of relief. He would, for a short time at least, be safe here.

During the meal, Aptekar declined to discuss his situation and instead asked questions about their life in Canada. All in all, he thought, listening to them, they were not doing too badly. Sergei had taken a job at a sawmill along the waterfront and had risen to foreman. A far cry from his pre-war life as an archaeologist working in Novgorod. They, like so many, had fled east, but they had taken refuge in Japan, and as war broke out, made their way to Canada. Darya missed the old country and still struggled with English. She found Vancouver small and provincial.

"But we are safe, my love." Sergei reached over to take her hand.

"Yes, we are safe. Safe to spend every day missing our dead son, safe to remember the life we lived, the home I lost. Yes, perfectly safe."

Aptekar shook his head sympathetically, thinking of what his friend must endure daily from his unhappy wife. Well, who was he to judge? His work had helped him to keep his life free from entanglements, and he had been able to ride the waves of conflict and keep himself useful. There had been one person only, and he had known—even as it was going on—that it would be doomed by history. He had been preparing for the end right from the first glance he'd had of her at the ball her mother had hosted before he went into the Mikhailovskaya Academy in 1898.

Darya shooed him away when he tried to help her with the dishes. "You go. You men have things to discuss, I'm sure."

"It was a lovely meal. You are kind to take me in like this." He was acutely aware of his borrowed and frayed clothes and his unkempt hair and beard.

"You are our friend," Darya said. "And I will say this. At least we can take you in here without fearing for our lives. It is something I don't miss about the old country. What I remember, it is gone forever." She shook her head and took the dishes he'd been holding. "Now, run along."

Aptekar sat in front of the fire with his friend Sergei. It had been miraculous when he had seen Sergei walking by the courthouse in Vancouver the previous winter. He had lost track of this friend of his youth just after 1919 and was certain he must have died, either in the war or after, at the beginning of the purges. Aptekar had rushed out of the dining room of Hotel Vancouver and onto the street, calling his friend's name. It had taken a moment for Sergei to recognize him, but they had embraced as only men can who have long thought each other dead.

"So now, what are you doing here, Stani?"

"It is a long story."

"I will bet that it begins with your luck finally running out, eh? You were with the Soviet consulate as I recall."

"It does. I was set to defect. I know. Don't look at me like that. After all these years, I suddenly want to abandon the mother country. But I am being practical. It is not safe in Russia, no matter what they say. They will think me a throwback, an embarrassment in the new Soviet Russia of dark suits and darker plans."

"But what happened?"

Aptekar had to be careful. His friend would not know the extent of what Aptekar did. He had told Sergei he was attached to the Soviet Consul General. He shrugged.

"I was going to leave through Yugoslavia, but I was arrested. They seemed to know exactly what I'd be doing. Who knows, the MGB seems to know everything. I had been given a fancy medal at the Kremlin almost on the same day, if you can believe it. Diplomatic service to the country. I don't know why I was arrested, really. Or why the show of a medal. But these people never take the short and direct road when a long and complicated one is available. One minute you are in, the next minute you are out. But you know this, or you wouldn't be here."

Aptekar did not say what he knew to be true: the authorities were afraid of what he knew, and if they found him in

174

Canada, his life would be over.

"So, what will you do now? Listen, I didn't want to say this in front of my wife, but you are probably not safe here. A friend called Fedorov who was on the run from the MGB has disappeared. That is not a good sign. He was here under an assumed name. He was calling himself Gusarov. Someone here is watching us. I think there has been some sort of trouble about a defector in Canada, and it has dredged up the muck. Everybody on both sides is watching us now."

"It seemed like such an, I don't know, innocent country when I was here before, officially." Aptekar shook his head. "I don't want to impose on you, Sergei, but I need clothes, a little money. There is one person I think can help me. I must get to her. She is the only one I feel I can trust."

"Well, thank you very much!" said Sergei in mock outrage.

"You know what I mean, my oldest friend. I am indebted to you, and I don't even know if I will ever be able to repay you."

"You have repaid me already, by calling me your oldest friend."

1898

STANIMIR BOWED AND then offered his hand. "I am honoured to be invited, sir," he said.

"I understand from your uncle that you are off to the academy?"

"I am. Tomorrow, in fact." Stanimir could hear the orchestra playing a Polonaise in another room and could smell pipe tobacco. People in the reception room were laughing and greeting each other like long-lost friends. Electric chandeliers sent light flickering off the glasses and silver and created a shimmering tapestry as it picked up the glitter of the jewels of the women moving through the room. He was entranced with the effect. His uncle held doggedly to gas and candles. It was Stanimir's first ball.

"Good lad. I hear you are an academic genius. Been abroad. A little soldiering will provide some balance, eh?" The host gave him a pat on the shoulder.

Stanimir bowed again and prepared to move toward the ballroom. He had seen his friend Sergei pass by with a glass of champagne and wink at him, lifting the glass as if to say, "We can drink all night at someone else's expense!" His host, who had been about to greet the next guest, turned back to the young recruit.

"Please introduce yourself to my wife. She is in the black over there, and if you have the courage, try my daughter. She does not like the vapid young men of the upper classes. It will be a challenge for you, eh?"

Stanimir bowed yet again and made his way toward the woman in black, who was talking with a group of women her own age. If his own mother had lived, she would be this age now, he thought, imagining the lithe and fragile woman who had been his dear *mamochka* until her death when he was seven. She would be stouter now, but still handsome, as this woman was. He was trying to think of what to say by way of introduction when she glanced over and saw him. She lifted her hand and beckoned him.

"Ah! You have come. Aptekar's nephew. You are

welcome, Stanimir Vadimovich Aptekar. How is the count?"

"He is very well, thank you. He sends you his warmest greetings. It was kind of you to invite me, madam." She must, he thought, have been very beautiful when she was young, though her face was set now along indomitable lines.

"You are to have a wonderful time. I understand you are for the academy. I hope you will consider spending some of your holidays with us."

Stanimir bowed again, beginning now to wish he could stay upright. The new uniform was stiff and demanded an erect posture. He was surprised by the invitation. He knew his uncle had a wide acquaintance among the aristocracy, but he had been so immersed in his studies—and had spent the last two years at school in England—that he had no real notion of the society with which his uncle expected him to conform. He was about to respond when someone behind him accidentally banged into him. He turned, and an older man apologized and continued on to where he saw a friend waving for him.

It was then that he saw her. She was sitting in a chair by the door into the ballroom, looking as if she were hoping to remain undiscovered there. She was wearing a pale blue gown, and she had one leg crossed over the other, swinging her foot impatiently and watching the proceedings with a haughty look that suggested she would rather be nearly anywhere else. She was beautiful in a way he had never imagined a girl could be. A fine oval face, dark eyes, and a look of lively intelligence. She had a fan in her hands, but unlike the other girls on show, she did not use it for its intended purpose. Instead she tapped it impatiently on her lap and looked straight into middle distance with her chin up, as if defying anyone to try to speak with her.

"Ah. You have espied my daughter. I challenge you, young man. If you can get her to stop fidgeting and dance, you will be a better man than any here!"

"She does not look like a girl who wishes to dance, madam. She looks like a girl who wishes she were in her room with a book and a cup of chocolate."

"You see! I knew you were the right sort of man. You understand her completely. Perhaps she will talk to you. She is overeducated. You may have a great deal in common. I should warn you, she is practically affianced to a young man who is not here, but I cannot have her ignoring everyone all night. Do be a dear and bring her out of herself a bit."

Stanimir could feel the eyes of the girl's mother on his back as he walked across the room. He had thought he understood the reason for the invitation he had received. He had assumed they were trying to unload a reluctant girl onto a suitable young man. He was relieved to learn that his only obligation was to entertain her. He took a chair and pulled it up next to her.

"I have been sent to try to get you to dance. I can see already it will be futile. Stanimir Aptekar."

"I know who you are. We met when we were children."

"Did we? I feel as if I should have remembered someone like you."

"If you are going to indulge in fatuous flattery, you can take yourself off. You are just like all the others. Pretty, ignorant, bound like sheep for your military careers."

"I didn't mean it as a compliment, though I thank you

for yours. I don't think I have been called 'pretty' before. No, I meant to say that you are like an Amazon. I imagine you must have been fierce as a little girl."

For the first time the girl turned to him.

"My name is Tatiana Danilovna. I was studious as a little girl. The ferocity is recent, now that I understand how the world is. You see, look around you. This is yet another evening designed to bring suitable families together by sacrificing their children into marriages, the only function of which is to ensure that land stays in the hands of the nobility. It doesn't matter to them that they live on the backs of the oppressed."

"I see," said Stanimir, smiling. "But you are determined to resist and throw your lot in with the oppressed?"

"Now you laugh at me. You know, I'm surprised they sent you over and have not realized the danger. Mother wants me to marry Arkady Orlov. He is out of the country, thank heavens, otherwise I would be stuck with him all evening. She must be hedging her bets."

"I wish you every happiness in advance. What danger has she not realized?"

"That you are not stupid. Let us astonish them all. Take me to dance. I will smile and laugh, but I will be telling you that all this," she waved her fan to take in the entire glittering scene as she stood up, "is about to end."

"I know that already. I would much rather learn about the man your mother wishes you to marry."

CHAPTER SEVENTEEN

ORLOVA WATCHED LANE'S CAR DISAPPEAR up the road and then turned back into the house. She was beginning to think it was no use. How long could she draw this out? She had already told them it was likely a waste of everyone's time. She went into the kitchen and filled the kettle and was about to sit down when she saw the little table where Lane had a typewriter, a jar of pencils, and a stack of paper. She had not seen Lane working at this table since she had arrived. Was she a writer? She shrugged, feeling slightly guilty. If Lane were a writer, having an unexpected guest underfoot would certainly be an impediment. She pulled open the drawer and found a manila file. Poetry! Well, now. That made her almost Russian.

Orlova put the file down because the kettle was boiling. She turned off the stove and went into the cupboard where Lane kept the tea. The poetry surprised her. She poured water over the tea leaves and then went to sit on the chair by the writing table. The first poem on the pile was called "Re

Past." Orlova inclined her head in a slight nod of approval at the unusual construction.

The bread was almost black
A shadow now in my memory
Mrs. Krumins is locked there, forever
Kneading dough for our house
Like a woman in a painting
Only there is no nostalgic shaft of sunlight
From a nearby window, only a question

The poem seemed unfinished, and Orlova reread it, out loud now. Had Lane been writing about her childhood? What question remained unanswered for her beautiful hostess? There was sympathy, certainly, for this baker of brown bread. But it was the reference to the painting that arrested her. She was back suddenly in her own sitting room with her papa, looking at the painting of the peasant women harvesting in a world that was gone forever. She felt such a stab of sadness and nostalgia that she could scarcely move. More than fifty years since she had sat with him. What was she now? She had always been certain. From childhood, she had had certainty as her sword and her shield. Through everything, she had known what was right, had seen her view vindicated by history, had fought to . . . to what?

She shook her head and stood. She would take her tea into the sitting room. Lane kept her mail there in a shelf with glass doors. Relieved that the debilitating feelings engendered by her sudden memory had left her, she thought, it will happen. I will be ready. That had always been the truth. It always would be.

OXLEY PULLED THE car up in front of the Penrith Boatworks. A sandwich board on the sidewalk advertised purchases, repairs, and rentals. The door was open. It took a moment to adjust to the murky light in the crowded shop. A man cleaning an outboard motor looked up from the row of parts he had neatly lined up on the workbench in front of him and put down the rag he was holding.

"Can I help you, gentlemen?"

"I'm Inspector Darling of the Nelson Police," Darling said, showing his card. "This is Constable Oxley. Are you Mr. Taylor?"

"That's me. If you've come about that boat someone took off me, it's too late. The thing was found wrecked down the river from here."

"No. We're here on another matter. Raymond Brodie was found dead yesterday."

Taylor sat down with a thump. "Ray? Dead? Dead, how?"

"When was the last time you saw him?" countered Darling.

"If you want the truth, I haven't seen him for a couple of years, not since, well, since we had a bit of a falling out. I was never too keen on him."

"Yes, your ex-wife explained about that."

"I bet she did! But poor Cassie! How is she?"

"As you'd expect, I should imagine."

"Look, Inspector. If you're coming here thinking I had anything to do with it, you're sadly mistaken. If anyone should be dead, it's me. He hates me, or hated me, I suppose, and if my bloody ex told you, then you know why."

"She implied you hated him," Darling said.

"I did. He was married to the woman I loved, still love, and he treated her like an unpaid servant. I never did understand why she stayed with him. But I wouldn't have killed him. I wouldn't do anything that could hurt Cassie, do you understand?"

"Can you account for your movements in the last, say, seventy-two hours?"

Taylor waved his hand to indicate his shop. "I've got more work than I can keep up with, Inspector. I work late, and then head up to the hotel bar for a beer, and then go to the rooming house I live in. Mrs. Metcalf will be happy to vouch for the time I spend there." It would have to do.

"Thank you, Mr. Taylor. We will speak with her. Were you open on Sunday?"

"As it happens, I was working here, as usual. A local fisherman brought me his motor to work on. He was mad because he'd been planning to go out on the Saturday, and he hoped I could fix it in time for Monday. He came around and talked my ear off while I worked on it."

"Until what time?"

"I don't know," Taylor said impatiently. "You know, you hear these radio dramas where people get asked the time and they always know it. Innocent people, Inspector, don't know the time they were somewhere most times. It was getting toward dusk. That's the best I can do."

"We'd better have his name as well, then, and the address of your rooming house."

Darling and Oxley waited while Taylor wrote down the information on the back of a receipt. He handed the paper to Darling.

"I don't understand, though, how did he die? When?"

"Thank you, Mr. Taylor. We'll be in touch if we have any further questions," Darling said, turning toward the door.

Back in the car, Oxley started the engine. "He doesn't seem like the romantic type. I mean, he's kind of old."

"The world is full of mysteries, Constable. The question is whether he's the type of man to knock off his rival. There is something about him I don't find all that convincing."

"I bet he's lying. If it's true he hasn't seen Brodie in two years, it seems strange that he would suddenly drop everything and go kill him," Oxley observed. "No. He's seen him recently, mark my words."

"It does indeed seem strange. But, strange is what we deal in. Let's go see his landlady."

ORLOVA ASSEMBLED HER painting gear and put it into the cloth bag Lane had provided her with. Her hostess had offered it as an alternative to the more ungainly suitcase. If she but knew. She might as well make the best of it. She would go up to the Hughes house and paint their blasted garden. The rain had stopped, and the sun had warmed the damp ground, creating a slight mist that hovered above the grass. Orlova turned the handle on the door, just as the phone rang. She listened. Two longs and a short. It was for Lane Winslow. Should she let it go? She could not take the risk of missing him, as reluctant as she was to expose herself. She put down her bag and took the earpiece off its hook and talked into the horn.

"Hello?"

Silence.

Orlova waited, then, "Hello?"

She heard the click of the phone being rung off. Slowly she put the earpiece back on the hook and looked at her watch.

DARLING AND OXLEY, having confirmed with the landlady and the man with the broken motor that Verne Taylor had been exactly where he said he'd been, made their way back to the station—Oxley to write up the notes and Darling to search out Gilly to see what he had to say.

The coroner was just washing up when Darling found him.

"Well-nourished man, late forties, good solid meal of canned pork and beans—"

"Yes, thank you, Gilly. Cut to the chase. What killed him?"

"You seem a little edgy. You all right?" Gilly turned and looked closely at Darling.

"I'm perfectly fine, thank you. I have a dead man on hand and would like to know what killed him. Now, can we get on?"

Darling knew he was being more impatient than usual. He also knew that it was because he was worried about Orlova. He was expecting Lane, and if he examined his own thoughts closely, he would see that he wanted the relief of seeing her come into the station and of knowing that nothing had happened to her. He also suspected he was being ridiculous. Lane was an experienced British agent. If she couldn't deal with an elderly woman, she'd be a sorry excuse for one. Speaking with Ames had reminded him about the possible inconsistencies in Orlova's story and of the anxiety he felt at the thought of something happening to the woman he loved—and of how much simpler life had been when he hadn't loved anyone.

"Right," said Gilly, glancing once more at Darling. He was not convinced by Darling's protestations. "His throat was cut, admirably, if you like that sort of thing, quickly and cleanly. Death would have been instantaneous. Someone was either extremely experienced or extremely lucky. I'd have said the killer was considerably taller than the victim, or the victim was kneeling or sitting, based on the upward movement of the weapon, though neither of these is consistent with the way you found him, stretched out and prone. You didn't find a nice sharp knife?"

"We did not. We scoured the place." Darling looked at the shrouded figure. "The family bread knife, or something more military?"

Gilly shook his head. "Not the bread knife, certainly, if by that you mean the serrated one. A slenderish blade, and very, very sharp. Could be military, though I'm not familiar with the full range. Was he followed up into the bush?"

"We've spoken to his one clear enemy who was apparently busy fixing boat motors right here in Nelson when this might have happened. Time of death?"

"At least forty-eight hours. He was brought in late yesterday, so put it thirty-six hours from the time you found him, roughly?"

"If it was someone he knew, that's a long, complicated slog through the forest to kill someone. But, I suppose, if you didn't want him found right away, you might crash around in the underbrush following him. But what if it was someone whom he surprised? There was no sign of a struggle at all. It must have been expertly done by someone he didn't even hear coming. My God! People at King's Cove will need to be on alert. I'm expecting Miss Winslow any minute, but I might phone through to the post office and ask them to pass on the message."

"AH, MRS. ARMSTRONG. It's Inspector Darling."

"Goodness, Inspector, this is a pleasure. How are you?"

"Thank you, very well. Listen, we have become a bit anxious about the death of that hunter. We don't know who is responsible, but he may still be in the area. Can you do me a big favour and get hold of people there and ask them to stay close to home? He may have been murdered by someone who knew him and followed him. In fact, it seems the much likelier scenario, but we can't entirely rule out some sort of random attack."

"Goodness me! Certainly, Inspector! I shall institute a sort of telephone tree and try to get the word out as quickly as possible. Does Miss Winslow know?"

"She is on her way here at the moment, so we will tell her."

"Oh, good. Yes. But her guest? In fact, I just saw her a few moments ago making her way up the path to the Hugheses' with her little painting bag. She doesn't speak a word of English. I'll try to get Gladys to hang on to her till Lane gets back. I know she's quite apt to take long walks, and she doesn't really know our area. Oh, dear!"

"You can tell Mrs. Hughes that the countess likes cake," Darling said.

187

ELEANOR ARMSTRONG'S PHONE tree had the almost instantaneous effect of having people gather at the post office. She had called Mabel Hughes and Robin Harris, and as Robin could not be counted on to call anyone, Mabel had called Reg and Alice, and Reg had called the Bertollis.

Angela Bertolli, who'd taken the call had said (predictably, Reg thought), "Horrors! The children!"

Glenn Ponting wasn't on the telephone, but she would tell him as soon as he came up for his mail, and in any case, he'd been part of the original search party.

Countess Orlova, who had been in Gladys Hughes's garden on a kitchen chair in front of a magnificent stand of lupines, had watched the older daughter of old Mrs. Hughes come out and call to her mother and sister, who were with the chickens and pigs behind the garage. She had watched Mabel hurry down the path she herself had come up, perhaps on the way down to the post office. She had seen out of the corner of her eye that old Mrs. Hughes and her other daughter (Gwen, was it?) were now standing together talking nervously and glancing in her direction. That unsettled her. She'd have liked to be closer to hear properly what they were saying. Clearly there was something going on. It would be artificial for her to sit, unconcerned, painting lupines with all the fuss going on around her, but what was she to glean when she understood only Russian?

She got up, turned her shoulders stiffly to loosen her back, and walked to where Gladys and Gwen stood, their faces registering anxiety about how they all were to communicate.

"Is problem?" Orlova asked.

Gwen leaned forward, frowning, trying to understand Madam Orlova's nearly impenetrable accent.

"Oh! Problem, yes, I see! No, I mean yes, actually. The police have rung through and said we all have to stay close to our houses because some madman is running around in the woods with a knife. You know, that poor hunter was killed and—"

"Gwen, she doesn't speak English, does she?" said Gladys. "Can't understand a thing you're saying. Well, we are unlikely to get snuck up on drinking tea in our kitchen, so let's get her into the house." She offered Orlova a peremptory smile and raised her voice. "Come! Tea. In house." She indicated with her head that Orlova should follow her.

Too bad, really, Gladys thought as she strode toward the kitchen door, her wellingtons flapping against her calves, she was making good progress on those lupines.

"NOW, I DON'T think we need to panic," Eleanor was saying. They were all standing outside the post office. "Inspector Darling just said we should stay close to home. I'm sure whoever it is is long gone."

"Unless he's up to no good in the bush," Robin said glumly.

"Now, Robin," said Kenny, "what could anyone be up to in the bush around here? I'm sure . . ." But he wasn't at all sure. A man had, after all, been brutally murdered while he was innocently out hunting.

"What about the dogs?" Alice Mather asked.

Mabel grunted a nearly silent "Ha!" The dogs in King's

Cove were more in danger, she thought, from Alice herself, in her mad hunts for cougars. She'd nearly shot one of the Bertolli collies a couple of years back.

"The dogs had better be kept close to home as well, I suppose," Eleanor said. "Just till this blows over."

"And what about that old lady of Lane's? She's always tramping everywhere."

"I'm sure Lane will explain to her in Russian."

"She's up with Mother and Gwennie right now. I'd better be getting back, or I'll miss the cake, since you don't seem to have anything to add."

"No, quite," Eleanor said, a little apologetically. "Just that we should all take care."

"HONESTLY," SHE SAID to Kenny a little later, when the people had trooped back to their own houses, and they were seated at their own tea in the kitchen. "It's a case of kill the messenger, isn't it? You could see they thought it was my fault somehow." She looked down and stroked Alexandra who was tucked into a perfect little circle on her lap, and cooed. "We'd better keep you indoors, hadn't we?"

CHAPTER EIGHTEEN

A MES WAS SURPRISED WHEN THE two men appeared beside him. He had not seen them come up. One of them took him by the elbow and guided him away from the other students that were all milling in the hall loudly talking across one another, clearly giddy from the relief of their exam being over.

"Hello?" Ames said. "Do I know you?"

"Just come along with us, kiddo. Here, we've been given a room along here," one of the men said.

He was shorter than Ames, and squat, like a wrestler, and smelled of cigarettes. His trench coat was undone and floated around him like a cape. The second man, dressed in the same style, seemed content to follow close behind Ames and keep an eye out. He took out a cigarette and lit it, closing one eye against the initial stinging stream of smoke. He shook the match and dropped it on the floor.

Ames was ushered into a room at the end of a hall. He saw at once that it was an interview room and looked behind him nervously. Because he wasn't from Vancouver, he really hadn't made friends among his classmates, and now he felt a little sorry about that, because no one would care if he disappeared.

The men were polite enough. He was asked to sit down, and the two of them sat opposite him. He wondered if they'd take their hats off. He put his own in front of him on the metal-topped table. Finally, one of them spoke.

"You have been a busy boy, haven't you?"

It was clear to Ames that they had the advantage on him in every way, and they seemed to know it. He suspected they were police, or detectives perhaps, who were very much his senior.

"Who are you, again?" Ames asked.

"We're from the RCMP, Intelligence Division. Now you, I've discovered, are a constable from Nelson, who's trying to move up in the world by taking your sergeant's exam, and more power to you. I bet your mom is proud. But instead of studying like a good policeman, you've been all over the map visiting Russians. What's the big interest in Russians?"

"Could . . . could I see some identification?" Ames wasn't sure he was on solid ground with this one. And it might make him seem more suspect. What the hell were they suspicious about?

"My God, you are a pill. Here." The short one pulled out his warrant card and showed it to Ames. Geoffry Carston, RCMP ID—with ID standing for Intelligence Division, Ames supposed.

"Come on, Dave, show him yours." The second man

languidly pulled his card out of his coat pocket and held it up. David Segal, RCMP ID.

"Now then, would you mind telling us why you've been tramping all over the place visiting Russians?"

"I was asked to inquire about a Russian man by my boss in Nelson, Inspector Darling. Apparently an old lady has turned up there looking for her brother. She's some sort of refugee."

"Lot of those around," Carston said glumly. "And?"

"Well, nothing doing."

"What sort of nothing doing?"

"I mean, no one has seen her brother, and as a matter of fact, no one has seen her either, which I thought was strange."

"Did you now?" the smoking one asked, leaning closer to Ames over the table. "How was that?"

Ames was silent for a moment. He felt a rebellious desire to not tell these pushy men everything, but he knew that that made no sense at all. They were clearly all on the same side. Maybe he was just cross about being sandbagged in this way. If he told them everything, he might get to go home to his boarding house and pack. Carston, the wrestler, stirred impatiently.

"My boss told me that the old lady supposedly had been all over Vancouver looking for him, the brother I mean, and I was surprised when I went to the only two Russian communities in the city and they hadn't seen her at all. But then, well, that's it, really."

"He's a smart one, eh? So you thought something might be wrong, and?"

"Well, I got a call from one of the churches and I spoke to a very frightened man who said the man in the picture, the brother, was a Soviet agent who'd interrogated him none too kindly back in the thirties. With the dead Russian in the cooler here, it just seemed like too much of a coincidence."

Both men sat up. "What dead Russian?" Carston asked.

Ames hesitated. It wasn't his dead Russian, after all, even though he'd been the one to notice that he might not have died naturally.

"There's a dead guy in the cooler here in Vancouver. He might not have died naturally. I lost interest when I found out he wasn't the man I was looking for."

Best not tell them about his little discovery, Ames thought. No doubt the coroner here would take the credit for it.

"Segal, look into that, will you?" Carston said. Segal got up, grinding the stubby remains of his cigarette into the tin ashtray, and left the room.

"So what's this about a Russian woman in, where are you from?"

Ames suspected his interrogator was being annoying on purpose. He knew perfectly well where Ames was from. "I only know what my boss told me. She's elderly and she's lost her brother."

"Only it seems like she lied to your boss, eh? She never was around here looking for him, according to you, so what's she doing all the way over in Nelson? Who's the person who called you from the church on Seventh Avenue?"

Look at that, Ames thought. He knows where I'm from and he knows the priest called me from Seventh Avenue.

What else does he know? With a sudden chill, he understood he'd been followed for who knows how long.

"Father Dmitry. But I expect you already know that. Is there anything else I can help with? Only I have to go home and pack. I have a train to catch."

"Not so fast. I need to see your photograph, the one you've been showing around."

Ames reached into the inner pocket of his jacket and extracted the photo. Carston took it and gazed at it, his mouth working. He pointed at the man leaning on the car.

"So this is the guy that is supposed to be the agent? The one who beats people up?"

"I can only tell you what that man told me."

"Hmmm," said Carston. He slid the picture into his own pocket and then got up and stretched, banging his chair noisily into the wall behind him.

"Hey," Ames said. "I need that."

"No, you don't, you're going home now. I'm sure your boss has one you can use. So, thanks. And stay away from things that don't concern you. If you read the news instead of just the funny papers, you'd know this. There's a war on."

Carston put his hands in his pockets and tilted his head, looking at Ames, who was now standing like a child waiting to be allowed to leave.

"Don't get me wrong. To me you look just like what you say you are, but others might not think so." He shook his head, his face set in a look of sympathy. "They'd be asking themselves why a young man like yourself, a low-ranking policeman with a salary to match, is running back and forth talking to Ruskies. 'What's he doing?' they'd be asking themselves. 'What's he passing back and forth?' So I'd be careful. I'd pack my bags and go straight home. Get back to your regular life, enjoy your sergeant's salary. You don't have to do anything special to show you're as innocent as you seem. We'll keep an eye on you."

Ames had wanted to be first out the door, but Carston preceded him, giving him a friendly pat on the back on his way out. Ames, feeling slightly wobbly, sat down with a thump. They just, if he wasn't mistaken, suggested he might be some sort of spy. His anxiety gravitated to anger. He tried to still the persistent suggestion his mind was offering that this was all Darling's fault. All he wanted to do was come out to Vancouver, take his course, write his exam, and get home, and now he was suddenly a perfectly innocent citizen who was being watched, apparently. "There's a war on," Carston had said. He hadn't heard that since the actual war had been on. What sort of war? Feeling a sudden surge of resolve, he made his way to the library, which was very nearby on Main Street. It would calm him down before he had to phone Darling. He didn't trust how he was feeling just yet.

DARLING SAT BACK, looking out the window, tapping the desk with his pencil. Lane sat opposite him.

"You said you wanted to discuss one problem," she said. "Now it's two. You're concerned about what my countess is up to, and now you think there's a man running around King's Cove with a bayonet that he knows how to use. Anything else I should know about? I'm not finding this all that relaxing. And I'm sure my neighbours, as plucky as they are, and as apt to come together to pass buckets of water in a chain during an emergency, are not either."

"I never said it was a bayonet. We don't know what it is."

"As to his running around King's Cove, you don't know, really, that Mr. Brodie was not killed by someone who wanted him dead, specifically. It's a singular circumstance, in my view, that he was killed way out in the bush in a place where no one could have known his whereabouts unless he'd been followed. It doesn't follow that whoever it is will now proceed from house to house executing people. He could have done that right at the beginning without the trouble of crashing about in the underbrush."

"That's a funny word to use, executing." Darling turned back to Lane. He had mostly stopped being uneasy about her former life, but her use of the word "execute" once again stirred his anxieties about what sort of life she'd been used to. "Is there something about what I've told you that makes you think the man was executed?"

"That clean cut, I suppose. I don't know much about throat-cutting, of course, but I suspect people often make a mess of it. People in general are not expert killers, even with military training. You'd be surprised how many shots taken during the war missed altogether. From that we can surmise that the average civilian, or even the average veteran, who doesn't know how to shoot properly, or has surprised someone during a robbery and has no time to think and so on, is unlikely to go around murdering people in quite this way. This seems to me to show that the killer had time, and the element of surprise, perhaps, and a very high, not to say professional, level of skill."

She pulled her chair closer and drew a line on the desk with her finger. "Let's say this is the creek. You found the man on this side, where he might have been sitting in the shade of that big outcrop you mentioned, maybe even dozing, if this was an afternoon killing. He must not have heard whoever it was until it was too late. If he was the intended victim, he must have been followed by someone very patient who waited until it was safe to sneak up on him. If he was a random victim, then he must have stumbled on something someone didn't want him to see, or maybe was trying to protect. A cache of money, for example. Has a bank been robbed recently? It might tell us something about the circumstances."

"It doesn't tell 'us' anything. It tells me and my men something. You don't come into it. All I need you to do is be careful, and while you're at it, find out what is going on with your guest. She is not what she seems."

"I'm not sure I entirely agree with you. She seems like an old lady, and indeed, she is. Maybe she didn't go about trying to find her brother in Vancouver the way you or Ames, professional policemen, might have." Lane stopped there. She knew in her heart she wasn't entirely convinced herself. The question she had about whether Orlova was pretending not to speak English was niggling, but if there was really nothing to be concerned about, she didn't want to add to Darling's anxieties. She'd keep an eye on her guest, and obediently stay near the house for the time being. "Darling, I survived the war, and I do know how to look after myself."

"I dare say, but you can't be satisfied with her story about asking around Vancouver for her brother, when no one has heard of her. You can carry on being plucky if you want, but you can't fool me. You know that there's something not quite 'comme il faut,' as they say, about her story or her for that matter. And with a lunatic armed to the teeth running around in the bush, I confess I'm not entirely comfortable with the whole set up."

"I promise to be as careful as can be. We still don't know her story isn't true. She has expressed genuine sadness about the possible fate of her brother. I don't think she's making it up. You can't expect a woman who's been running from danger and possible death to be entirely honest, even in a situation you and I think is safe." There. She'd done her best to reassure Darling, but she would be on her guard. "Now let's get down to brass tacks. Have you asked Ames to be your best man yet?"

"Certainly not. I didn't want to disrupt his studies. Who knows how he'll react."

"Time is ticking by. I've asked Angela to stand up for me. She is, as you can imagine, over the moon and planning something that will equal the upcoming wedding of Princess Elizabeth."

Darling groaned. "I rather thought we were having a quiet wedding. If you've unleashed Angela—"

"I haven't 'unleashed' her. And anyway, there's a limit to the damage she can do with the resources at hand in King's Cove. The worst that can happen is that Eleanor Armstrong and Mabel Hughes will fight over who makes the cake. Have you asked your brother and his fiancée and your father?"

"Not yet. I will though, I suppose," said Darling, "but it's a long way to come."

"They will come for you. I bet no one thought you'd ever marry!"

"I bet you're right. I suppose you're planning to invite the whole of King's Cove?"

"I can't invite one and not all the rest, even Reginald Mather and his mad wife. Who will you invite from here?"

"Ames," Darling said. He looked to the sky. "God, I can't believe I'm saying that. Can you imagine the best man's speech? The rest are going to have to stay back and man the station. I'm sure they'll get together and buy me a cup of coffee when it's all over."

"I think we should have Lorenzo and Mrs. Lorenzo, don't you?"

"Yes, I was thinking about that. I'm certain he had us married in his imagination from the first moment he saw you. Will they be able to leave their restaurant? Will they be offended if we don't ask them to cook something? All these social niceties. I'm not cut out for this sort of thing."

"I wonder if they could make a cake? They'd have to haul it up the lake in the back of their little van or whatever they drive, but it would save us from a falling out between Eleanor and Mabel."

"You know, he might feel honoured to do it. Good idea. I'll ask, shall I? But you'll have to take care of things down at your end, at the Cove. We'd better have this situation in hand by then. I won't be easy till we've found this beastly man with, as you so quaintly put it, the bayonet."

AMES WAS SEATED, finally, at a library table with a pile of papers going back to 1945, which he'd gained access to after the rather clumsy start of asking the librarian if there'd been anything in the papers about Russians lately. After learning that ships from Vladivostok and other eastern Soviet ports were coming to Vancouver to get repairs, and that the local churches had organized a big picnic on Russian Orthodox Easter—on a different day from what he thought of as regular Easter—Ames was reminded that there was indeed a state of unease between Canada and the Soviet Empire, but who didn't know that? We're fighting the communists and all that, after all. The librarian had come up to him as he'd explored, without success, anything that might account for his peculiar afternoon.

"Is this any good?" she said.

CHAPTER NINETEEN

December 1918

THE FIRST AWARENESS THAT TATIANA Orlova had was of the sound of some metal object falling. She tried to open her eyes, but one was completely covered over with something. Only an oily yellow blur was visible through the other one. She tried to talk, but her throat felt as if it had been laid out to dry in the sun.

"We thought you might not make it," said a male voice in a matter-of-fact tone.

She did not recognize the voice. She had no energy or will to respond. Where was she? She moved her hand toward the bandage over her eye, but felt it pulled back.

"Nuh-uh. You'll hurt yourself. Just try to lie still."

Tatiana turned her head toward the voice, trying to open her one uncovered eye, but it made her head thunder, and she closed it again, leaving her skull motionless on the pillow.

"Don't try to talk. You're lucky we found you. In one regard, we might have been too late, but that comrade of yours that you work with saw what was happening and managed to get away to get help. It was fortuitous, really. We've had our eye on you."

Tatiana tried to understand how she was feeling. The pain in her head wiped out any other sensation. She tried to imagine what she'd been saved from, and if she was even happy about it. She wasn't. It would have been better if her rescuers had left her to die. She was sure, even without remembering anything about her life before this painful moment, that she probably had no real reason to live.

DARLING WAS LOOKING at a file of some local murders, trying to find any evidence of another death similar to Brodie's when his phone rang. Irritated, he pick up the receiver.

"Darling."

"Sir, I'm on my way home on the morning train."

"Goody. Did you flub that exam?"

"I don't think so. I was finished before most of the other people," Ames said.

"That's not necessarily a good sign. When do the results come?"

"They said a week or so. But it's what's happened since the exam that I'm calling about."

Darling frowned and pushed the file aside. There was nothing in it that was helpful. A few unsolved murders, mostly old, mostly firearms or ersatz weapons like bats, and nothing similar in the solved ones. "You just wrote the thing this morning."

"Yes, and right after it I was wrangled into an interview room by a couple of RCMP heavies and, I don't think it would be an exaggeration to say, interrogated."

"You mustn't be rude about our colleagues. Why? What have you done? I wonder if I should have left you alone in the big city."

"If I'd done something in the big city, the Vancouver Police could have taken care of it. These guys said they were from the RCMP Intelligence Division. They wondered why I've been running around the city talking to Russians. And they swiped my photo of the old lady's brother."

"Now that is interesting. Did they say what they were concerned about?"

"I've gone over and over it in my head, but they were peppering me with questions, without telling me anything. They implied I might be on the take to augment my lousy constable's salary. I think they were suggesting I might be some sort of spy."

"This better not be a ploy to get a raise. Did they have you followed?"

"That's what I don't know. They certainly knew where I'd been and when. I can't make out if they had their eyes on the local Russians and saw me visiting, or if, maybe, one of the Russians is reporting back to them."

"For God's sakes, Ames. Can't I let you off the lead for five minutes? Okay, listen, haul out that little notebook of yours and use your time on the train home to write down every single thing about your Russian investigation. Let's see if we can make head or tail of it when it's all on paper. And include the questions the heavies asked you. When you get back, there will be no lollygagging. There's work to do. I have an unsolved crime here that might, I say *might*, be along the lines of an execution. That idea, by the way, ludicrous for our gentle part of the world, comes from your friend Miss Winslow."

"Yes, sir. I went to the local library to look at some back issues of the papers. I think I might have found out why the RCMP is fidgety. Last year there was a big spy scandal, and Canada, Britain, and the US all arrested a bunch of people in a big spy ring. We might not have known about it except some Yank reporter talked about it on the radio. The prime minister apparently set up a commission of some sort to investigate how this all happened. I bet the heavies are part of the commission's work. They seemed to be trying to root out as-yet-undiscovered spies. I certainly felt as though I was being rooted out. Apparently, there's a general fear that the commies are trying to get at our nuclear secrets." He paused. "Something one of the heavies said made more sense after that. He said, 'There's a war on.' He meant between Canada and Russia."

"I see," said Darling. "Well, that could complicate things. I had no idea we even had nuclear secrets. All right, Ames."

Darling paused. It was now or never. Clearing his throat, he said, "Listen. I have another little job for you, one that will not depend on you becoming a sergeant."

"Sir?"

"The fact is that Miss Winslow has agreed to marry me—"

"Aha!"

"Ames," Darling said dangerously.

"Sir."

"We're just having a small wedding at that rickety church out at King's Cove, but I'll need some sort of best man."

"Me, sir?"

"Yes, you. Who do you think I meant? Don't make me regret this."

"No, sir! Yes, sir! I'd be very honoured. May I say, sir—"

"You may not. This is costing money. Just get home. Oh—and thank you."

AMES HUNG UP the phone and leaned against the payphone wall in the grip of a tumult of feeling. Never in all the world would he have expected Darling to ask him to be his best man. He pushed open the door and felt the cool September air on his face. It smelled like rain. He looked at his watch. A gift! He tipped his hat happily at a woman waiting to use the booth and, feeling as fizzy as an ice cream soda, turned toward Woodward's Department Store on Cordova Street.

October 1923

APTEKAR HAD ONLY half an ear to the speech. He had, he thought, heard it all before, but he kept his face set in ways that suggested interest. It was his eyes that wandered continuously to two rows in front and slightly to the right of where he was sitting. He was looking at the back of a head he was sure he recognized. He had been grumpy about the continual need the government had to gather everyone into massive red-flag-draped rooms for speeches. He wanted to get back to where he'd been assigned to keep an eye on a German counterpart whose embrace of socialism had seemed to him to be overzealous. The German travelled often to Leningrad, and it was his current trip that had brought Aptekar back. Unfortunately, the German had decamped, and Aptekar was temporarily stuck, asked by his bosses to attend the conference. He had wanted to say to his divisional head that it was a waste of time, and that his German could be getting up to anything, but he suspected the head knew that and was merely responding to some sort of pressure from above about the discipline of field personnel.

Someone next to the woman he was watching said something to her, and she turned her head. Aptekar's heart turned over. He had never thought he'd see her again after the day she married, but here she was, in a drab grey serge suit, her hair pulled back severely away from her beautiful face.

He turned his eyes back to the speaker who was citing some eye-watering statistics about production, and thought about his own almost ungovernable madness leading up to that wedding. It had begun on his first holiday from the military academy. She had begun it, he thought now, looking at her profile, and then her neck as she turned back to look at the speaker. He felt again the astonishment and passion of his own undoing that night so long ago in her father's garden. For a moment he wondered that she had not sensed him behind her, and then smiled slightly at his own vanity. She was married now, had children, no doubt, and would not remember him. It was only when the wave of applause rose and then fell, and the swell of conversation started up as people began to rise that he thought, What does it mean that she is here at an event laid on for people who work for the MGB?

"WELL?" THE DIRECTOR was scowling at the telephone on his desk, his voice tense as he talked to Vancouver.

"Well. Nice-looking woman, I'll say that."

"You're not judging a bloody beauty contest, Hunt."

"Absolutely no evidence of anything. She says she didn't tell him anything, and she doesn't know where he is, though she did concede that if he were looking for her, he'd probably know where to find her. And sir, I'm inclined to believe her. Wasn't she one of your top girls?"

"Yes. Well, top girls can be toppled." But in his heart, he knew Hunt was probably right. Lane Winslow had never been wobbly. If she'd seen Aptekar, she would have said.

Hunt continued. "The local intelligence people have the wind up, I'll tell you that. That network of informants that was arrested last year has everyone on edge. People are seeing spies under every bed. There is quite a community of Russian expats here. I imagine it's keeping the RCMP busy." He didn't say he had his own little network of informants who alerted him if any of the Russians on the ships tried to defect.

The director was silent for a beat. "Bloody Russians everywhere. I expect I'll hear from my local man that Aptekar's fetched up here, but just in case, keep an eye out at the port of entry. He's probably travelling under an assumed name, but something might turn up."

"Why is he so important? He was coming over anyway, wasn't he? Why not just let him run to ground?"

"Thank you, Hunt. Keep me posted." The director put the receiver into the cradle definitively. It was happening all over since the war ended. Even Canada. British citizens had been got at, he knew, and he was under pressure from the home office to produce some names. "Have to justify your salary, Dunn," the home secretary had said with only a thin veneer of humour.

"**HELLO? IS THIS** the police?"

"Yes," said Constable Oxley. Of course, it bloody is. "Who is this?"

"Oh. Yes. Mrs. Metcalf? Mr. Taylor's landlady?"

Oxley sat up straighter and pulled a pad of paper forward. "Yes, Mrs. Metcalf. Did you think of something else?" She certainly hadn't got much when they talked to her.

"I don't like to speak out of turn . . ." Mrs. Metcalf hesitated. Oxley waited. "It's more that I forgot, really. You see I turn in quite early. Before Mr. Taylor. He rents the room downstairs near the kitchen."

"Yes, I remember you showed us the room."

"Well, I woke in the night. Sometimes I can't sleep, you see, and I went downstairs to the kitchen to make myself some hot milk. It's very soothing. It works like a charm."

Oxley, who was maintaining a polite patience, wrote "charm" across the top margin of his paper and drew a glass of milk. For good measure he added a few wisps of steam coming off it.

"Are you there?" Mrs. Metcalf sounded anxious.

"Yes, absolutely."

"That's when I noticed that Mr. Taylor's door was open, and the light was off. And, well, I peeped in while the milk was heating, and he wasn't there. I think the disaster of the milk boiling over put it right out of my mind. It took ages to clean up. It burns onto the stove, you see."

Oxley did see—but didn't care. "What time was this, Mrs. Metcalf?"

"Oh, it would have been one or one thirty."

"Was he there in the morning?"

"Well, I went around and checked that the doors were locked. I like to have Mr. Taylor here, as I'm a widow and live alone since Mr. Metcalf died. Naturally, I was very tired once I finally went to sleep and I didn't wake up till almost nine in the morning. Of course, he'd be at the shop by then. He is a very early riser."

"Do you usually make the bed, Mrs. Metcalf? Had it been slept in?"

"Oh no, I make it a strict rule that the tenant has to look after all that sort of thing. I do the washing once a week on a Monday, and I make breakfast and supper."

"So, was the bed slept in?"

"That's what I'm trying to say, Constable. I wouldn't be able to tell you. He is very good about making his bed and keeping his room tidy, but, I don't know, I did feel when I looked in the morning that he'd never been there at all."

Oxley wrote up the rest of his notes and went to stand outside Darling's door.

Suddenly aware of Oxley haunting his threshold, Darling rolled his eyes. "Can we establish that you knock, Oxley? What is it?"

"The landlady, sir. Taylor, it turns out, was not at home overnight as she had thought."

CHAPTER TWENTY

"**I DON'T BELIEVE THERE'S ANYONE RUNNING** around with a knife," Eleanor said. "Do you? If you'd done that to someone, you'd be off like a greyhound. Why hang around waiting for the police to come looking for you?"

Eleanor, Kenny, and Lane were sitting on the back porch, enjoying the warmth of the afternoon sun. Alexandra was asleep at Eleanor's feet. The tea plates were empty but for the crumbs of the currant scones that had engaged their attention earlier. Orlova had returned to the Hugheses' garden to finish up some sketches.

"I'm inclined to agree with you," Lane said. "I really do think that whoever killed that poor man was after him specifically. Mind you, if I'm a narcotics importer or something equally unsavoury, there'd be no better place to hide than in the bush up above our little settlement."

"There'd be no point in a narcotics outfit establishing itself here," Kenny reasoned. "We're miles from anywhere. You'd want to be near one of the big places, like Vancouver.

No, I agree with Lane. Someone wanted him dead, and we have nothing to worry about."

They maintained a friendly silence for a bit. Alexandra, always an alert sleeper, turned on her side and stretched her neck to look out at the garden, now a riot of fall colour. Black-eyed Susans, mums, late delphiniums. Lane wondered how they'd look in a modest little bouquet.

"Actually, I do have a little news of my own." Would this ever get easier? "I, well . . . I'm to be married. The inspector—"

But whatever else she would have said was lost in Eleanor Armstrong's delighted cries. Alexandra was up barking, and Lane's hand was being pressed in earnest congratulations by Kenny, and Eleanor's enormous false teeth were displayed in a beaming smile. Lane was pleased to note that Angela had actually managed to keep it a secret. The surprised reaction of her neighbours was quite genuine.

"But where? Oh. I suppose you'll be off to the coast. Doesn't the inspector have family there?" Eleanor asked, preparing to be disappointed.

"No, actually. Mr. Stevens, our very own vicar, has agreed to do the heavy lifting, and we're going to be married right here at St. Joe's. I did tell Angela yesterday because she's going to be my matron of honour, and I must say I'm impressed she managed to sit on it all this time."

"That is absolutely splendid!" Eleanor said. "I won't mention a thing till you've told everyone else."

"I suppose I'd better send out some invitations. I might as well have the lot. You can stick them in everyone's mail boxes and have the excruciating pleasure of having to talk about it endlessly."

"Listen, where you and that inspector are concerned, the gossip is already pretty endless, but never excruciating. Oh." Eleanor sat back, an expression of dismay on her face. "I suspect this means you'll be leaving us."

"No, it won't. Darling and I have agreed to live here. I couldn't bear to leave."

"Now, you just hold it right there. This calls for a celebration." Kenny got up and went into the house, followed by Alexandra. He was limping a little.

"It's nothing," Eleanor said, seeing Lane's eyes following him. "He gets a bit of a twitch in his hip when he gets up. It wears off in no time. It comes to all of us, I'm afraid. Oh, I am happy to know there will be a family next door. You and that lovely inspector and—"

"Steady on! The lovely inspector and I, and maybe a dog."

Kenny had a bottle of sherry and three exquisitely engraved glasses. "Now, then, I've been into the glass cabinet for these. They only get an airing on very special occasions." He put the tray down on the bench and poured three glasses. "To Miss Winslow and Inspector Darling!"

THE NEXT MORNING there was a substantial gathering at the door of the post office. Normally people came down to collect their mail in dribs and drabs as their work and chores allowed, but this morning some collective sense seemed to permeate King's Cove and most had turned up at the same time.

"Didn't someone say they heard a shot the other day?" Glenn Ponting asked. "It's amazing that I was up in the bush nearish to there, and I didn't hear it. But I might have missed it; I was collecting samples and that involves a fair bit of hammering away on rocks."

"You're lucky you weren't dispatched," remarked Mabel. "I thought that shot was in all likelihood," and here she dropped her voice into a whisper, "Alice shooting at her imaginary cougars."

"That was Angela," Lane said, raising her voice slightly to speak over the approach of Robin Harris grumpily bumping down the road toward them on his tractor. Both he and the tractor were smoking.

"Angela was shooting at cougars?" asked Gwen, looking surprised.

Reginald Mather came out of the post office and looked disapprovingly at the gathering. "Nothing wrong with my hearing. It was not my Alice, so you can stop that for a start. I've put the rifle out of reach, and she was at home."

"No one thinks it was Alice, Reg," said Lane soothingly. "I only meant, it was Angela who heard the shot. But the man who was killed was a hunter, and he was hunting in the mountains just north of us here, so it's not surprising someone heard a shot. She was worried because my guest was out walking, and Angela thought she might want to be careful."

"Ah, yes. Your Russian," Reg said without further comment, but leaving his disapprobation of this foreigner in their midst hanging in the air.

"She's all right," Gwen said. "She's painted some lovely pictures of the garden. Even Mummy is impressed." She leaned over to Lane and said *sotto voce*, "Mummy doubts she's much of a gardener. She was very smug about it."

214

Robin got down off the tractor and spoke through the cigarette in his mouth. "When are the ruddy police going to catch this man? We aren't safe in our beds. We've all got work to do now picking season is here. We're sitting ducks. This idiot could pick us off one by one."

"For God's sakes, Robin. To what end?" Gladys said.

"I don't know, do I? He's already killed a completely innocent hunter. What's to say he's not an escapee from a loony bin? Likes to kill people? What's going on with your tame policeman?" He addressed this peevishly to Lane.

Lane wished she could still the rising anxiety, but she didn't have much knowledge of what the police were thinking, and what she did have, she felt unable to share.

"I'M AFRAID THEY might find out about us," Verne Taylor said. They were sitting on a boat dock in a secluded patch of lake near Balfour. They met there often.

Cassie Brodie looked at him, frightened. "But they already do. Arlene told them. Do you think it matters? The police think it was over five years ago."

"I know, but what if they discover I was with you all night? I mean, my landlady told them that—"

"Wait, what do you mean all night?" Cassie Brodie had put her hand over her mouth. "It was not even two when you went back to town. Oh my God, Verne, just tell me the truth. Did you do it?"

"How could you think that?" Taylor said. He could hear his own voice shaking. He hadn't told her where he'd been. He took her hand and looked at her imploringly. "I love you. Isn't that all that matters? I don't know what happened to him. But you have to believe me, I would never have killed him!"

Even as he said it, the lie tasted bitter in his mouth.

"I couldn't bear it if I thought you'd done it. I couldn't bear it, Verne! It would be the end of everything!"

She tried to pull her hand away, to lean away from him on the upturned rowboat on the pier next to her, to hide the anguish she felt.

"Hey, hey, hey! There now. I'm not going to lie to you, Cass. Not about anything. Come here."

He pulled her into his arms, feeling, with a combination of anger and pity the slenderness and fragility of her body. It had been the last straw, that Friday night a couple of weeks before, when Brodie had come home and found his wife lying down, a cold compress on her forehead from a violent headache. He had been enraged to find the stove unlit, the table unset. She had gone to a neighbour the next morning and managed to call him, using their usual code. When they met, he had seen the bruises on her arm and cheek.

"And you know what? I'm glad he's dead. When I heard I felt so happy, Cass. So happy that we would finally be able to be together. We just have to wait till this all blows over and they catch the guy. But Cassie, I need you to do something for me. I need you to tell the inspector that I was with you all night. It won't really be lying because I wasn't off killing anybody."

"Oh, but—"

"Cass, you need to trust me, no matter what. No matter what, do you understand what I'm saying to you? You need to trust me that I didn't do this!"

"SO, SIR, HOW would you like to proceed on Taylor? He was out somewhere in the night. He could have been killing Brodie."

Darling considered this. "Perhaps. Though we think it more likely that Brodie died in the afternoon, and even if Taylor had developed, shall we say, special skills during the war, he would have had difficulty pulling it off in the pitch dark. But, it's not completely out of the question. The time of death is not one hundred percent certain."

Oxley chewed his lip. That was true enough. He wanted to get this right.

Darling said, "This new information means he lied to us. The question is, why? I'm going to pop around and see him. You, if you'd be so good, are going to find out if he had special training during the war."

Darling put on his jacket and hat and clattered down the stairs. "O'Brien, I'm expecting Miss Winslow in the next forty minutes. I shall probably be back before then, but if she arrives, please ply her with tea and try to be interesting."

TAYLOR WAS NOT immediately in evidence as Darling entered the engine repair shop after his short walk down the hill, but he heard a crash and some swearing coming from some sort of storage area near the back door.

"Oh, sorry, Inspector. One of my bloody shelves came down. Place is falling down around me. Is there something you want?"

"There is indeed, Mr. Taylor. I'd like to know why you didn't tell me you didn't get home till late on Sunday night, if at all?"

Taylor coloured and put a drill down on his workbench. "I don't see how it is your business," he said finally.

Darling watched him, saying nothing.

"It has nothing to do with Brodie's death," Taylor tried.

"Where were you, please?" Darling asked, his voice taking on a studied patience.

"It's not what you think," Taylor said, sitting down heavily.

"I don't know what to think," Darling said genially. "Perhaps you'd better tell me the truth. I do have an appointment I need to get back to, and I'd sooner not have to escort you up to the station to answer more questions."

"I was with her, all right? With Mrs. Brodie. My ex-wife can't know. She thinks it was over with years ago."

"I see. Was this unusual, or was it a regular arrangement?"

"Whenever we could. He went hunting a couple of times a year, so those times I'd stay over."

Darling nodded, his hands in the pockets of his jacket. "So you were over there both nights that Mr. Brodie was meant to be away? What time would you leave?"

"Early, to get back here. I'd sneak into my room at the house and then come to work as usual."

"That's a lot of sneaking around for a grown man to do," Darling commented.

Taylor said nothing for a moment, then finally, "What are you going to do?"

"Talk to Mrs. Brodie, I expect. And if you'd be kind enough to lend me your telephone, I'll call the station and get some lads to come down and look this place over."

"You have to believe me, Inspector. I had nothing to

do with Brodie being killed."

"That's as may be. I think for starters, though, you are no doubt more pleased than not that he's dead."

Darling waited while Oxley and Ward came down from the station. "Constable Oxley you've met, and this is Constable Ward. Do you have any objection to their taking a look around? I can, of course, get a warrant, but it would be altogether quicker if we just got on with it."

With ill-grace, Taylor agreed to the search, and after letting Oxley know that Taylor had had trouble with the shelving in his storage cupboard, Darling turned to go back up the hill. He wondered if he should have just brought Taylor in, but the fact was that, according to the landlady and the man whose boat Taylor was fixing, Taylor had been in town during the time it was most likely that Brodie had been killed. On the other hand, he had been having an ongoing affair with the dead man's wife. That was certainly reason enough in some quarters to cut a man's throat.

London

"LOOK HERE, DUNN, it's not good enough, is it? Cambridge practically has a graduate degree in espionage. You should be able to stand outside its hallowed doors and collect them in a bucket as they're coming out." The home secretary leaned forward on his desk with his hands clasped.

He'd been having trouble with his eyes, so the heavy drapes on the tall windows were partially shut, giving the room a gloomy air. Dunn was trying, with subtle adjustments, to sit in a way that maintained some dignity, but there was no denying it: he was before the headmaster, and he had not a lot to say for himself. So he said nothing.

"Anyway, I thought you handed over some spy of theirs who was going to defect to the West," the home secretary said.

"Yes, sir. And they arrested him. But he's apparently got away."

"Well, that's not our lookout, is it?"

"They think he's here. Or in Canada. They've sent someone to look in both places."

"That's just wonderful. This whole country is overrun with communist spies, domestic and foreign. Why Canada?"

"One of our people has retired there. A very talented girl. I tried to get her to work as a double agent, but Aptekar, their spy who was supposed to be running her from that side, told her he wanted to come to the West instead. I've sent Hunt to speak to her because she apparently has some Russian émigré staying with her."

"You're still in contact with her? I thought you said she retired."

"Yes, sir. She was excellent during the war, but she is adamantly retired. I understand she is to be married to a local policeman." Dunn said no more on that subject.

The home secretary had changed since the debacle of Darling's arrest for murder in London during the summer. The previous home secretary had not been kind to Dunn, who had made what his boss had called a "bungled attempt" to cover up the misdeeds of one of his field men, who turned out to work for the other side. Getting this exchange right was critical, or Dunn would be put out to pasture. The universities weren't just producing spies, they were producing eager, thrusting young men who were after his job. Women too for all he knew, he thought bitterly.

The home secretary let out a massive sigh. "You seem to have this woman under pretty close surveillance if you know who her house guests are and what her marital plans are. You obviously think this Aptekar is going to turn up there?"

"I do have a channel, yes, sir. It's only one possibility. If he does make his way there, we'll get Canadian authorities to pick him up and hand him back to us."

"What happens if the Ruskies get to him first?"

This was a sore point. Dunn had seen Soviet tactics. They had surprised him with the move to send Aptekar to a labour camp. That seemed to Dunn like overkill. Unless he had information they could not afford to lose sight of. Then they were likely to kill him as soon as look at him. If that happened, they might renege on the deal. His contact had told him the whole thing was getting to be too much trouble.

"As you know, Home Secretary, the Canadians had a bit of a spy crisis of their own a couple of years ago. They are very careful right now about who they let in. Our man Hunt is keeping an eye on all the coming and going in the Vancouver port. The Royal Canadian Mounted Police are on the job there. They should get to him."

"Yes, I know all about that spy crisis. What we learned from it is that Canada is already full of people willing to work for the Soviets. They're supposed to be getting nuclear secrets, but I'm sure some of them wouldn't mind a little side trip to eliminate a traitor. Best get on it."

Best had, Dunn thought glumly, getting up and making for the door. "Home Secretary."

CHAPTER TWENTY-ONE

DUNN LOOKED AT THE CABLE. Well, that was something, anyway. He'd set up a meeting with his dour Russian counterpart. The Russian could call off his dogs. On the other hand, this made it vastly more complicated, having to do everything at a distance. He wasn't surprised, all in all, and had some satisfaction in knowing he'd been right about where their man would go to ground. He stood and took up his hat and Mackintosh. At least it wasn't raining.

The bench by the Serpentine looked out on the water. The two men sat side by side watching the ducks flapping and swimming in circles near the grassy bank. A child was feeding the birds scraps of bread.

"What did those ducks do during the war, I wonder?" the Russian said. He lifted his chin but still did not look at Dunn. "Well, you were in a hurry to see me. You've made me walk half an hour just to get here."

"We think our man landed in Vancouver. One of your ships had to sail back to Vladivostok a man short, so you can stand your people down in Hong Kong. And here for that matter."

"Good. Is there anything else? It is my lunch time."

"Yes. I want your undertaking that no matter what happens, you will follow through with our deal."

"You mean, if he is accidentally killed, yes? The minute one of our people lays eyes on him, you will get your list. You know, Director Comrade Dunn, you people should ask yourselves why your brightest and best-educated college men, and women, for that matter, want to come to the Soviet Union, eh? People want something to believe in. Look how many of your people secretly supported Hitler." He shrugged and waved his hand at the water and trees. "It's a pretty country, don't get me wrong, but young people don't want all those archaic institutions you're so proud of. They want the future, they want idealism and justice. They want to be in a country where the government has the power to make the changes that are so necessary. Your government is always flailing." He let this sit for a moment, and then he stood. "Well then, until next time."

The Russian turned north toward Bayswater Road and walked away without looking back.

Dunn sat on for some moments. He'd been young once. Had he been filled with ideals? The truth suggested itself to him, and he wondered for a moment if he should feel any shame about it. No. It had been what his father had taught him, what he believed in to the core of his being. He had been filled with ambition. That was what young men ought to be driven by. Ambition.

LANE SAT WITH Darling in a window booth at the café by the station. It was what her neighbours would call tea time, and so it was quiet, as the bulk of the café's patrons visited for breakfast and lunch. She'd been hankering for pie. She would take a piece home for Countess Orlova. It was apple today. She shifted her attention back to Darling. He was in a mood.

"Any news of when we might be able to move the countess out of your spare room?"

"The vicar is working on it, darling. We'll have to be content with that."

"I suppose you're wondering how we're getting on with the murder?" Darling asked.

"I was, but I didn't like to ask. I know how you feel about interference."

Darling ignored this invitation. "Sordid extramarital affair sort of thing. It makes it less likely there's a random killer lurking around King's Cove." Darling seemed disinclined to say anymore.

"Ah. So like most murders, I expect, someone he knew. As dangerous as the subject of marriage has suddenly become, I've picked up these little cards and I will issue invitations to my neighbours. How many will you need? I'm sure your family would like to get theirs in a card instead of the scraps of paper you'd no doubt write to them on."

Lane pulled a card out of her handbag—a simple white card with an embossed floral design subtly suggesting celebration and marital harmony. As Lane spoke, she was aware of another pool of anxiety she was keeping at bay. Her conversation with Hunt. She felt, by not telling Darling what had happened with Hunt, that she was lying to him.

"My poor family would be lucky to get scraps of paper from me. I'm afraid I'm not much of a correspondent."

"Even better, then. This will be a thrill for them. Will five do?"

"Two will do. No, maybe three. I should invite Ames's mother. I'm afraid my old housekeeper, Mrs. Andrews, has never forgiven me for revealing her son as a murderer and a spy, so she's out." Mrs. Andrews had been Darling's housekeeper since he'd returned from the war, but she had refused to talk to him again when her son had been arrested. "Now, can we talk about your houseguest? You've been avoiding it."

Lane put down her fork. She had been avoiding it. She was keenly aware that she was about to enter into a marriage with a man from whom she would wish to keep nothing, and yet already she had information that may or may not be relevant to the situation, information that she could not share.

"Yes, I suppose I have, a bit. I've been as puzzled as you by your information that Orlova may not have gone around Vancouver looking for her brother as she claimed, and even more by the news that her brother, or the man in the picture, might have been an MGB interrogator, and not a refugee at all. Indeed, the very opposite. And is he even her brother? And to top it off, I'm not actually sure she doesn't speak some English."

"Well, I can see you don't need me filling you with alarming questions. I'm relieved that you seem to have some native caution."

"The vicar did sound hopeful. And it's silly for her to be sitting out in King's Cove. She's not going to find the man she's looking for miles from anywhere. Anyway, I'm still sure she poses no danger to me. Don't forget, I was randomly found simply because I speak Russian. Stevens could have called anyone." Even as she said this, Lane felt an anxiety she could not quite identify.

"I hope you're right about the vicar finding something. I wasn't looking forward to the spare room being full of her. I was hoping to use it as a place to store my two suits. Didn't you mention something else that you were concerned about?"

Lane nodded. "I'm not sure concerned is the right word. Maybe 'puzzled' again. It's about her suitcase. She had two of them when I collected her from the vicar, and she stores them under the bed. Only, the other day when I went in to put her cardigan on the bed, I saw only one."

"Putting her cardigan on the bed required you to look under it? If it weren't about to be nepotism, I could hire you on at the Nelson Police."

"It's not like that. All right, maybe it is. It wouldn't have struck me as odd because she used to always take her painting supplies in the suitcase. Except the problem is I'm not quite sure about this time; I thought I saw her going up to the Hugheses' with a cloth bag I gave her, which she said she was going to be using from now on, so I was a teensy bit puzzled about why there was only one suitcase."

She longed to tell him that the most puzzling thing of all was how Hunt had known she had a Russian guest in her house, but she knew she couldn't. Anything to do with her old work in intelligence could never be shared with anyone. Even though her stint was over, she knew she was under the provisions of the Official Secrets Act. It was not a suggestion. It was the law.

"And anyway, she does do the loveliest paintings. And there are many things that could explain the situation. She could have stopped looking when she realized people knew him as MGB, and she concluded she wouldn't get any answers. He, in fact, may have got tired of the whole Soviet empire and fled."

"Yes, but here's the thing. Why is she here? If no one would talk to her about him because they were afraid, who told her he'd come *here* because isn't that what she told you?"

"It doesn't follow that someone didn't tell her he'd come here, but you do make a good point. Did someone lie to her? Were they trying to get her away from Vancouver for some reason? Is her brother the MGB man actually there, but doesn't want to be found? Poor thing. I'm sure I'm going to be able to bring her here in a couple of days, and she'll have to decide what to do next. What's the sordid extramarital affair, anyway?"

"You won't get that out of me that easily. I've work to do, much as I'd rather stay here eating pie with you."

"There will be plenty of time for that after we're married. One of us could learn to make pie so we won't even have to come all the way here to eat it." Lane took his hand. "Don't forget to write your invitations."

"I won't. I love you."

"You always say that. Off you go. I'm going to get some pie for the countess. I was going to attempt to make

228

some, but this is much easier. We will use it to celebrate her removal to town." Lane spoke lightly, but weighing on her was Hunt and his suggestion that Aptekar might be on his way here, and the oh-so irritating information that Hunt seemed to know all about her activities.

Lane stood on her porch looking out at the lake. Peace of mind was all she'd ever really wanted, but here, in a very paradise, it was as elusive as the mythical phoenix she'd so hoped to emulate when she had first moved here after the war. A new land, a new life. She felt a swell of resentment at being put into this situation. It was one thing when she had been a child in Latvia and been somewhere on the grounds of her childhood estate in Riga where she'd been forbidden to go, feeling this guilt and anxiety. And there was the normal tension and anxiety of the war, which she was slowly learning to leave behind. But, now this—she had done nothing to deserve this renewed inquietude. Her musing was interrupted by the telephone. It was the vicar saying he thought he'd found a place for her guest. That was something, anyway.

She phoned Eleanor and told her that the vicar had found a place for the countess, and Eleanor insisted they come to the cottage for supper so Lane didn't have to worry about trying to cook something. Orlova was back at the Hugheses' yet again, painting a view of the lake from the back porch. She must have a dozen pictures of those vast gardens by now. With a sigh of relief at not having to cope with dinner, Lane hung the receiver on its hook. No one needs me for anything just at the moment, she thought, so perhaps a walk. She would find temporary succour from the mess of questions and irritations that assailed her in the quiet of the forest and the soul-soothing views of the lake.

She took a sweater out of her drawer, tied it around her neck, and set out up the hill. She would take her favourite path to the old schoolhouse and sit on its rickety front steps. There the view did not encompass the lake, but rather the cascades of forest stretched out below. It was the absolute natural quiet she loved when she sat there. She had once imaginatively felt that the slight whispers of the trees were the fading voices of the children who had been schooled there in those early years before all the wars that were scarring the twentieth century. It was a place of complete isolation and innocence.

The sun was standing off a very black bank of clouds just above her behind the mountain that rose up at the back of King's Cove. The golden intensity of the sun and the contrast between the deep blue of the sky and the charcoal cloud mesmerized her. She had often thought that the whole place would be claustrophobic were it not for the fact that the hamlet opened out toward the lake with the mountain behind it, almost, she thought, protecting it. Relieved to be on her own, she took long steps through the tall grass, breathing in the warmth of the Indian summer. The school appeared through the trees above where she stood. It was a scene of such solitude and silence. She made for the steps and sat on the top one and leaned back, her face toward the sun.

She had to think through what it meant to be going into this marriage with Darling still carrying secrets. Even the thought of it made her heart a little heavier. But in a way, they were not her own. They were British government secrets, after all. Darling had to keep secrets as well. For example, he wasn't really supposed to give her as many details as he often did about his cases, however often she was involved in them. But look at this case. He gave only the vaguest response when she asked him about it, and that was as it should be. He was keeping police secrets, she was keeping intelligence secrets. There. That wasn't so bad after all. They both had to keep things from each other for work. Perfect. Thus resolved, she closed her eyes and let the sun play on her eyelids, its cleansing heat pushing her troubles away for a few blissful moments.

CHAPTER TWENTY-TWO

A week earlier

THE DOOR TO THE SHOP, already open to let in the mild fall air, slammed against the wall, causing Verne Taylor to jump and drop the screw he was trying to insert into the workings of the outboard he was fixing. He looked up to see Brodie looking at various tools laid out on the counter with an unreadable expression on his face.

"It's been going on the whole time," Brodie said. He picked up a slender iron hammer, considered it, and put it down.

"What's been going on the whole time?" Taylor asked wearily. His initial anxiety caused by the banging of the door was waning. "Now I've lost the bloody screw on the floor here somewhere." He started to bend over, but Brodie suddenly lunged at him, grabbing a handful of his shirt.

"My wife!" he shouted. Brodie was strong and had managed to pull Taylor so that he was leaning awkwardly over the counter and was using his hands to try to keep from falling forward.

"Look—" Taylor began, but Brodie struck him hard on the side of the head with the palm of his hand, stunning him, making his ear ring.

"Don't bother to deny it. She's changed toward me. She's like a bitch in heat."

At this Taylor violently shrugged himself free of Brodie's grip and pushed him so that Brodie staggered back a step. Neither one of them saw the two men who had come into the shop and now stood mesmerized and uncertain just inside the door.

"Do not use that kind of language about Cassie! No wonder she's looking to me. You treat your animals better!"

"I'm warning you, Taylor. You stay away from her. She's my wife, and I can do with her what I like!" Brodie started toward the door, angrily kicking a round gas can across the floor. The two customers had scurried out.

Taylor sprang over the counter and was bearing down on the retreating Brodie. He stopped at the door and shouted after him. "You lay one hand on her again and you'll be sorry!"

Brodie, who had parked his truck on the wrong side of the street so that his driver door was facing the shop, got into the truck, started the engine, ground the gears, and with a rude gesture, peeled into the street, narrowly missing an oncoming car that swerved and honked.

"HOY, LOOK AT this!" Oxley was in the equipment closet where the shelving had fallen down. Ward was on his hands and knees looking into the far recesses of the shelves under Taylor's workbench. He pulled his head out.

"What?"

"I've found something, is what. I think this will put the thing to bed."

Ward stood up, rubbing his right knee, and went into the closet where Oxley was holding what looked like an old rag rolled into a bundle. He was holding it aloft with a pair of tongs. Ward frowned at it in the semi-dark of the cupboard. "What is it?"

"Let's find out, shall we?" Oxley indicated Ward should get out of the doorway, and then he strode to the workbench. Taylor had been sitting on a stool in the corner with his arms crossed watching the comings and goings of the two searching policemen impatiently. "Now then, Mr. Taylor. Can you tell me about this?" He put the cloth on the workbench and used the tongs to unroll the bundle. "And would you look at this?"

Ward watched the cloth unfold and then pulled his head back suddenly as he realized what he was seeing: an old white shirt clearly covered in large patches of dried blood, in the centre of which was a hunting knife. The shirt showed evidence of an attempt to wash it out. Taylor stood, nearly knocking over the stool. He shook his head violently.

"No! No. I've never seen that before. It's not even mine!"

"Is that right?" Oxley said, his voice calm. "Then can you tell me how it came to be stuffed behind one of the wall boards in your closet? In fact, when my boss was here, weren't you dealing with the shelves having collapsed? I wonder why that was?"

"I don't know. I don't understand! It's not mine!" Taylor walked around the counter toward the cupboard convulsively, as if looking into it would make sense of what he was seeing.

Oxley rewrapped the knife, pushed the bundle toward Ward, and then wiped his hands together as if happy to pass it off to an underling. Ward paused for a split second, looking at his partner with a nearly imperceptible narrowing of the eyes, and then moved slowly to put the bundle into a paper bag.

"You'll have plenty of time to explain about the shirt and the knife and anything else you'd like to tell us up at the station. Officer Ward has a nice pooch who might even be able to tell us if this is Mr. Brodie's blood." He shook his head. "Didn't anyone ever tell you? You need to start with cold water if you want to get blood out of a shirt."

TAYLOR RAN BOTH of his hands through his hair and then slumped forward, his arms resting on the interview table. Darling was seated on the other side, and Oxley was taking notes. Unlike Ames, who usually sat against the wall, Oxley had pulled his chair up to the end of the table.

"You can't be surprised to find yourself here, Mr. Taylor. You lied about where you were the other night, and you are lying about evidence found in your shop: a blood-stained shirt and a weapon. I'm not surprised by the blood; it's a messy business cutting someone's throat. And you had, from your point of view, good reason to want him out of the way. You have been having a long-standing affair with his wife. Now, I wonder if you could just walk us through the events of that day. What might have happened to push you over the edge after all this time? Did it come out? Did you and Brodie have words?"

"Yes, we had words. But I would never," he paused and wrinkled his face, disgust written on it, "do that to anyone."

"Tell me about the words," coaxed Darling.

"He came barging into my shop, if you must know, about a week ago, and tried to start a fight. He struck me quite hard. My ear is still ringing. He said he knew about me and Cassie and he warned me off."

Darling looked at Oxley, who nodded. He turned back to the prisoner. "One of your neighbours on that block heard an argument. Did you threaten Brodie?"

"It seems you already know, so I don't know why you're asking me. I told him he'd be sorry if he laid a hand on her."

"And did he?" Darling asked. "You said you were with her the first night Brodie was away on the hunting trip. Did she say anything to you?"

"No," Taylor muttered. "I thought I saw some bruising on her arm. I asked her about it, but she said she banged it on the corner of a cupboard. I don't know how she banged her arm hard enough to leave bruises on the front and the back of it."

"So, why wouldn't she say something, I wonder?"

Taylor was silent. He leaned back with his arm flung over the back of the chair and looked at the window that gave onto the alley.

"Is it because she was afraid of something like this?" Darling suggested.

"She knew she didn't have to be afraid of me. She was afraid of him. That's what she was afraid of. And with good reason."

"Perhaps she had good reason to be afraid that you

would do something to protect her. Brodie is dead, after all, and we have strong evidence linking you to that death. You're a hunter too, aren't you?"

"I wasn't hunting him, if that's what you're implying. I'm not an idiot. When I said he'd be sorry, I meant that I would take her and move away."

Darling nodded. "I see. But that wouldn't really be a permanent fix, would it? Divorces are messy and hard to get, and in this case, the infidelity of the wife would come out in court and be very punishing for Mrs. Brodie to go through. No, I really meant, you have hunting equipment. Rifles, hunting knives, that sort of thing. And you know his route, because you used to go with him when you were still friends. Can you tell us your inventory?"

"Oh my God. I have two rifles—a Winchester my father left me, and a Savage I bought for myself in '36. I have one knife, a Randall I just bought last year to replace one I lost. They're in the shop, as if your officers don't know. They tore the place apart. But that one you found is not mine. I've never seen it before."

Darling turned to Oxley.

"Sir, we found the rifles and one knife neatly stowed, so this is the second knife." Oxley opened his hand, indicating the knife found with the shirt.

Taylor threw himself back in the chair. "No, it's not. That's a lie. My other knife was lost years ago. This is not it. How can I make you understand?"

"Don't worry. We'll dust it for prints," Oxley said. "Though I'm sure you cleaned them off. I know I would have in your shoes. Too bad you tucked it into your shirt.

A smarter man would have tossed it away somewhere."

Darling glanced at Oxley, a slight pulling together of his eyebrows indicating disapproval of his flippant tone, then he turned to the prisoner. "Mr. Taylor, I am officially charging you with the murder of Raymond Brodie. If you wish to speak further, I recommend you call a lawyer. We can let you make a phone call from here."

When the phone call had been made, and the prisoner led back to the cell, Darling stood with Oxley in the interview room. "This is not hanging together very well for me. Although it can never be a hundred percent, we have an estimated time of death, most likely in the afternoon sometime, give or take some hours. But Taylor lied about being out overnight, which, even stretching those time-of-death hours, would not get us into the wee small hours, so he wasn't out there killing Brodie then. What are we missing?"

"Not a damn thing, sir. He follows and kills Brodie, let's say in the late afternoon, when he'd normally have finished work, and then he goes back to make sure, or revisit the scene. He doesn't have an alibi for every hour of the afternoon after all. Maybe his conscience is working overtime, or he's in shock because he can't believe he's done it, so he feels compelled to go back. Maybe he left the murder weapon and is afraid it will be traced to him, so he brings it back to clean it and is going to think of a way to get rid of it later. No one says criminals are that bright. Of course he's lying about it. We now have him squarely at the scene of the crime. It beggars belief he wasn't the murderer, all things considered."

"Hm," was all Darling said.

IT WAS SEVEN in the evening and the hotel bar was full. There was a jukebox playing Hank Williams in the far corner from where officers Ward and O'Brien were having a beer. The clack of a pool cue against a rack sounded behind them and someone laughed. Ward was not in a laughing mood.

"When is Ames coming back, anyway?" he asked.

"Should be any time now. His exam was yesterday, I think. Don't tell me you miss Ames!"

"I didn't till that Ox turned up. I don't like him."

"He seems pleasant enough," O'Brien said, raising his empty glass toward the waitress and holding up two fingers. Ward was evidently in a funk and needed an ear.

"Yes. That's what he shows you and the boss. Pleasant, eager. Butter wouldn't melt. But he's different when we're away from the station. He has an edge. He ordered me about like he'd been made king. He was, I don't know how to say it . . . harsh, threatening almost when we were searching that guy Taylor's shop. I don't trust him. I think Ames should watch his back. He's going after his job. You mark my words."

"You're overstating it, my friend. Taylor has been arrested for murder. I'm not surprised Oxley wasn't treating him with kid gloves. Anyway, Ames will be a sergeant and the boss loves him."

"I'm not saying anyone should be treated with kid gloves. It's just, I don't know, he's trying to wheedle into the inspector's good graces. You watch him one day, you'll see what I mean. Throws his weight around. I just don't trust him. Look at the way he was out washing the car the other day."

"Yeah, I saw that. The car did need a good scrub. You know what those roads are like."

"But did it really look completely clean? I think he just does the least he can do and tries to get away with it. He goes out a lot, too. Pretends to be working, but you go to find him, and he's nowhere to be seen. I saw him the other day at the soda fountain when I was on my way to send a wire."

O'Brien, who'd seen a little of that himself in Oxley, nevertheless thought there was no percentage in complaining about a fellow officer. Oxley may not be Ames, he'd concede that, but he did his job and seemed smart enough.

"Here, Ward. Drink up. Don't hurt yourself. Give that brain a rest. I think the only thing wrong with Oxley is that I don't reckon he's going to stay here. He's looking for the main chance. He was back east. I bet he finds us pretty small potatoes."

"Looking for the main chance. I couldn't have put it better myself." Ward drank deeply, satisfied that O'Brien seemed to agree with his assessment of Oxley and pulled out his cigarettes. "One more and I'd better get home to the missus."

LANE WAS IN the sitting room with Countess Orlova. They were watching the day end on the lake below with glasses of sherry. There had been a thoughtful silence between them. The place in town that might have accommodated Orlova was run by a prim middle-aged woman who kept house for her son and rented out her spare rooms. At the last moment she had called the vicar in an anxious flurry saying she didn't think she'd be able to accommodate Countess Orlova after all, what with the language barrier and all. Finally, Orlova spoke.

"It is pointless for me to stay on. Your policeman has found no trace of my brother. I must give up. And I have now become a nuisance to everyone."

Lane found herself at a loss. Competing in her mind was the worry that Orlova really had no place to go, and the possibility put to her by Darling that she might have been lying about who her brother really is. Was he in the country because he'd fallen afoul of his MGB employers? He certainly wouldn't have been the first. But that meant that a possibly brutal former Soviet interrogator was seeking some sort of asylum in Canada. This idea appalled her. How could she approach this with Orlova?

The ringing of the phone saved her from any immediate response. It was for her.

"KC 431, Lane Winslow speaking."

"Oh, Miss Winslow!" The next part of the sentence was drowned in sobs.

"Hello? Are you all right?" Lane said. She did not immediately recognize the voice.

"I'm so sorry. I'm so upset. I didn't know who else to turn to. They've arrested Verne! It's all wrong! He wouldn't do something like this!"

It took Lane a moment, but then she realized it was Cassie Brodie. "Mrs. Brodie, can you take a breath and tell me from the beginning?"

"Yes, I'm sorry. I know I'm not making any sense. The police. They found out we were still having an affair, and they got it into their heads that he killed my husband for me. But he wouldn't, not like that. Not any way. Oh my God, this whole thing is my fault! I told them Verne was with me at night when my husband was up the mountain, but I admitted he wasn't there all night, so they got the idea he was off killing him. But he wasn't! I know it. You have to help me!"

"I . . . I don't know how I can help, Mrs. Brodie. The police must have some evidence." Her voice trailed off. She could hear Cassie Brodie's panic, but she also heard what she hadn't known at all, that Verne Taylor and Mrs. Brodie had been having an ongoing affair. She wondered where Cassie had parcelled the horror of her husband's murder, that she should now be begging for her lover. From the back of her mind came the memory of the glimpse of the bruises on Cassie's arm as she had sat down to await the news from the search party. There was much, Lane realized, you can never really know about people's lives.

"But what evidence can they have? He didn't do it!"

"Well, I suppose it could be the circumstance of his having some time that is unexplained when he was not with you. I don't really know, I honestly don't."

"But you're friendly with the policeman. That's what I heard. Can't you find out? Please?"

Lane's heart sank. Was she to be put in this invidious position because she was to become the wife of a policeman?

"Please, Miss Winslow. I have no one else!"

With enormous reluctance Lane said, "I can try to see what I can learn, Mrs. Brodie, or better yet, get the inspector to speak with you directly. I am really not privy to anything at all from the police end."

When she had hung up the phone, jiggling the hook for the earpiece, which she still had not fixed in the nearly year and a half since she'd moved to King's Cove, she leaned against the wall, frowning, wondering how to approach something that she knew would only upset Darling. Furthermore, she thought, he would be right to be upset.

"Is something the matter?" Orlova asked as Lane came slowly back to the sitting room.

"That was the wife of the man who was killed. Apparently, she is the lover of the man they have arrested for killing him, and she is positive he would never do something like that."

"But this is good news! They have made an arrest. Everyone here in this charming little place can relax and not be in fear of their lives. As for the widow, well, a man's lover is bound to say he is innocent, no?"

Lane drank the dregs of her sherry. Yes, she thought. A man's lover is bound to say that, especially if she believed she knew he could never do such a thing. When Darling had been charged with killing someone, she had been sure he was no murderer, and she had been right. What if Cassie Brodie was right?

CHAPTER TWENTY-THREE

L ANE WAITED UNTIL THE FOLLOWING morning when
Countess Orlova was safely in the upper field overlooking the lake with her paints before putting a call into
the police station. She breathed a sigh of relief when she
heard Darling put through. She had had a rough night of
sleep, wondering how she could even pose the question
without sounding like she was interfering, and she finally
gained some sleep when she decided on the truth, delivered straight up. After all, she was just passing on a request
from a frantic woman, not trying to persuade Darling of
anything untoward on her own account.

"I've heard that you've made an arrest," she began when
the greetings had been fondly exchanged.

"Well, that's pretty fast. It was only yesterday afternoon."
Darling said this with a slight tone of inquiry.

"I had a call from a desperate Cassie Brodie last evening.
She wanted me to persuade you that Verne Taylor would
never do such a thing, and that you have the wrong man.

She seemed very sure. She was sobbing to such an extent that I very reluctantly said I would call you. So I am."

"Good. Thank you. Is there anything else I can do for you?"

His tone was good-natured, but Lane did not miss its intent. She paused. She'd certainly done nothing at all for Cassie Brodie. "May I tell the anxious residents of King's Cove that you've made an arrest? Everyone here is on tenterhooks."

"You may. But only that we have made a sure arrest. You may not tell them what little I'm prepared to tell you now: we have solid evidence, and I am quite satisfied, in spite of energetic denials by the suspect."

Lane stood looking out the door into her yard. She really hadn't helped at all.

"Lane, I appreciate your position," Darling said into the silence.

"I was just thinking of how sure she was. How deeply she believes in his innocence."

"Are you about to draw a parallel of some sort between you and her? I wish you wouldn't. This is not the same."

"There was solid evidence against you as well, they all thought. Mistakes can be made."

"I wish you'd trust me. He's denying it, as people often do, but the physical evidence is extremely compelling. However, the case is far from closed as there is still the crime scene to consider and some questions about the time of death. We will continue to interview him, and probably his hapless lover as well, until we are satisfied about how it all came to this."

Stung by the suggestion that she did not trust him, she examined her own conscience for a split second and knew she did, utterly.

"I do trust you, darling. I think I just feel terrible for her. Her whole world has crumbled into a sordid mess from which she is desperately trying to find an escape. Her life as she knows it is over."

"Murder destroys lives, it's true. I nearly hate myself for asking this, but you don't have any 'feeling' about this one do you?"

"Good heavens, no. As I said, it's more the force of her complete confidence that he could not have done this. I realize she has, like so many before her, been deceived. In her case by both her husband and her lover."

"I have to get on. Do keep me abreast of anyone else importuning you on this matter. If it is of any comfort to you, I will interview her again, and she can tell me directly how innocent he is. I will need to anyway now that we have charged him. In the meantime, you can tell your neighbours they're safe."

"Yes, I will. Thank you for listening."

"I still love you."

"I know," Lane said, "me too."

WORD SPREAD QUICKLY that an arrest had been made, and there was a palpable return to good cheer as people gathered at the post office that day. Lane had told Eleanor Armstrong, knowing that everyone else would know within the hour.

"Shocking!" Mabel Hughes said to Lane, relief evident even in her exclamation. "I heard he was shot."

Lane was surprised to realize that the gruesome manner of his death had not been broadcast through the usual means and spared a grateful thought for Glenn Ponting, who had been in the search party and seen the corpse, but had evidently told no one, and the Armstrongs, in whom she herself had confided the grisly details, as far as she knew them.

"I'm not sure, but I am as relieved as the rest of you to know we don't have to worry."

"Wasn't the body brought to your house?" Mabel pressed.

"It was wrapped in one of my sheets, so I didn't see it, I'm happy to say. Someone did hear a shot in the afternoon of the day before." Might as well keep that illusion going.

"Yes. Though that could have just been him hunting. Still and all, I'm happy it's over. We've had to move our afternoon tea indoors in this lovely fall weather just in case there was someone lurking in the upper orchard with a rifle waiting to pick us off. I guess your Russian countess can resume her country walks. She may be safe from a mad gunman, but she should mind the cougars."

"Perhaps I could get Alice Mather and her trusty rifle to go along with her," Lane said, smiling, wondering who in the world would ever want to "pick off" the wonderful Hughes trio.

Lane sat on her veranda with a cup of tea at her elbow and her pile of invitations on her lap. Orlova had still not returned, and Lane had not called Cassie Brodie, knowing that Darling was no doubt already on to it. She wanted to put behind her the pressing worry of what would become of Orlova, and the still-lingering impression of Cassie's absolute certainty about her lover's innocence, and focus instead on her own innocent activity: writing her wedding invitations. It must be killing both Eleanor and Angela to keep quiet, and at least she could put them out of their misery.

DARLING WAS BROODING in his office. The weather offered support for his mood by suddenly turning to black clouds. The people on the street below him were pulling jackets and sweaters more closely around themselves as a cooler wind had picked up. The idyll of the warm September seemed to have disappeared completely and suddenly with the downturn of his mood.

He could see no fault in Lane's phone call. She was, after all, a kind person who hated to see someone in such distress. On the other hand, he wondered again at their closeness and her interest in his work. Would there be other times when he would have to rebuff her, however gently? But that wasn't it, he knew. He actually trusted Lane's sense of judgement. It was more the juxtaposition of her phone call about Cassie Brodie's absolute certainty and the vigorous denials of the prisoner.

He accepted that people, especially people with little conscience, could look one in the eye and deny their crimes. But Taylor didn't strike him as a man without a conscience. Indeed, he struck Darling as a very emotional man. One who loved a woman he could never fully be with, and who agonized over the ill treatment she received from her husband. Emotion like that could indeed drive a man to kill the hated rival, but it would, in Darling's experience, also make him unable to deny it once confronted. A man like that would be more likely to break down and use the excuse of his love and fear for the woman in the picture as justification.

Yet, Taylor denied it absolutely, and there was a tiny corner of Darling's mind that wanted to believe him. But the bloody shirt and possible murder weapon needed to be explained. And there was certainly no one else even remotely on the suspect list. He tried to shake the idea that something was amiss in how Oxley was handling it. No doubt it was because Oxley felt so sure about it. He reminded himself to take a step at a time. He would interview the prisoner and expand his interviewing to Mrs. Brodie and back to the landlady and the two men who'd inadvertently witnessed the original fight.

He would start with Oxley and Ward. Have them give him more detail about finding the shirt and weapon. He knew this would most likely serve to confirm the connection between the damning evidence and Taylor's guilt rather than cast any doubt on the matter, but he wanted to be absolutely clear in his mind. He'd also get Gilly on to testing the blood.

In an unusual move, Darling went next door to the office Oxley was occupying. It was empty. Pushing aside the complications he would be facing when Ames returned—any minute now, he reckoned—he called down the stairs.

"O'Brien, where's Oxley?"

O'Brien came to the bottom of the stairs and shook his head. "Gone out, sir."

"Gone out where?" Darling asked, irritated.

"He's about police business, I assume, sir. Ah. The

prodigal returns," he said, as Darling heard the door to the station open and close. "But your golden boy is back, sir. Shall I send him up?"

Ames did not wait for an answer but bounded up the stairs. "Good afternoon, sir. Have the phones gone down? You don't usually stand at the top of the stairs shouting for underlings."

"Oh. It's you. It's not you I want right now. But you'd better come in, I suppose. I'm sorry to say your office has been sublet. We'll have to make arrangements. You may have to double up for the time being."

Ames looked into his office and shrugging, hung his mackintosh on the coat rack and perched his hat on the top of it. He didn't relish sharing his office, but he'd seen how big city police organized themselves, and he knew he'd been lucky to have an office at all. All in all, he thought, he'd be happier to set up a desk downstairs somewhere rather than trying to share one desk with someone he didn't know.

"Well?" asked Darling once they were seated in his office. "Any other news on the Russian front?"

Ames shook his head. "It's pretty much what I told you, sir. It looks like the old lady didn't really go around asking about her brother, which is odd, and the RCMP intelligence people swiped my photo of him, which is odd, and the dead Russian turns out to have possibly been murdered."

"Which, I suppose you are about to tell me, is odd."

"Well, it is. Why should the intelligence Johnnies be interested in this woman's brother?"

"Presumably because he's some sort of Soviet secret service operative. More concerning to me, is that this puts the supposedly innocent old lady cluttering up Miss Winslow's house in a very dubious light."

"Oh, and congratulations on that, sir! I'm very happy, and very honoured—"

"Can you keep your focus, Ames? I've got a murderer in the cell I'm in the middle of investigating and a good deal of anxiety about what that woman may be up to. And I don't like not knowing what we are dealing with. The RCMP will be sure to tell us absolutely nothing, and then blame us for bungling their case if the whole thing goes south."

Ames hid a smile. It was good to be home. "I understood she is extremely old. How much could she be up to?"

"I tell you what. How do you fancy a drive up the lake? I want you to take the car and drive up to see Miss Winslow. You can use the excuse that you're to be the best man or that you want to congratulate her. I'm sure you'll think of something absolutely charming. I want you to get a feel for things. This countess was supposed to be offered a place in town and something went wrong with that, I don't strictly know what. We haven't found her brother, and we aren't going to. Certainly not before the RCMP do, if he's even over here, so she has no reason to hang on here. Let the good countess know that the RCMP have taken up the task, see how she responds. I haven't got time for any of it as Oxley and I are going to have to re-interview all our witnesses now that we have a solid suspect. Where is that blasted man anyway?"

Darling picked up the phone and dialled down to the front desk.

"Any sign of Oxley?" He listened for a moment. "Has he taken the car?" Another pause. "All right. Give the keys to Ames."

He slammed down the receiver. "Oxley has apparently gone off to send a wire. Take the second set of keys. Run along. In the meantime, I'll get someone to sort the office business." Darling waved his hand at the door.

"Have you talked to Miss Winslow about your concerns about her guest?"

Darling shook his head impatiently. "Of course, I've talked to her, as much as I can, but she's never alone, and I don't trust her damn phone. The old lady goes around painting people's gardens. That might give you a chance to catch her alone."

Happy to be of use immediately upon his return and even happier to be seeing Miss Winslow, Ames collected the keys and went around the corner to get the car. It wasn't until he was on the ferry going across to the west side of the lake to join the road that led to King's Cove that he thought about how unusual this assignment was and wondered if he should be offended not to be in on the real action: the murder. But, in fairness, he'd done some digging in Vancouver, so he might get a feel for whether the old lady was involved in anything, or completely innocently looking for her brother.

LANE HAD DRIVEN to the Balfour gas station to fill the car and pick up some biscuits, and now instead of driving smartly home she found herself taking the road straight up toward Angela's. It was generally accepted that one didn't drive up this road, but only down it, in case of meeting cars, but there was so little in the way of traffic in King's Cove, she knew she was quite safe.

She drove past her friend's palatial log cabin and continued up the road to an abandoned house near the top of the road. She still shuddered at the thought of the house. After the discovery of long-buried bones in the Hugheses' root cellar in the cold and miserable spring, Lane had explored it thoroughly and gotten a sense of the hopeless poverty and struggle of a family trying to make a go of it in the years before the Great War. She stopped the car and got out. There was a path that went up north-northwest, she knew. It crossed a meadow and led to an abandoned cabin above Ponting's cabin, and then continued upward, into the forest. She was surprised that even at the outer edges of King's Cove, the path was clearly visible. It must be one of the paths Ponting used, she realized, to get at the areas he was prospecting.

With her hands in her pockets, she looked toward that forest now. Ponting must have been farther above that forest when he found the horse. Did he say he'd been in a meadow? She listened and heard the creek flowing just below her. Could she find the place where the hunter had been killed?

Shaking her head, she turned back toward the car, but she could not forget the sound of Cassie Brodie's plea. She knew she would find nothing at the scene, assuming she could find it. She turned back again toward the forest. Looking behind her, as if Darling himself might be standing there and frowning with utmost disapproval, she set out up the path toward the meadow that met the dark bank of trees.

"Meadow" might be a generous word for the scraggly piece of territory Lane now stood in. It was open, yes, filled primarily with low bushes and rocks rather than waving grass and alpine flowers. Based on what Ponting had said, the body hadn't been here, only the horse; Brodie had been found on the other side of the gully carved by the creek. She picked her way through the underbrush until she reached the trees along the upper bank of the gully, which now lay in shade. She could see the sun illuminating the open area visible through the trees on the other side. And she could see a granite outcrop. Did that look like the place where the body was found?

Lane drummed her fingers on the side of her leg. It was madness to go, she knew. For one thing, there would be nothing to see, except, she realized with a shudder, possibly the dried blood of the victim, and for another, whoever had done the throat cutting could even now be squatting in the area. Except, she reasoned, Ponting would have seen traces of someone if they'd been attempting to survive in the bush. Without allowing herself to think much more, Lane plunged down the hill toward the creek and then up the steep rise to the other side.

She stood completely still and listened when she arrived at the bottom of the outcrop. Silence. The sun shone down, bleaching out the drying grass and warming the rock. A crow fluttered suddenly out of a nearby tree. Cautiously Lane advanced along the base of the outcrop and then stopped and held her breath. That dried, black mess was surely the hunter's blood.

"Well, that's fine," she said out loud. "You're quite a clever clogs, aren't you? So what?" The police had been, after all, and picked up every bit of evidence, what had she been hoping to gain? Almost embarrassed by not being sure herself, she moved around so that she could sit on the top of the outcrop. Cross-legged, she looked down toward where the man had been found and tried to imagine the murder. Judging by where the blood was, he must have been looking northish when he was surprised from behind. Could he have been standing? she wondered. If he'd been sitting, he would have had his back to the outcrop, resting against it. Because of the way it slanted outwards slightly at the top, no one could have surprised him from behind if he'd been sitting.

"What are you doing there?" she asked quietly. "What are you looking at?"

She slipped off the rock and stood about where he must have been standing if he'd fallen forward when he died, and looked out. But there was nothing unusual. Twenty yards on, the forest started up again. She looked around, puzzled, and then in a fit of nerves looked behind her. It wouldn't do to be snuck up on oneself! Turning back, she took one last look at the stain of dried blood, and it was then she realized that there was a kind of shelf of rock, low down, at the base of the outcrop just ahead of the blood.

Skirting the dark mess, she went around to the other edge of the flat stone and knelt down. Had there been something there? She sighed. Fruitless. Why had she bothered? And then she saw it—a tiny scrap of brown cloth the size of her little fingernail, flattened into the rough surface of the rock. Was this something? She tried to lean closer, but somehow the more she looked at it, the more it seemed like nothing at all. She started to reach for it, and then stopped herself. If it was anything, Darling could decide. It could be a scrap of the hunter's clothing for all she knew, and Darling would have seen what he'd been wearing.

Memorizing the details, she got up and looked around the area again. Already she was trying to imagine how she could possibly explain to Darling her reasoning for coming up to the scene of the murder. She scarcely understood it herself. But she would have to phone him and tell him.

CHAPTER TWENTY-FOUR

PTEKAR ACCEPTED THE KEY FROM the motel clerk, who
eyed him with some misgivings. "You stay more than
a week you're going to have to pay up front every time."

"Thank you. I should not be that long."

"Don't wipe your shoes on the towel," the man called
out as Aptekar went out the door.

Wondering what sort of reprobates the motel was used to
accommodating, Aptekar threw his small bag on the single
bed and opened the curtains to try to reduce the dinginess
of the place. Well, he'd wanted dingy. The motel was a
mile out of town by the side of the road between Nelson
and nearby Salmo. He would have to think about how to
proceed. He'd been lucky and caught a ride with a truck
driver who was making the full journey from Vancouver
to Castlegar, and then he'd picked up another ride to this
nearly unoccupied motel.

Now that he had come this far, he was filled with misgivings. He had thought that if he could find Lane, she would

know whom to contact in the government, but then what? Someone had known he was to meet the British agent. Had he been followed from the minute he was so ceremoniously "retired"? Or had someone in Britain betrayed him to the Russians? He had thought he would seek asylum with the Canadians, but could they be trusted any more than their staunchest allies, the British? No doubt they worked hand in glove. His only safety lay in having enough to trade on, and he was certain they would be interested in the information he had, if not in him. It had only been two years since he'd learned of the Russian embassy man who'd turned himself over to the Canadian authorities with a list of all the Canadian and Russian operatives at work in the country. It was the list of new recruits that he had in his head, and the urgency to get to Lane had only grown when he'd seen the lie of the land in Vancouver. Soviet operatives were at work there as well.

Aptekar lay down on the bed, feeling with annoyance the metal springs through the thin mattress, and closed his eyes. He was on the last leg of his trip. The idea that he had been betrayed by someone in Britain had taken a firm hold, and this betrayal had set off the workings of the Soviet machinery, which he had seen work so well when he was on the right side of it. Now he was the rat they were chasing. The country near here looks innocent, he thought, but he had seen the persistence of the Soviet machine. They would be here. Nowhere was safe for him right now. Maybe ever again. Lane lived far out in the country. He had not the means to hire a car. He would have to find another way to get to her. His survival would depend on his being able to spot the people chasing him before they spotted him.

"BLAST!" AMES POUNDED the steering wheel with his fist and pulled over to the side of the road. The flapping sound of the punctured tyre stopped, and the car settled with a tilt to the back-passenger side. He got out and walked around to look at the damage. It must have been a massive nail, he thought. The rim was resting right on the completely deflated tyre. Looking in either direction he could see no traffic, not that he'd want to see anyone. Indeed, he'd rather not. He had always thought changing a tyre was an undignified procedure. It somehow suggested a failure to look after the vehicle properly in the first place.

He removed his jacket and rolled up his sleeves, casting a warning look at the sky. The clouds of earlier had dissipated somewhat, and the threatening storm had not broken but rather taken itself off somewhere over the mountains, but there was still a dark roll banked on the west. The trunk was surprisingly full of things he'd never kept in it. A bucket and a stiff dried cloth, some boots caked in drying mud that must have been part of the murder investigation.

His every sense of propriety was outraged. He had babied this car when he was in charge of it. Cleaned it, checked the equipment and the oil and the instruments. And he never would have left dirty boots and an unsavoury looking bucket in the trunk. He took these out as they covered the wheel well, and then pulled away a blanket that covered the spare tyre. To his utter chagrin, instead of a spare tyre, there was a small brown suitcase. Absolutely puzzled, and with his irritation climbing to indignant anger, he lifted the suitcase by its edge to see if the tyre was impossibly somehow jammed under it in the wheel well. Who the

259

blazes put anything but a spare tyre where the spare tyre should be? Emitting a volley of bad language, he slammed the trunk shut and considered what to do next. He knew that the Balfour store and gas station was a good two miles off, the last half mile up a long steep hill. But they might have a spare, or a tow truck—at the very least he could call the office to report and then call Miss Winslow. She might pick him up, though to what end he wasn't sure just yet.

He was reaching into the back seat to collect his jacket when he turned and went back to the trunk and opened it. He pulled the case properly out of the wheel well. It was heavier than he expected. It had two brass latches that could be locked, and he pushed them outward to release the catches. Whoever had put it there had not bothered to lock them. They slid sideways, and the locking mechanisms snapped up smartly. The sight that greeted him mystified him completely.

The suitcase seemed to be full of some sort of electrical equipment. There were two black boxes, one of which had some sort of glass dial, and in a cavity left by the boxes, a jumble of wires had been shoved. Carefully Ames pulled out the mess of wiring and saw a small tidy pair of ear phones entangled in them. He pushed them back and frowned at the whole affair. Was this new police equipment? It was obviously some sort of communication device, but it seemed peculiar that he'd not been told. Of course, no one expected he'd have a flat tyre, but it seemed to him very short-sighted of whoever had stowed the new equipment to replace something so essential as a spare tyre. And why had it been covered with a blanket? Granted, expensive new equipment could not be left lying around on the back seat of a car for anyone to see. Even putting a spare tyre in the back seat of the car could indicate to any miscreant that there was something valuable in the trunk of the car.

He was still staring into the trunk when he heard a vehicle rattle to a stop behind him. It was a Ford runabout truck from the late twenties. An older man with a heavy growth of beard leaned out the window and surveyed the scene.

"Can I give you a lift somewheres? Looks like you got trouble with that tyre. I'm headed up to Bales's store. He might be able to help you," the old man said genially.

"Oh, yes, thanks! That would be great. Someone's taken the spare out of the trunk, if you can believe it. Just two ticks." Ames closed the trunk, and on consideration locked it, and the rest of the car.

Once the truck putted back to life and was progressing slowly up the road the old man said, "Now who'd go and take the tyre out of the car? Isn't it your car?"

"No. It belongs to the Nelson Police. I've been away out at the coast, so I guess someone else has been driving it."

"Police, eh?" the old man chuckled. "You'd think you fellows would be a bit more organized!"

"Yes, you would," said Ames.

DARLING HEARD OXLEY go into his office, and called out, "There you are. Step in here please, Oxley."

There was the sound of a desk drawer opening and closing, and then Oxley was at Darling's door. "Sir?"

"Sit. Now that we have Taylor in custody, I'd like to be clear that we have a solid case against him. We will re-interview Mrs. Brodie, Taylor's ex, and the landlady, for a start, and I'll just have you go over again your visit with Ward to the shop where you found the shirt."

"Why?"

"I beg your pardon?"

"Why? Why do all that? We have what we need. Motive, opportunity, the best evidence I've ever seen. What jury would not convict?"

Darling sat for a moment looking at his subordinate, trying to weigh the man's sense of conviction against his own caution, but also surprised by his tone. Dismissive, Darling would have called it. He was not pleased.

"There are problems with our case, Constable, and if you had been able to keep an open mind thus far you would see them. Obvious questions around the crime scene alone might be turned into reasonable doubt in the hands of a qualified defence attorney. And so if you don't mind, I would like to look more fully at everything we have. Now then, would you be good enough to find Ward and send him up to me?" Darling knew he was being petty, making Oxley wait, sending him to fetch Ward. "Oh, and by the way, Constable Ames is back from Vancouver so will likely need his office back. We'll sort something later."

"Sir."

OXLEY STOOD IN the now-disputed office he'd been occupying and drew in a few deep breaths. He should have been more careful. The word "insubordination" repeated itself in his mind. He would much rather be in the thick of things in Ottawa, but he'd been sent out here. Insubordination was the word they'd used. He knew success here would help him get back to where he belonged. He would have to be much, much more careful. He knew he'd miscalculated in assuming that police in a small town on the other side of the country would be easy for a man like him to deal with. Ward was easy. Darling was not. He would almost admire the inspector if he weren't so angry.

WATCHING VAN EYCK'S pickup truck trundle off up the road, Ames thought again of the life of a country policeman. In Vancouver it would have been the work of a moment to find a garage and get the tyre fixed. Here a good two hours had passed. Bales didn't have tyres, but had given him a ride to the Van Eyck garage where Van Eyck's daughter, Tina, the lady mechanic, as Ames thought of her, had assessed the situation and, clucking at the incompetence of the police not having a spare, had taken the spare from the trunk of her father's car. Together they'd driven back to where his car was still listing on the side of the road.

He thought about Tina now, watching her drive off, leaving a cloud of dust. He'd met her during a previous case when a man called Carl Castle had gone missing from a nearby farm. He'd been surprised that she was a mechanic and had taken a good deal of jibing from Darling on the subject of his backward views on women. She'd been crisp and efficient, and not a little teasing on the subject of the poor preparedness of the police, and wondering aloud how they could solve crimes when they couldn't even keep their cars in order.

She had been standing looking at the flat tyre with

her hands on her hips. "If you want to be helpful, you can hand me the spanner, otherwise stay out of my way." She'd accompanied this with a dazzling smile that had quite unnerved Ames, who had had to figure out what a "spanner" might be.

"Wrench, you nincompoop. I haven't got all day." Tina had wrangled the damaged tyre off the car and had a good look at it. "This one's kaput. For one thing it's worn to nothing, and for another it's torn along the edge where this nail went in here, see?"

Ames leaned down to look at where Tina was pointing and tried to ignore the faint scent of lavender emanating from her. He saw what she was pointing at.

"I see. Well, I can put this one on. No need for you—"

"Don't be ridiculous. Just stay out of my way and hand me things," Tina said with finality. She stood up and held the damaged tyre. "I'll take this thing back and put a new tyre on it. I better have that spare back by tomorrow!"

Sighing, and trying not to think about how pretty she'd looked with her blond curly hair falling onto her forehead out of her business-like turban, and how lovely her voice was, mocking him though she had, Ames started the car and resumed his trip to King's Cove. He'd have to phone Darling from Miss Winslow's to explain about the mishap with the spare, and once he got back he'd find out who the devil had taken it out of the car in the first place.

WARD SAT IN front of Darling, thinking more about the dog, who needed a walk, than about the arrest of Taylor. So much so that he'd had to ask Darling to repeat the question. "Sorry, sir. My mind was somewhere else. The dog needs his walk, and he gets a brush down at the end of the day."

"He's earned it, finding our missing man like that. I won't keep you long. Can you just go over your visit to Taylor's repair shop again? I'm interested in particular if you went over every part of it, as I'm wanting to make sure we got every piece of evidence. At the moment, we have a missing hunting rifle, as you know. No, no," Darling added, seeing Ward's face fall. "I don't think you've been negligent, I just want to make sure we've covered the ground."

"Right, of course, sir." Ward took out his notebook. "We entered the premises at approximately two thirty. I was directed to tackle the workbench as it has a number of drawers and cupboards. It was a big job, sir. The drawers were quite deep and full of tools and the like. I could see that, if I was looking for a weapon, I would need to unpack everything to go through them properly. I decided to check the cupboards that were under the drawers first. These were full of larger objects, outboard motor hulls and parts and so on, so I could be done with those quickly and then get on with the drawers."

"And Oxley? What did he tackle?"

"He went straight for the closet. I think he mentioned later that because the shelves had fallen down when you'd been there before, he guessed that the suspect might have upset the shelves when he was hiding something there."

"Good. So you went through the cupboards and then through the drawers, but found no trace of the rifle, or anything else, is that right?"

Ward paused, looking nervously at the floor. "No, sir. Not exactly. You see Oxley found the shirt with the knife bundled into it in short order and brought it out. He was holding it with a pair of tongs and when he spread it out on the counter it was clear that there had been plenty of blood on the front of the shirt, and with the knife . . . well, we arrested Taylor and came away after that."

"So Oxley went straight for the closet, found the shirt and knife, and that was that? The rest of the shop was never searched?" Darling studiously kept a neutral face that was in direct conflict with what he was feeling.

Ward realized what they had done, or failed to do, and looked crestfallen. "That's about the size of it, sir. I'd better go back and complete the search."

"Yes, you had, and take O'Brien with you. He never gets an airing. And take the dog. You never know, he might do a better job than the two of you did. We're still looking for that rifle." Even with the dodgy behaviour of their prisoner regarding the murder weapon and the night-time visit to Brodie's camp, finding the missing rifle at Taylor's shop would really seal the thing.

When Ward had left his office, Darling chewed the end of his pencil and shook his head. He was interested in the word Ward had used, that he'd been "directed" to go look into the workbench. His thoughts on this were interrupted by the ringing of the phone. O'Brien said Ames was on the line.

"Yes, Ames, what is it?"

"I just wanted to tell you it's all taken a bit longer because I got a flat."

"Forgotten how to change a tyre, have you? How long could that take?"

"Two hours, sir, if you count the fact that the spare tyre has been removed from the car and replaced with some newfangled policing equipment. I had to get that Tina Van Eyck to come and bring me a new one. It was embarrassing standing around watching a woman change the tyre. Luckily there wasn't much traffic."

Darling hated to miss a chance to tease Ames, but he was on the alert. "What newfangled police equipment?"

"That radio transmitter thing. I should ring off. I understand from Miss Winslow that her guest could return at any moment."

WHEN HE HAD hung up, Ames went into the kitchen in the hope of finding something cold to drink. Lane motioned Ames to sit down. "Did I hear you telling the inspector that the police now have radio transmission equipment? That's frightfully modern. How will it be used?"

"Search me. It was stuffed into the wheel well instead of my spare. You should come have a look. No one told me about it, that's what's so strange. Mind you, I was dispatched here the minute I stepped into the station this afternoon."

"I'd be very interested, seeing as I'm marrying into the police."

"Oh, Miss Winslow! I should have congratulated you right away! The tyre business put it out of my mind. I could not be happier. I guess you know the inspector asked me to be his best man?"

"I certainly do, and I approve heartily. It's a sign of his quite correct regard for you."

"Oh, I wouldn't go that far."

"I would. The big question now is will you bring a guest?" Lane almost winked. The ups and downs of Ames's love life were a constant source of speculation and not a little teasing by the inspector.

AMES OPENED THE trunk and pushed aside the boots and bucket to lift the blanket off the wheel well. "See? Can you beat that?"

Lane leaned forward and put her hand on the surface of the case. "You know, I don't think I can," she said, her voice low and suddenly grave. She pulled the case out of the wheel well. "Is it locked?"

"No," Ames said. He snapped open the latches and opened it. "Look."

Lane looked, and then she closed it and settled it back into its spot and pulled the blanket over it.

"Listen carefully, Constable. Do not talk to anyone about this. Let's go back into the house. I'm going to give a quick call to the inspector, and I'm going to ask you to pick up my two deck chairs and set them up on the bottom of my lawn around the back of the house. Wait for me there."

Now more mystified than ever, Ames nodded. Her tone brooked no questions. She stopped by the phone and nodded toward the back porch where the deck chairs were set up next to a little table, and then she rang through to the exchange, with her fingers crossed.

"Ah," she said when she heard Darling's voice. "Listen."

Darling waited. There was a tone of warning he'd not heard before in that word.

"That package you sent out with Ames? It's meant to be a surprise, so don't tell anyone just yet. I'd hate like heck to ruin it." She didn't use the opportunity to tell Darling she'd been at the scene of the murder. It didn't seem to matter so much now, with this astonishing discovery in the trunk of the police car. Maybe she'd mention it to Ames and leave it at that. Who needed a dressing down from Darling just now?

OXLEY HADN'T, STRICTLY speaking, "moved in" to the office. It would be just as well, at this point, to be downstairs at one of the unused desks in the main office. He took a deep breath, pulled his few things out of the desk drawers, took his jacket and hat, and went into the hall. Darling's door was shut, and he could hear him talking in a low voice. Should he be worried? He paused, but he could not make out what the inspector was saying. Could Darling be talking to that good-looking woman of his up the lake? If that was the case, he wouldn't have to worry.

Downstairs he was surprised to see O'Brien not at his usual place. Someone else was sitting by the phone at the front desk. This person looked up at him. Oxley wished he'd done a better job remembering who everyone was.

"Is that desk over there anybody's?"

"Nope. Did you get the bum's rush because Ames is back?" the young man asked.

"Yup. Where's O'Brien?"

"Dunno. He went out with Ward and the dog."

Oxley looked up to where the keys of the car were kept, and his heart jolted. "Where are the car keys?"

"Ames took them. He said he was going up the lake. I don't know where the other ones are. You could see he was happy about it. He loves that car. Looks after it like a kid. I bet he missed it while he was out in Vancouver."

CHAPTER TWENTY-FIVE

August 1947

"**I HOPE YOU'RE NOT HERE TO** try to get out of this assignment. I told you, you're the man for the job," Oxley's supervisor said. It annoyed him to have to jimmy this one along. He should just do what he was damn well told.

"Of course not, sir," Oxley said. He had been minding his p's and q's for months, so he hoped he could be trusted again, but with this assignment he'd be out of the centre of everything.

"Well, cat got your tongue? Nothing to say on this matter?"

"No, sir. But I had hoped with what was developing here—"

"I don't know what you're making such a fuss about. You come from out there somewhere don't you? You can visit your dear old mum."

"Yes, of course, sir."

"We need someone who speaks the lingo, just in case. We need eyes and ears, understand? And if what we suspect actually transpires, we'll need a good deal more than that. Your counterpart is on the way. We've made the arrangements with the local police. Let's hop to it."

LATER, IN AN apartment in Ottawa near the Soviet embassy, two men sat over drinks, spent cigarettes filling the ashtray between them. "He's the hardest type to deal with. Smart, willing, well-trained, to be sure, but that tendency to overconfidence."

"Overconfidence you call it? It's more than that. He thinks he knows better than anyone else. He could become a danger in time. But you were maybe right to send him out on this. He can think himself in charge and he won't shy away from bold action. I hope he doesn't bungle it. Everything depends on him right now. Nevertheless, I think we would be wise to make what you people call a fallback."

"I DON'T KNOW how much I can say, Ames. No, I do know. Nothing. For one thing, I don't understand; for another, if I did, I may, nevertheless, be under an obligation."

Ames frowned. "Is this something to do with the war? That's all over, isn't it?"

"It's never all over, I'm afraid. And I couldn't say if it is anything to do with the war. I suspect not. Now then, you weren't sent out here to congratulate me on my upcoming nuptials. Darling would never countenance the waste of petrol. So why are you here?"

They were sitting at the bottom of the lawn, looking out toward the lake, and not for the first time, Ames felt himself soothed by the view, by the green around him, by the bank of

272

daisies along the edge of the garden, and he tried to imagine himself living in such a place, and as before, knew himself to be too much of a townie. This would be great for a holiday. He quickly swatted away a sudden image of himself on the lawn of a country cottage with Tina Van Eyck.

"I guess the boss told you that, while I was in Vancouver, he had me look into anything I could find about your old lady's brother. I think because of what I found, or didn't find, he's uneasy about her. I think he wants me to find out what you think. I mean, do you think there's anything fishy about her?"

Put directly like that, the question challenged Lane. Darling had told her that Ames discovered that Orlova's brother might be an MGB interrogator, and that the countess perhaps did not go around looking for him in Vancouver as she had suggested she had. On the surface these discoveries appeared to be in contradiction to what Orlova was saying about herself, and Lane could not shake the idea that disparate things were beginning to add up to there being something wrong about her guest.

She would expect someone in Orlova's position to be evasive. She'd known nothing but repression and persecution under the Soviets, so she would have adopted evasion as a necessary shield to protect herself. The MGB brother, for example, perhaps had fled the country, having found his own situation untenable. Madam Orlova could have feared exposure and instigated her own search for her brother in Vancouver. But that left one question still hanging: if she had spoken to no one, how would she have learned that he might have come here? And now . . .

"I don't really know how to answer that question, if I'm honest with you. I would have told you that even with your information from Vancouver, I could well imagine someone in her situation, a refugee who is fearful for her life, might well behave exactly in that way: evasive, untruthful even."

"So you don't have any doubts about her?" Ames asked.

"No. I'm not saying that exactly. I am beginning to have questions, certainly. But I'm not completely sure that they add up to her being sinister in any way. Except, I suppose, that she said someone told her the brother had come out this way, to Nelson. What you're saying contradicts that."

"Not necessarily. I went directly to the two churches in Vancouver to talk to their priests. She could have talked to someone else altogether."

"That's true, I suppose. Ah! Madam! You are back." Lane had seen Orlova coming around from the front of the house holding a portfolio. She continued in Russian. "Look, this is the young man who is going to be the best man for Inspector Darling at the wedding. He has been away getting his sergeant's qualifications."

Ames leaped out of the chair he was in, impressed as always by hearing Miss Winslow launch into another language as if it were her mother tongue. He bowed slightly at the minute old lady and offered his hand. He had to admit, she did look absolutely harmless. She said something, smiling, and Ames nodded, mystified.

"She says you are a most handsome man and that the inspector chose well. Now listen, I'm going in to get something for us all to drink. You entertain Countess Orlova and I'll be right back."

"Oh, hey . . ." Ames said, raising his hand in protest, but Lane was already halfway across the lawn. He smiled again at Countess Orlova and waited for her to sit down, and then sat down himself, wondering if this day could get any stranger or more difficult.

In the kitchen, Lane pulled the iced tea she had made from the fridge and put it on the table, and then stopped and leaned on the table with both hands. It was no good. Things were not all right with Orlova. She moved to the window and looked down toward where Ames and the old lady were sitting.

Orlova seemed to have taken the lead and was showing Ames her watercolours. He was nodding and smiling, looking like he genuinely admired them. Lane gave a slight smile. A little culture would do him good. Then she darted, her heart pounding, toward Orlova's room.

APTEKAR WALKED INTO town pulling up the collar of his jacket. He watched people bustling on the street, cars going by, could hear the whistle of the train, could see the traffic on the lake. The September sun threw a light that was reflected back on the few leaves that were beginning to turn. We always think seasons are beginnings, he thought. Autumn, we go back to school. Winter, we begin with new resolutions. Spring, we clean to welcome the new world. Summer is the beginning of rest. For him, any of these now could be a time to die.

He walked down to the edge of the lake and sat on a bench and tried to calculate his risk. He was certain that if there was to be trouble, he was the cause of it. Both the British and the Soviets knew of his connection to Lane Winslow. He was sure they would have sent someone. The British, perhaps, to warn her. They had someone in Vancouver, he was sure. But the Soviets, they could have someone on the ground already, and they would send someone he didn't know.

He had to see her. To place the names in her hand, and maybe even, but here he laughed grimly, seek asylum in Canada. He was no fool. That would not be the outcome. Pulling down his hat, he walked up the hill to the post office. The man at the motel had told him where it was. He had seemed surprised that someone as scruffy as this man had something to mail. "I can post it for you," he'd offered.

"Thank you. I will go. I need some exercise."

"It's going to be a couple of miles," the man had warned.

"I can manage. Thank you."

"Suit yourself." The man had shrugged. Old guy like that. Bound to keel over with a heart attack. Good thing he'd prepaid.

Aptekar watched the letter thrown into a bag that was going out in the afternoon mail. He would wait.

HER HEART POUNDING, Lane turned the doorknob and pushed gently on the door. How had she never noticed the squealing of the hinges? She stopped and looked behind her and then slipped into the room. Orlova had pulled the curtains, throwing the room into a green shade. She could hear, through the open window, Orlova talking slowly and loudly outside, and she took a relieved breath. Poor Ames! There would be silence any moment as both gave up the unequal battle with mutual incomprehension.

Under the bed there were the two suitcases her guest had come with. Orlova had put her cloth bag with the painting supplies on her dressing table. Lane thought she knew for certain now that when Orlova was out with the suitcase, she was not out painting. She dropped to her knees and gently moved each suitcase and then selected the one that seemed full and pulled it forward. It was very similar to the one she had seen in the car. She snapped the latches and they sprang up, making a noise, she thought, like a saucepan falling, so loud did it seem.

Inside Lane saw what she'd expected to see, what she'd dreaded. Very familiar transmission equipment. She sat back staring at the dials, the neatly folded wires. These had a range of what, fifty miles? More than enough for Nelson, but in this mountainous country probably not much more. Even then, she would probably have had to take the equipment to higher ground. Lane could see herself again as if it were yesterday working with the communications people in France, demonstrating the equipment, dialling in frequency, hearing the often-muffled reply from a distant machine, the squeak and buzz of electrical interference.

Lane snapped out of her memory with a jolt. What she heard now was complete silence coming in the window. Ames and her guest were no longer talking. With a massive effort of will she stilled the sudden racing of her heart—how had she ever done this during the war? Willing her hands to be steady, she pressed the lid closed and snapped the latches into place. She could hear footsteps coming up the stairs of the porch. Praying that Ames would find a way to detain Orlova, something that would be a fortunate accident since he did not know she was skulking about in her guest's room, she pushed the suitcase under the desk, slipped out the door, closing it with her breath held, and ran on tiptoes into her own room.

She opened a drawer—she would use the pretence of needing a sweater—and looked into it, seeing nothing but the dials on the transmitter. She could hear Orlova coming up the hall, going into her own room. She lunged at a blue cardigan, her movements jerky with panic. What if Orlova had left the suitcases in a certain alignment? She would know instantly. It meant that her guest was a spy, a trained operative. That her "accidental" placement with Lane was deliberate. No, she told herself. Calm down. The radio certainly meant something like that, but no need to add the panic that she had taken the precaution of positioning her things in a manner that would allow her to detect if anyone had been in her room. After all, she had not locked the suitcase, so she must still think herself safe and undetected.

This thought calmed Lane considerably. She put back the blue cardigan, closed the drawer firmly, and took up her usual green one from where she had tossed it on the chair. Coming out of the room she saw that Orlova's door was ajar, and she could hear her moving about. She turned down the hall toward the sitting room, saying as casually and cheerfully as she could, "I've put out the iced tea, and now I'm wondering if it's the right thing. I can definitely feel that fall chill in the air."

Ames, who had been standing at the window looking at a picture, turned. "I know what you mean. That's why we came in. Look, she's given me this."

He handed Lane the watercolour. It was of the lake from, she guessed, the top of her north field, right near the fence that separated her property from Robin Harris's. It was lovely. Masquerading she may be, Lane thought, but she was a damn good artist.

"Well, lucky you! You'd better get it to the framer as soon as you get back."

"My mom will love it. We don't have any real art in the house."

CHAPTER TWENTY-SIX

L ANE HAD NOT SLEPT WELL. Knowing what she now knew, she wondered about staying in the house at all, but claiming suddenly that she had to go up to town for the night would tip her hand. It would suggest she thought herself in danger and clearly Orlova, as dishonest as she was, did not pose any actual danger. She was wracked with indecision, though. Should she confront her guest? Or sneak off to town to see Darling? By the time her bedside clock read three in the morning, she had decided the better part of valour was to go to Darling. She thought she knew why Orlova was here, though she resisted the notion with every part of her being.

She woke with a jolt at seven, a new thought filling her with a visceral fear. There was something about the suitcase. Then the glance she had seen of the dead Brodie as they had loaded him into the van came to her memory, but then, as she became fully awake, she shook her head and smiled grimly. Things were bad enough. No point in absolute hysteria. Brodie's murderer had been arrested, and in spite of Cassie Brodie's protestation Lane trusted that Darling must think the evidence against Brodie was strong enough to warrant the arrest.

She put a compressed hot washcloth on her eyes to soothe them, and then went back to her room to dress. This was out of the norm, a sign of her sudden caution. Normally she padded to the kitchen in her slippers and bathrobe to make coffee or tea, whatever her mood dictated that day. Today it was tea, strong, lots of sugar, as if she were treating herself for shock. It would suit her guest, too, strong black tea, she thought with a touch of annoyance. Very Russian.

Relieved that the countess seemed not to be stirring, Lane took her tea onto the porch. The mornings were increasingly chilly, so she put on her thick green sweater. She couldn't bear to be in the house just now. She walked to the railing and put her cup of tea on it, and then moved her deck chair so that it was at the outer corner of the porch, where she could turn to see the lake without having her back to the house.

Now then. Time to be practical. She held her cup with both hands to warm them and drank her tea. What she could know for sure was that Ames had found a radio transmission device in the car where the spare tyre should be. First question: who used that car while he was away? Or maybe the first should be, were the police instituting some new equipment? They ought to, they were jolly useful, as she knew only too well. She had trained people in occupied France to use a version of these transmitters that had been developed in Britain.

The other thing she knew was that Countess Orlova, her innocent dear old thing, had one as well. She had seen it. Lane's mind wandered back to the tension of trying to carry on as if last night were a normal evening. The supper together, the nightcap, the goodnights, her own long sleepless night.

One obvious conclusion, however implausible, was that Orlova was communicating with someone right inside the police force. If that was the case, Darling had to be warned. She wished now she'd said something to Ames as he'd left, a warning to Darling, maybe.

A second, less mystifying conclusion was that the transmitter in the police car was genuine equipment that Ames, recently back, simply had not been briefed on, and Orlova was in contact with someone else. This one made more sense, though here, on a beautiful peaceful morning in out-of-the-way King's Cove, it seemed almost impossible. But Lane herself had been warned by the British consul, Hunt, that a Russian spy might be on the run, and might turn up here.

Her first thought had been that Orlova was here to watch for Aptekar, but if so, to what purpose? What did Aptekar have that they would want so badly? Hunt had said Aptekar had never turned up at the meeting place. She was certain from her last interaction with Aptekar in Berlin that he was absolutely genuine in wanting to defect. She had believed him when he told her that he intended to retire from the whole game. She saw that this had led her to think, perhaps mistakenly, that he was being pushed out, and no longer had a serious role to play. The world order had changed, and fresh new people would be on the job. But maybe he did have something important that both sides wanted.

A more worrisome question, perhaps, was how had he been betrayed? No one could have known his plans to go to the Yugoslav border, unless he'd been followed. No, Hunt had said he never even arrived there. Something had gone wrong earlier.

Lane looked at her watch. It was nearing eight on a Thursday. The sternwheeler would be coming in with supplies and mail. Kenny would drive his truck down to meet it in another hour. She wanted desperately to go to the Armstrongs' where she would phone Darling. The idea that among Orlova's deceptions was that she spoke English after all, loomed larger. She no longer trusted that Orlova might not understand her phone calls. But she could not do anything to arouse her guest's suspicions. She would have to wait, carry on with the morning routines.

Everything became a matter of suspicion. Why had Orlova's plans for a room in town fallen through? Was it coincidence, or had it somehow been engineered so that she would have to stay here, with Lane, waiting, as Lane now guessed, for Aptekar.

The French door opened, and Orlova came out, pulling her black sweater around her. "Good morning, my dear. What a lover of the fresh air you must be! It is quite chilly."

"Ah, Countess. Good morning. Let me put the water on. I am having tea today. I know, it is cooler. I think I am clinging to the idea that if the sun is shining it is still summer. The winter will close in soon enough!" Lane got up, smiling. "Did you sleep well?"

"Very, as always. I am thinking today that I will paint something more wild and natural. Perhaps it is this feeling of the autumn. It is so elemental, is it not? I have certainly done justice to the gardens, so I think I may leave them."

Inside, Lane filled the kettle again and put it on the stove. "Constable Ames seemed delighted with his picture. It was so kind of you to give it to him. He told me his mother would be thrilled."

Madam Orlova sat at the table and folded her hands. She smiled at Lane. "He reminded me of someone I used to know. Tall, young, handsome. So long ago. A story from another life."

Lane poured water over the tea leaves.

"How romantic. Can you tell me about it?" She glanced at the clock. *And could your story last another hour?* she wondered hopefully.

"It is nothing really, when I think about it. He was a young man in the military. I met him at a perfectly dreary ball my parents threw. He was not like the other men my parents thrust at me. He was intelligent, surprising, even. I was already engaged to one of those bores, but my fiancé was away that night at his father's estate. The young officer had that clear-eyed, almost innocent look of your young policeman."

Orlova put sugar into her cup and poured the tea over it and stirred. "I took him as my lover, of course, and then pushed my parents to bring my marriage forward, for the obvious reason. I pretended I could not be separated from Orlov for another minute. Orlov was a good man, dull as the others sadly, and he fell afoul of the authorities after the revolution. My child died of diphtheria. I decided I must get out, together with my brother. There."

Your brother, the ferocious MGB interrogator, Lane thought. "You never saw the young man again?"

"No. It is better that way. I never had to tell him he had a little girl who died, and I can keep forever the memory of him as he was when I first met him. Did you never have an unhappy love affair? Someone like you, so beautiful, in all the chaos of the war?"

Uncannily like what did happen, Lane thought, but she shook her head.

"There was someone I thought I might have loved once, but it was short-lived, and I was very busy during the war. Men were very flighty creatures then, and I was young. Now, well, there is the inspector." She got up and took a loaf of bread from her breadbox and put a frying pan on the stove. "Now, what do you say to a little breakfast? You're going to need it if you are going farther afield today. And I'd better get a start in the orchard or my neighbour will be very cross with me."

"You are very, very lucky. I wonder if you know how fortunate, to find real love."

"I do," said Lane. "I do, indeed."

AT THE POST office Lane leaned against the counter. She knew the mail, having just arrived, would still be in the canvas bag it travelled in, but she had to get to a phone she could trust slightly more than her own.

"You look all in, and it's barely nine in the morning," Eleanor said. Alexandra barked helpfully from the floor by Eleanor's feet. The postmistress leaned over and picked up the puppy and pushed her through the window. "Here, you can cheer up our Miss Winslow. So what's the matter, dearie?" she said when the dog transfer was completed.

Lane, under a barrage of cheerful licking and sniffing, said, "Something odd has come up. I didn't sleep a wink, I'm afraid. I've come over pretending to get the mail, but I really need to use your phone to call Darling."

"Nothing that will jeopardize the wedding, I hope?"

"No, no. Nothing like that."

"Anyway, you won't need to pretend about the mail. I had just fished this out of the bag before you came. A beautiful hand!" Eleanor handed the letter through to Lane, who had become preoccupied with socializing with the puppy. "You'd better come around to the kitchen," Eleanor said.

Lane put Alexandra down and went out of the post office and into the kitchen. Kenny Armstrong was pushing some wood into the stove. "A sight for sore eyes," he said by way of greeting. "I've got the kettle on."

"She can't be fussing around with cups of tea. She needs to use *our* telephone," Eleanor said, emphasizing the word "our" in a conspiratorial way.

Kenny looked pleased by the sudden mysterious turn in the conversation. "You don't say? I better show you through."

The Armstrongs' phone sat on a tiny table just inside the sitting room. It was certainly not the ancient trumpet model that Lane had in her hallway, but it, too, was old and dated from the mid-twenties. After Kenny had dialled through to the exchange in Balfour, Lane took up the instrument and asked for the Nelson Police Department, knowing full well that Lucy, the girl who worked the exchange out of the Balfour store, would no doubt go on a mad spiral of speculation about whether Lane was involved in another crime, or if this was the continuation of what she liked to tell her friends was the romance of the century.

While she waited, Lane looked at her letter and, with a gasp, realized that she was holding a missive from Stanimir Aptekar, franked at the post office in Nelson the afternoon before.

Lane stood in the sitting room, looking unseeing through the window while she waited to be put through. Finally, she heard Sergeant O'Brien.

"Nelson Police, O'Brien here."

"Good morning, Sergeant. Is the inspector alone? It's Miss Winslow. Please don't say my name out loud, just put me through to him if he's alone."

Darling picked up the phone. He'd been puzzling about their failure to find Brodie's hunting rifle, either at the scene or in Taylor's shop. But he was also puzzled by the knife. Anyone with brains would have tossed a knife in the lake, or hurled it far into the bush. Why keep it with the bloodied shirt? He was in the process of going through the murder in his mind and was mentally following the murderer out of the forest to his car. They hadn't searched his car.

"Yes?"

"Is Ames with you, sir?" O'Brien had already established that the recent occupant of Darling's office, Oxley, was even now at the corner desk on the main floor, trying to pull open the bottom drawer, which always stuck, which is why the desk was never used.

"No, Sergeant, he's not. If you wanted him why didn't you ring through to him?"

"One moment, sir."

"Inspector, darling. It's me. Are you alone?"

"Not you too. What's going on?"

"I'm at the Armstrongs', using their telephone. I've called to say you're right. There's something very wrong with the countess. She has the companion piece to the radio found in the back of your police car."

Darling had not been expecting this. So much so that he found he couldn't make sense of it at all. "Wait." Then Darling glanced at his office door. It was ajar. "Don't go away, I'm going to shut the door."

Lane waited, her brain whirring, following radio signals between King's Cove and Nelson, then where? In a bewildering moment she imagined Angus Dunn, picking up his phone, catching the signal that had crossed the country, crossed the Atlantic.

"Okay, now start again. Your countess has the same radio equipment as that from the back of the car."

"Yes."

"No. I still don't understand. Are you suggesting that she is in touch for some reason with a member of this force? She doesn't even speak English."

"Who's been driving that car since Ames has been away? Oxley. A recent member of your force. Where did he come from, again?"

Frowning, he tried desperately to fit two completely unmatched pieces of a puzzle together.

"Ontario somewhere. But why in God's name would they have to be in secret radio contact?"

He'd bloody well better find out where Oxley had come from, he thought, and if he spoke Russian.

Lane was silent for a moment, looking down, as puzzled as he was. She had put the letter she'd received on the telephone table, and her eyes lit on it now. She tucked the receiver between her shoulder and her ear.

"Just wait," she said. She pushed her thumb along the edge of the envelope and pulled out a single note-sized piece of paper.

I will take the boat on Saturday to King's Cove. Meet me at the landing. SA

"Oh," Lane said.

"'Oh' what?" Darling asked.

"I thought I might know why she's here. I think it's confirmed. It doesn't explain Oxley. But it explains, well, that's the trouble. I don't think I can say."

"You don't think you can say? You don't think you can say? I have some sort of interloper on my police force and you've got, whatever the hell she is, and you can't say?"

"Darling, try not to be upset. I need to think."

"No!"

"No what?"

"No, I will not try not to be upset. This is ridiculous. Outrageous, even. Is this your stinking Official Secrets Act rearing its head again? Because it's intolerable."

"Look, I understand why you're angry. I just—"

"Do you?" Darling interrupted. "Well, that's just splendid. We should get along like a house on fire! Maybe we should get married."

"I was going to say, I just need to think through this. You should try to find out about Oxley. Where he comes from. All I can tell you is that he's here on purpose. And I suspect he's here for the same reason she is. I'm not sure why they are in contact with each other. I need to make another phone call. I promise I'll call you back and tell you everything I can. Look, there's nothing I can do to change this right now. You have to trust me."

It sounded weak, even to her.

A sarcastic remark struggled for utterance in Darling, but it came to him that this was the moment, really. The true test. He knew she had a past. He knew she was obliged to keep secrets. He knew that if their life together was to work, he would have to trust her. Did he trust her? He knew in his heart of hearts that he did.

"I do," he said simply. "But you understand that this may be directly impacting my force here, and possibly even my current murder investigation since Oxley has been part of it. So, step on it, would you?"

"Oh, by the way," Lane said, trying to make it sound as casual as possible, "what was Raymond Brodie wearing?"

Frowning, Darling stared at the receiver. The complete change in tone threw him. "What do you mean?"

"I mean, was he wearing anything brown?" Lane paused. "Only when I was up at the site where you found him, there appeared to be a tiny scrap of brown cloth."

Lane saw the cloth in her mind's eye, suddenly, and didn't continue.

Darling was rendered almost, but not quite, speechless. "Come again?"

She toyed with mounting a defence, and then thought, hang it, I'm free to do what I want, after all, and so she tried a more direct tack.

"You're not intrigued by the possible evidence I found?"

"I am, as a matter of fact. I'm intrigued that my eager beaver Oxley didn't see it, but then again, it turns out he's maybe not a real policeman. I am more intrigued by what the devil makes you want to go and nose around a crime scene. I mean it, Lane, I genuinely don't understand. And it makes me worry, and worry makes me angry. How are you to be kept safe when you carry on like this?"

Lane thought for a moment. "Do you think it is your job to keep me safe?"

"I'm marrying you. Isn't that one of the manly tasks?"

"I don't see why. Who kept me safe before? Why should marrying me add to the burden of your tasks in life?"

"It's what you imagine, isn't it? The strong man protecting and feeding his family."

"Is that what we're doing?" Lane asked, with a ping of anxiety. "I don't have any experience with the sort of man you're describing. My father was hardly around. I always thought it was our cook who protected and fed us. I'm a little afraid that you are going to feel obliged to make yourself into that sort of man. I don't think it would be good for us, do you? How would your feelings about me change if you had to become some sort of protector?"

Darling sighed. She was right. What they had together right now was based on two full people coming together, interested in each other, independent, in love. The very thing he must have fallen in love with in the first place. He'd thought marriage would simply bring them together without changing that beautiful balance, but now he could see that somehow their being married, combined with his absolutely understandable, as he saw it, anxiety about her safety, was adding up to something else. Unmarried he would be anxious and frustrated, yes, but married he might become anxious and controlling. This would fundamentally change how he felt about her.

"My God," he said quietly. "You are, annoyingly, right. I almost feel a little ashamed, but it's a dilemma. How can I stop worrying if you are going to continue to, well, be you? I think I must be allowed to worry, as part of the bargain."

"Yes, I think I can allow that. It is your worry, after all. I have no right to it. And I must be allowed, as you so succinctly put it, to be me. A fair bargain?"

"A fair bargain," he said. "The poor vicar. He missed the boat entirely. This is what we should have been hashing out in his claustrophobic office."

"Should we tell him? He can get to work on it with his other couples. 'How marriage may make you into completely different people and change how you feel about each other.'"

"It would stop people wanting to marry altogether. He'd be out of business," Darling said. "And along those lines, do you still want to marry me?"

She smiled. "I do," she said.

"I'm relieved. I expect Lorenzo is already planning the cake."

"Oh," Lane said. "Sorry, did you tell me that the dead man wore brown? Only I just suddenly thought of something."

"I didn't, no, and he wasn't. Now what?"

"You know what, darling, it's all right. I'll call you back. I have to check something. No point in creating anxiety for no reason."

Lane put the receiver back onto the phone and took a deep breath. She may have saved herself a dressing down from Darling, but what she realized was much more grave.

WHEN HE PUT down the receiver, Darling counted to ten, determined to keep his focus, and then went to the door, opened it, and shouted.

"Ames!"

OXLEY DID NOT panic when he learned the car had gone. He could feel his face go opaque, expressionless with steely thought. It could not be long now, anyway, he thought. He tried not to race ahead to the conclusion.

CHAPTER TWENTY-SEVEN

Three weeks earlier

"LOOK HERE, OXLEY, THERE'S NO getting around the fact that you've blotted your copybook here with your insubordination, but you're a good agent. You can make everything right with this, do you hear? I know you're not happy about it, but this is extremely important. There's a good indication that a Russian agent is defecting, and he has the information we need to prevent another absolute debacle like we had with Gouzenko. There's a good chance he knows every traitor still loose in this country. He was meant to defect to England, but the Soviets may have got wind of it. He apparently has some connection with an ex-British agent living in, God help us, British Columbia, and word is he might try to find her. You're to go there and collect him and get him safely back to us. Is that clear? And I think at this point a brisk 'yes, sir' is all we want from you."

"Yes, sir."

"AMES, I WANT you to take over the Brodie business. I need to deal with Oxley."

Ames shifted his weight subtly where he stood in the doorway of Darling's office. "If I may, sir."

"Yes, what is it?" First Lane, now Ames.

"Well, I wonder," he said, slipping all the way into Darling's office and shutting the door. "I wonder if I should cozy up to Oxley. Take him to the bar, see if I can find anything out from his end. He strikes me, I don't know, as a little full of himself. I wonder if he'd slip up a bit if I expressed some admiration or envy for his big city background."

Darling considered this.

"Yes, all right. You can take him to the bar after you meet with him, Ward, and O'Brien to find out where we are. Play dumb, you've been away, et cetera. And try to get a feel for where we are. I have a sense Ward has some misgivings about the original search of Taylor's shop. I don't think there's any question we've got the right man, but I don't like loose ends. I can't make out why a killer wouldn't get rid of the weapon—or the shirt, for that matter. When you've finished, you and O'Brien re-interview Taylor. Maybe he'll be less cowed with a nice fellow like you."

"Very funny, sir." Ames started for the door. "Can I put the tab at the bar on account?"

"Get out, Ames," Darling said. It was good to have Ames back.

With Ames gone, Darling opened his desk drawer to find the letter that had accompanied the assignment of Oxley to the Nelson Police station. It annoyed him that he himself had just rubber stamped it without any real concern simply because he was short a man and too focused on his own personal business.

Having found the letter, he reached for his phone and then stopped. Perhaps it was the example of Lane going to the Armstrongs' to use a safer phone than her own might be, or that his own distrust of Oxley had reached alarming proportions. And there was the elephant in the room. That damn radio. It felt artificial to pretend he didn't know about it, but he knew he'd best wait on Lane. Taking up his jacket and hat, he went downstairs. He expected O'Brien to be manning the desk, but of course, he'd sent Ames off to meet with him.

"Back in an hour," he said to the quite new Constable Terrell, temporarily assigned to the front desk. He was the first black man to join the Nelson police force, and Darling thought he might make a good addition. He was quiet and efficient, and Darling suspected, better educated than most of the men.

Just as he opened the door, he looked back into the room. The meeting room door was closed, and there was no sign of Oxley. He glanced at the nail where the car keys usually hung. They were gone. Now what was he up to?

"Constable, do you know what's happened to Oxley?"

Terrell looked at a list in front of him. "Yes, sir. He's gone out on a complaint from a motel owner just outside of town about some derelict who might not pay his bill."

"Not a police matter just yet, surely?"

"I know, sir. But Officer Oxley said that the man seemed really agitated, and he thought it best to just go out and calm him down and prevent some sort of brouhaha."

"Quite right. Thank you, Constable Terrell."

APTEKAR WAS FINDING his stay at the Easy Two Motel a strain. There was a kind of sordid hopelessness about the small room with its single-bulb lighting and the empty parking lot indicating next to no visitors in spite of the cheerful sign advertising fishing and boating. Most people travelling to town simply stayed in town, he assumed. Perhaps this place was for summer holiday makers. To keep alert, he had instituted daily walks down to the lake, more of a river here, and along the road used to service the power station nearby.

This time he'd gone the other way, to a small general store to pick up a loaf of bread and a can of spam. Nothing that required cooking. He was climbing up the path toward the road. The motel, on the opposite side, had just become visible, when he saw a car pull up and park in front of the last room.

Aptekar stopped, almost holding his breath. A man in a police uniform got out and looked up and down the length of the building and then began to walk slowly past each room looking into each window, cupping his hands around his face to block out the light. He watched until the man went into the office. The police. What did this mean? The motel owner must have called them. Why? He'd been paying as he went. A day later and it wouldn't have mattered. Well. He wouldn't have to stay in that miserable room another night.

"NO, YOU WERE right to call," Oxley said. "Can I have a look at his room?"

"I guess so. I didn't think anyone would come out. I just wanted to know what my recourse was if he didn't pay. I mean he's paid so far, by the day, but he is a foreigner, and looks hard up and—"

"Listen, you had a good natural instinct to call us. Maybe he's been paying, but what is he doing here? He's not on his way somewhere like a good honest citizen would be, is he? He doesn't have a car, he doesn't appear to have any plans to go anywhere, isn't that what you said?"

"I guess there'd be no harm in it."

The owner led Oxley out of the office and they walked along the gravel driveway to the third room. "This is the room."

"Well, open it!" Oxley said with impatient sarcasm. "I don't have all day."

The owner fitted in the key, turned the lock, and pushed open the door. He was surprised by what he saw, and his misgivings about his own action in calling the police in the first place reached new heights. The bed had been neatly made, a small leather hold-all sat closed on the one chair, and two cans of beans were lined up neatly on the dresser. A can opener and a clean spoon lay beside them. He'd been worried that he might see a vagrant's room: full of garbage, smelling of dirty clothes, cigarettes, towels on the floor.

"You know, I think it's going to be all right. I don't think we should be in here." He started to back out the door.

"You run along. I won't be a moment," Oxley said dismissively. He already had the hold-all in his hand, and he turned it over, dumping the contents on the bed.

The motel owner stood a moment, uncertain what to do, and then went outside. His one concession to his sudden unease was to stay outside the door and not return to his office.

Oxley looked through the small pile of clothes, checking the pockets of the shirts and the one extra pair of pants, feeling the inside of the hold-all for a lining that was loose or someplace papers could be hidden. Annoyed, he left bag and clothes in a tumble on the bed and checked the bathroom. Toothbrush, comb, and toothpowder lined neatly behind the taps on the sink. He went back into the bedroom and pulled open all of the drawers in the dresser. They were empty. Frustrated now, he went outside and was startled by the manager leaning against the wall right outside the door.

"You call me the minute he comes back. Same number, but you ask for me, do you understand?" Oxley turned and walked back down the parking lot to the car and slammed the door. In the next moment he was out of the car and striding back toward the owner, who was tentatively locking the door of the room. "Listen. This man is a wanted man. This is as close as we've got to him. Don't approach him, don't talk to him. He's dangerous, and I expect he's armed. Just call, right?"

At this the owner looked anxiously up and down what suddenly seemed to him to be a lonely stretch of road, and at the looming bank of trees between the motel and the lake.

"Dangerous? No one said . . . okay. Yes. I'll call."

"Good fellow." Oxley gave the owner a slap on the shoulder and returned to his car.

Remembering about the letter, the owner hurried after the policeman. Oxley impatiently rolled down the car window.

"What is it?"

"Just that he asked me about the post office, day before yesterday. Said he had a letter to mail. I offered to send it, but he said the walk would do him good."

"Did you see the letter?"

"Well, no. But that's what he said. I did see him go off down the road toward town."

"Good man. That's helpful."

The owner watched the car peel out of the driveway and turn in the direction of Nelson, and then he hurried back to the office. It was just beginning to dawn on him that he would have to stay by his window watching for the return of the man who had been, he reflected now, foreign after all, and far too polite. He had been right to suspect he was up to something. He was glad now he'd phoned the police. He went into the small garage at the back of his own living quarters and pulled out his hunting rifle and a box of cartridges. No harm in having these close by while he waited.

Aptekar watched all the coming and going from his vantage point across the road, and wished he was close enough to hear what was being said. He sat down, facing the lake below and sighed. He'd be sleeping al fresco tonight.

"MR. HUNT. YOU'RE a hard man to get hold of," Lane said. She was sitting in the Armstrong parlour. She had waited to be connected to the British consular office in Vancouver for a considerable time, and then more time was expended waiting for Hunt to be tracked down. She had spent the nearly half hour looking at the titles in the bookshelf opposite from where she was sitting. "This is Lane Winslow."

"Miss Winslow," Hunt said, unable to hide the slight lilt of surprise in his voice. "I hadn't expected to hear from you. I can only assume this means our man has turned up."

"No, he hasn't. But something else has, and I thought you ought to know. Or alternatively, I thought you could explain." For reasons she wasn't quite sure of, she did not tell Hunt about her note from Aptekar. She would, she reassured herself, but not yet.

"Are you calling from your own phone?"

Lane suppressed an impatient sigh. "No, Mr. Hunt, I am not. Now can I get on with it?" Lane experienced only a slight frisson of guilt at her knowledge that Lucy, the exchange girl in Balfour, could well be listening in. But she wouldn't be able to make hide nor hair of their conversation, Lane reassured herself. Anyway, there must be times when Lucy did her nails or drank coffee and didn't pay attention to other people's phone calls.

"Yes, go on."

"If you are waiting for this man, Stanimir Aptekar, to turn up, you may not be alone. I suspect my Russian visitor might be too, and there's a policeman called Oxley, I don't know his Christian name, who has been recently assigned to the Nelson police force, who may be as well."

There was a moment's silence on the line. "Why do you think this?"

"Because they are both equipped with radio transmitters. It strains all credulity that this would not be a coincidence."

"I see."

"Well, I don't."

As Lane had contemplated this state of affairs, she had mentally run through the options. It was possible that Orlova and Oxley were either agents of the Soviets, or precautions put in place by the British. Hunt's sudden caginess made the latter suspicion take centre stage. "I suppose they are something to do with you? Of course, they are. How else would you have known I had a guest or that I was getting married?"

Another long silence. "Look, Miss Winslow—

"I am looking, Mr. Hunt. In fact, it was my looking that led to me finding the radio my guest has no doubt been using up in the bush somewhere, and the police have discovered a matching radio they are certain belongs to Oxley. I cautioned them to say nothing until I could ascertain what might be going on. I'm familiar with this equipment. I know exactly what kind of range it has and how to use it. But I expect you spent the war behind a desk."

This was uncalled for, she knew, but her ire at the circumlocutions of her former employers brought up memories.

On the other end of the line, Hunt was considering what would be for the best. If he didn't tell her, she and the police would continue mucking about and no doubt destroy their one chance to get hold of Aptekar. He had trusted what she presented when they had spoken by the lake, but the director seemed to be ambivalent about her and had implied she might not be trustworthy. He too, in that moment, suppressed a sigh at the infernal compartmentalizing and secrecy of the agency. If he did tell her, could he trust that she had been a good enough agent to do as she was told?

"Mr. Hunt," Lane said wearily into the phone. "There's no point in all this secrecy. I've had a note from Aptekar with a suggested meeting place tomorrow. If these are your agents, then I'd better know; if they are not, he is in danger. You were right that he would seek me out, though I don't know why he has, but I'm certain you will agree with me that he needs protection."

"Oxley is that protection. He's one of ours. You need to tell him about the meeting."

"There. Was that so hard?"

"You are an unknown quantity, Miss Winslow."

"You have no idea. And the countess?"

"Countess?"

"My Russian guest, Orlova."

"Oxley is running her. She is there as failsafe. In case Aptekar turned up directly to you, she was to contact him. This isn't a game, Miss Winslow. You must contact Oxley immediately with the details of the meeting. In fact, give them to me now."

Hunt's anxiety about Winslow had increased with every question she asked. Was she working with the Russians? Had she even been planning to tell him about Aptekar's note? Still. She had. And the director had been absolutely clear in his instructions: Aptekar was to be turned over to Oxley.

Lane looked at the note in her hand. Aptekar had said "tell no one." He had said he would meet her off the steamer that would dock at King's Cove on Saturday at around noon. Did "no one" include the man who was sent to collect him and keep him safe? Safe from whom? He had clearly been spirited away by the Soviets when he was supposed to meet the British near the Yugoslav border. He had escaped somehow and had made his way here, a journey that must have been harrowing and dangerous. He was feeling vulnerable and untrusting of anyone. Would it be a betrayal to tell Hunt his plans? She, on her own, would not be able to keep him safe if there were Soviet agents looking for him. If she told Hunt the details, he would contact Oxley. Would Oxley then tell Orlova? There would be no point. Orlova was only there as an extra set of eyes. Oxley could swoop in, collect Aptekar, and get him back to England. It seemed unlikely to her that he would involve her. But they were all unknown quantities, weren't they? Except possibly Hunt. He was the perfect British bureaucrat. The problem with him, she thought, is that he is being directed by Dunn, and *he* was an altogether too well-known quantity.

"I'll let you know, Mr. Hunt." Lane put the phone down and realized she was almost shaking. It had been a decision that came quite unbidden, surprising even her. But she knew it was right. And so was the next thing she would do.

CHAPTER TWENTY-EIGHT

"**YOU'RE BEING A CONFOUNDED NUISANCE,** Darling." The man on the other end of the phone was in Ottawa. The line crackled.

"It's my police station. I'm responsible for the men in it. I have every right to be as much of a nuisance as I want if someone has been planted here for some purpose about which I know nothing."

"He's a trained policeman."

"With a communication device he has been keeping secret from all of us, hampering the work of the department, as a matter of fact, since he replaced the spare tyre with it."

"Look, I'd like to tell you. I can't."

"Good. Well my usual man is back, so I can return yours to you. I'll go down to the station and dismiss him. My man can take over the murder investigation we've got going."

"Don't be an ass, Darling. You're making heavy weather of this. You can't send him back. If you must know, he's in the middle of an investigation for us. It's a matter of national security. There, I've said it."

Darling looked out his living room window at the peaceful city of Nelson lying below him in the golden light and sharp shadows of the autumn sun. Any place less likely to be in the grip of a national security crisis he could not imagine.

"Well, that covers a multitude of sins. Imminent Soviet invasion is it?"

"Look, just trust me. Leave Oxley in place. He's one of ours. He has a job to do—when he's done it, he'll be out of your hair. All I can tell you is that he is after an asset, and when he's collected him, he'll be done."

"Second time today I've been asked to just trust someone. I'm finding it difficult, I must say. I'm a veteran and the highest-ranked policeman in this district. How about someone trusting me for a change? Where is this asset to be collected?"

"Really, Inspector. I can't have you bumbling around making a mess of things. Just leave it, will you?"

"Only I'm wondering, will you be collecting that asset at the home of Miss Lane Winslow?"

The silence at the end of the line seemed to stretch. Finally, "Where did you get that name?" Darling was surprised by the anxiety he heard in the Ottawa man's voice.

"She's my fiancée, as a matter of fact." He knew he oughtn't to have said anything, but he felt a biting irritation with this patronizing apparatchik of the Canadian government.

"Well, that complicates things. We didn't know that she—"

"I don't see why it has to complicate anything. If Oxley is what you say he is, then he can finish up his job and get out with this 'asset' you're so keen on. In fact, I could help."

"I know you think you can help, Inspector, but you can't. This is a highly sensitive security matter. It's a bloody shame that the so-called ex-intelligence officer in question could not keep her mouth shut."

"Oh, she has 'kept her mouth shut' as you so graciously put it." Darling was furious on Lane's behalf. "I've put two and two together, which I wouldn't have had to do if you'd brought me in in the first place by telling me what the hell your swaggering man Oxley was doing here. You are welcome to him!" He slammed down the receiver.

Darling had gone home to make the phone call, and he stood now chewing on his upper lip, looking down toward where he could just see a narrow band of the intersection at Baker Street. The citizens of Nelson driving, walking, standing in groups, smoking and talking. I bet they'd be surprised there's a national security crisis unfolding somewhere nearby, he thought.

He reviewed what he knew now. Virtually nothing— except that Oxley was a creature of the security branch of the Canadian government and that he'd be collecting someone at Lane's house. Whom he was meant to be collecting Darling had no idea, and it infuriated him that he'd ostensibly been assigned a policeman, whose job it ought to be to be an actual useful policeman, only to have him be someone with only half an eye on his job.

That meant that it was none too soon for Ames to be taking over the murder. It was clear now that the incomplete job of searching Taylor's shop owed to Oxley's attentions being focused elsewhere. Not that Ward and O'Brien had found anything else in the shop. The problem of the missing rifle still loomed. Anyway, he thought, there was certainly no point in Ames taking him for that drink. If he was a government agent, he would not be undisciplined enough to reveal himself over beer and cigarettes at the local bar.

"HELLO? MADAM?" LANE called as she came into the house. She went down the hall to the sitting room and carefully positioned the envelope from Aptekar on the bookshelf with her other mail. "Hello?"

She saw her guest sitting on the edge of the porch, her sketchbook in hand, apparently drawing the clothesline that ran from the side of the house to a pole at the edge of a bank of fir that disappeared into a gully below.

"It is my daily habit to find some interesting problem of perspective to practice on." Orlova held up her drawing. "This clothesline offers some interesting challenges."

"But it is perfect!" Lane exclaimed. It certainly was. It was hard in that moment to see Orlova in the role of secret agent.

Orlova cocked her head in acknowledgement. "It is daily practice. Anyone could do it. I only learned to draw because it was an expectation for young ladies of my time. It was the only expectation I learned to love."

"I really doubt that I could learn at this late stage," Lane said, smiling. "I've just been up to the Hugheses' to find some eggs, but they're out, so I'm going off to Balfour to pick some up. Would you like to come?"

"No. I have planned to go up behind that lovely old schoolhouse of yours. There is a stand of birch whose leaves are just beginning to turn. This too reminds me of the land around my childhood home. I would like to capture that. The afternoon light will be perfect."

"All right. I'll see you when you come down. Happy painting!" Lane thought about what she had seen, and what she must do. She would pretend to drive away, wait, and then come back. She would know then, but it would make no sense; she knew this already. She got her handbag, then put it down again, threw her cardigan over her shoulders, and made her way to the car. It was only when she was in the car that she was aware of the anxious thumping of her heart.

Parking the car on the side of the road near the turnoff to the wharf, Lane waited. How long would it take Orlova to get her things together and be away from the house? At twenty minutes, she turned the car around and drove slowly back, pausing at the entrance to her driveway. The house looked still in the quiet of the afternoon, the sun beginning to make long shadows on the lawn. She pulled the car forward and stopped, waiting one for moment, and then she ran to the house.

"Countess?" she called. "I forgot my handbag, can you believe it?" But there was no answer. She looked into every room, and then, her heart pounding, she pushed open the spare room door. There, under the bed, was one suitcase. Her heart sank. She'd been so sure, suddenly, and now . . . but then she saw it. They were old suitcases, battered by travel and use. Especially the one with the radio. It must have gone through the entire war. Flecks of the brown leather were peeling off, and there, near the bedpost, was a tiny scrap of that brown leather.

AMES WATCHED OXLEY lift the counter and come through into the main floor office area. Oxley hung up the car keys and threw his hat onto the desk.

"Do you mind, Oxley? I need to talk to you about the Taylor case. I'm taking it over."

"Bully for you," Oxley said. "I'm busy, as it happens."

"Well you can unbusy yourself and come up to my office."

"Fine," Oxley said gracelessly.

As they reached the top of the stairs, Darling came out of his office. "Oxley. A word, please."

"I am Mr. Popular today. Ames here said he wanted to talk to me. Which is it to be?"

Darling stilled his rising anger at Oxley's tone. It was clear the "mission" he was on must be nearing an end. He felt no need to be respectful to anyone. Darling indicated with a jerk of his head that Oxley was to step into his office smartly.

"You can stand the attitude down, Oxley. I've been speaking to your keepers in Ottawa. I understand you're with the secret intelligence branch. I'd like to know the state of your enterprise, and when I will have you out of my hair."

"It would hardly be a secret then, would it!" He leaned back in his chair and languidly looked at his hand. "If you must know, I expect to be finalizing everything tomorrow. I'll need the car, I expect. The person I'm here to collect is meeting someone up the lake. Once I've got him, we'll be on the train and away."

"Someone, who? And where?"

"Sorry, sir."

"I have a right to know where you're taking our car."

"I'm afraid you don't, actually."

"Do you have anything to do with that Countess Orlova who is staying with Miss Winslow in King's Cove?"

"Who?"

"Only she's Russian, and we can't quite make out what she's doing here. Her story is not panning out. I'm assuming now she's something to do with you."

This was unexpected. Oxley looked down at his shoes.

"Look, sir, I appreciate your situation. I do. I really can't tell you anything more than you already know. Suffice it to say we'll be done tomorrow, and I'll be gone."

Darling fumed. He was not going to push this puppy on the subject of Lane Winslow. He already had the information he needed. But Lane knew something more. He needed to contact her. Not that she'd be any more forthcoming.

"Look, sir, I know this is frustrating. We're all on the same side here. Just step aside and let me do my work."

Darling considered this. It was, after all, true. He was angry because he'd been deceived, and his police equipment used freely for someone else's secret purposes. He was used to being in charge, being the one with the information. His pride was hurt because he now knew Lane was completely involved with the same operation. Perhaps she'd known about Oxley all along, as well. And Orlova. Is that why she'd not reacted sufficiently to the concern he expressed to her about Orlova's dishonesty about the so-called search for her brother?

"Fine. And you will kindly take that equipment out of the car and replace the missing tyre. Now go and brief Ames on whatever you have on the Taylor case."

Oxley lingered.

"Thank you," said Darling with finality, scooping up the papers in his "in" box.

"I'M AT BALES'S shop. Can you talk?"

Darling looked around what he had always thought of as his sanctuary. His door was closed. He could hear the rumble of indistinct conversation coming through the wall from Ames's small office. He suddenly thought of the phrase "the walls have ears."

"I suppose so. I don't really know anymore."

"I wanted to tell you what I can about the radios."

"Let me save you the trouble of having to skirt around what you can and can't tell me. I got through to some prat in Ottawa, and apparently Oxley works for some intelligence branch I've never heard of. He's here to collect an 'asset,' whatever that is, and he's apparently certain it will all conclude tomorrow. And I'm pretty certain from Ottawa that it's all going to be taking place at your lovely house. There. Does that help? Does it fit in with your radio business?" Before she could respond, he continued. "I spoke to Oxley, who has the manners of a gangster, and is now acting like he owns the place, and he confirmed all of that, and refused to tell me about your guest, but I read between the lines that she is part of this whole thing somehow. Anything you'd like to add?"

"I think it's safe to say that that explains the radios."

"I'll tell you what else I read between the lines. You've likely known about this all along."

Lane sighed. She wanted to reassure him. She wondered if she should tell him to just send Oxley out in the car. He could pick up Aptekar and the countess and they'd be done with the whole business. She wanted to reassure him that she had nothing to do with it. But something was making her uneasy.

"Where's he been today?"

This was unexpected. "I talked to him a few minutes ago, and this morning he was out talking to a motel owner about some vagrant."

"What sort of vagrant?"

"It must have come to nothing. He didn't tell me about it. The owner of the motel had someone staying there he thought might not pay the bill."

"And he told you what when you talked to him?"

"That he needed the car to drive up the lake to pick up this asset."

"He said that, 'up the lake'?"

"Yes."

What was making her uneasy was simple, really. How did Oxley know that's where Aptekar would be? She had the note from him in her handbag. The only way he could know is if he'd followed Aptekar or traced the note somehow. And if he'd followed Aptekar, then he knew where he was and could have just collected him from town. Probably at that motel. Why all the mess of letting Aptekar follow through with his meeting with her? What could she tell Darling?

"Something's not quite right," she said finally.

"You're telling me."

"Okay. Listen but don't talk. Where is he now?"

Darling was suddenly aware that the voices next door had stopped. "Just wait." Darling put down the phone, went to the door, and opened it. Ames's office door was ajar. He stuck his head in.

"Where's Oxley?"

Ames looked up from the case notes Ward had given him. "Downstairs, I think, sir. He's given me the shirt and knife he found at Taylor's shop. Said that's all I needed to know. I don't care for his tone."

"Me either. I'll talk to you in a minute. I'm on the phone."

Back at his desk, Darling picked up the phone again and said, "He's gone downstairs."

"Here's what I don't understand," said Lane. "I have a note from that asset telling me he is going to meet me at the pier in King's Cove when the steamer comes to dock there tomorrow. Which, before you ask, I just got this morning. Until that moment I didn't know what was going on. As far as I know, no one else has this information. Are you with me?"

"Go on."

"But your man told you he was coming up the lake tomorrow to pick him up. How does he know? He must have followed him to where, for example, you would buy your ticket for the boat. In fact, it makes sense to me that the so-called vagrant may be the man he is here to collect."

"So you are asking yourself why he doesn't just pick him up here because he already knows where he is?" Darling suggested.

"You could do this in your sleep," Lane said.

"I like to sleep in my sleep. So what does this mean, exactly?"

"Why go through the charade of coming out here? One thing suggests itself. He has tried to find him, but the asset is one step ahead of him, has seen him, and doesn't trust him. That is not necessarily bad. This asset probably trusts no one."

"Except you. You obviously know him."

"Look, you need to stop Oxley from coming here. Tell him I will bring the man in myself. If he sees someone else, he'll try to flee."

"I don't understand any of this. Why is this man coming to see you? Who is he?"

"I'm really sorry, darling. I can't say. I've probably said too much already, but I don't want him spooked."

"I'm spooked. I suppose that doesn't matter to you. How do I know he's safe?"

"I can tell you this much. He's a very old man. I'm perfectly safe." She wanted to tell him he'd been a friend of her father's, but she couldn't, and on further consideration, it wasn't really true. He'd been a long-term colleague.

"I talked to some man in Ottawa about Oxley, and I think I let my manly pride get the better of me. I hate being pulled about like a trap pony by arrogant government men. I suggested this asset was going to be collected at your house. That shut him up for a minute. He demanded to know where I got your name. I suspect he was worried about Oxley. I told him you were my fiancée, always assuming that after all this is over that is still true. I was more gratified than I can tell you by the fact that he didn't seem to know that."

"I'm afraid we are going to have to go through with the

wedding. Everyone at the Cove got an invitation today. We can't back out now." Lane paused. "Listen. This man is meant to be taking the steamer to the Cove to meet me tomorrow at noon. Then Oxley thinks he's going to come along and collect him. You couldn't pop out to that motel and see if he's there, could you? His name is Stanimir Aptekar. He may be travelling under an alias. I just have a feeling he needs protection."

"He's got protection. Ottawa in the form of Oxley is protecting him."

"I don't trust him completely."

"The man at the motel might just be a vagrant."

"Yes," Lane said. "But if he isn't and Oxley thinks it's the man he's after, he hasn't told you that, has he? Are you familiar with the motel?"

"There's only one on that road out of town."

"The man we are looking for is tall and slender and has a full head of white hair. He speaks English with a kind of central European accent. He is extremely polite. Call me if you find him. Orlova will be here, so I will be circumspect on my end."

"You said you had something to tell me about the radios?"

"Yes," Lane said hesitantly, "but I don't know what it means."

"Spit it out."

"I had this idea about that brown fleck of cloth I found, and when you said the dead man wasn't wearing brown, I suddenly realized where it might have come from, so I checked. It's just possible it came off the suitcase that contains the radio. Of course, she said she's off painting, but she's taken the radio with her. I found a tiny scrap of the same material under her bed where she shoves the suitcases."

"What are you saying?" Darling asked flatly.

"I don't know. I suppose only that possibly Orlova used the outcrop in that open field to contact Oxley. I don't know that it means anything. You have your killer, your motive. It's just such a coincidence."

LANE PUT HER handbag in her room then called out for Orlova and was greeted with silence. A tour of the house and garden revealed that she was still gone. In the sitting room, she saw her pile of mail, still where she'd left it. Only the envelope, into which she had slipped a blank piece of paper, had been moved. Well, tit for tat, she thought. I've been sneaking about looking in her room, she's no doubt been looking at my mail. There was no point in all this secrecy now. When Orlova got back, they would sort it out. With an instinct she didn't fully grasp, she went back into Orlova's room and stood silently in the doorway, looking carefully at the almost monk-like space. She tuned her ear to sounds.

The house was silent.

So much so that she felt it ringing in her ears. Then she moved swiftly to the closet and opened the door. Neatly hung on hangers were two dresses and a wool jacket, as before. She moved these aside and took in an involuntary gasp of air. She stood frozen looking at the rifle propped in the dark corner of the closet. She wanted to reach in, to identify it, but was almost fearful that if she touched it then it would change everything, that it could never be unseen. She had a momentary illusion that if she closed the door, it would be as if it had never happened.

CHAPTER TWENTY-NINE

L**ANE STOOD IN THE KITCHEN,** looking unseeing at the peaceful view through the windows. She struggled to understand what she'd discovered. The rifle could have been there all along. She tried to remember if she'd ever really looked in the spare room cupboard. Kenny might know. She thought through it carefully and then dismissed the idea that the rifle belonged to her guest. She had arrived with two suitcases and nothing else. Lane took a deep breath and told herself to back away from the cliff of her own anxieties. It must be easily explained.

She would make a cup of tea and sort out her thoughts. The rifle might not be any part of this. She would try to work through her concerns by mapping them out. There were enough unanswered questions besides the rifle. She filled the kettle and put it on the stove and took up several sheets of foolscap. And then she put them down and hurried to the spare room. She might as well know what sort of rifle it was. Glancing out the glass panes of her front door at her undisturbed yard, she went into the room, opened the closet door, and then stopped. She took off her sweater and gingerly took the gun by the barrel using the sweater so that she didn't touch it with her hands. It looked like something from the Great War. She did not understand all the insignias, but she knew a George V insignia meant it had been made early in the century. She felt a sense of comfort from this. She took the rifle and moved across the hall to her own room, and put it into her closet, behind the hanging clothes. Her thought was that the vintage made it all the more likely the gun belonged to Kenny, or his mother. A decommissioned military rifle from the Great War. She took her sweater from the bed and closed the door of her room. She would make her tea and carry on with her map plan; later, she would examine more closely why she wasn't comfortable with the rifle being in the closet of Orlova's room.

Tea made, and a soothing cup to hand, she took up her paper again and began. She drew a circle and wrote "Vancouver" and then "Brit. Con. Hunt there to watch for Russians." Then she drew a ship at the edge of the circle. Then "Orlova searching for missing brother?" She sat back. No. There was no missing brother. Or there was a brother, but not missing. The truth of it was that Orlova was here to find Aptekar. But then why the picture of the so-called brother, who turned out to be a feared MGB agent?

She looked at the activity around that Vancouver circle. Orlova appears and then Aptekar arrives there, after who knows what kind of journey, and now is here. She wrote "Aptekar arrives from? Vladivostok?" She took up a second piece of paper and drew a circle and wrote "Nelson," and then drew a line linking one with the other crossing both pages. "Aptekar arrives, is possibly the vagrant. Oxley, Canadian agent. Sent to pick him up." Now then. For the first time she wondered why the Canadians were involved at all. She was sure Hunt had not mentioned the involvement of the Canadians. The only possibility was that the British were looking for Aptekar, and had alerted the Canadians to be on the lookout, in the one likely place he'd turn up: with her. Her blood ran cold. With deliberation she wrote "Dunn" on a third piece of paper. At the bottom of the paper she wrote "Vladivostok" and drew a dotted line between them.

Aptekar was a defecting agent who was turning himself over to the British to retire. They'd arranged to collect him, only he'd never arrived at the meeting point in Yugoslavia. Instead he engaged in some harum-scarum flight across the whole of Russia, not to mention an ocean, to get here. Why? What did he have that warranted that flight, and all this elaborate to-do from the Canadian government to pick him up? And if the Canadians are, practically speaking, the British, why was Aptekar not comfortably turning himself over to them, instead of engaging in this desperate bid to see her?

Lane sat stock still in front of her map. The silence of the house seemed to intensify. She shook her head, as if to clear it, but the question would not reshape or resolve itself. How had Hunt known about her marriage? She had resolved the matter of him knowing about her guest; the man in Ottawa must have said something to Dunn, who was conveying all the instructions to Hunt in Vancouver. Or had he? She struggled now to remember if Darling had said whether the Ottawa man had said anything about Orlova. Perhaps, if Darling hadn't brought it up, he wouldn't have either. But the marriage? Here was the central question: if the man in Ottawa didn't know they were getting married, then how did Hunt know?

Feverishly she took another piece of paper and wrote two names at the top: Angus Dunn and Ottawa Man. She drew a line of communication between them. Then she drew a line of communication down, from Dunn to Hunt and from Hunt to herself. The line descending from Ottawa Man took her to Oxley and then to Orlova. These lines of communication should be the normal ones. Dunn contacts Ottawa; he thinks a Russian agent set to defect might run to ground in Canada, seeking out a retired British agent called Lane Winslow. Ottawa Man then goes into action. He doesn't tell Dunn how he's going to do it. He just reassures him he'll take care of it and then uses his own people.

Yet, somehow Dunn learns something that Ottawa Man doesn't know. That she is getting married. She knew it must be Dunn because there is no reason for Hunt to know it independently. He gets all his information from Dunn.

Her flowchart wasn't helping. She looked at it again and then, with a kind of illumination, saw what wasn't quite right. Orlova wasn't quite right. Everyone else made sense. She didn't, though she was clearly the "eyes on the ground" so that she could notify Oxley with her little radio transmitter if Aptekar turned up.

On the surface, that explanation made sense; even the charade about her brother made sense. Poor old dear looking for her missing brother, a White Russian refugee fleeing the advance of Communism into Asia. Orlova had told her the stories about her childhood and her flight from the Bolsheviks. Those had a ring of truth, she admitted. What wasn't true was the brother. The brother turned out to be an MGB agent and, very likely, not her brother at all. Then, what? She wondered if she should try to reach Ames to ask him to just go over what he'd learned in Vancouver.

The other thing that was starkly clear was that the one person who knew she was getting married to the inspector was Orlova herself. In her flow chart, Orlova would tell Oxley and Oxley would then go up the line to Ottawa Man. But Ottawa Man hadn't known. Hunt could only have heard from Dunn.

Dunn had been jealous and petty when Darling had been released from jail in London early in the summer. He most certainly knew she and Darling were in love. Had he speculated to Hunt in one of his communications about a possible wedding? But no, Hunt had congratulated her on her upcoming marriage. He knew quite specifically that it was to take place. She took her pencil and drew a short line of communication from Dunn and ended it with a question mark. Where had he learned of it?

What was the line of communication between Orlova and Dunn? Her head felt congested with unformed and unanswered questions. One thing was clear. There was a whole layer of communication invisible in the background somewhere that she could not put her finger on.

Ames first. Lane took all her papers and looked around the kitchen. There was really no place there that she could keep them completely safe from her guest. She felt the urgent need for precaution, even though, apparently, her guest would be gone by some time the next day, when she herself would meet Aptekar and take him and Orlova for the rendezvous with Oxley. Finally, she went to her bedroom and pushed the papers under the mattress, and then went into the hall for the phone.

Not knowing how much time she had before Orlova came back from her painting expedition up the hill near the schoolhouse, Lane stood impatiently waiting to be connected to Constable Ames. She turned her body so that in spite of having to face the trumpet to talk, she could keep an eye on the front door, where she would be able to see when Orlova came back.

"Constable Ames."

Relieved, Lane said, "Oh, Constable, it's Lane Winslow. I'm so sorry to bother you."

"Now that's one thing you never need be sorry about, Miss Winslow. What can I do for you?"

"Can you tell me, just quickly, about what you discovered when Darling asked you to check into the Russian community in Vancouver? I know that the picture turned out to be an MGB agent and someone you talked to had met him and been interrogated by him and was frightened. Was there anything else odd in your research?" Lane stopped and then quickly added, "Is Constable Oxley anywhere near, by the way?"

"No. He's downstairs. The other really odd thing was the body, but I don't think it has anything to do with anything. Otherwise it was just me hitting blank walls. Most people, besides the frightened guy, had never even seen your old lady. I mean, that was peculiar certainly, since I understood from the boss that she'd been all over town looking for her brother."

"Body? What body?" Lane glanced through the panes of glass up her driveway. No Orlova yet. She noticed that some of the leaves in the maple trees interspersed among the bank of birches at the edge of the driveway were starting to turn. The cozy comfort of red and orange was in such contrast to her own anxiety.

"Like I said, I don't think it has much to do with this . . . more of a coincidence really, but it turns out there was the body of some Russian guy in the morgue. I asked to see him in case he was the brother, but he wasn't. I did actually help with that one, as a matter of fact. They thought he'd died of a heart attack, but I saw a thing that looked like a rash on his neck, and when I mentioned it to them, they pooh-poohed it. But a week or so later when I was coming out of my last session the guy from the morgue came to tell me they now thought he'd been poisoned, and the poison was likely administered by something spread on his skin. I felt pretty good, I don't mind telling you!"

"I'm not surprised, Ames. I've always thought you were the bee's knees. When do you hear about your exam?"

"A couple of weeks still, I guess. And thank you. Is there anything else?"

"No, that's splendid, thanks, Constable! Oh, and thank you for being the best man. It's so kind of you."

"I nearly died when he asked me. I'm terrified of making a mess of it."

"You could never mess it up. You will be wonderful. And I hope that by then we'll be calling you Sergeant Ames!"

Lane stood in the hallway after hanging the earpiece on its hook. Ames's news had not been in the least bit reassuring. That death in Vancouver. Something about her time at the Russian desk during the war nudged at her. That was it. There had been rumours that the Soviets had a secret facility where they manufactured barbaric chemical weapons and tested them, likely on political prisoners. But it didn't follow that this man's death had anything to do with Orlova at all. If she understood what Hunt had said, there was substantial Soviet activity in the country. The dead man could have been a dissident polished off by one of these Russian sailors that seemed to always be coming into the Vancouver port.

Could she try to get hold of Hunt in Vancouver? Could she risk another long phone call before Orlova got back? The shadows were beginning to descend along the mountains behind King's Cove. Even a determined painter would not stay out in the woods as the light and temperature fell. Was she even painting? She may be painting, Lane thought grimly, but she's also on the transmitter. Presumably to Oxley. Telling him she'd found an envelope from Aptekar in Lane's mail pile. Telling him that whatever note it had contained had been substituted with a blank piece of paper. Telling him they needed to be cautious because Lane was suspicious. And he was no doubt telling her that he knew that Aptekar would be arriving tomorrow. And still the irksome question: how had he found out? He must have followed him or learned something from the motel owner—but what? And why, oh why, did Oxley not just pick him up in town?

She suddenly felt being inside was making her claustrophobic, blocking her capacity for thought. She needed air, so she wrapped herself in her green sweater and went to sit on the porch. She had to come up with a plan that would not raise suspicion but would protect Aptekar, if all of this was adding up to his needing protection. The centrepiece of her plan rested on Darling either finding Aptekar himself or preventing Oxley from making the trip out.

DARLING WAS IRRITATED to find the car was out. "Well where is it?" he asked O'Brien.

O'Brien shrugged. "Oxley has it. He didn't explain himself to me, I'm afraid." He sniffed in a slightly hard-done-by tone.

"I need to get to a motel just out of town on the Salmo road."

"I did bring my car today, sir. I have to run over to pick up some apples from a farmer for the wife. She cans apple sauce. I could drive you."

"I need to go alone. Can't explain."

"Yeah, of course, sir." He reached into his pockets and took out the keys. "Blue '39 Studebaker. Parked up on Cedar. The gear shift is a little creaky going into third."

"Thanks, Sergeant."

Darling stood on the sidewalk looking up and down the street. Where had Oxley gone? Off using that blasted radio?

All Oxley's absences, irritating at the time, now added up to a man who was using his police station and his police vehicle for whatever he wanted. How had Darling not put two and two together? He set off for Cedar and found O'Brien's car parked facing downward toward Baker. As he eased onto the main road, he thought about cars. He ought to get one. No, he had to get one. The days of Ames driving him around like a grandee were over. He'd be living up the lake with Lane, and Ames would no longer be quite the underling.

The motel looked gloomy and faded in the shadow of the hill it was built against. One pickup truck with a wood-slated bed was parked in front of the long low building. Now that summer was over, and school was back in, the motel's season had come to an end. How did a place like this stay in business the rest of the year?

"Hello?" he called, when he'd stepped into the office. He was rewarded with the sound of the front legs of a chair crashing to the ground, and a clearing of the throat.

"Coming." It was the voice of a man who smoked and drank pretty liberally. "One night?" the man said, when he'd made an appearance.

Darling took out his card and held it up. "I'm looking for a man who may have stayed here. Tall, white haired, accent."

"Had another one of you guys here yesterday looking for him. Heard the foreigner was dangerous, so I'm glad to tell you he hasn't been back, and I don't know where he is. He left his carry-all here. I got it in the back."

"What do you mean dangerous?"

"Cop told me he was a wanted man, armed and danger-ous. Not to approach him but to call the station and ask for him if he turned up. I told that other cop that the man mailed a letter but otherwise seemed harmless enough, but you never know, do you? Turns out he's a crook. Do you want his stuff? I sure don't need it."

Darling sat in the car after he'd parked back on Cedar. According to Lane, Aptekar was not in the least dangerous. Perhaps Oxley had described him as a wanted man to underline the urgency of finding him. Oxley knew he was going to be in King's Cove the next day. How? Logical. He must have gone to the post office, and somehow from there been redirected to the steamer office. Likely Aptekar would have asked the post office where the steamer office was. If that was the case, why would Oxley not just take his man before he boarded the steamer? Why go through the charade of having him travel all the way to the Cove to meet Lane?

"Thanks, O'Brien," Darling said, handing back the keys. "Oxley back?"

"Yes, sir. Shall I send him up?"

"Yup."

Back in his office, Darling took out the file on the Taylor case and looked, unseeing, at the notes contained therein. A knock, followed by the door opening brought Oxley into the room.

"You wanted to see me?"

Suppressing the "no" that came to him, Darling said, "Yes. Sit down." He waited for Oxley to sit and then took a long breath. "I've spoken to Miss Winslow. There will be no need for you to go to King's Cove tomorrow. She will bring the man in and that probably bogus countess as well. Your job will be done, and you can take yourselves off to Ottawa. Though, since you seem to know where he's going to be and when, I'm at a loss to understand why you don't take him before he boards the steamer."

"You done, sir? Not possible, I'm afraid. I don't expect you to understand. I'll be going out, as I planned."

"Why?"

Oxley considered this.

"Will that be all, sir?" Then, not receiving an answer, he stood up and made for the door. He turned back to Darling. "By the way, I've replaced the tyre. I won't need your car, you'll be happy to learn. I've hired one of my own."

Fuming at this entirely unsatisfactory conversation, Darling sat, trying to breathe away his irritation. Finally, he picked up the phone and had a call put through to King's Cove.

When the phone rang, Lane waited and then said, "Mine. Excuse me." She and Orlova had been preparing vegetables for dinner in the kitchen. "KC 431. Lane Winslow speaking."

"That swine Oxley can't be stopped. He's going out tomorrow as he planned. I don't really see how I can prevent it. He, after all, does not belong to me. And by the way, I went to the motel, and Aptekar never came back after he left yesterday. I have his bag, which he left behind."

"Oh, yes, I know. We're having an early dinner ourselves. We've some lovely carrots from the garden. I don't know how the deer left us any. We must have spooked them by sitting in the garden. They left one carrot half eaten and ran." Lane made this pronouncement in a cheerful and enthusiastic voice.

"Oh. I wonder if he somehow saw Oxley talking to the motel owner and decided it was unsafe to return. But that would only be because he trusts no one but you. It looks like you will be the go-between tomorrow. I should be there."

Lane considered this. Something wasn't right, but did it follow that it was anything more than the usual secrecy? Having more people there wouldn't help. According to Hunt, Oxley was an agent of the Canadian government, so there was nothing more to do. Just make sure Aptekar understood he was in safe hands and let them all get in a car and go away.

"No need, thanks. We have lots. Happy supper yourselves."

It was only when she'd hung up that she remembered about the rifle. Well, she couldn't have said anything anyway. Besides, she hadn't yet had a chance to talk with Kenny. She would slip out later and ask Kenny about it. If it wasn't his, he could call the police without fear of being overheard.

CHAPTER THIRTY

"**IT'S GO. I'LL MEET YOU** at the airfield. Between one and one thirty, just in case of loose ends." Oxley listened to the voice on the other end.

"Da, tovarich. Spasiba. Pakah."

KENNY HELD THE piece of paper Lane had given him and hovered over his phone. He was not comforted by her reassurances about the rifle. He had told her in no uncertain terms that the rifle had nothing to do with him and certainly had not belonged to his mother. Lane had told him that it could not belong to Orlova because she had only the suitcases when she arrived. Fretfully, Kenny took up the phone and asked to be put through to the police. His request to speak to either Darling or Ames was unsatisfied, as both were no longer at the station.

"Listen, it's critical that they get this note the minute they come in the morning. Tell them Miss Winslow . . . yes, Winslow, has found an old rifle in a closet in her house . . . no, wait, say 'in her guest's closet in her house.' Do you have that?"

Eleanor looked at him when he came back into the kitchen.

"I'm not at all easy in my mind," he said. He repeated this observation to Alexandra when she came and jumped onto his lap wiggling and wanting to lick his face.

LANE AND ORLOVA sat with the remains of glasses of wine in front of their empty plates. There was a feel of *The Last Supper* about the lingering silence between them.

"Countess. The secrecy must stop. I know who you are; at least I think I do. And I know why you are here. I would prefer if you told me yourself. I'm not an enormous fan of guessing games."

Orlova smiled and handled the stem of her glass.

"You remind me of myself," she said. "When I was young. I was beautiful, smart, inventive. I was even in love, only once, and forever."

"With whom?" Lane asked.

"With a wonderful young soldier, I told you, I think, before. I had his baby, though my husband did not suspect. At least, I assume he didn't. It is so hard to know, is it not? I never told him I had been in love with Stanimir, and I could never love anyone else the same way, but he was a good man, Orlov. I didn't want to hurt him."

Lane tried not to register the surprise she felt. "Stanimir Aptekar?"

Orlova shrugged and gave a slight nod.

"Obviously you are not a countess. Were you an agent

332

of the Soviet government?" Lane asked.

Orlova shook her head, as if at fate. "I would have been a countess, you know, if not for the revolution, on my own family's account and on Orlov's. He would have inherited his father's title. It's funny, I was wild to throw off the aristocratic trappings when I was a girl. Now I feel almost wistful, looking back on that vanished world."

"And the brother? I suppose there is no such man?"

"You must have some things that are true, do you not think, when you are undercover? My brother is real, but he is dead. He worked for the MGB as I did, but he was shot in the street. They told me it was a counterrevolutionary, someone who had lost a family member perhaps. I don't think so, myself. He had become difficult? Maybe. I don't know. But I had to become more loyal, do you see? So I would not be tainted by whatever he had done. It becomes quite a game, trying to stay alive. But you see, I made it. I think being small, and a woman, makes one less important. And now I am here to help with Stanimir."

"Is that why you are here? Because you will recognize him?"

"I volunteered," Orlova said, "when I heard he had disappeared."

"Who are you working for?" Lane watched Orlova's face.

The countess smiled and shook her head very slightly. "I know, it seems crazy to you, after all these years, I am sure. But I got tired of . . . I don't know . . . how intense the Soviets are. Life looked more relaxed on the other side. I have long since lost all my status, and I am now being handled by one of the many people who live in this country and work for us, but my life is more peaceful, not so violent. After this I will retire, well and truly."

Lane looked down, hiding a smile of her own. How typical that answer.

"So you work for the British."

Orlova inclined her head. Suddenly breaking into English, she said, "You have been a remarkable translator. It is a sign of your great integrity, I think. Never a line I didn't speak, never a joke. I have come to respect you. I already liked you of course. You have aristocratic manners."

Lane laughed at hearing her guest speaking English.

"Touché. You had me completely bamboozled."

"What is this word, bamboozle?"

"It means completely deceived."

"Ah. Bamboozle. Though when I finally become just a painter, I will not need it. I will be bamboozling no one."

"I like you too, Countess. It would be hard not to. But I cannot help feeling that you continue to deceive me."

Orlova regarded Lane. "Of course, you are a spy. Well, an ex-spy. Suspicion never leaves, does it? I must remember this. I don't want to live my remaining days looking over my shoulder. But why should you be suspicious? I have told you everything."

Lane shook her head and reverted to Russian. "I don't think so. How did you engineer being placed here with me?"

"That was child's play. My Canadian contact, Oxley, nicely disguised, picked me up at that train station pretending to be a taxi driver. He merely dropped a hint to the nice priest about 'the lady up the lake who speaks Russian.' And here I am."

Lane reached for the wine bottle and offered some to her guest.

"How easily we were all duped."

"No, thank you. Not for me. Do not think of it as being duped. You sell yourself short. Look at you now. You seem to know everything, and we can go forward on an honest footing. You have searched my room, I have looked at your mail and listened to your phone calls, but here we are, all cards on the table. Your phone calls, by the way, are charming. All your lovely neighbours calling about carrots. That is the life I want. You have done well for yourself. I would like such a life. I could not live out here, however. It is so far from everything. But perhaps in Ontario, or even Britain."

"If our cards are on the table, perhaps you can tell me where you were doing your transmitting? I honestly believed you were off painting, until I saw your radio."

"There was a troublesome problem. The mountains are a difficulty. But I did eventually find a meadow where I could make a connection. It was clear of trees, with a good outcrop and high enough to make the connection."

"As it happens I found it. Do you know it is where the dead hunter was found?"

"But that is remarkable!" Orlova exclaimed. "If I had known I am sure I would have tried to find another place. When the killer was arrested, I felt safe to return there, knowing there was no madman on the loose. It never occurred to me—"

"I'm surprised you didn't see the dried blood there."

Orlova shuddered. "I'm glad I didn't. How gruesome!"

"And what did you talk about, you and Oxley?"

"Nothing very much. The radio was to alert him when Stanimir came, so before that we experimented until we could get a good connection, and we made a few calls to make sure it was working. I told him what he could expect out here, a little bit about you, of course."

"Like that I was getting married?"

"Yes, certainly. That was important, no? You are marrying the police inspector. Oxley needed to know that."

Lane let this sit. "Why is it so important for Aptekar to be picked up? Why can he not be left alone?"

"I know. I wish for this as well, but after the last time . . . " She sighed, shrugging.

"After what last time?"

"Ah, yes. Well, you were not to know. You were not here, yet, I believe. It happened right after the war, in '45. It was discovered that this country had many people working for the Soviets. A defector told your government everything. Now he too has disappeared. That's all I can say, really. But I suspect Stanimir must have something or he would not require protection."

Lane tilted her glass this way and that. Should she put one of her last cards down? She was afraid to, she knew. It was almost comforting and certainly convenient to believe what she was being told now, though it was discomfiting to know that Orlova even knew she had arrived in Canada in '46. But she would not be safe, Aptekar would not be safe, if she did not know the whole truth, or at least have enough to guess at it.

"You see," Lane said, "the one thing in all of this that

I don't understand is how the British agent in Vancouver knew I was going to marry."

ORLOVA SAT ON her bed with her hands folded in her lap. She could feel her chest rising and falling with her own breath. The only emotion she could discern was a layer of anticipation somewhere under the stillness. She would see Aptekar, after all this time. She saw herself, suddenly, at eighteen, her hair pulled out of its pins, falling over his face, his arms around her bare back. It was like a picture of some other people now, so long ago was it, filled with passions she had long since lost. Only something did remain, not that youthful ardour, something almost more primal, a physical need to be with him, like lovers who are buried together. It was likely they would be.

She had volunteered for the assignment and they had accepted her immediately. What she told them about how she would manage it had made sense. She could pose as an émigrée, paint her pictures, keep an eye on things, and protect the mission if need be. She had done that. She felt some regret about the man. She had never quite squared the idea of killing in peacetime, but in a way, it was a war still.

It was too bad about Miss Winslow. She had not lied to her. The girl did remind her of her younger self. She had heard they had tried to bring her over. Winslow's excellent Russian, her disaffection for her wartime employer. She would have been a catch. And she was clever. Orlova unclasped her hands and stroked the bedcover briefly, the only sign that she was unsettled. The girl was on the verge of understanding. She could tell by the kinds of questions she asked. And she had found the rifle.

She contemplated killing her now, while she slept, but that would have impractical ramifications. If Aptekar did not find her on the wharf, he would be suspicious. He might be armed. She lay back on the bed fully dressed, pulling the blankets over herself. Her bags stood by the door, packed. They had agreed. They would wait until she met him, and then they would take him. His papers had been prepared as had the cover story that he was ill and had to return to Vladivostok. She knew he would be sent back to a gulag, but he would be alive. That was the bargain she'd struck. Sparing one last thought for the girl, she slept.

AMES SAT AT his desk. He liked the mornings; they felt settled, and he could think better than he could later in the day when things that needed attending to started crowding in. He had laid the shirt with the dried blood out on the desk, and the knife to one side on a piece of paper, and he was looking at them with distaste. Gilly had performed some sort of test on them and they were waiting for the results. He looked at his watch. It was eight thirty. Gilly would have something any moment. Ames shook his head. If he had cut someone's throat, he'd have thrown the knife as far into the bush as he could and burned the shirt.

Perhaps Taylor had been planning to burn the shirt, but it was found before he got the chance? But why not toss the weapon immediately?

He would have a go at Taylor. Maybe after all these days in the clink he'd be more willing to talk. He stood up and stretched—and then something about the shirt came into focus from this new perspective. Frowning he leaned forward, and then sat down again. He was about to try to sort what he'd seen when Gilly appeared at his door. He hadn't even heard him coming up the stairs.

"It's Brodie's blood on the shirt, all right, as near as we can tell. So I expect you have the murderer's shirt there," he said. "But the knife? I'm not convinced. This blade is quite thick. I'm pretty certain the work was done with a much slenderer sort of blade."

"Wait, are you saying this is not the murder weapon?" Ames struggled to understand what that meant.

"I wouldn't say so, no. That shirt's pretty messy as well."

Ames looked at the shirt, frowning. "Come here a minute. Turn around. Now if I'm going to cut your throat . . . wait, Brodie was kneeling down or something, according to you. What was he doing?"

"He was squatting or kneeling. The assailant was above him, from the way the cut was angled. Why? And do I have to start my day having my throat cut? The wife is expecting me home for lunch."

"This'll only take a minute. I need your expertise. If you prefer, you can cut mine. Yes, let's do that. You've seen the cut, you'll know exactly how it was done." Ames kneeled on the floor. "Like this?"

"Good enough." Gilly pulled Ames's head back by the hair, eliciting an "ow" and then made a swiping motion. "Okay, fall forward." Gilly stood up and watched Ames fall over. "Ah!" he exclaimed. In the position that Ames had been in on his knees, he tumbled forward and then sideways, because his bent knees prevented him from lying flat.

"'Ah' what?" asked Ames, getting up and dusting off his knees and arms.

"I have a photo of the body taken at the scene. It was lying flat out, face down. Even if he was squatting instead of kneeling, he'd have ended up on his side."

"Convulsions?"

"There is no time for convulsions with a cut like that. Death would have been instantaneous. Is this why we've done this little charade?"

"No, but it adds to my puzzlement. I wanted you to cut my throat and then tell me where all the blood would be on that nice white shirt of yours."

"If I'm a professional, which I am, by the way, if the cut is anything to go by, there won't be much blood on me. It will all have poured outwards and onto the ground. Photos show that to be the case. Once the victim was down, the rest of the blood would drain away. Now, the victim's shirt would be a right mess because he'd be lying in it."

"But the victim was wearing a shirt when he was found. Look at this thing. This is the shirt with, you now tell me, the victim's blood. Look where it is. It looks like whoever was wearing this was dancing the tango with the victim."

Gilly smiled thinly, and then went serious again.

"It's perfectly possible that having committed the murder, the killer regretted it and turned the body over, wept over it, turned it back. That would account for the way he was found. Didn't you say they used to be friends?"

"Good point. I just can't square why there'd be this

practically assassin level of clean, efficient murder, and then all this folderol with the body. I'm going to talk to him again. And the knife is a whole other barrel of fish, if what you say is true."

TAYLOR SAT WITH his hands clasped, chewing his bottom lip. He knew why he was there now, with this policeman he'd never seen. They'd charge him officially now.

"I'm Constable Ames, you know O'Brien, I think?"

Taylor nodded, and looked at the table.

"I just need to go over some things, if you don't mind."

"Are you going to charge me, or what?"

"Probably, but you need to answer some questions."

Taylor shook his head. "The one question you can ask is, did I kill Brodie, and the answer is still no."

Ames leaned forward. "I know, you've said that before. However, our pathologist, Mr. Gillingham, has told me this morning that the blood on the shirt found in your cupboard belongs to your old friend Brodie. If you didn't do it, how can you explain that?"

Taylor was silent. He rubbed his right thumb over the knuckles of his left hand. Finally, he said, "I didn't do it. I wanted to often enough, but I didn't."

"Then you need to adequately explain this shirt business. Your shirt, his blood, your cupboard."

"And that knife that was with it has nothing to do with me!" Taylor exploded, and then turned away with a groan.

"There we go. Now we're cooking with gas. How did it get there then? And if you didn't kill him, why is the shirt covered with his blood?"

"Look, if I tell you this, she can never know. You have to promise me."

"Can't do too much in the way of promises, I'm afraid. When things go to trial it all tends to come out. If, as you say, you didn't do it, you won't need to worry about a trial."

"I did go up there that night," Taylor said quietly.

O'Brien shifted forward in his chair against the wall by the door to the interview room.

"I did. And I was going to kill him. He'd come around threatening me, and he'd hurt Cassie one time too many. I knew where he usually made camp. I took my revolver and hiked up. It was getting dark, so I had my flashlight. Only when I got there, he was already dead. I nearly passed out at the sight of him. His head hanging like that, blood everywhere. I—"

"Just a minute, Mr. Taylor. Why don't you describe exactly how the body was?"

"Uh, it was kind of weird. He was on his side with his knees drawn up, kind of, his head rolled back." He shuddered.

"Then what did you do?"

"I can hardly remember, I was so upset. I sort of forgot that I was angry enough to kill him, and all I saw was someone I used to be friends with. I tried to move him. I don't even know why, now. I think I was trying to feel his pulse or something. I couldn't take in that he was dead. But the blood . . . I realized I had it on my hands and shirt sleeves. I ripped off my jacket and shirt and tried to cover his neck with the shirt. I was like a crazy man. Part of me knew he was dead, but part of me didn't want to believe it."

342

"Did you do anything else to the body?"

"I don't know. Yes. I . . . I think I tried to straighten it out, turn him face down so I couldn't see that ghastly wound any more. It seemed, I don't know, more dignified."

"Then?"

"I ran. It suddenly occurred to me that someone had slit his throat, and that person might still be around. Especially as there was still blood. I must have come on the scene not too long after."

"And the shirt?"

"It was covered with his blood. I took it and crumpled it up and shoved it in my jacket. I was planning to burn it when I could."

"And the gun?"

"What gun?" Taylor said, puzzled.

"Brodie's hunting rifle."

Taylor shook his head. "I didn't see it. But it was dark. He could have propped it up somewhere. To be honest with him lying cut up like that, I didn't think about his rifle."

"You were a bit out of your head. Are you sure you didn't take it with you?" Ames asked.

He shook his head vigorously. "I know I didn't. I swear I didn't. I didn't kill him! You have to believe me!" Taylor was overcome, now, and began to sob, coughing and wiping his nose.

"Mr. Taylor, which policeman found the shirt?"

"That short, bossy one," he said, coughing again. "I've seen the other one, Ward, but I'd never seen this one."

"I'll leave you a few minutes to recover. O'Brien, can you get him some water?"

"Right." O'Brien got up, stretching his back, and the two policemen left Taylor to his regrets.

Outside in the hallway by the stairs up to the main floor, O'Brien said, "Well, that's one for the books! I can't imagine he thinks we'll believe him."

"That's the thing, O'Brien, there may be some reason to. Get him his water. I'm going to see the boss."

THE WATER DELIVERED, O'Brien went back to the phones to await developments. When the call came, he put it through to Ames. Then he remembered Ames had said he was going to see Darling, so he tried to put the call through there, with no result. "Where the heck is he?" he asked himself and then shouted up the stairs for him. "Ames! Vancouver calling!" Still no answer. "Sorry, can't find him. Can I take a message?" O'Brien listened carefully and wrote it in the notebook.

Ames, as it happened, had found Darling just outside the station's front door, heading to the café for a cup of coffee. "Sir, something is very wrong," Ames said simply. "Where is Oxley?"

"Hasn't been in," said Darling, walking briskly. Ames caught up with him and they walked together. "I expect we've seen the last of him. Gone up the lake to collect his Russian spy," He glanced at Ames. "What do you mean, wrong?"

"For starters, I think Oxley planted the knife in Taylor's shop. Taylor has confessed that he went up to find Brodie to kill him but found him already dead. His shirt got covered in blood because he was messing around moving the body, and he shoved the shirt in his cupboard till he could find an opportunity to burn it. But Gilly says the knife that Oxley found in the shirt probably wasn't the murder weapon. That means Oxley must have put it there."

Darling frowned. "What was Oxley playing at?"

"Planting evidence to secure a conviction? Not honest, but it's been known to happen."

Darling shook his head and said, "No, he was trying to cover up. He knew who killed Brodie."

"But why?" asked Ames. "Who was Brodie to him? Who was the killer to him, for that matter?"

Darling paused, having arrived at the café, and he and Ames stood just outside the door. "That bloody Russian woman! They were busy keeping contact with each other with those bloody transmitters, supposedly agents waiting to capture a defector. Either Oxley killed Brodie, or he thought she'd killed him and was covering up. He didn't know about Taylor, but finding that shirt provided a perfect opportunity to secure him as the murderer. He must have had that planted knife on him when we went to investigate."

"But I still don't understand why Brodie needed to die."

"Because, Amesy," Darling said, the promise of coffee now forgotten, "he must have stumbled on something while he was out hunting bears. Orlova is a seasoned agent. As tiny as she is, I bet she can kill like a pro. Which means that you are absolutely right, something is very wrong indeed. We need to get out there as fast as we can!"

CHAPTER THIRTY-ONE

September 1947

FEDOROV, WHO COULD STILL NOT fully embrace his assumed name, Gusarov, would not have called himself religious, but here, in exile, being at the church, talking to the others, fed some atavistic memory from his childhood.

"Checkmate, I think, Anton," he said. "Tea? One of the old ladies has brought zakuska. No vodka, of course."

His companion shook his head at yet another defeat and shrugged. "Why not?" He moved to stand.

"No, no. Sit. I will bring it." Fedorov got up, both happy and unhappy to stretch his bad leg. He muttered "oof" when he stepped on it at first. This too gave him memories, ones he tried to block out, of his time in Minlag Prison. He had never told his friend how he had gotten away from there, whom he had killed to escape.

He didn't know what made him swivel his head to the door. It felt like some sort of fate when he thought about it after, during the brief time remaining to him. But he saw her, and he felt his innards go loose with a fear he did not think he would have to face again. He wanted to turn away, to leave, forget the *zakuska* and Anton and the chess, but she was looking at him, her face blank.

"You look white as a ghost. What's the matter with you?" Anton asked his friend when he collapsed in the chair, the tea sloshing out of the cups onto the tray.

"I thought I saw someone I knew before, but I don't think she recognized me. If she did, I'm done for. No. Don't look. She is like Medusa. You will turn to stone. She is an old woman, but I would know her anywhere."

At that, Anton did turn. "That? She is like my babushka."

"If your babushka is an interrogator for the MGB, then, I suppose."

Later, when she passed by with a glass of water, she stumbled and apologized. A little water had spilled on the back of his neck. She was so very sorry. He did not look up, but only muttered.

The last echoing sound he heard over the excruciating pain in his chest was his friend Anton shouting, as if from far away.

"Gusarov! Gusarov! Someone call an ambulance!"

"Anton," he wanted to say, "Anton, let me die as myself."

DARLING AND AMES rushed down the stairs and made for the door of the station. Ames stopped to take the keys, and O'Brien, watching the commotion, stopped Darling on the way out the door.

"Before you go bashing off, I found this note. The night man must have taken it."

Darling seized the paper, read it, and groaned.

"Rifle found, anyway." He pushed open the door, only to find Ames coming back from where the car was parked.

"Ames, like the wind!"

"Tyres slashed, sir. All four."

"My God! We have no time to lose! O'Brien, can—"

"Don't have to ask, sir. Here are the keys. Parked where it was yesterday. By the way, Ames, I had a call a few moments ago. Someone from a morgue in Vancouver calling to say they'd solved the case of the murder of the Russian." Here O'Brien took up his notes. "It appears he was a dissident who'd escaped, and he was likely killed by an old woman. He called because he was wondering if it might be the old woman you had been asking about, and he suggested you be careful, as she might be lethal. He was quite droll about that part."

WATER LAPPED AGAINST the wharf, the morning sun making it a shimmering emerald green against the shadows underneath. Lane stood, watching the steamer approach. There was no one boarding from the Cove, and she could see the tourists along the railings, pointing and admiring the smattering of homes just visible on the green rise. It was not a usual delivery day for the Cove, but they would drop, she hoped, the man she was expecting, and soon thereafter it would all be over. Aptekar would be safely delivered.

Orlova was standing behind her at the top of the wharf, still and watchful. Lane had left early, nosing her car as noiselessly as possible down the road, past the church, over the main road, and onto the wharf. Orlova must have walked down when she'd seen the car gone, Lane thought.

Hearing a car coming down the road, Lane turned and saw it pull up next to Orlova. It was Oxley. He didn't get out. The boat crunched against the dock, the wood emitting a loud squeal of protest as the boat slid to a stop. A gangplank was lowered, and Lane saw him waiting, watching her. Stanimir Aptekar.

How different he was from the expensively dressed, suave operative whom she had met in Berlin. He was wearing workmen's clothes with heavy boots, and he had several days' growth of beard. He didn't even have a bag with him. She approached to meet him, and with utter clarity, she understood why Oxley did not pick him up in town. She shook his hand. He bowed and kissed hers.

"I find you at last," he said.

"You do. But I am not alone, as you see. We are not safe. Is there something you need to say to me alone, or shall we join them? It is Madam Orlova and a Canadian agent called Oxley."

Aptekar stood still, frowning.

"Orlova? Here?"

He looked behind him as the gangplank was being slid back into the boat, as if his hope of escape was cut off. He took her arm and leaned in, whispering. "We will walk slowly, and I will tell you, no matter what happens, there is a motel outside of Nelson; below it, a path to the lake. There is a green shed for oars and things. Under it, at the back. Don't forget."

Lane felt her chest compress. She continued to lean in, smiling as if he were still talking, but she swivelled her eyes toward where Orlova stood, her hands clasped behind her.

"Something is wrong," she said. A statement.

"I can't believe it is her. After so many years." His voice caught. He stopped and looked at Lane, his voice almost inaudible. "Yes," he said. "Something is wrong." He walked forward, firmly, his hands out. "Tatiana Andreivna Orlova! You are as beautiful as ever."

Orlova looked at him with a deep sadness.

"Stani. I am sorry." She seemed to choke on the last word, as she lifted the rifle she had hidden behind her back.

Lane had been moving toward the car where Oxley was sitting, and then she saw Orlova raise the rifle. She felt her blood drain. She was going to shoot Aptekar! It took a moment for her to understand that the rifle was trained on her.

"I am sorry, Miss Winslow. You have been a wonderful hostess. This is a poor way to repay you." She cocked the gun.

Lane felt everything go into slow motion. She could see Oxley out of her peripheral vision. He looked up, panic written on his face, and then looked down at something on the seat. She heard the car door open and felt her head swivel from him to the rifle Orlova had pointed at her. Her eyes took an eternity to see Orlova's finger begin to press the trigger. She almost wanted to smile at her own stupidity in not taking the rifle out of the house. The countess had found it and now she was going to die. When the shot came, she felt deafened and thought only of Darling standing alone by the church.

But it was not she, but Madam Orlova who lay on the ground, the rifle unfired and dropped beside her. Aptekar sprang forward and knelt down beside her, lifting her head, trying to rouse her, but Oxley had aimed with deadly accuracy and she was dead.

Lane pulled her eyes away from the dead woman, still not fully comprehending what had happened. For one moment she thought Oxley had saved her life. Oxley stood, leaning on the door, holding a revolver. He inclined his head, and then shook it.

"Kind of touching, really, don't you think?"

"Why do you need that revolver? He's not armed," Lane said. She tried to move closer to the car as if she was approaching him to talk. Oxley laughed mirthlessly. "Who knows, eh? She was. She did a fine job on that hunter."

Lane wanted to react, to understand what he was saying, but he was raising the revolver, pointing it at Aptekar.

"Best get on. I don't have all day," Oxley said crisply, aiming the weapon, then he turned it toward her. "When this is over, you're coming with me. I don't see why, personally, but I do what I'm told." Then he trained the gun back on Aptekar, steadying his hand on the top of the car door.

Lane threw herself at the door, shoulder down, as hard as she could. Oxley fell back heavily against the car, his head cracking on the edge of the roof, the gun flying out of his hand. Lane leaped toward it, picked it up, and aimed it at Oxley, backing toward where Aptekar knelt over Orlova.

"She's dead. She was meant to kill me, but she is the one dead." Aptekar seemed uncomprehending.

"We have to do something about this man," Lane said. She did not want to look away from Oxley, who was dazed and rubbing his head. This standoff with her holding a gun to Oxley could last indefinitely. Aptekar would have to pull himself together, she thought. Then Oxley looked behind him, and Lane heard it too. A car roaring down the narrow road, coming to a noisy and dusty halt. Darling and Ames leaping out, O'Brien climbing out of the back seat.

"The cavalry," said Lane. "Late as usual."

DARLING HAD WANTED more than anything to hold Lane, to stop the shivering that had begun almost as soon as she had relinquished the revolver she was holding, to reassure himself that she was alive, as it could so easily have been a different outcome. But there was work to be done. Instead he had taken off his jacket and placed it around her shoulders, saying very quietly, "Darling."

"It's all right. I'm fine," she had whispered back. "I'll be over there." She could feel herself beginning to really shake and she didn't want him to feel he had to stay with her.

She sat on the edge of the wharf next to Aptekar. Behind them the business of police work unfolded. O'Brien had been sent to the Armstrongs' to call for a van for Orlova's body. Oxley had been handcuffed and placed, scowling, into the back of the car he'd driven. Ames was writing in his little book. Darling was leaning against the front of the car, waiting.

"I knew when I saw her," Aptekar said. "They must have known all along that I was coming here."

"She told me she had come over to the British, that she was working with Oxley to bring you in."

Aptekar shook his head. "Tatiana would never have defected. It was not in her. I met her about twenty years ago at a Soviet conference for the intelligence people after years of not seeing her. She was as devoted a communist as Lenin himself. She would not have changed. It is why she was prepared to kill you, and probably me. It was her job. She would not think of our past. She was quite cold-blooded. I always try to remember the woman she was, but perhaps she had too much tragedy. There has been a lot to go around."

"I know this much: she loved you. She said she never stopped."

"And yet, she was part of this attempt to find me, to eliminate me." He shrugged. "Well, such is my business."

"I think she surprised Oxley. He looked dismayed when he saw that she intended to kill me. His orders were to kill both of you, and apparently to bring me along. I'm not convinced he wouldn't have shot me in the end, because I could see he didn't really see why I had to be taken along. I don't even understand it. Did the Russians think I had something to tell them?"

"I don't think we will ever know. Maybe the gods didn't want to ruin your wedding." Aptekar smiled and put his arm around her. "You are cold."

"No. I expect I'm just a bit shaken by how close it all was. I don't think Oxley had thought about what Orlova's orders might have been," Lane said. "I wondered why he didn't just pick you up in town once he knew where you were, but if your mission is to eliminate several people, it is better accomplished far from anyone."

"As soon as you said his name, I knew it might all go bad. He is on the list of names I left hidden. Canadians who are working for the other side. What I can't quite understand is how they knew I would come to you."

Lane thought back to Hunt's visit. "The British consul in Vancouver, a man called Hunt, came to see me, to warn me you were on the run and might come here. He got that from Dunn, the director in London. I assumed that if Oxley and Orlova were acting for the British, that's how they knew. But they weren't, were they? They were acting for the Soviets, and whoever sent Oxley out here was working for them as well." Lane took a deep breath and thought about her map, with a line of communication from Dunn to a question mark.

Then she nodded as the piece fell into place.

"You see, I was puzzled about how the British consulate knew I was getting married. The only person in this story who knew that was Orlova. If she was working for the Soviets, it means that when she told Oxley, he told his keepers up the chain. It got from the Soviets to someone in England. That someone, a Russian spy, is in direct contact with the director." She turned and looked at Aptekar. "I believe the man who betrayed you was Angus Dunn, and I very much wonder why."

THERE WAS NO using the telephone at King's Cove. It was busy all the time. Lane's invitation had hit like an explosion of confetti. Gladys had immediately called Eleanor and declared that the only place for the party must be her house, Eleanor claimed the right to arrange the flowers at the church, Angela busied herself looking for dresses in magazines. Kenny eyed the ivy growing uncontrollably along the garden fence and imagined it decorating the wagon he had used to pull the mail up the hill before he got his truck, with himself driving Lane to the church.

Even Alice Mather saw a benefit in the celebrations, declaring to a group chatting outside the post office, "Well, it will get her out of circulation anyway. I suppose I'll have to wear a frock."

Gwen and Mabel Hughes busied themselves with lists of projected canapés and reached into their dark armoires to pull out tablecloths and napkins to be aired.

"Mid-October is a bit late," Gladys complained. "Why not do it when the gardens are perfect?"

"Quit fussing mother. It's not like you. You know how lovely the light is in the fall, and with the trees turning it will be absolutely golden."

"Provided we don't get a heavy early snow," Gladys said. "Remember '35? We were positively buried in it."

"In fairness, Mother, it wasn't early. That bad snow was in January, not October," said Gwen. "What do you think of this? We haven't used it since I can't remember when." She held up a cloth with lace edges that had been beautifully pressed when it was first put away, and now was a checkerboard of creases.

"Oh, yes," said Mabel happily. "Just the thing for a wedding. Give me that. I'll get those creases right out."

At the post office, Kenny's curmudgeonly cousin Robin Harris stood holding his quarterly veteran's cheque and a newspaper under his arm and watched Kenny snipping the hedge at the bottom of his garden.

"Lot of fuss over nothing, if you ask me."

Kenny straightened up and mopped his brow. "We think it's something, don't we, Alexandra?" He addressed this to the dog, who was sitting at attention watching the trimming. She wiggled appreciatively at being addressed. "You see? And if you examined your own conscience, you'd see you think so as well. Lane Winslow has had the patience of Job with you."

"What if she has that foreigner give her away?" Robin asked, apparently determined to be disgruntled about the whole thing, though he recognized the truth of what Kenny was saying. She had been quite nice to him, what with one thing and another.

"We don't know that he will. But apparently he was a friend of her father's, and since her father died in the war, I think it would be quite nice. She doesn't have much family, poor thing. Some grandparents in Scotland, but they are getting on a bit for a trip like that."

"One of us could have done it," Robin muttered, nearly under his breath, a remark that astonished Eleanor when she was told of it later, over tea.

"Well, you amaze me! He said that? I think the old coot must be getting soft."

LANE, THE SUBJECT of all this happy speculation, was in town, looking thoughtfully at some dresses in a window. She had come in to meet with Stanimir Aptekar, for whom rooms had been found, clothing bought, and a shave procured. For now he was being allowed to recoup his energy, and had been given reluctant permission to stay on for the wedding. Hunt, at the British consulate in Vancouver, had been in a tussle with Canadian intelligence officials about the disposition of Aptekar, the Canadians insisting that the British had lost the moral high ground with the betrayal perpetrated by their director.

Hunt had somehow won the day and conducted the interrogation that revealed the names and positions of Soviet sympathizers in Canada. Hunt handed the list to the dismayed intelligence services in Ottawa. They had just been through an ugly scene two years before with Canadians, some quite prominent, on a list of people trading secrets to the Soviets through the embassy. The new list included Oxley.

Lane glanced at her watch. She had twenty minutes before she had to meet Aptekar at Lorenzo's. Could she decide in that time? She knew Angela was wild to be involved in the dress decision, but she was wary of what that might mean. She really didn't want anything fussy. Angela wouldn't be able to argue if Lane came back to King's Cove that afternoon, dress in hand. With a sigh, she pushed open the door of the shop.

"How can I help you, miss?" a woman with a grey cardigan draped over her shoulders asked.

"I need something to get married in," Lane said, a little hesitantly.

"Oh! Lovely! Now over here, and these have just come in, are two of this season's most gorgeous wedding dresses."

Lane was led to the dresses and regarded them for a moment. She shook her head. "I think what I want is a very smart cocktail dress," she declared.

Later, bag in hand, she found Aptekar waiting outside the restaurant. He removed his hat and opened the door for her.

"This time you will allow me to treat you," Lane said, smiling as she saw Lorenzo approaching. "I owe you after Berlin."

"My dear Miss Winslow!" Lorenzo cried, seizing her hand. "And with a bag from our most expensive dress shop. May I guess?"

"You guess right, Signor Lorenzo," Lane said, smiling. "May I introduce you to an old friend of my father's, Mr. Stanimir Aptekar. Mr. Aptekar, Signor Lorenzo. This would be the finest restaurant in any town no matter where it was."

"You are very kind, Miss Winslow. The missus is thinking of nothing but wedding cakes, but I am sure we have something good, eh?"

"I don't know how it is, but no matter when we come here, the best table seems to be magically available," Lane said a few minutes later when they were seated.

"I believe you have that kind of magic, Miss Winslow. Look, you have tamed a grizzled old Russian spy."

"Never grizzled, Mr. Aptekar, and I'm sure never tamed! In fact, you look remarkably like your old self. It is very kind of you to stay on to see me married, especially after what you have endured here."

"I do it in part for my old friend, Stanton Winslow, of course, but mostly for his remarkable daughter. It is an honour I had never imagined."

"Tell me about the countess. What was she like when you first met her?"

Lorenzo appeared at the table with a bottle of champagne and made a great show of opening it.

"Goodness! What's this in aid of?" asked Lane.

Lorenzo only winked at Aptekar and poured.

Aptekar lifted his glass. "A wedding, an unexpected meeting, an unexpected reprieve from death. What is there not to drink to?" He smiled sadly and shook his head. "She was beautiful and ferocious. And engaged. She claimed she was drawn to me because I was not vapid. I was, you know. Poor thing was the only daughter of a count and a charming mother who was alert to class distinction like no one I've ever met. If we had stayed together, she would have learned the truth, that I was as vapid and empty-headed as all the other aristocratic young men. They had engaged her to Orlov by the time she was seventeen. But they didn't know that she had her eyes on the future. She dreamed of a world of justice and equality, a world that would eliminate forever the very roots she came from. I was only her first rebellion. Maybe not even. She told me she was barely seventeen when she heard a young Lenin speak in a hall."

"Did she . . . ?"

"You are going to ask about the child, yes? She told me twenty years ago, in quite a bloodless manner. These great political movements spare no one, do they? I had a daughter I never met, but so many daughters and sons died. They will never be able to count the millions who have disappeared forever. I learned from another man in my division that Tatiana was a particularly skilled assassin. Would she have gone down that road if her . . . if our child had lived? I don't know. But let us speak of happier things."

When the food arrived, a gnocchi dish Lane had had and loved before, she asked, "What will you do?"

"I am no longer in possession of secrets. These have been

removed by your Mr. Hunt, so I am no longer radioactive. I think I will proceed to a farm in Sussex as I had originally intended. Provided your old boss does not forbid it."

"I suspect my old boss is in quite a bit of trouble. According to Hunt, he fooled everyone. He was trying to stay in power in a postwar world where all the rules were changing, so he traded you for a few names of British would-be Soviet sympathizers so that he could look like he was on the job and flushing out British traitors. Like all vain men, he thought he was getting the better of the deal. He thought you were a washed-up spy and of no use to anyone. He had no idea of the value of the information you were bringing over."

"Now," said Aptekar holding up his glass, "I am happier than I can say to be nothing more than a washed-up spy. I am already planning the layout of my garden. I will develop a new rose and call it by my daughter's name, Kira."

IN LONDON, THE fall had descended into days of drizzle. The leaves in Hyde Park, on the verge of putting on a golden autumn show, instead cascaded in wet piles to the ground. Angus Dunn sat with his hands folded on his desk, struggling with a feeling he had never experienced before; in fact, so unfamiliar was it that he could scarcely give it a name. *Disintegration* came to his mind. He became conscious of how tightly he was clasping his hands, as if holding himself together. He had never known failure; he did not allow for it and could not summon the resources needed to deal with the feelings it engendered. He glanced at the clock on the shelf, and then pushed himself to his feet, pulling his double-breasted jacket down firmly and standing very erect. He was due at the Home Office.

Did his secretary have a look of sympathy as he handed him his umbrella? Was his driver a little distant? He felt a bubble of panic that he could not tell any more, could not read the faces of those around him.

"Well, Dunn. Here we are."

Dunn wanted to say "Where, sir?" He adjusted himself in the chair opposite the home secretary so that he was leaning back nonchalantly, his leg crossed, but now this position felt foreign and he could find no comfort in it.

"Sir."

"You've had a good innings. Changing times, what? Let some of these young chappies into the game, I think."

"Sir, if I could explain." Dunn hated hearing himself ingratiating, bargaining.

The home secretary leaned forward, his hands flat on a thin file; then he lifted them and brought them down with the gentlest and most final slap.

"Cock up all the way around, I think you'll agree. Not your first, I understand. That business in the summer nearly put us all into a bind when you lost control of that little German agent. Let's leave it at that, shall we? Every dog has his day. You've had yours. Time to enjoy the gardens up at that place of yours. We'll want your office end of day tomorrow."

"I'll need time to sort through the files, the confidential material, the—"

"No need." The home secretary stood and pressed a buzzer on his desk. "All done, while you were here. You just have to pack up the personal paraphernalia. That will be all."

CASSIE BRODIE STOOD with a cup of coffee looking out the kitchen window, her lips clamped and turned down. She was feeling—she couldn't quite place it, because she had never felt anything like it before—hardened, she supposed came closest. She wondered what her life would have been like if she had been more tough like this when she had been married to Brodie. Would she have been able to stop his cruelties? Leave him? But no. She had been like a child, trusting a man would look after her, and being crushed when she learned the truth. You earn your hardness, she thought.

She knew her neighbours, at first sympathetic and then standoffish, must have heard the gossip about her affair with Taylor. But perhaps they knew all along and felt sorry for her, as if she was owed a little happiness the way her husband carried on. Maybe she had made them standoffish with the way she had refused their initial kindnesses, had said she just wanted to be left alone.

She heard the car bumping down the road. This was it, she thought. She would have to decide. She had told herself that she could never love Taylor the same way, knowing he'd actually planned to kill her husband. She had been sure, in the long sleepless hours at night, that she would tell him they were through, that that was the right thing to do. But in the morning, she knew that her cousin Arlene had been right.

"Don't be a fool. How will you support yourself on your own? So what if he was going to kill him? He didn't, and he loves you. And don't you worry about me. As far as I'm concerned, you're welcome to him."

Cassie watched him get out of the car, saw the look of anxiety on his face, put down her coffee and smoothed her apron. For starters she would tell him they would be moving. He could fix boats anywhere.

CHAPTER THIRTY-TWO

THE DAY OF THE WEDDING, with the bloody-mindedness often attributed to weather, dawned cloudy and damp from an overnight rain. Lane woke feeling groggy and was, for a moment, convinced that her guest was still sleeping in the next room—then remembered what the day was. She felt a strange mixture of regret and horror at the thought of the silent, empty room where Madam Orlova had slept and from which she had left some weeks prior to murder a man who had stumbled on her transmitting equipment during the course of his annual hunt. That state of war had never left Orlova, Lane thought. A peaceful part of Canada, to be sure, but in the countess's head, it was a war she carried with her always, ready to be fought wherever she perceived an enemy. That was the danger of war. For some people it never ended.

"Pull yourself together," she said out loud. She put on her dressing gown and padded to the kitchen to decide, on this of all days, whether she should say goodbye to her old life with coffee or tea. She knew, as she stood gazing out at the clouds and the long grasses at the edge of her lawn, now bent with the rain, that she was indulging in gloomy thoughts because she was nervous. Deciding on the gentle support of tea, she put the kettle on and went to the spare room. Madam Orlova's bag of paints and the pile of pictures she had done in King's Cove were on the bed, now stripped of everything but the bedspread and a pillow. Her suitcase and the transmitter had been taken by the police, and from there passed on to the RCMP intelligence branch, as was any further investigation into the murder of the hunter, Brodie.

Lane remembered that morning when Orlova had been shot by the lake. After the police had sorted everything out, had handcuffed Oxley and Aptekar and driven up the hill, Darling had stayed behind. He'd been leaning on the car Oxley had rented and which he was to drive back to town. Lane had stood beside him. He had held her hand as if he would never let it go.

"I thought she would kill you," he had whispered, as if he couldn't bear to say it out loud. She had turned toward him, and they had stood in an embrace, the quiet of the now deserted beach enveloping them.

She picked up the paintings and went through them: her house, her garden, the lake, the Hugheses' lupines, the stand of trees near the outcrop where she had apparently been transmitting messages to Oxley—where that unfortunate hunter had bled into the ground, a victim of a war he could not have begun to imagine. She was a wonderful painter, Lane thought, and she wondered if it was odd that she should want to frame and hang the pictures Madam Orlova had personally given her, knowing what she now knew about her.

Gladys might like the paintings of her flowerbeds. She wouldn't mind if Orlova was an assassin and a spy, in fact she'd relish it. But the rest of the pictures ought to go to Aptekar. He could put them on the walls of his cottage in Sussex. Her kettle whistled, and she went back to the kitchen and poured the water over the tea leaves. She would drink her last cup of tea as a single woman in the perfect peace and silence of her beautiful house, looking out at the myriad of greys that reflected on mountain and lake on rainy days like this, relishing the green scent that trees exude after a rain.

Darling had called her the night before. They had been silent together on the line after the initial greeting.

"Are you sure you want to go through with this?" he'd asked her finally, his voice soft.

"Are you?"

"That's not an answer. You're making me nervous."

"Neither is that," Lane had pointed out, smiling with sheer happiness. "I'm terribly happy. Does that count?"

"It will have to, I suppose," Darling had answered. "As it happens, I'm even happier than you."

"You don't know that."

"Yes, I do. I'm getting you, but you're only getting me."

"You say that now," Lane had said, "but you'll be tired of me in no time."

"I can tell you with absolute certainty that I will never, ever be tired of you. Though I confess I am already tired of you nearly getting shot. Could we go a few weeks without that sort of thing, do you think?"

There was another silence after this, and then Lane had said, "See you tomorrow, then?"

"Tomorrow."

The weather was not going to match Lane's thoughtful mood. As she watched, her throat catching at the memory of the phone call, the clouds lifted and the rising sun sent golden rays shooting across the lake. She nearly laughed at how it lifted her spirits. Angela would be by in a couple of hours, ready to fuss over her hair and decide on shoes, and ask again if she was sorry she'd not opted for the traditional white satin wedding dress Angela had so wanted her to wear. Lane smiled, and taking her tea, went to the closet and pulled out her dress and hung it on the door. She would never be sorry she had bought this dress. She had felt quite extravagant buying a deep blue taffeta dress with a generous skirt. It had a draped upper bodice and sleeves, and pulled in tight at the waist. The skirt was wide, but not voluminous. Just right, she thought.

"I can't go waltzing into a church wearing white like an ingénue," she had said when Angela had first seen it and exclaimed over its shimmering loveliness and complete inappropriateness as a wedding dress. "I'd feel like a complete fraud. Anyway, I can use this again."

"Yes, indeed," Angela had said. "For all those cocktail parties we throw here at King's Cove."

AMES PULLED UP in front of Darling's house. He set the brakes for the steep hill and went to the door. He was about to knock when the door was opened by a young man to whom Ames had been introduced the day before. Darling's brother, Bob.

"Good morning, Constable Ames. We are all ready, though Father could not be persuaded into a suit. Fred, your constable is here!" he called into the house behind him. "This is Isabel," he added, "my fiancée."

Ames shook hands with a lovely, delicate strawberry blond woman dressed in crème satin, with a matching hat, whom he was prepared to like immediately, until he detected a determination in the set of her jaw that reminded him too much of his recent girl, Violet, with whom he had parted ways.

"Miss," he said with courteous caution.

Darling appeared, pulling his shirt cuff even with the suit sleeve. He stopped short and looked at Ames. "What's that?"

Ames held it up. "It's a boutonnière, sir, to wear in your *bouton*. As you see, I have one."

"It doesn't mean you're going to get me into one."

Darling's brother took the offending item. "Come along, Fred. Don't be obstreperous. Do as you're told."

Ames held the door as the party left the house, Darling last, and he leaned in to whisper, "You look very handsome, sir. She's a lucky woman. And before you ask, I have the rings." He patted his pocket. "Got your speech?"

"For the last time, Ames, I am not making a speech. I thought the whole point of getting a best man was to have him do the speeches."

"Just kidding, sir!"

"Please don't. It's extraordinarily unhelpful."

Smiling inwardly at seeing his boss in a state of nerves, Ames set off for King's Cove. The overnight rain had made the usual dust on the roads lie down. They should get there looking as fresh as daisies.

GWEN WAS UP the hill putting the finishing touches on the layout for the wedding party, and wondering if it really mattered that the three of them would be wearing the same best dresses they wore for every event. Well, it was Lane's day. What mattered was that they would be able to get their crystal and best china out for an airing. She noted, with approval, that the sun had decided to cooperate and the rain had not knocked the garden around too much.

"We haven't had a wedding here for a donkey's age," Mabel said, coming in with a pile of exquisite Royal Albert Imari side plates. "Whatever prompted Mother to buy fifteen place settings? Where did she think we were moving to in the nineties?"

"We've never had a wedding here," corrected her sister. "I suppose you and John would have tied the knot here, though. I expect that's why Mother bought all that china. She thought her daughters would have big weddings."

John had been killed in the Great War, which had put an end to all of Gwen's hopes, and bad fortune had left Mabel a spinster as well, though neither dwelled on it after all this time.

"What do you think she'll wear?" Gwen asked. "Angela hasn't breathed a word."

"She did say it was a rather surprising choice, though. Do you think it's possible she won't wear a proper wedding dress?"

"Anything is possible with our Miss Winslow," Mabel said.

"WHAT DO YOU think, Mother?" Kenny asked, surveying his cart, now bedecked in ivy.

"Very nice. You will bump her to death on the way to her wedding. I'll be walking, if no one minds."

"Look at the sun and that long rim of blue sky! Could it be more auspicious? Will we like having him as a neighbour, I wonder?"

"Certainly. It is always comforting to have a gentleman living next door. He has exquisite manners. We'll be as safe as houses, having a policeman in King's Cove. There, now. What do you think of this?"

Eleanor held up a bouquet of fall flowers. Dahlias and late roses provided layers of orange and gold, and some sprigs of late lavender and greenery made a perfect balance.

"Lovely. Should I put a crown of ivy on Alexandra?"

"Only if you want to irritate her. I'm going to run this over to Lane now."

WHEN KENNY PULLED his wagon next to the path to Lane's house, the sun had fully emerged. Lane had been listening anxiously to the sound of cars pulling up the hill toward the church. She had had a battle to keep Angela from fussing too much with her hair and had wanted to have as little makeup as possible, on the grounds that she would like the groom to be able to recognize her.

There was a brisk knock on the door, and Kenny, in a very snug but becoming grey wool jacket, bowed. "Your carriage awaits, madam." And then he followed this up with "Whew! Don't you look a sight!"

Lane had topped the wedding ensemble with a neat blue hat with a veil that came to just above her chin. Eleanor had lent her a mink stole, covering the required "something borrowed."

"Will I do?"

"I've said it before and I'll say it again: he's a lucky man!"

"Well I hope someone on the other end is telling him I'm a lucky woman because I am."

Angela came up behind Lane carrying the bouquet. "Oh, how perfect! These deep oranges with that gorgeous blue of your dress! Such complementary colours!" She held the bouquet next to Lane's dress. "I hope poor David has managed to wrangle the boys into their clothes. I have a feeling there was a real donnybrook about the bow ties! What if they forget what they're supposed to do?"

"No one will notice. They'll all be looking at our miss, here. Hop in, Angela. Best get moving. Don't want to frighten the groom by being late," Kenny said.

The decorum of the bride's arrival was slightly marred by Angela's boys, who had been waiting outside the church, galloping inside, and shouting all at once, "They're here!"

Lane stood with Kenny at the door of the church, her arm through his, bouquet in hand. The organ, played by Gwen, sounded the first stuttering chords of the wedding march and Kenny gave her hand a little pat.

"Now then, we're on," he whispered.

Darling and Ames were at the end of the aisle, looking toward her. The wooden pews creaked as everyone else turned and there was a gentle gasp and murmuring. Lane heard a scarcely contained "Che bellezza!" from Lorenzo, and she smiled. Ames was beaming, and had clearly bought a new suit for the occasion, as had Darling, who was dressed in a deep charcoal grey, a match for his eyes, which were turned toward her. She wasn't sure what she wanted or ought to see in the eyes of the man she was about to marry, but the look of almost devastated longing would do. And then she was there, and Darling reached for her hand.

"IT'S OVER PRETTY fast," remarked Alice. "No time to think it through and wriggle out while you can. Very good eats, these. Did you make these sausage rolls, Mabel?"

The afternoon had become warm enough that people were standing in the garden with plates of canapés and glasses of champagne. The boys were chasing each other around the islands of flowerbeds, causing Gladys, who was standing with Gwen near the kitchen door, to wince.

Mabel nodded at Alice and continued a theme she'd developed in her mind during the ceremony. "I don't know that it's entirely appropriate in this day and age to have women passed from man to man like some sort of parcel, do you? At least they dropped the dreaded 'obey.'" The vicar, Darling, and Lane were helping themselves to sausage rolls and something made with mushrooms that Mabel had brought around.

"It was only Kenny," Alice pointed out. She was set to say something else, but the sausage rolls demanded to be eaten.

"I'll tell you something: I was extremely glad of an arm to lean on. I was much more nervous than I thought I'd be," Lane said.

"I'm not surprised, with me at the end of the road. What do you think, Vicar?" Darling said.

"Well, of course, it is a very long tradition, with no doubt disreputable origins from when women were chattels. I think it's probably good to bring new eyes to bear on this sort of thing. You've certainly flown in the face of tradition by electing to continue to be called Lane Winslow despite the name on your marriage certificate. I imagine it could create awkwardness from time to time. I'm not sure the world is ready for that sort of thing." He looked as though he might be worried about the brave new world and what might be set to replace the flawed old one.

Lane smiled. "I think we just thought that with his name being Darling, and us calling each other darling all the time, it would be too much of a good thing if I too went about calling myself Darling." She glanced at her husband. It had been their final resolve. Lane had loved Darling the more, for his only slight resistance to the idea. "But I don't promise it will entirely eliminate my desire to protect you," he'd warned.

Gladys surveyed the success of her party from the steps. She and Gwen had plates of tiny squares of sandwich, egg, sardine, ham, which they were about to disperse into the crowd. "We've already got the one Russian foreigner, but who's that other little foreigner?" Gladys asked Gwen suddenly, nodding in the direction of Lorenzo, who was talking to David Bertolli.

"Mother, please, I told you, they made the cake."

"Yes, but why has the baker been invited to the wedding? That's not usual, is it?"

"They are very good friends of the inspector and Lane."

"Peculiar sort of friends if you ask me," her mother remarked, "but the cake looks decent, I'll say that."

"Really mother, peculiar? Have you looked at this lot lately?" Gwen waved her hand to encompass the Mathers, Robin Harris, the Bertollis, the Armstrongs. "The guests from Vancouver are the only normal people here!"

"And who the devil is that?"

Gwen swivelled to where her mother was pointing. Ames was talking to a blonde who wore an extraordinary hat with a pair of partridge feathers on it that swooped around toward her chin, framing her face in a most becoming manner. Her suit was bright yellow, and pulled in charmingly at the waist, and seemed to complement, rather than compete with, her curly, very blond hair.

"That is a lady mechanic. Constable Ames brought her. She's very lively. He'll have to watch himself! The Van Eyck girl, do you remember? We used to see her at the church picnics in the early thirties when she was a girl?"

"Rather odd headgear, but she has a lovely smile," Gladys conceded.

"I HAVE AN old colleague from my early policing days who lives in Arizona," Darling said. They were sitting, alone at last, in the armchairs in front of the Franklin in Lane's house, the fire throwing flickers of light along the walls of the darkened room. "We'll need a honeymoon. It might be nice to be there when the weather gets dicey here."

"I'll go anywhere, as long as I'm with you. Is that too clichéd for words?"

"Only when other people say it. It was very nice of Ames to drive my father and brother and his fiancée back to town. I hope his lady mechanic didn't mind. I thought it was a rather good do altogether."

"As did I. Some of the locals were a little surprised to be served that divine flakey and creamy sort of Italian wedding cake. I'm sure they all expected a rock hard square of fruitcake with marzipan and white icing in the British tradition."

"Miss Winslow, the fire is dying down. Should we be spending the evening talking about cake?" Darling asked. He reached for her hand and entwined his fingers through hers.

Lane, her shoes off, leaned toward Darling with a rustling of taffeta, and kissed him. "Not if you don't want to," she said, her lips grazing his again, so that his heart leapt.

ON MONDAY MORNING, Ames pushed into the café next to the station, whistling despite another wave of inclement weather. It was the fall after all. The wedding had gone off beautifully, and Darling would be away until Thursday, though everyone had encouraged him to take at least a week off. Darling had explained that they were going to honeymoon in November, and crime wasn't going to stop just because he'd gotten married.

April looked up, and smiled a greeting, making Ames wish he could have worn his new suit. He looked exceedingly smart in it. At least, so Tina had said.

"You're in a good mood. How did the wedding go?"

"Like clockwork."

"You didn't forget the rings then?"

"Very funny. I think I'll have the full breakfast today. Being a best man is hungry work."

April smiled and poured Ames a coffee. "Do you think this will improve his mood? That Miss Winslow is the most beautiful woman I've ever seen."

Ames toyed with "not as lovely as you," but worried it would reignite the discomfort of their brief courtship and unfortunate break up. And there was Tina Van Eyck to consider. It was just the sort of thing that probably got him into trouble in the first place.

"I hope so," he said. "But maybe if I ever get my sergeant's letter, that might do it. I'd like a 'first class.' Probably too much to hope for." He spooned sugar into his coffee.

"Probably. You know he already thinks you're first class, don't you? I bet dollars to doughnuts he still stiffs you with the breakfast bills, though!"

AMES WAS FEELING slightly annoyed on his way down the hill to the station on the Thursday Darling was due back. He was already anticipating that he would still not have received notification about his exam results, but when he walked into the office, imagining having to make an angry phone call to Vancouver, O'Brien handed him a letter.

"Get in trouble with the police while you were there?" O'Brien asked.

"Oh, jeepers. This will be my results!" Ames bounded up the stairs and closed his office door. And in the next instant opened it again and bounded into Darling's office.

"I did it, sir! I mean, good morning." Ames sat down, feeling a little faint, and leaned back in his chair. He looked down again at his letter, then passed it to Darling.

"Well done. Won't you sit down? No, you can't put your feet up on my desk. This will never entitle you to that," Darling said.

Ames leaned over and pointed at a line on the letter. "First class, sir. What do you think of that?"

"Very creditable. I suppose you'll be swanning around wanting to be addressed as Sergeant from now on." Darling looked past Ames and gave a slight nod to someone outside the door.

Ames turned and saw no one and resumed the happy perusal of his letter.

"I wouldn't describe me as 'swanning,' sir, would you?"

"Every time you get a new pair of shoes, Ames."

They were interrupted by the sound of light hammering. Darling waited till it stopped.

"Run along and quit cluttering up my office. I have to finish the paperwork on this Brodie business." He watched Ames leap out of the chair and start toward the door. "Oh, and Ames, about figuring out that Oxley had planted evidence . . . not bad, all things considered. There might be hope for you yet."

Ames tried unsuccessfully to keep himself from beaming. "Thank you, sir. And about the wedding, I want to thank you again—"

"Later, Ames. Beat it." Darling waited until Ames had left and then smiled. He had a great deal to smile about, he thought.

Ames made it as far as his office door and then stopped. There, above the door, was a new wooden plaque with gold lettering. It read:

SERGEANT D. AMES.

ACKNOWLEDGMENTS

THE OTHER DAY I WAS going through my bookshelves and found a notebook in which I must have been practicing some '80s-era visioning. In 1987, after years of scribbling, and with no publication to my name (and little hope of any), I drew a stick-figure cartoon of myself sitting at a table with a pile of books and a great crowd of people lined up to have me sign their copies of my "best-selling" novel. It's taken almost thirty years and at least three careers, but now I can say I have lived that scene many times since I took up with Lane Winslow.

This hasn't happened because I'm clever or prescient. It's happened because of the people who believed in me from the start of this series, taking these books from a someday dream to a lovely, tangible reality. These people include the talented and absolutely delightful people at TouchWood Editions: Taryn Boyd, a publisher who envisions what could be; Renée Layberry, the sharp-eyed and infinitely patient in-house editor; Tori Elliott, the industrious publicist who seems as delighted with the writers' success as the writers themselves. I must also thank the other brilliant editors who have prodded me, challenged me, and been kind enough to enjoy what I have written: Cailey Cavallin, Warren Layberry, and Claire Philipson. They have helped make *A Deceptive Devotion* as good as it can be.

Thanks as well to designer Colin Parks and any number of others at TouchWood Editions who squirrel away making beautiful books a reality. The cover illustrations, which elicit exclamations of delight from anyone who has seen them in my travels across Canada and in the US, are done by Margaret Hanson.

I must also thank my initial readers, Sasha Bley-Vroman and Gerald Miller, who always give me that first intimation of how the book might go down with the public. A special thanks to my son Biski, who reads my books with astonishing enjoyment.

And finally, of course, I thank my kind, clever, and long-suffering partner Terry, who willingly drops whatever he is doing or thinking to listen, sage advice at the ready, when I burst out with "What if I . . ."

IONA WHISHAW was born in British Columbia. After living her early years in the Kootenays, she spent her formative years living and learning in Mexico, Nicaragua, and the US. She travelled extensively for pleasure and education before settling in the Vancouver area. Throughout her roles as youth worker, social worker, teacher, and award-winning high school principal, her love of writing remained consistent, and compelled her to obtain her master's in creative writing from the University of British Columbia. Iona has published short fiction, poetry, poetry translation, and one children's book, *Henry and the Cow Problem*. *A Killer in King's Cove* was her first adult novel. Her heroine, Lane Winslow, was inspired by Iona's mother who, like her father before her, was a wartime spy. Book #7 in the series, *A Match Made for Murder*, won the Bony Blithe Light Mystery Award. Visit ionawhishaw.ca to find out more.

THE LANE WINSLOW MYSTERY SERIES

IONA WHISHAW
A KILLER IN KING'S COVE
A LANE WINSLOW MYSTERY

IONA WHISHAW
DEATH IN A DARKENING MIST
A LANE WINSLOW MYSTERY

IONA WHISHAW
AN OLD, COLD GRAVE
A LANE WINSLOW MYSTERY

IONA WHISHAW
IT BEGINS IN BETRAYAL
A LANE WINSLOW MYSTERY

IONA WHISHAW
A SORROWFUL SANCTUARY
A LANE WINSLOW MYSTERY

IONA WHISHAW
A DECEPTIVE DEVOTION
A LANE WINSLOW MYSTERY